Wrath of a Mad God

Raymond E. Feist

W F HOWES LTD

This large print edition published in 2008 by
W F Howes Ltd
Unit 4, Rearsby Business Park, Gaddesby Lane,
Rearsby, Leicester LE7 4YH

1 3 5 7 9 10 8 6 4 2

First published in the United Kingdom in 2008
by Harper*Voyager*

A CIP catalogue record for this book is available
from the British Library

ISBN 978 1 40740 149 2

Typeset by Palimpsest Book Production Limited,
Grangemouth, Stirlingshire
Printed and bound in Great Britain
by Antony Rowe Ltd, Chippenham, Wilts.

FSC
Mixed Sources
Product group from well-managed
forests and other controlled sources

Cert no. SGS-COC-2953
www.fsc.org
© 1996 Forest Stewardship Council

To Lacey,
With thanks for sticking around
and keeping your sense of humour.

ACKNOWLEDGMENTS

As always, I could not have completed this work, another chapter in the vast Riftwar Cycle, without the foundation given to me by the original creators of Midkemia.

Again, my family and friends, for providing much-needed balance in my life and keeping me sane, or as close to it as I'll get.

Jonathan Matson, who has been a rock upon which I have built a career and without whose sage counsel and patient attention I would not have come half as far.

And, especially, I wish to thank my editors at HarperCollins, Jane Johnson, Jennifer Brehl, Katherine Nintzel, and Emma Coode, for always understanding, especially in times of difficulty, that it's about the work and for showing their willingness to adjust to chaotic times and provide vital support to me. I hope your faith in me remains justified and your passion for the work never flags. I absolutely could not have done this without you.

Raymond E. Feist
San Diego, CA   2007

CHAPTER 1

ESCAPE

Miranda screamed.

The searing agony that seized her mind relented for the briefest moment, and in that instant she found what she had been seeking. The preponderance of her awareness was occupied with the battle of wills with her captors, but a tiny fragment – a disciplined fraction of her consciousness – had been readied. Over the days of interrogation and examination she had used every respite to partition off this one sliver of her intellect, to somehow overcome the blinding pain, and observe. During the last four encounters with the Dasati Deathpriests she had achieved that detachment and willed her body to withstand the pain. It was there, she knew, inflamed nerves protesting about the alien energies coursing across the surface of her mind, probing it, seeking insights into her very being, but she had learned to ignore physical pain centuries before. The mental assaults were more difficult, for they attacked the root of her power, the unique intelligence that made her a supreme magician on her home world.

These Dasati clerics lacked any pretence of subtlety. At first they had ripped open her thoughts like a bear pulling apart a tree stump looking for honey. A lesser mind would have been savaged beyond recovery on the first assault. After the third such onslaught, Miranda nearly had been reduced to idiocy. Still, she had fought back and knowing there was no victory if there was no survival, she had focused all her considerable talents first on endurance, then insight.

Her ability to shunt aside the terrible assault and focus on that tiny sliver of knowledge she had gained kept her sane. Her determination to overcome her captivity and return with that knowledge gave her purpose.

Now she feigned unconsciousness, a new ploy in her struggle with her captors. Unless they possessed finer skills than she had so far encountered, her charade was undetected: to them she appeared incapacitated. This counterfeit lack of awareness was her first successful conjuration since her captivity began. She risked just enough body awareness to ensure that her breathing was slow and shallow, even though she suspected the Deathpriests who studied her still knew too little about humans to understand what physical signs to observe. No, her struggle was in the mind, and there she would eventually triumph. She had learned more about her captors than they had about her, she was certain.

Individually the Dasati were no match for her,

nor even for one of her more advanced students back home. She had no doubt without the snare concocted by Leso Varen to disorient her, she would have easily disposed of the two Deathpriests who had seized her. But Varen was a force to reckon with, a necromancer with centuries of experience, and she alone would be hard pressed to best him: three times one of his bodies had been killed that to her knowledge, by multiple foes and taken by surprise, but still he survived. Between Varen and the Deathpriests, she had been quickly over-whelmed.

Now she knew the Deathpriests for what they were, necromancers of a sort. Throughout her life, Miranda had chosen to ignore clerical magic, as was common for most magicians on Midkemia, as being some sort of manifestation of the gods' powers. Now she regretted that oversight. Her husband Pug had been the only magician with whom she was familiar who had some insight into clerical magic, having made it a point to learn as much about it as he could, despite the tendency of the various orders to be secretive. He had learned a great deal about this darkest of magic because of his repeated encounters with the Pantathian Serpent Priests, a death cult with their own mad ambitions. He had confronted several attempts on their part to wreak havoc throughout the world. She had listened indifferently to several discussions on the subject, and now she wished she had paid closer attention.

Now, however she was learning by the minute; the Deathpriests were clumsy and imprecise in their investigation and often revealed as much about their own magical nature as they learned about hers. Their lack of subtlety worked in her favour.

She heard her captor leave, but kept her eyes closed as she slowly let her consciousness return to the upper levels of her mind, every instant clinging to the insight she had just achieved. Then clarity returned. And with it, pain. She fought back the urge to cry out, and used deep breathing and mental discipline to manage the agony.

She lay up on a slab of stone, but stone that had its own evil nature, a sense of energy alien to Miranda. Simply touching it was uncomfortable, and she was strapped to it without benefit of clothing. She was drenched in perspiration and nauseous. Her muscles were threatening to cramp and with her limbs restrained, the additional pain was unwelcome. She employed every trick at her disposal to control the urge, calm herself, and let the pain flow away.

For almost a week she had undergone the Dasati examination, enduring humiliation as well as pain, as they sought to learn as much about her and the human race as possible. She was secretly grateful for their heavy-handed approach for it provided her with two advantages: they had no experience with human guile and they vastly underestimated her.

She put aside her speculation on the Dasati, and

4

turned her attention to escape. Once trapped by Leso Varen and the Deathpriests, she had quickly realized that her best course of action was to give her interrogators just enough truth to make credible everything said. Varen, his malignant consciousness currently inhabiting the body of the Tsurani magician Wyntakata, had not appeared since she had been taken, a fact for which she was grateful, as he would have given the Dasati a far greater advantage in dealing with her. She knew he had his own mad agenda and had only been in league with the Dasati for as long as it suited him, and cared nothing for the success of their insane ambitions, only for his own.

She opened her eyes. As she expected, her Dasati captors were gone. For an instant she had worried that one might have lingered quietly to observe her. Sometimes they spoke to her in a conversational manner as if chatting with a guest, at other times they subjected her to physical violence. There seemed little pattern or sense to their choices. She had been allowed to keep her powers at first, for the Deathpriests had been supremely confident and had wished to see the scope of her abilities. But on the fourth day of her captivity, she had lashed out at a Deathpriest with the full fury of her magic when he had presumed to touch her naked body. After that, they had reined in her powers with a spell that had frustrated every attempt at using her magic.

The screaming nerves of every inch of her body

reminded her that they were still in torment. She took a long, deep breath and used all her skills to lessen the pain until she could ignore it.

Miranda took another deep breath, and tried to see if what she had just learned from her captors was true or merely grasping at vain hope. She forced her mind to work in a new fashion, applying a minor spell, saying it so softly there was barely any sound. And the pain slowly leached away! At last she had discovered what she had sought.

She closed her eyes, reclaiming the image she had gained while being tortured. She knew intuitively that she had found something critically important, but she was still uncertain of exactly what it was. For an instant she wished she could somehow communicate with Pug or his companion Nakor, for both had keen insights into the nature of magic, down to the very bedrock of the energies used by magicians – what Nakor insisting on calling 'stuff'. She smiled slightly and took another deep breath. She would have laughed had she not been in so much discomfort.

Nakor would be delighted. Her newfound intelligence on this realm of the Dasati was something he would take great pleasure in: the 'stuff' of this realm was similar to those energies familiar to every magician on Sorcerer's Isle, but it was . . . how would Nakor put it, she wondered? It was *bent*. It was as if the energies wanted to move at right angles to what she knew. She felt as if she were learning to walk all over again, only this time she had to think 'sideways' to move forward.

She reached out with her mind and let mental 'fingers' touch the buckles of her restraints. It took almost no effort for her to unfasten them. Quickly she freed herself.

Sitting up, she flexed shoulders, back and legs, feeling circulation returning and a soreness that seemed to run to her marrow. Miranda had lived a lifetime measured in centuries, but she looked no more than forty years of age. She was slender, but surprisingly strong, for she took delight in walking the hills on Sorcerer's Isle and taking long swims in the sea. Her dark hair was dusted with a little grey, and her dark eyes were clear and youthful. The effects of magic, she had come to believe, gave a long life to certain practitioners.

She took another deep breath. The churning in her stomach subsided. At least the Dasati hadn't used hot irons or sharp implements, being content for the time being merely to beat her when they thought it might provide better information.

If she ever saw Nakor again she'd kiss him, for without his insistence that magic was somehow composed of a fundamental energy, she would never have understood what made it work differently here within the Dasati realm . . .

She was certain she was still on Kelewan, in the black energy sphere she had observed moments before she was captured. This 'room' was nothing more than a small compartment and high above was an inky void, or at least a ceiling so high it vanished into the gloom. She glanced around, studying what she should see clearly, now that she wasn't lashed to the slab. The enclosure was curtained off, but she could see the curve of the dome rising above her head, for the stanchions and rods holding the curtains were only about ten feet high. The material was uniformly dark grey-blue in colour, if she could judge from the light in the room, a pulsing glow from an odd-looking grey stone placed upon a table nearby. She closed her eyes and let her mind extend and after a few seconds she encountered what could only be the shell of the sphere.

How then, she wondered, had the familiar rules of magic been replaced by Dasati rules? It was as if they brought their own world with them . . .

She stood up. Suddenly she understood. They weren't just going to invade Kelewan; they were going to change Kelewan, convert it into a world in which they could comfortably live. They were going to colonize it!

Now it was imperative that she get free of this prison, find the Assembly at once and return to warn the Great Ones. The Dasati needed only to enlarge this sphere. It would not be easy, but it was straightforward. Given enough energy and this sphere would encircle the entire world, converting it into one like those in the second realm of reality, or at the least turn it into one like Delecordia, the world Pug found that somehow existed between the two realms.

She sent out her mental probes. Keeping them tiny and weak, preparing to withdraw them the instant they touched anything sentient, lest they alert a Deathpriest or some other Dasati that she was free.

She glanced around the room, saw her clothing tossed into a corner and quickly dressed. While she had no problem appearing naked in the halls of the Assembly of Magicians, and while the Tsurani were far less concerned with nudity than many of the cultures on Midkemia, there was something simply undignified about it.

Miranda hesitated. Time was pressing, yet she wished she could linger, investigate more, and return to the Assembly with better intelligence. For a moment she wondered if she could contrive a spell to make her invisible, so as to creep around in this . . . bubble. No, better to carry the warning and return with the might of the Assembly behind her.

She closed her eyes and probed at the shell above her. It was painful, and she quickly withdrew, but she had learned what she needed to know. It was the boundary between her realm and the Dasati realm, or at least the part they had carried with them to Kelewan. She would be able to traverse it, but she required more time to prepare.

Wondering how many captors were with her, she sent out a tiny fibre of perception, a minuscule feeler to sense life energy. It should arouse no notice if she managed it correctly. She felt a brushing of energy as faint as a dandelion seed carried by the breeze touching the cheek, and she recoiled instantly, lest she be noticed. That was one. Again and again she quested, until she was certain that only two Deathpriests were presently in the dome.

She took a deep breath, and readied herself. Then she hesitated. She knew the wise choice would be to flee, to find her way to the Assembly as quickly as possible and then return with a host of Black Robes to crush this intrusion into Kelewan. But another part of her wished to know more about these invaders, to better understand who they faced. A sense of dread in her completed the thought: in case Pug did not return from the Dasati world.

She was confident in her power that she could overcome both Deathpriests, and perhaps take one of them prisoner. She would welcome the opportunity to return the hospitality shown to her. She knew however that Varen had most likely returned to the Assembly, and when asked as to her whereabouts, would have simply said she had returned to Midkemia unexpectedly. It could take weeks for word to reach Kelewan that she hadn't returned home and then the Assembly would begin enquiries into her disappearance. One of the disadvantages of being who she was, of being an agent for the Conclave, was the secrecy associated with much of what she did. It could be a month or more before she was missed.

She studied the 'wall' nearest to her. Probing

gently with her senses, she tried to feel the rhythm of the energies. This would be a tricky proposition as she knew little of the surrounding terrain, and a long-distance jump to a familiar spot, say in the Assembly, through the dense magic sphere also presented unknown problems.

She decided it was wiser to jump a short distance away, to a rise she remembered because the lordsbush flowers were in vivid bloom, something she had noticed just before cresting the rise and seeing the sphere.

Then she felt a presence. At once she turned only to find a Dasati Deathpriest raising a device of some sort, pointing it towards her. She tried her best to apply what she had learned about magic here and sent out a spell which should have merely knocked him off his feet. Instead, she felt energies rush from her, as if yanked from her body, and saw the shocked expression on the alien face as he was slammed by an invisible force that propelled him through the curtain.

Beyond the curtain was a wall constructed of some alien wood. It exploded as the Deathpriest's body crashed through it and into the cubicle beyond. His lifeless corpse left a bloody smear on the floor and Miranda was surprised to note that Dasati blood was more orange than red.

The unexpected ferocity of the attack had one unanticipated benefit. The second Dasati Deathpriest was lying on the floor, stunned senseless by

11

the impact of his companion as he had flown across the gap between them.

Miranda quickly inspected the two Dasati, and confirmed that the first was dead and the second unconscious. She looked in all directions to see if anyone else might have escaped her probes but after a moment she accepted that she was now alone with a corpse and a potential prisoner.

With one wall shattered and another knocked flat she finally saw her prison in its entirety. The sphere was no more than a hundred feet in diameter, partitioned by wooden walls and curtains inside which were two pallets with bedding, a table with writing materials and another of those alien stone lamps, a chest and a large woven mat over the earth floor. She quickly scouted the other spaces and found an almost incomprehensible array of items. The one thing she failed to discover was the device that had provided the means to make the journey from the Dasati realm to Kelewan. She had anticipated something large, similar to the Tsurani rift machines, or at least something like a pedestal upon which to stand, but nothing presented itself as an obvious choice.

She was already angry, and now the frustration of the moment drove her to the edge of rage. How dare these aliens come into this realm and assault her! All her life Miranda had battled a violent temper, a heritage from her mother and while she maintained a relatively calm demeanour most of the time, when she finally lost that temper her family had long since decided that giving her a wide berth was the only practical choice.

A stack of papers, oddly waxy, lay around the floor, and Miranda knelt to grab a handful. Who knew what was written upon them, in this alien language? Perhaps some insight into these creatures might be forthcoming.

She heard a soft groan, and saw the still-living Deathpriest start to twitch. Without thought she stood up, took one step and kicked his jaw as hard as she could. 'Ow!' The side of the Dasati's jaw felt like granite. 'Damn me!' she swore, thinking she had broken her foot. With the papers in one hand, she knelt next to the unconscious form and gripped the front of his robe. 'You're coming with me!' she hissed.

Miranda closed her eyes and turned the entirety of her attention to the walls of the sphere she was probing until she felt the peculiar flow of energy and then attuning herself to it as if turning pegs on a lute to change the pitch of the strings.

When she judged herself ready, Miranda willed herself outside, a short distance from the other side of the wall. She screamed as her entire body was torn for a moment by cascading energies, as if ice were cutting into her nerves, then she found herself kneeling on the dry grass in the hills of Lash Province. It was morning, which for some reason surprised her and she could barely stand the pain that came even from breathing.

Her entire body protested the reversion to her

13

native environment. Whatever the Dasati had done to provide her with the means to live in their realm, or that piece of it under the dome, the translation back was agony.

The Deathpriest appeared to have also survived the transition. She knelt beside him, clutching his robe as if it were the only tether she had to consciousness. A moment passed and the pain lessened, and after another, she felt herself beginning to adjust. Taking a deep, gasping breath, she blinked to clear her vision before immediately closing them again. 'That's not good.'

Taking another deep breath, she ignored the searing pain that opening her eyes had caused her, and willed herself to the Pattern Room in the Assembly.

Two magicians were in the room when she appeared. She cast her captive down in front of them. 'Bind him. He is a Dasati Deathpriest.' She did not know if these two were privy to the knowledge Pug had passed to the Assembly since the Talnoy had been brought to Kelewan for study, but every Great One living had heard of the Dasati. Finding one lying unconscious at their feet caused them to hesitate for a moment, but then the two Black Robes hurried to do her bidding. The stress of escape and bringing a captive had taken Miranda to the end of her already-depleted resources. She took two staggering steps, and then slumped unconscious to the floor.

★   ★   ★

14

Miranda opened her eyes and found herself in quarters reserved for her or Pug when they came to visit. Alenca, the most senior member of the Assembly of Magicians sat on a stool beside her bed, his face composed and untroubled, looking like a grandparent waiting patiently for a child to awaken from an illness.

Miranda blinked, then croaked, 'How long?'

'One afternoon, last night, and all this morning. How are you?'

Miranda sat up, gingerly, and discovered that she was wearing a simple white linen shift. Alenca smiled, 'I trust you don't object to our having cleaned you up. You were in quite a state when you appeared before us.'

Miranda swung her legs out of bed and carefully stood up. Her cleaned, pressed robes waited for her on a divan in front of a window overlooking the lake. The afternoon sun sparkled off the water. Unmindful of the old man watching her, she slipped off the shift and put on her robes. 'What about the Dasati?' she asked, inspecting herself in the small mirror on the wall.

'He is still unconscious, and it appears, dying.'

'Really?' said Miranda. 'I didn't think his injuries that severe.' She looked at the old magician. 'I need to see him and we need to call as many members as you can to the Assembly.'

'Already done,' said the old man with a chuckle. 'Word of the captive quickly spread and only those members too ill to travel are absent.'

'Wyntakata?' asked Miranda.

'Missing, of course.' He waved Miranda through the portal to the hallway and followed her, falling into step beside her. 'We assume he is either dead or had some hand in this.'

'He's not Wyntakata,' said Miranda. 'He's Leso Varen, the necromancer.'

'Ah,' said the old man. 'That explains a great deal.' He sighed as they rounded a corner. 'It's a pity, really. I was fond of Wyntakata, though he tended to ramble when he spoke. But he was clever and always good company.'

Miranda found it difficult to separate the host from the parasite that occupied it, but realized the old man was sincere in his regret. 'I'm sorry you lost a friend,' she said, 'but I fear we may lose a great many friends before this business is over.'

She stopped at a large intersection and glanced at her companion, who indicated they should turn down a long corridor. 'We have the Dasati in a warded room.'

'Good,' said Miranda.

Two grey-robed apprentice magicians stood guard at the door. Inside the room a pair of Great Ones stood beside the figure of the Dasati Death-priest.

One, a man named Hostan, greeted Miranda while the other kept watch over the unconscious figure on the sleeping pallet. 'Cubai and I are convinced something is very wrong with this . . . man.'

The magician inspecting the Deathpriest nodded. 'He has not shown any signs of reviving, and his breathing appears to be more laboured. If he were human I would say he has a fever.' He shook his head in dismay. 'But with this creature, I don't have a remote idea what to look for.'

Cubai was a magician who was far more curious about healing arts than most Black Robes, since it tended to be the province of healers of the Lesser Path of magic and clerics of certain orders. Miranda thought him an ideal choice to be watching over the Deathpriest.

Miranda said, 'While a prisoner, I deduced some things about these creatures.

'The Dasati are not that different from humans, at least in the sense that elves, dwarves and goblins are similar: roughly human-like in form, standing upright on two legs, eyes in the front of a recognizable face, all the rest you can see, and I know they have two genders, male and female, the women bearing their young within their bodies. I gleaned that much while being closely examined by the Deathpriests. I can't speak their language, but I did pick up a word or two along the way and now have some sense of what they presume about humans.'

She turned to a handful of magicians who had come into the room when word had spread she was up and with the Deathpriest. She raised her voice so all could hear. 'They are physically stronger than us by a significant margin. I judge it to be a quality of their nature magnified by their presence on this world. But I think they have some difficulty with the differences between the two worlds, hence the dome of energy they created in which to reside. But one of their average warriors can overpower all but the most powerful human, be it Tsurani warrior or Kingdom soldier.' No time like the present to start planting the idea of Midkemian help, she thought.

She looked down at the Deathpriest and tried to reconcile what she saw with what she had observed while he and his companion had experimented on her. 'He doesn't look well, that is clear.' She leaned over and saw a sheen of moisture on his brow. 'I think you're right about the fever, Cubai. I think his colour is pale, but that may be the difference in light in the two . . .' Her voice trailed off as she saw the creature's eyelids flutter. She stepped back. 'I think he's waking!'

Instantly two magicians began incanting words while others readied spells of confinement, but the Dasati did not awake or rise. Instead, with a low moan of agony, his body arched and began to convulse. Miranda was hesitant to touch him and that hesitancy prevented her from stopping him from flopping off the pallet onto the floor.

As he thrashed violently now, his skin started to blister. Not quite sure why, Miranda shouted, 'Stand away!'

The magicians drew back. Suddenly a flame engulfed the Deathpriest's body and then a huge discharge of heat and light nearly blinded those standing nearby, singeing hair and causing everyone within proximity to fall back.

The stench was that of sulphur and rotting meat being cooked, and many were gagging from the smell. Moving backwards from the site of the immolation, Miranda saw only the faint outline of a body in white ash on the floor.

'What just happened?' asked Alenca, obviously shaken by the experience.

'I don't know,' answered Miranda. 'I think that outside the dome they are unable to deal with the abundance of energy that we take for granted. I think it proved too much for him and . . . well, you saw what happened.'

'What now?' asked the old magician.

'We go back to the dome and investigate,' answered Miranda, assuming command of the situation without being asked. 'That incursion is a threat to the Empire.'

That alone was reason enough to mobilize the Great Ones of the Empire. Alenca nodded. 'Not only must we investigate, we must eradicate this dome.' He turned to another magician and said, 'Hochaka, would you be good enough to carry word to the Light of Heaven in the Holy City? The Emperor must be made aware of what is taking place, and convey to him our intentions of providing a fully-detailed report after we finish.'

Miranda was amused by the steely tone taken by the old magician: in his youth he must have been an impressive figure. He was the type of man who often surprised others when he took control, a quiet authority figure, effective at gaining attention when other louder voices are demanding it and being ignored.

Miranda followed his lead. Quietly she said, 'I had to . . . sense my way around inside the dome before I could escape.' She paused for effect before saying, 'I ask that you allow me to guide you in this.'

The Great Ones in the room looked taken aback by the request – a woman, and an outlander at that, leading them? But others looked to Alenca who quietly said, 'It is only logical.' With those four words he handed the power of the Assembly of Magicians, the single most puissant gathering of magic on two worlds, over to Miranda.

She nodded. 'Please ask as many of the Assembly as can be here to gather in the Great Hall of Magicians in one hour's time. I will tell what I know and suggest what I think should be done.'

Magicians quickly left to use their arts to summon as many of the members of the Assembly as they could reach. Miranda knew that whatever else might be true, once word of a threat to the Empire reached even the most distant member, all would return to hear her warning. Only those out of touch or too ill to travel would not be in the Hall when she explained that the Empire of Tsuranuanni, and the entire world of Kelewan, now faced the gravest threat ever known.

Miranda retired to her quarters. She slumped down onto the soft divan. She dared not lie down on the bed as she knew she would quickly fall asleep again. One night's rest and a meal didn't undo the damage the Dasati had wrought on her. She had to stay focused on the task at hand using fear, pain and the need to act quickly as if they were food and drink, for she knew time was working against them.

Whatever processes the Dasati had begun would only become more difficult to interrupt as time went by. A knock at the door announced the arrival of a grey-robed apprentice, one of the few young women now a student of magic. She carried a tray bearing a porcelain pitcher, a cup, and a platter of fruits and breads. 'Great One, the Great One Alenca thought you might need refreshment.'

'Thank you,' said Miranda, indicating that the girl should put the tray down. As soon as she left, Miranda realized she was starving. She fell to eating and quickly felt energy returning to her aching, damaged body. This was one of those times she wished she had been more disposed to study clerical magic, as her husband had. Pug had called upon those arts several times and Miranda knew he would soon have had her feeling as if she had slept a week and had not endured days of humiliation and torture with an incantation or a draught of some foul-tasting but effective elixir.

Thinking of Pug made her pensive. She couldn't imagine three people better able to withstand the journey into the Dasati realm – the second level of reality as Pug called it. Yet she worried. A complicated woman with complex feelings, Miranda loved her husband deeply. Not with the passionate abandon of youth – she had outgrown that when Pug was still a child – but rather with a deep appreciation of his unique qualities and why they made him perfectly suited for her as a life companion. Her sons had been an unexpected benefit of powerful life-magic, and had proven a blessing she had never anticipated. She might not be the best mother by some people's judgment, but she enjoyed being one.

Caleb had been a challenge, when it was discovered he possessed no overt talent for the magic arts, especially after Magnus proved to be such a prodigy. She loved both her sons – with that special feeling for a first-born she had for Magnus, and that equally special feeling for the baby of the family, amplified by her awareness of how difficult Caleb's childhood had been in a community of magic-users. The other children's pranks had been especially cruel, and Magnus sticking up for his younger brother had been both a blessing and a curse. Still, both children had grown to be men of exceptional qualities, men she looked upon with pride and love.

She sat silently for a moment, then stood up. Those three men – Pug, Magnus and Caleb – were as much a reason as she needed to destroy the Dasati world if need be, for they were more important to her than any three beings in her long history. She found herself growing angry and knew that if he were here, Pug would be telling her to rein in her fiery temper because it only clouded her judgment.

Miranda stretched, ignoring protesting muscles and aching joints. She would find time later to deal with her own physical discomfort. Right now she had an invasion to deal with.

A knock at the door announced Alenca's arrival. 'They are here,' he said.

Miranda nodded. 'Thank you, old friend.' She walked with him to the Great Hall of the Assembly of Magicians.

As she anticipated, nearly every seat was filled and the low murmur of voices fell away as Alenca took his position on the podium.

'Brothers . . . and sisters,' he began, reminding himself there were now female Great Ones scattered around the room. 'We are here at the behest of an old friend, Miranda.' He stepped aside letting her take his place. No one in the Great Hall needed to be told who Miranda was. Pug's status as one of the Great Ones had been established even before Alenca had been born, and Miranda benefited from this association as well as being a powerful magic-user in her own right.

'Kelewan is being invaded,' Miranda said without preamble, 'At this very moment, a dome of black energy is being expanded in a vale in the far north. At first I saw it as a beachhead, much like the rift your forebears used to invade my home world.' The reference to the Riftwar was intentional. She knew that every student in this Assembly had been taught the entire tragic history of that ill-fated invasion in which the lives of so many had been spent in a bid of raw political power. The deadly 'Game of the Council' had seen thousands of Midkemian and Tsurani soldiers dead as a ploy on behalf of a political faction in the High Council. Several Black Robes had been party to that murderous plot, to establish the then Warlord and his faction in an unassailable position of power. Only the intervention of Pug, and the rise to power of a remarkable woman, Mara of the Acoma, had changed that deadly game.

Miranda continued. 'Each of you here knows why the Riftwar was conducted, so I will not lecture you on what you already know. This is not an invasion for political gain, wealth in booty, concessions in victory, or any sort of conventional war.

'This is not merely an invasion, but the beginning of a colonization, a process that will end with the complete annihilation of every life form on this world.'

That brought a collective intake of breath and murmurings of disbelief. Miranda held up her hands and continued. 'Those who have studied the Talnoy and the Dasati Deathpriest prisoner, I urge you to disseminate to as many of the other members as to what you know.'

She paused, looking around the room, making

eye contact with as many members of the Assembly as possible. Then she said, 'Here is what I know. The Dasati wish to remake your world. They will change it, utterly and completely, to resemble their own. They will seed every square inch of land taken with their own world's creatures, from the smallest insect to the largest beast.

'The water will become poisonous to drink, the air will burn your lungs, and the touch of even the least creature from that world will pull the life out of your body. This is no tale made up to scare children, Great Ones. This is what the Dasati are already doing under that black dome from which I escaped.'

One of the younger members shouted, 'We must act!'

'Yes,' agreed Miranda. 'Quickly and certainly, but not in haste. I suggest a group of those among us who are most masterful in the arts of light, heat and other aspects of energy, along with those of us who are masters in the arts of living beings – and perhaps we need the most powerful of the Lesser Path magicians we can contact, as well – must go at once to that valley to weigh and study the threat, and then we must destroy the dome.'

'When?' asked the young magician who had spoken out.

'As soon as we can,' said Miranda. 'We must contact the Emperor, and we will need soldiers. The Dasati will not sit idly by, I fear, and let us destroy their dome. We are likely to face beings who are unafraid to die, beings who are able to counter our magic, and we will need strong arms and swords to deal with them.'

Alenca said, 'I suggest you break up in to smaller groups and discuss what has been said and tonight we will reconvene here, after the evening meal. At that time we will discuss Miranda's warning and choose the course of action most appropriate to this threat.' He slammed down the heel of his walking stick on the stone floor, emphasizing that the meeting was over.

Miranda turned towards the exit and whispered to Alenca, 'You asked that youngster to stir things up?'

'I thought his timing was perfect.'

'You are a very dangerous man, my old friend.'

'Now we wait,' said Alenca. 'But I think we'll have a full agreement tonight, and I cannot see any other course of action than the one you suggest.'

As they walked back towards Miranda's quarters, she said, 'I hope so, and I hope my plan works. Otherwise we must ready the Empire for war against the most belligerent warlord in your history.'

Two hundred men stood ready, honour guards from four of the nearest estates in the province, answering the call of the Great Ones of Tsuranuanni without hesitation. They were arrayed in two groups, each under the command of a Great One awaiting orders from Miranda. While peace had reigned throughout the Empire for more than a generation, Tsurani discipline and training remained unchanged. These were tough, determined men ready to die for the honour of their lords' houses.

Miranda and a dozen Great Ones walked slowly up the ridge to where she had first caught sight of the Dasati dome. She spoke softly, 'Everyone ready?'

Men nodded and glanced at one another. Not one living Great One of the Empire had seen any sort of conflict: the last Great One to die in combat had done so in the Riftwar, more than a hundred years ago. These were scholarly men, not warriors. But these magicians were those best able to bring incredible power to bear if the need arose.

Slowly the thirteen magic-users, arguably the most powerful practitioners of the arcane arts, moved up the hill. At the rise, Miranda actually stood up on tiptoe to peer over, and then she said, 'Damn!'

Before them was an empty vale, the only evidence of Dasati occupation being a large circle of blackened earth where the sphere had been.

'They're gone,' said one of the younger magicians.

'They'll be back,' said Miranda, turning her back. Taking a breath, she said, 'I suggest you spread the word to every house in the Empire, that every village and farmstead, valley and dell, every isolated nook and cranny be inspected, searched, and searched again.' She looked at every face nearby. 'They will be back, and next time it won't be a small dome. I think next time they'll be coming to stay.'

CHAPTER 2

GAMBIT

Jommy frowned.

Sitting under a canvas cloth hastily rigged to provide shelter from the pitiless rain, he hugged his knees to his chest, he said, 'But what I don't understand is why?'

Servan, huddled next to the young officer, replied, 'We don't ask why; we simply follow orders.' They sat on a hillside, overlooking a distant cove: a vantage point that prevented anyone from arriving without being noticed. The problem for the moment was that the rain shrouded the area and lowered visibility to the point at which someone was required to sit close by; in this case, that someone was Servan, and Jommy had been selected to sit with him.

His dark hair matted wet against his forehead, Jommy regarded his companion. In the last few months his slender face had aged dramatically. An arduous life on the march had drained pounds from his youthful frame, while days in the sun and sleeping on the ground had given a tough, leathery quality to his skin. The court-bred noble who Jommy had come to know well over the last few months had been replaced by a young veteran embarking on his third campaign in as many months.

Never friends, the two, along with their other four companions – Tad, Zane, Grandy and Geoffry – had come to appreciate one another as reliable colleagues. In the relatively short time since they had been unceremoniously taken from the university at Roldem and cast into the role of young soldiers of rank, they had received an intensive tutelage in the realities of military life. To Jommy's unending irritation, Servan had been appointed senior for this campaign, which meant Jommy was expected to follow his orders without question. So far there had been no hint of reprisal for the mischief Jommy had inflicted on Servan during the last operation, when Jommy had been appointed senior, but Jommy just knew it was coming.

The two young officers had been detailed to a position low in the foothills of the region known as the Peaks of the Quor, a rugged, mountainous peninsula jutting northward from the eastern side of the Empire of Great Kesh. About a hundred men, including these two young officers, had been deposited on this beach a week earlier, and all Jommy knew was that a landing was expected here, though the exact identity of the invaders had not been shared with the young officers. All Jommy knew was they wouldn't be friendly.

Jommy also had aged, but as a farm youth and caravan worker, already used to a harsher life than his companion, he revealed less dramatic evidence of his recent experiences. Rather, his already cocksure brashness had evolved into a quiet confidence, and his time spent with the other young officers from the university at Roldem had taught him a fair dose of humility; all of them were better at something than he was. Even so, one part of his nature remained unchanged: his almost unique ability to see humour in most situations. This one, however, had tested his limits. The downpour had been unrelenting for four days now. Their only source of warmth was a fire built in a large cave a mile up a miserable hillside, and the enemy they had been told to expect had shown no evidence of arriving on schedule.

'No,' said Jommy, 'I don't mean why are *we* here. I mean why are we *here*?'

'Did you sleep through the Captain's orders?' came a voice from behind them.

Jommy turned to see a shadowy figure who had approached undetected. 'I wish you wouldn't do that,' he complained.

The man sat down next to Jommy, ignoring the fact that half his body was still outside the scant protection offered by the make-shift shelter. 'I wouldn't be much of a thief if I couldn't sneak up on you two in a driving storm, would I?' he replied.

The newcomer was only a few years older than them, yet his face showed premature ageing, including an unexpected sprinkling of grey hair in his dark moustache and beard, a neatly trimmed affair that revealed a streak of vanity in an otherwise chronically unkempt and slovenly person. He was nearly as tall as Jommy, but not quite as burly, yet his movement and carriage betrayed a lean hardness, a whipcord toughness that convinced Jommy he'd be a difficult man to contend with in a stand-up fight.

Servan nodded. 'Jim,' he acknowledged. The young thief had somehow managed to get caught up in the same net of intrigue that had bought Servan and Jommy to this lonely hillside. He had put in an appearance the week before, arriving on a ship with supplies for what Jommy had come to think of as the 'Cursed Expedition'.

Servan and Jommy were both currently serving in the Army of Roldem, though Jommy came from a land on the other side of the world. Servan was nobility, royalty even – somewhere in line to be king, should perhaps ten or eleven relatives expire unexpectedly. Yet they were now assigned to what could only be generously called an unusual company, soldiers from Roldem, the Kingdom of the Isles, Kesh, and even a contingent of miners and sappers from the dwarven city of Dorgin, all under the command of Kaspar of Olasko, former duke of what was now a province of the Kingdom of Roldem. Once a hunted outlaw with a price on his head, sometime over the last few years he had managed to rehabilitate his reputation and now had special status with both Roldem and the

Empire of Great Kesh. His adjutant was a Roldem captain named Stefan who happened to be Servan's cousin, which also made him another distant cousin to the King of Roldem.

The arrival of the newcomer had revealed another puzzling aspect of this expedition. Jim was one of half a dozen men who were not by any stretch of the imagination soldiers, yet were billeted with the soldiers, sent out on missions with soldiers, and expected to follow instructions without question, as if they were soldiers. All Jommy and Servan could get from the usually voluble self-confessed thief was he was part of a special group of 'volunteers' who were here to train with the combined forces of Roldem, Kesh, the Kingdom, and a scattering of officers from the Eastern Kingdoms.

The usually curious Jommy was beside himself with curiosity to discover what was going on, but the last few months of serving with various forces from Roldem had taught him that a young officer's best course was to keep silent and listen. Servan had that knack by nature.

Still, Jommy's curiosity couldn't be entirely stemmed, so he thought perhaps a different approach to the subject might get him some hint of what was going on. 'Jim, you're from the Kingdom, right?'

'Yes,' said the young thief. 'Born in Krondor; lived there all my life until now.'

'You claim to be a thief—' began Jommy.

Jim shifted his weight, lightly brushing against

Jommy, then with a grin held up Jommy's belt pouch. 'This is yours, I believe?'

Servan tried hard not to laugh while Jommy snatched back his belt-purse, which had been tucked up under his tunic. 'Very well,' he said, 'you are a thief.'

'A very good thief.'

'A very good thief,' Jommy conceded. 'But what I want to know is how a very good thief from Krondor finds himself out here on the edge of the world.'

'That's a story,' said Jim. 'I've travelled a lot, you see.'

'Oh?' said Servan, welcoming the distraction from the tedious rain.

'Yes,' said the agreeable thief. 'Been to some very odd places.' He smiled, and years dropped away from his visage, showing an almost boyish glee. 'There was this one time when I was forced to seek shelter from just this sort of driving rain in a cave on a distant island.'

Jommy and Servan exchanged a glance, and both smiled and nodded, silently communicating the same thought: not one word of what they were about to hear would be true, but the story should be entertaining.

'I was . . . taking a journey out of Krondor.'

'Business?' asked Servan.

'Health,' said Jim, his grin widening further. 'It seemed like a good idea to be out of Krondor for a while.'

Jommy tried not to laugh. 'So you went . . . ?'

'I took ship out of Krondor, bound for the Far Coast, and then in Carse found a likely bunch of lads who had come by some information on a . . . venture that would net all involved a handsome living.'

'Pirates,' said Jommy and Servan at the same moment.

'Freebooters, out of Freeport in the Sunset Islands.' Jim nodded. 'At the time the captain claimed they sailed under a letter of marque from the Crown, though I never saw it. But being a trusting lad at the time, I took his word.'

Jommy doubted there had been a single moment in the thief's life when he had ever been a 'trusting lad' but he let the comment go.

'Well, I find myself on this island, in this cave, with this elf lass . . .'

'Did you leave something out?' asked Servan.

'Oh, a lot actually, but I'm talking about strange *places* I've been.'

'Let him go on,' said Jommy with ill-concealed mirth.

'Anyway, the lads I had shipped with were out looking for me, as I had tumbled to their less-than-honourable intentions as to my share of the treasure—'

'Treasure?' began Servan, but Jommy held up his hand. He wanted to hear this story.

'Well, that's another part of the tale,' said Jim. 'Anyway, as I was saying, I was hiding in this cave when I encounter this elf lass, name of Jazebel—'

35

'Jazebel,' echoed Jommy.

'Jazebel,' repeated Jim. 'And she had her own story of how she'd got there. She was trying to keep from being killed by these bears, only they weren't rightly bears, more like big furry owls.'

'Big furry owls,' said Servan, open astonishment now on his face. Jommy could barely contain himself, all cold, wet misery forgotten in the moment.

'Well, as I was saying, it was an odd place, far outside the Sunset Isles. She was gathering eggs for some elf magic. But anyway, she and I managed to fend off the creatures long enough to let my bloody companions pass by the cave, then we slipped out and got to a safe spot.'

'How did you ever get home?' asked Jommy.

Jim grinned. 'She had this magic stone, some elf thing, and once we were where she could do some magic, it took us to Elvandar.'

'Elvandar? Is that near Cloud Land?' Servan asked, invoking the name of a mythical land from children's tales.

Jommy said, 'Elvandar's real, Servan. I know people who've been there.'

'Next you'll be telling me you know some elves, too.'

Jommy smiled. 'Not personally, but I know people who do.'

'Well,' said Jim. 'As I had helped save the girl and all that, the Queen and her husband feted me with a supper, gave me their thanks and told me I was welcome any time I wanted to come calling. Then they helped me get to the outpost at Jonril – the one up in Crydee Duchy, not the one in Kesh it's named after – and from there I got back to Krondor.'

'Amazing,' said Jommy.

'More than amazing,' said Servan, shivering again. 'Unbelievable.'

Jim reached inside his tunic and pulled out a leather cord around his neck bearing a beautifully carved trinket. 'The Queen herself gave me this,' he said. 'She said any elf would recognize it and I would be named Elf-friend.'

Both Jommy and Servan leaned forward to inspect the trinket more closely. It was a pattern of interlocking knots, carved in what looked to be bone or ivory, and there was something about the design and shape that seemed more than human.

Suddenly serious, the thief said, 'I'm a lot of things, lads: rogue, adventurer, thief and, when needs be, downright murderous thug, but no man has ever called Jimmyhand a liar.'

'Jimmyhand?' asked Jommy.

'My . . . professional name, as it were. After a famous old thief from back in the day, Jimmy the Hand. Some say I'm a lot like him. Others say he might have been my great grand-da – but I think that was my mum trying to make me feel special. So, when I was a wee tyke I'd say, "I'm Jimmyhand", 'cause I never quite got the "the" part right. So it stuck. I'm rightly named Jim Dasher.'

In the time he had spent with Caleb and his family at Sorcerer's Isle, Jommy had heard a fair number of 'back in the day' stories from the old timers, not a few of which revolved around the notorious Jimmy the Hand, a thief who according to legend became an agent of the Prince of Krondor, then later was given a noble title, rising to the rank of Duke of both Rillanon and Krondor, the two most powerful offices in the Kingdom after the King.

Jommy studied the thief. He hardly knew him, but found him agreeable company, his outrageous stories were a welcome relief from the tedium of days spent waiting for an enemy who might never appear. He had no doubt Jim was every bit as dangerous as he claimed to be, but there was a quality under the surface that Jommy had learned to recognized at an early age out on the road alone: an instinct about who he could trust and who he couldn't. He nodded, then said, 'Jim, I'll never call you a liar until the day I catch you out.'

Jim stared at Jommy for a long moment, then the grin returned. 'Fair enough.'

Servan turned his attention back to the distant beach they had been assigned to watch. 'How much longer?'

'As long as it takes,' said Jommy.

'Which won't be much longer,' said Jim, pointing off into the rainy gloom. 'Boat coming.'

'How can you—' began Servan, then he saw it, a tiny dark speck that grew larger by the moment as a longboat came into the cove.

'Must be a ship lying off,' said Jommy.

'I'll tell the Captain,' said Servan, scrambling from under the lean-to. 'You watch them.'

Jommy also got out from under the shelter. 'Let's get a little closer.'

Jim held him back. 'Wait. There's another boat.'

After a moment, Jommy could see a second long-boat coming out of the gloom, following the first by a dozen yards. 'Now,' whispered Jim, though they were far too distant to be overheard, 'what do you think of that?'

Jommy said, 'Well, I can say the intelligence the Captain received was correct so far.'

'Not about the second boat,' corrected Jim.

'Picky,' Jommy muttered.

The two longboats rowed in to shore, and men leaped out of each and pulled them up on the sand, securing them with stakes and ropes. 'Looks like they plan on being here for a while,' said Jommy.

'What's that?' asked Jim, pointing to the second boat.

The crew of the two boats were dressed like common seamen, though each sported a black headcloth, tied behind the left ear. Most were bare-foot, marking them as sailors, though some wore heavy boots. But the last man leaving the second boat wore robes of dark orange trimmed with black. His features were masked by a hood, but the other men seemed deferential to the point of fear. None offered to help him exit the craft and all gave him a wide berth as he came ashore.

'Magician,' said Jim, almost spitting out the word, 'I hate magicians.'

'I've met a few I like,' Jommy said quietly.

'Well, I haven't. Damn near had my head removed by a magical trap down in Darindus one time. There's no trap made by the hand of mortal man I can't puzzle out with enough time, but magic . . .'

'Well,' said Jommy, 'I've met a few who are all right.'

Jim fell silent as the men in the boat spread out. It was clear that they were checking the surrounding area to see if they were observed. Jommy and Jim reached up and quietly took apart the hastily constructed lean-to, hiding the canvas behind the tree, then they both moved to a denser stand of bushes to the right. Without a word, they shared the same thought: in a few minutes an armed company of men, numbering twice those on the beach, would come over the rise behind them, but until that moment, it would be a good thing not to be seen by these men.

Jommy felt Jim's hand tighten on his shoulder. Jim pointed at himself and Jommy, then back up the hill. Jommy pointed to a small outcrop a hundred feet back up the trail, and Jim nodded. They moved through the rain which was letting up a bit, causing Jommy to curse under his breath. He wanted more cover, not less, and the weather had picked a very inconvenient time to become more clement after days of punishing him.

When they reached the outcrop they both lay

down, ignoring the soaking mud. The men from the boats had spread out to form a perimeter and a few began unloading what looked to be supplies.

'Looks like they plan on staying a while,' repeated Jommy.

'A third boat!' whispered Jim.

The third boat put in to the right of the others and more sailors leaped out, hauled it on to the beach and quickly began unloading provisions. More crates were passed along and Jim observed, 'They may be murderous dogs, but they're disciplined.'

Jommy observed their efficiency without comment.

Jim whispered, 'Those head-scarves. Saw something like that on some corpses down in the south Sunsets, about a week's sailing out of Freeport.'

'Who are they?'

'Wouldn't rightly know: these are the first ones I've seen who weren't dead. We came across a smoking hulk, burned down to the waterline, beached on an island with no proper name. The ship was known to my captain, but the corpses wearing those head-scarves were unknown to any sailor on that ship. Bit of a mystery as no man living was around to tell us the story of what had happened. We can only assume that the captain and crew of the burned ship had been carried off as slaves.'

The sound of movement from behind them caused both young men to turn around. Kaspar and Captain Stefan were coming down the hill in a crouch. Stirrings amongst the undergrowth revealed that men were moving into position to encircle the landing party.

'How many?' asked Kaspar, his eyes scanning the cove.

'About thirty,' said Jommy, 'and they have a spell-caster of some kind in their midst. The crew seems downright afraid of him.'

Jim said, 'Looks like some pirates out of the Sunsets, General.'

Kaspar muttered, 'What are they doing here?'

Jim whispered, 'If you sail straight west out of the Sunsets . . .'

'You end up in the Sea of Kingdoms,' finished Kaspar. 'I know how they got here. What I want to know is why.' To Captain Stefan, Kaspar said, 'Pass the word. I want prisoners. Especially that magician if we can manage it.'

'Magicians,' said Jim, as if it were a curse word.

Jommy exchanged glances with Kaspar. 'I said I've known some good ones.'

Kaspar's smile was rueful. 'And I've know some who were bloody monsters,' returned the General. 'Captain?'

'Sir?'

'Are the men in position?'

The Captain turned and made a slight hand gesture. Wherever he looked up on the hill, Jommy couldn't see the returned signal, but the Captain said, 'In position, sir.'

Kaspar nodded. 'Captain, whenever you're ready—'

'What is that?' asked Jim, pointing.

The others didn't need Jim to explain what 'that' was, for they saw it too. The magician was holding a staff above his head and a pillar of light appeared around him, reaching up into the clouds. A hollow voice speaking in a language unfamiliar to either onlooker answered seemingly from the air around the magician.

Then a figure appeared before the spell-caster, a shadowy thing draped in smoke. Even through the constant sound of the rain they could hear the air thrum with energy and crackle as if sparks were dancing off metal. The thing spoke and again that hollow voice echoed alien words. The magician replied in the foreign tongue and the creature looked around, surveying the area.

The hair on the back of Jommy's neck stood up as it seemed to lock gazes with him. The figure began to resolve itself into a man-like form, easily seven feet tall. Its shoulders were impossibly broad, and it appeared to have no neck. The creature's 'skin', dark-grey blue without any apparent blemish, rippled and pulsed, as if air flowed under a silk cloth, and the face was featureless, save for two red flames where eyes should be. The skin hardened and began to look like black rock.

'Now, Captain,' said Kaspar softly.

Captain Stefan stood up, holding a white cloth

43

in his left hand, and made a single chopping motion.

Chaos erupted.

From the ridge behind them shouts rang out, while arrows arched through the air to strike several of the men on the beach. Instantly three things occurred, as Jommy drew his sword. The men on the beach fanned out in precise order, not panicking, keeping their wits about them, and seeking cover wherever possible – behind the bulwarks of the boats, ridges of sand, and some large piles of driftwood. Several bowmen on the beach returned fire, but they were shooting blindly into the thicket on the hillside while those above had clear targets on the sand.

Men raced past Jommy's position, soldiers wearing Keshian and Kingdom tabards, and Jommy leaped to his feet, shouting, 'Come on, Jim!'

The conjured creature roared. It stood defiantly, arms spread as if ready to charge or be charged, and the men approaching could feel waves of heat coming from it as the volume of smoke rising from its black-rock skin increased.

Men faltered as they raced towards it, whilst those waiting for the onslaught were emboldened. Jommy half-ran, half-fell down the hillside, passing several soldiers who were brought to a halt by the demonic being's outcry. Suddenly he realized he was passing the vanguard and in front of him waited weapons poised to cut him down, plus some creature from an impossible nightmare.

Jommy started to back away, but one of the raiders charged him, ignoring arrows that were still raining down from the hillside. The raider took a step forward then was impaled by a long shaft which knocked him backwards. Jommy crouched, waiting for the others to catch up. He glanced backwards, and saw the soldiers were either motionless or retreating.

He understood why a moment later. The conjured creature was growing! The thing was now a good two feet taller than it had been before and much broader across what Jommy considered to be its shoulders. The arms appeared brawnier, and decorated with what seemed to be burning metal bands, twisting rods of some hot metal that gave off so much heat that Jommy could feel it through the rain. Cracks in the rocky 'skin' now appeared and from them tiny flames issued.

'Jim!' shouted Jommy, 'Let's get out of . . .' He glanced around and realized Jim Dasher was nowhere in sight. 'Damn,' muttered Jommy as he quickly backed away. 'He's either a coward or a lot smarter than I am!'

A pirate raced at Jommy and swung a vicious overhead blow with a weighted cutlass, a blow that was likely either to break Jommy's blade or cleave him from shoulder to stomach. Training and experience lent the young man the reflex to knock the blade to the right while dodging to the left, avoiding most of the force. The sand on the beach was terrible footing, so Jommy ignored the impulse to spin and slice the man's spine, instead electing to throw a right elbow at his jaw. Pain shot up his arm to his shoulder as he connected, and the man's eyes glazed over. Stepping back, Jommy slashed sideways with his blade, slicing the man's neck. As blood spurted upwards, Jommy continued to back away, unable to take his eyes off the horror that rose up before him.

Kaspar's voice cut through the air: 'Hit them hard: now!'

The soldiers were well trained, and despite their growing sense of dread as the conjured being rose up to a height of nearly nine feet, they charged. Those on the beach were dedicated, fanatics even, but they were not trained soldiers, and suddenly the left side of their defence collapsed.

With nowhere to retreat, they fought viciously, but within seconds the soldiers of Kaspar's command had killed half a dozen and had the rest retreating through the water to the scant protection offered by beached boats. Jommy faced a more determined defence, as soldiers from the Kingdom, Roldem and Kesh joined him in attacking the middle, mere yards away from the creature.

The raiders fought like men possessed, as if they were more afraid to retreat back to where the smouldering creature waited than die facing mortal men. Then the creature strode forward, and the man next to Jommy howled in agony as the diabolical being snatched him up by the neck. The sound of searing meat replaced the choked-off cry and the apparition tossed the soldier aside like a broken toy. Jommy saw flame coming from the creature's hands and could feel heat waves emanating from it as its appearance continued to evolve. The grey-blue skin was now crisscrossed with glowing red cracks, looking like nothing so much as molten metal under a rock crust, and where rain struck it sizzled and gave off tiny explosions of steam.

Jommy leaped backward, almost falling as he crashed into a soldier coming up behind him. 'Sir!' the man shouted in his ear. 'Another two boats have put in to the north and more of the bastards are coming down on our right flank.'

Jommy hesitated, then realized the soldier must be waiting, and that he was a senior officer, or at least as far as the men near him were concerned. Something had to be done to avoid a total rout. 'On me!' he shouted. 'Rally to me!'

Men hurried to him while the now-flaming monster snagged another screaming man and ripped his arm off while his torso was engulfed in fire.

'Form circle!' shouted Jommy, and the men nearby gathered in a tight knot around him. To the soldier who had warned him of the move on their flank, he shouted, 'Find the General, and tell the others to fall back to wherever he is. We'll hold them here! Go!'

The messenger ran off.

'Shield wall!' was Jommy's next command, and

the trained soldiers linked shields and suddenly he and two others, both irregulars from Krondor, stood in a tiny fortress of shields.

He had no faith in his order. Jommy knew that should the advancing monster strike the front of the shield wall, several of them would be instantly incinerated and the defensive position would collapse. But it was the only thing he could think of doing to buy a few minutes for the rest of the men to fall back to wherever Kaspar waited.

The creature stood motionless for a moment, and the magic-user pointed at the men clustered around Jommy with his staff and shouted something in the alien tongue. The creature took a great stride towards them and Jommy shouted, 'Steady!'

The creature halted for a moment, and raised his fist up high above them. Jommy shouted, 'Turtle!' He dropped his sword and sat down hard, yanking the two men next to him down to keep them from injury.

The men raised their shields overhead, and braced themselves as they would for a barrage of falling arrows. The flaming monster's fist, now the size of an anvil, crashed down on a pair of shields, causing one man to go to his knees and the other to collapse completely.

'Bloody hell!' said one of the irregulars, his eyes wide in terror.

'Scatter!' shouted Jommy: confusion was the only way to save as many men as possible. The two irregulars crawled away, while the soldiers did as they had been trained, each man running off directly away from the centre of the turtle, putting as much space as possible between themselves and their comrades. Those in the front fell straight back, then turned and fled.

Kaspar's own archers had attempted to hurt the creature, but their arrows were having no effect, the iron heads bouncing off the thing's hide while the shafts burst into flame. Waves of heat rolled over Jommy, as if he were standing before an open oven.

With a sweep of arms now as long as a spear, the creature knocked men aside as if he were playing with children. Whatever he touched burst into flames: men lay screaming and dying.

As Jommy pulled back, the creature seemed to notice him, and started towards him. Jommy braced himself, sure that in an instant he would be either crushed or burned to death. As he raised his sword to defend himself he saw beyond the creature a figure rising out of the surf. Water dripping off his face, his clothing soaked through, Jim Dasher seemed to appear out of nowhere as he came up from a low crouch to stand behind the magician. With a deft move so fast Jommy could barely follow it, the Krondorian thief raised his hands before him, crossed at the wrist, and flipped something over the magician's head. Suddenly the spell-caster was yanked backwards as Jim brought his knee up into the magician's spine, and even with the pounding of the surf, the tattoo of the rain and the screams from dying men Jommy could hear the snap of the man's spine. Blood sprayed from the magician's neck and he waved his arms for a brief instant before going limp.

As the magician died, the creature faltered, and then stopped and looked around as if waiting to be told what to do next. He howled, an echoing sound that grated on the ears and sent shivers through Jommy's body. Then the monster lashed out, first one way, then another. Men scattered, even those wearing the black head-cloths more intent on putting space between themselves and the apparition than in continuing the fight. Jommy threw himself backwards, avoiding a sudden reversal of direction by the flaming creature, and rolled on the sand, coming to his feet in a crouch, his sword ready.

Then he saw Servan running in his direction, shouting something that Jommy couldn't make out, but pointing directly at him. At the same instant Jommy sensed someone behind him and realized that Servan wasn't pointing at him, but at something behind him. He fell to his left, rolled and turned, seeing the blade cut through the air that would have taken his head had Servan not warned him.

Jommy didn't even think of trying to stand, but instead lashed out with his sword, cutting the man across the heel, severing the tendon. The man screamed and almost fell on top of Jommy. Jommy now shoved his sword point into the raider's armpit. Blood flowed down the man's side as the raider tried to retaliate with a looping blow designed to take Jommy's arm off.

Jommy rolled again hearing the sword strike sand. Now he was on his back. Knowing this was as poor a position for a fight as could be, Jommy kept rolling until he could again see his opponent. Then someone stepped over him and a sword point thrust down, ending the raider's life.

Servan reached down and pulled Jommy to his feet. 'We've got to fall back!' shouted the young nobleman. 'That thing is still killing anything near it, and it's getting hotter by the minute.'

Jommy didn't need his companion to tell him that; he could feel waves of heat rolling off the creature. Steam exploded from every step it took in the wet sand. Men on all sides were still locked in struggle, but there was nothing remotely organized about the conflict, and Jommy knew there was no way to co-ordinate any sort of counter-attack or even organize an orderly withdrawal. 'We need to have everyone fall back to that big rock over there!' Jommy shouted, pointing with his sword.

Servan nodded. 'I don't know where the General or the Captain are.'

They paused and looked up and down the cove, until Servan cried, 'Up there!'

Jommy saw Kaspar and Captain Stefan fighting back to back twenty yards up the hillside as half a dozen pirates circled them. Jommy looked at Servan.

'What now?'

Jommy was a good leader in the field and had a rudimentary grasp of tactics, but Servan was a born leader, a first rate strategist as well as an instinctive tactician. 'That big rock is our rally point, and I'll try to get to them—'

Jommy looked over again to where Kaspar and Stefan fought, and saw Jim Dasher – again seemingly out of nowhere – appear behind the two men fighting Kaspar. With a dagger in each hand he stabbed both men in the back of the neck, and they dropped instantly to the ground. Suddenly it wasn't six against two, but four against three, and as one of the men turned to see what happened to his companions, Kaspar ran him through and it was three against three.

Jommy shouted, 'I'll go this way, you go that, get the men moving! Get word to the General where we rally!'

Servan nodded and ran off, circling away from the flailing tower of flames that howled and lashed out in all directions. Jommy headed down the beach to where a knot of his men faced off against an equal number of pirates. Both sides seemed more concerned with getting untangled than with killing one another. Jommy shouted, 'To me!'

Breaking off the fight, his men retreated towards him, and within moments a fairly orderly withdrawal was underway. Moving to the agreed-upon position, Jommy motioned for the men to follow. 'Rally at that rock. Look for the General!'

Now the conjured creature, burning as brightly as the hottest fire Jommy had ever seen, lumbered in his direction. 'Watch out!' he warned and motioned for his men to move off and circle around to the rally point.

As they pulled away from the flaming monstrosity, men shouted that another boat was landing. 'Things are getting out of hand,' Jommy said to himself. As he glanced to see where the raiders were positioning themselves, he realized he was being flanked. If he wasn't careful, the enemy he had left behind would use his retreating men as a screen, allowing them to loop around and hit Kaspar's position from the rear.

'You, you, and you,' Jommy said pointing at the three nearest soldiers, two from Roldem and one from Kesh, 'follow me.' He gave a great war cry and charged at the closest raider.

From behind him he heard one of the soldiers from Roldem shout, 'Are you mad?'

Jommy shouted back, 'I want them to think so!'

The others followed and Jommy raced straight at the pirates who, seeing the men running straight at them, braced themselves for a charge. Just short of contact, Jommy shouted, 'Run!' and turned and fled back up the beach towards the hillside where Kaspar and Stefan were organizing a defensive position. A quick glance over his shoulder made Jommy wonder at the futility of that: the creature was becoming ever more enraged, thrashing out at anyone within reach. The only benefit this gave to Kaspar's forces was that the raiders now had to consider the monster as much as the men they were fighting. The difference was that Kaspar could organize his forces and pull them up the hillside to the base camp on the ridge a mile away if he had to. The raiders had nowhere to go but try to launch the boats, but now two of them were flaming from the horror's touch and no man looked willing to brave getting past it to the remaining boats. Some would no doubt flee up the coast to where the fourth boat had landed, but Jommy doubted it could hold all who wanted to escape the monster.

'They'll be coming this way in moments,' he shouted. 'Get to the General and dig in!'

Already fatigued from the short but intense struggle on the beach, men ran uphill in the mud, and suddenly Jommy realized there was no sound of fighting behind him. All he could hear was the echoing bellows of the monster, the rain in the woods above, and the panting of men nearly out of breath as they struggled to get to safety.

They reached Kaspar's position and saw men furiously making defensive positions, with brush and rocks and digging small trenches with swords and daggers. All the while the bowmen struggled to keep their strings dry enough to be effective against the enemy who were surely only moments behind those coming up the hill.

'Here they come!' shouted Kaspar.

Jommy reached the first line of defenders and

turned. A knot of raiders had formed at the base of the path and were fanning out to attack. He glanced to the north and saw another band of raiders fleeing for the remaining boat. As if reading his thoughts, Kaspar said, 'If we get through this we'll send a squad that way to round up any stragglers.'

'Why shouldn't we get through this, General?' asked Servan, still out of breath.

'They're attacking uphill and we're ready,' said Jommy.

'I'm not worried about those cutthroats,' said Kaspar. 'It's the thing following them that bothers me. It's stopped getting bigger, but it's setting fire to everything it touches.'

'And we're standing uphill,' said Captain Stefan.

'Ah, maybe we should pull back and get on the other side of the ridge?' observed Jommy.

'No time,' said Kaspar. 'Archers!' he shouted.

A few arrows arched overhead and the attackers scattered, but the bow fire was ineffective. 'Damn rain,' said Servan.

The men hurrying up the hill looked at those waiting for them and just kept coming. Jommy flexed his knees, his sword ready to parry or strike; and then it struck him. The only battle cries were from his own men: those coming at them were labouring, their panting breath barely able to meet the demands of the climb, let alone enabling them to shout or scream. There was a grim resignation on their faces. They were determined but they didn't show the usual edge of madness that Jommy had seen in other confrontations. These men knew they were going to die.

Jommy made his way back until he was next to Kaspar. 'General, those men are going to let us kill them.'

The former Duke of Olasko nodded. 'They have that look, don't they?' He turned and shouted, 'I want prisoners!' Then with an eye on the flaming monstrosity behind them, he quietly added, 'Should any of us survive.'

The creature had wandered aimlessly lashing out at anything it could, but now it seemed to have turned its attention to the hillside. Jommy said, 'I think it's seen us.'

'I have no idea if the thing even has eyes,' said Kaspar, 'but we'd better get this under control, because it's definitely coming this way.'

The first half a dozen raiders to reach the defenders threw themselves forward with manic ferocity. Several of Kaspar's men were wounded, but every attacker was cut down. Jommy waited, but no one approached him directly. He saw there were a dozen corpses on the ground just below where he waited, and farther down the hillside a knot of perhaps two dozen men watched. One of them said something and others nodded, then they broke forward, and now Jommy could hear shouts and cries. He did not recognize the language, but the intent was clear: they meant to kill as many of Kaspar's men as they could before dying in their turn.

56

Jommy saw one of the raiders turn, run down the hill and taunt the creature. How he had managed to do this, Jommy couldn't imagine, but it mattered little because the man had attracted the monster's attention. He slowly led the fiendish being up the hill and then waited. Jommy's eyes widened in astonishment as he saw the raider put down his sword and let the creature crush him as a man would an insect. The man's scream was short and high-pitched and came to an abrupt halt. His body had exploded into flames a second before the creature's fiery hand had touched him: even at this distance, those on the hillside could feel the heat.

A second man raced down, halfway between the monster and Kaspar's position just as the attackers reached the defensive position. But this time instead of a furious assault, the tempo was more that of a probing attack, something Jommy had come to understand was what soldiers did at times when they were trying to gauge the enemy's strength.

Suddenly he understood. 'General!' Jommy shouted.

'Yes?' replied Kaspar as he easily slapped aside a half-hearted thrust from a raider who had got between two soldiers. The General slashed with his blade and the raider fell dead, his throat fountaining crimson.

'They're bringing that thing up to us! They're dying in order to bring it here!' Jommy said.

'Idiots,' said Servan, but he looked distinctly nervous.

Jommy was forced to admit their tactic was effective, if you didn't mind dying to make it work. A third raider had now given himself up to the creature, and the ferocity of the heat was almost unbearable.

As if recognizing the hopelessness of their position, a handful of the enemy feigned attacks and purposefully left themselves open for killing blows.

'Prisoners!' shouted Kaspar. 'Keep one of them alive!'

Jommy couldn't stand his ground; everyone started to retreat before the forge-like heat of the monster. At the same time the raiders advanced and Jommy was forced to fight while backing up a steep hillside. The footing was wet and treacherous. Jommy killed one man only to almost die as another man shoved his companion into Jommy's blade. Only a quick blow over Jommy's shoulder by another soldier gave him the seconds he needed to pull his blade free.

Jommy almost lost his balance as his heel caught on a rock, and he barely avoided an enemy's sword thrust. He lashed out wildly and even though his opponent was willing to die, he pulled back out of reflex. When he sprang again Jommy was ready and the man died silently.

A desperate struggle ensued as men wishing to live tried to give way to men willing to die. Jommy felt the tempo of the conflict change and he recognized a difference in the battle around him: panic was imminent. The men of Kaspar's company were becoming desperate as they attempted a nearly impossible organized withdrawal, and the attackers were becoming frantic as they sought to keep from being captured while leading the monstrosity to their foes.

As they struggled to retreat up the hillside, a loud thrumming filled the air.

The creature was abruptly bathed in light as a shaft of white brilliance shot down from the clouds. It became transfixed, unable to move, and several men took wounds because they had stopped fighting in order to watch it.

Jommy killed a man in front of him, and glanced over the dying raider's shoulder. The enemy appeared to have sensed that the day had been lost, and they began to back away.

Abruptly both sides disengaged. Jommy shouted, 'General?'

'Wait,' came the order and Jommy did so. He watched the creature below as the raiders moved towards it, never taking their eyes off Kaspar's men. The rain now appeared to be cooling it off, as if the creature's mystic fire had lost its power. The sizzling sound of steam exploding off its surface diminished and its colour faded from a brilliant hot yellow back to the red-and-black appearance of molten rock. Jommy looked over his shoulder at Kaspar, and saw another figure high on a rock behind him. 'Look, General,' he said, pointing.

A being dressed in buckskin leather, with long flowing golden hair, stood holding a staff above his head. He appeared to be chanting. It was obvious to Jommy and Kaspar this was the author of the mystic light.

With a shudder, the creature dissolved like hot rocks falling apart. Great clouds of smoke filled the air.

'Prisoners!' shouted Kaspar: too late. The raiders, seeing no escape, wordlessly turned their swords on one another.

Jommy had seen enough men die in fights to know killing blows when he saw them. He turned to Kaspar and shook his head. The General's expression was a mixture of disgust at losing his prisoners and open relief at the intervention of the newcomer, who was obviously a magician. With a sigh, he said, 'Must be one of Pug's, come to look out for us. Good thing, too—'

Jommy shook his head. 'I don't think so, General.'

Captain Stefan and Servan both came to stand by their commander as the figure on the rock put his staff down. 'It's an elf,' said Servan. 'As I live—'

Kaspar said, 'I think you're right, Lieutenant.'

The elf said something, a question from the tone of it.

'I speak more than a dozen tongues and I don't recognize it,' said Kaspar.

The elf walked slowly down from his position above them, then halted half a dozen paces above

Kaspar and studied them for a moment. 'I said, who are you to be trespassing on the Peaks of the Quor?' He spoke the tongue of Kesh, but with an odd accent and cadence.

'I'm Kaspar, former Duke of Olasko and commander of this company. As for trespassing, I'm here with the permission of the King of Roldem and the Emperor of Great Kesh, both of whom claim this region.'

The elf's features showed no emotion, then after a second resolved into an expression of dark humour. 'Your masters' vanities do not concern me. This land belongs to the Quor.'

Trying to remain civil, Kaspar said, 'I want to thank you—'

'Before you thank me for anything, human, realize I did not save you from the elemental creature. It was a thing of magic so foul I needed to dispose of it before I deal with you.'

'Deal with us?' said Kaspar.

'Yes,' said the elf. 'You are all my prisoners.'

Instantly, men took combative stances, for while there was only one elf, they had just seen him vanquish the monster with seemingly no effort. Kaspar said, 'And do you, alone, intend to capture all of us?' There were still thirty combat-ready soldiers behind him.

'No,' said the elf and then he raised his voice and said something in the other language.

As if by magic elves appeared from behind rocks and trees, at least twice as many as Kaspar's band.

The one thing that stood out most about them was their appearance: all were blond, had sun-browned skin, and the same sky blue eyes as the magician. And all of them wore the same buck-skin so that it was almost a uniform, save for a slightly different cut to a tunic or fringe on the sleeves. Some elves had feathers or polished stones woven into their braids or a warrior's knot, and many wore their hair down, long past the shoulders. Most carried bows, with arrows pointed at them, and another half a dozen carried staves. Kaspar was certain they were magic-users like the elf before them. After a moment he said, 'Throw down your weapons.' Reluctantly the men obeyed, and Kaspar said to the elf, 'We surrender.'

The elf nodded. 'Gather your wounded who can travel, and come with us.'

It took a few minutes to find those able to move and render them aid so they could travel. A dozen men were too injured to move and the elf said, 'Leave them. They will be attended to.'

Kaspar nodded and when his men were ready, elves began escorting them up the hillside, along the same trail that led down from the cave Kaspar had used as his base of operations. As they reached a point where the elf had first revealed himself, a strangled cry from behind them caused Jommy to flinch. As he started to turn, he felt a strong hand grip his arm. Jim Dasher said, 'Don't look. It's better not to.'

Jommy nodded. The men too injured to move

were being killed quickly by the elves, and although Jommy knew it was probably kinder than letting a man die slowly from a gut wound or exposure, he still hated the thought of it.

Slowly the captives wended their way up the hillside high into the mountains above.

The rain continued.

CHAPTER 3

UPHEAVAL

Pug looked at the sun.

He shifted his perception through the visible spectrum and then into the other energy states he could now recognize. No matter how hard he tried, he could not find true words to express what he was seeing. He had been on the Dasati home world for two weeks, hiding in a complex of rooms under the protection of Martuch, a Dasati warrior and secret follower of the White. He had taken the opportunity to fine tune his control of his abilities in this realm.

Nakor the Isalani, his companion and long-time friend, sat on another bench in the little garden, watching Pug. His charge, the strange young warrior Ralan Bek, was with Martuch, practising his role as Martuch's protégé and mastering more of the subtleties of being a Dasati warrior.

Magnus, Pug's older son, sat on the bench beside his father, lost in his own thoughts as the three magicians contemplated their mission. He trusted his father implicitly, but still had no idea what had brought them into this dark realm, to a place to which no human had ever travelled, seeking only

64

his father knew what. Magnus recognized the threat posed by the Dasati, yet he had no concept of what they could possibly accomplish here, on a world an unimaginable distance from home. Distance, he corrected himself, was meaningless in discussing where they were. There was a good deal of proof that this world would have a twin in their own universe, perhaps even a world known to Magnus, but how they would get home to their own plane of reality was beyond Magnus's understanding.

That last awareness sparked concerns in the young magician; he was, after his mother and father – and perhaps Nakor – the most powerful practitioner of magic on the world of Midkemia, and some day would most likely surpass even them. But for all his ability, talent and knowledge, he had no idea how they would return. He had tried to understand the nature of the magic employed to bring them here, and bits of it were . . . familiar, echoing things he knew about transporting the body from location to location, as well as being reminiscent of rift magic, but how it all came together, that was lost on Magnus. Martuch had indicated that in one way it was an easy transition to make, but had been vague on details.

As much as Magnus knew he must trust this Dasati renegade, deep within he harboured doubts. While they seemed to be serving roughly similar causes, they were not entirely after the same goals, and Magnus had no doubt that

Martuch would put serving his own people's needs ahead of the lives of the four humans from Midkemia.

Now the other reason for Magnus's discomfort entered the tiny garden. It was, if he was to believe what his father had told him, his grandfather, the legendary Macros the Black. But the man who stood before him was not human, but Dasati. Yet the man had memories that could have only belonged to Macros, spoke flawless King's Tongue, Tsurani, and Keshian, as well as any number of other languages from Midkemia and Kelewan, and in so many things demonstrated that he had the mind of a human from his home world. Yet the entire question of Macros's presence on this world, in this form, raised questions that went far beyond troubling. Secretly, Magnus was frightened.

Macros had been absent most of the time since Pug and the others arrived, and Pug and he had had only minutes at a time to speak. The tall Dasati nodded a greeting and came over to stand before Pug and Magnus. 'May I sit?' he asked.

Magnus nodded, moving over on the stone bench to make room for the Dasati magician.

'Even after weeks, my mind is reeling,' said Pug. 'I realize you have . . . changed, yet I can see . . . you are still you.' He studied the features of the Dasati sitting next to him. 'I've been, by any reasonable measure, patient, I think you'll agree.' He glanced at his two companions. 'We understand from what we've pieced together that you are the leader of a group constantly in peril, and that you have many responsibilities. But you are here, now, so as we have this time, why don't you tell us the complete story?'

Nakor rose from his bench and walked over to sit down before Pug. 'As much as I enjoy a good story, it would be useful if we heard only the truth this time, Macros.'

Macros smiled. 'Perhaps my most grievous sin was lying. At that time . . .' He looked away as if into a painful memory. He took a breath. 'It was so many years ago, my friends. I was an arrogant man who refused to trust others enough to tell them the simple – or in some cases not-so-simple – truth and let them choose whether or not to do the right thing.

'I manipulated people with lies, so that I could ensure . . .' He shook his head. 'Another sin was vanity, I'll confess. I was so certain back when . . . when I was young, when I was human.' He waved his hand in a general circle. 'This experience has been humbling, Pug.' He looked at Magnus. 'I've a grown grandson and I have missed every day of his life.'

'You have two,' said Magnus. 'I have a younger brother.'

'Caleb,' said Macros to Magnus. 'I know.'

Pug was still grappling with the fact of his alien existence, forcing his mind to accept what he could see with his own eyes. Once past that amazement, he was still left with another issue: that the man before him was Macros the Black, his wife's father.

67

As he had just openly admitted, he was a man who had used people as one might use tools, and shamelessly lied to gain advantage. He had put people in harm's way without their consent, and had made choices for others that had resulted in pain, suffering and death. As a result, trusting him was a difficult task. Then again, Pug had watched Macros die defending others against Maarg, the Demon King. It had been the highest act of sacrifice and almost certainly had saved Midkemia from horrors for which the Serpentwar would have been but a mild prelude. Maarg would have almost certainly destroyed the entire world given enough time.

Macros spoke calmly. 'The time for duplicity is over.' He looked at Magnus and reached out, his hand gently touching his face. 'I'm younger than you, in this body,' he said with a bitter smile, 'despite being hundreds of years in memory, I'm but thirty years as the Dasati measure time.' He took his hand away from Magnus's face. 'Around the eyes, you resemble your mother.' Magnus nodded slightly. Macros's gaze went from his grandson, to Nakor, then to Pug.

'Start at the beginning,' said Pug.

Macros laughed. 'For this story, the beginning was my ending. As I told you, I died at the hands of Maarg, the Demon King.' He looked across the garden, and gazed into the distance, focused on memory. 'When I died . . .' He closed his eyes. 'It is difficult to remember, sometimes . . . the longer

I live as a Dasati, the more . . . distant my human memories are, the feelings especially, Pug.' He looked at his grandson Magnus. 'Forgive me, my boy, but whatever familial ties I should be feeling are absent.' He lowered his eyes. 'I haven't even asked about your mother, have I?'

'Actually, you did,' said Magnus.

Macros nodded. 'Then I fear my memory is fading very rapidly. Ironically, for a human who has lived the span of more than nine hundred years, it would seem that I am dying.'

Pug's shock could not have been more evident. 'Dying?'

'A disease, rare in the Dasati, but not unheard of; should anyone besides our group and our Attenders suspect, I would be killed out of hand for weakness. The human ailments of the elderly are alien to the Dasati. Should the eyes fail or the memory fade, the person so afflicted is killed without thought.'

'Is there anything—' began Magnus.

'No, nothing,' said Macros. 'This culture is about death, not life. Narueen said there may be something the Bloodwitches could do in their enclave, but that's a continent away and time is of critical importance.' He smiled. 'Besides, if you've already died once, death is hardly something to fear, is it? And I'm interested to see what the gods have in store for me this time.' He winced slightly as he shifted his weight. 'No, death is easy. It's dying that's the hard part.' He looked around. 'Now, as

I was saying, my memory seems to be fading, so I'll tell you what you need to know and then we can see if we can serve a common cause.' Looking at Nakor, Macros said, 'The gambler. The one who cheated me! Now I remember.'

Nakor smiled. 'I told you how when you revived from your ascension to godhood.'

'Yes . . . you slipped me a cold deck of cards!' Macros looked amused at the memory. Then his eyes narrowed and he studied Nakor more closely for a moment. 'You are more than you seem to be, my friend.' He hiked his thumb in the direction of Martuch's home and said, 'As is your young friend. He has something within his being that is dangerous, very dangerous.'

'I know,' said Nakor. 'I think Ralan Bek contains a tiny fragment of the Nameless One.'

Macros pondered this and then said, 'In my dealings with the gods and goddesses I have come to understand a little of both their abilities and their limitations. What do you know?'

Nakor glanced at Pug.

'We believe that the gods are natural beings, defined in many ways by the form of human worship. If we believe the god of fire to be a warrior with torches, he becomes that,' Pug answered.

'Just so,' said Macros. 'Yet if another nation sees that being as a woman with flames for hair, then that is what the deity becomes.' He looked from face to face. 'In ancient days, the Dasati had a god or goddess for almost every aspect of nature you can imagine. There were the obvious major gods: the god of fire, death, air, nature, and the rest of it – even a god and goddess of love or at least the fundamental male and female urge to create offspring. But there were also so many minor gods it would give a scholar a throbbing head just to catalogue them.

'There was the goddess of the hearth, and the god of trees, and the god of water was served in turn by the god of the sea, and another god of rivers, a goddess of waves, and another for rain. There was a god for travel, and another for builders, yet another for those who laboured under the ground in mines. As I understand it, there were shrines at every street corner and along the roads, and votive offerings were placed upon them by a worshipful populace who dutifully attended the prescribed public worships, festivals, and dedications.' He took a deep breath. 'The Dasati were a race of believers who also had a sense of duty that would shame a Tsurani temple nun. They created a pantheon of thousands of gods and goddesses, and every one had their appointed day of celebration, even if that consisted only of laying a flower on an altar, or hoisting a drink in a tavern in the god's name.

'It is important to remember that these gods and goddesses were as real as any you've encountered in Midkemia, even if their realms were minute. They had a spark of the divine within them, even if their mandate was only to ensure lovely flowers in the field each spring.'

Of Pug, he asked, 'What have you learned about the Chaos Wars since we last met?'

'Little. Tomas has a few more of Ashen-Shugar's memories to draw upon, and I've found an odd volume or two of myth and legend. But little substantial.'

'Then listen,' said Macros. He looked directly at Nakor. 'The truth.'

Nakor nodded once, emphatically, but said nothing.

Macros began. 'Before humanity came to Midkemia there were ancient races, several of which you know about, such as the Valheru, rulers of that world and masters of the dragons and elves. But other races existed as well, their names and nature lost before the dawn of human memory.

'There was a race of flyers who soared above the highest peaks, and a race of beings living below the oceans depths. Peaceful or warlike, we will never know, for they were destroyed by the Valheru.

'But above all others rose two beings: Rathar, Lord of Order, and Mythar, Lord of Chaos. These were the two Blind Gods of the Beginning. The very fabric of the universe around them was their province, and Rathar weaved the threads of space and time into order, while Mythar tore them asunder, only to have Rathar reweave them, over and over.

'Ages past, Midkemia was a world in balance, the hub of that particular region of space and time, and all was well, more or less.'

Nakor grinned. 'If you were a being of incredible power.'

'Yes, it was not a good time to be weak, for it was rule by might and no hint of justice or mercy existed,' responded Macros. 'The Valheru were far more an expression of that epoch than they were evil; it can even be argued that good and evil were meaningless concepts during that time.

'But something changed. The order of the universe shifted. More than anything I wished to know the reason for this shift, yet it is lost in time. A fundamental reordering of things took place – it's impossible to say what the scale of time involved was, but to the races living on Midkemia at the time the result of that reordering seemed abrupt. Vast rifts in space and time appeared, seemingly from nowhere, and suddenly beings unknown on Midkemia entered the world: humanity, dwarves, giants, goblins, trolls and others as well. And races that came but did not endure, as well.

'For years a war raged across the universe, and we mere humans . . .' He stopped and laughed softly. '*You* mere humans could only apprehend the tiniest part of it. What we know is legend, myth, and fable. Shreds of history may be enmeshed in them, but no one will really know the truth of it.'

Nakor laughed. 'For a man who can travel in time, you had a simple enough means to discover that truth.'

73

Macros grinned. 'You would think so, wouldn't you? But the truth is I do not have the ability to travel in time, at least not in the fashion you'd imagine.' Looking at Pug, he said, 'I remember when you and Tomas came to find me in the Garden, at the edge of the City Forever.'

Pug remembered. It had been his first encounter with the Hall of Worlds.

'Had I the ability to travel in time, I never would have permitted the trap sprung by the Pantathian Serpent Priests to fling us backwards through time.'

'Yet you instructed me how to accelerate its unfolding many times, until we reached a point at which time was meaningless,' observed Pug.

'True, and while I lacked *your* talents in that regard, I also lacked the skills to manipulate time as the Pantathians had.'

'In all our encounters with the Serpent Priests,' said Pug, 'we found them clever, but hardly brilliant, dangerous in numbers, but never individually.' He mused for a moment, then added, 'I never considered that the time trap was actually a spell of majestic complexity and required skills beyond their abilities. At least one of those priests was inspired.'

'All things return to the Nameless One,' said Nakor. 'As he has touched Leso Varen, he must have so done with a Pantathian high priest. There was your inspired genius.'

Macros waved his hand. 'Yes. Had they all had

that level of talent, the war would have turned out very different, but other than that one savant, they were always a nuisance at most—'

'Nuisance?' interrupted Pug. 'Tens of thousands died over the course of two wars because of that *nuisance*.'

'You mistake my meaning,' said Macros. 'They created chaos, but as Nakor observed, it was the Nameless One at the root of it all.'

Macros stood and walked a pace, turned and said, 'There is so much to tell, and it's difficult to know where to begin.' He glanced from face to face. 'Should a question occur to you, perhaps it were best if you leave off asking until I make this following point.' He waved his hand in the air, and a globe appeared, an illusion that Pug instantly recognized, for he had used such things to teach students at the Assembly on Kelewan, the Academy at Stardock, and upon Sorcerer's Isle.

'Consider this globe to be all that can exist,' said Macros. 'Surrounded by the void, it represents all of what we comprehend.' He waved his hand and the globe was now banded with shades of grey, from a nearly black band at the bottom to an off-white one at the top. 'Each layer represents a plane of reality, with the centremost one being our own . . . *your* own,' he corrected himself. 'As you noticed on Kosridi, it's a physical match for Midkemia, as this world is a match for Kelewan.'

'Kelewan,' said Pug. 'I had no inkling.'

Macros nodded. 'You sit within a garden that is roughly in the middle of the great hall in the Emperor's palace in the Holy City of Kentosani, if I remember my Tsurani geography. There's an affinity between physical creations that I do not pretend to understand – it can even be argued that there is but only one physical expression and that the planes are overlays, spiritual realms that actually exist in the same space. It's all very difficult and borders on the abstract debates ordinarily suitable only for students of natural philosophy. But I can appreciate your not recognizing Omadrabar being analogous to Kelewan, because this world has been occupied by the Dasati a great deal longer than Kelewan has been home to humanity.

'Were you to rise up to a great height, you would find that while the seas would look familiar far more of this world is covered by construction.' He paused. 'Did you know that given the manner in which the Dasati farm, they've been forced to include gigantic farming enclaves within the cities, so they can feed the populace?'

Macros shrugged. 'Enough digression. These levels or planes of reality have been stable for . . . well, I guess since the dawn of time and as you see them.' He waved his hand, and suddenly there appeared a distortion, as if someone had stuck a long needle through the sphere from the bottom, pushing a small part of each layer upward, until it intersected the layer above. 'Then came something I can only call the Disturbance.'

Pug glanced at his companions, but said nothing.

Macros continued. 'Like the cause of the upheaval that brought humanity to Midkemia, we'll never know the cause of the Disturbance.'

Nakor grinned. 'Are they the same?'

Macros frowned like an annoyed schoolteacher. 'If you find out, please let me know. This Disturbance is an . . . imbalance, a pressure upwards from the lowest to the highest realm of reality. Just as the Dasati are attempting to manifest themselves into our . . . *your* realm, so are creatures from the third realm attempting to rise up into this one.'

'You're describing a cataclysm of unprecedented scope,' whispered Pug.

Macros nodded. 'Yes, my friend. The entire fabric of the universe is being rent apart, and we must stop it before it gets worse.'

'How?' asked Magnus quietly.

Macros sighed, a very human sound coming from a Dasati. 'I have no real knowledge, just intuition, and even that is . . . not compelling.' He waved his hand and the conjured sphere vanished. 'The Chaos Wars appeared to have been an attempt at reordering the balances within the entirety of reality, from the highest to the lowest plane. We can only speculate on what occurred in the other realms of reality, but I suspect balance was restored, else the crisis we face would be even more catastrophic. We've had no evidence of any interaction between your native realm, the one I used to live in as well, and the one above it, the first heaven.'

'Because the Nameless One is imprisoned?' suggested Nakor.

'Most likely,' said Macros. 'So, the chaos comes from the lower realms. His Darkness, the Dark God of the Dasati, is so powerful in his supremacy that whatever incursions from below threatened this plane have almost certainly been dealt with.'

'If I might ask a question?' inquired Magnus.

'What?' asked his grandfather, barely hiding his impatience at the interruption.

'Why here? Why Kelewan and Midkemia?'

Macros paused, then said, 'Not a bad question.' He smiled. 'I suspect there must be a locus somewhere, or loci, where the incursions from one realm to the next manifest first, analogous to the first Tsurani rift into Midkemia, in the Grey Towers Mountains.

'Remember, the gods of each realm are local expressions of a much vaster entity, spanning universes. The Nameless One is a manifestation of evil on an unimaginable scale, one that spans the entirety of the universe within which Midkemia resides, a universe of billions of worlds, with countless creatures on them, multitudes having visions of that evil, giving it a legion of guises. Yet, we can assume with some degree of certainty that just as the Nameless One was confined in Midkemia, so he was in many other places, the result of the conflict which seemed to centre on that world.

'I expect the further one travelled from Midkemia, the less likely it would be that the history of the Chaos Wars remained unchanged. Remember the sphere? If you were at the extremities the ordering of the planes of existence seemed normal, unchanged. Yet if you were at the point of the incursion, you would be amidst chaos.'

'You build a persuasive argument,' said Pug. 'But what I wish to know is how this applies to us, finding ourselves here?'

Macros nodded and smiled. 'To the heart of the matter.' He looked directly into Pug's eyes. 'The Nameless One is confined, but as you have witnessed, not without influence, even some power, albeit limited by the other surviving Greater Gods, the Controllers.

'He doesn't appreciate the incursion from 'below' by the Dark God of the Dasati. As much as possible, he's working in concert with the other gods of Midkemia to restore the proper order of things.'

'We're working on behalf of the Nameless One?' asked Nakor.

'In a manner of speaking, yes,' replied Macros. 'It is my belief that ultimately we all play a part in the Nameless One's plans.'

'That plan being?' asked Nakor.

Macros's expression became grimmer than before. 'I believe we are seeing a struggle between gods, my friends. And I believe in some fashion we are weapons.'

'Weapons?' echoed Magnus. 'We are just three magicians and a . . . ?' He glanced at Nakor.

'Bek may be a weapon. There is little about him that is natural.'

'There is a prophecy,' said Macros. 'A Dasati lord will rebel against the TeKarana, and prepare the way for the God Killer.'

Pug said, 'You think Bek . . .'

'Is the weapon,' said Nakor. 'It is almost certain.'

'What I don't know is if he is *the* weapon.' Macros coughed, fighting back the impulse even as Pug saw his chest tighten and the spasm hit him. When he finished, he said, 'Even the lowest of the low would attack me if they saw such an overt sign of weakness.'

A servant hurried in, and moments later a warrior in the garb of the Sadharin followed. 'Master,' said the servant. 'Something—'

The soldier interrupted. 'Word from Martuch. You must flee. Within the hour the announcement will come from the Palace. At sundown we shall begin a Great Culling.'

Macros drew himself up to his full height, his will overcoming his weakened body. 'You know what to do,' he said to the servant. 'Take only what you must and get our people to the closest sanctuary.'

'Master,' said the servant, bowing his head and running off.

To the soldier he said, 'Return to Martuch and tell him to meet me at the Grove of Delmat-Ama as soon as he is able. If possible, have him bring Valko and anyone else he thinks will serve. It is close to the time, I think.'

The young warrior nodded respectfully, then hurried off. Macros said to himself, 'Please the gods they survive.'

Pug asked, 'What is it?'

Macros said, 'Get your things. We leave within minutes. The TeKarana has called the Great Culling, and at sundown everyone within the Dasati Empire will have licence to kill whomever they may. All truces are abated, all alliances put aside, murder is the will of His Darkness.'

'What does it mean?' asked Magnus.

Macros looked troubled. 'It means the Dark God is hungry. It means the usual slaughter of his subjects is not enough to feed him. I fear it means he is ready to begin his invasion into the next realm.'

Pug, Nakor, and Magnus exchanged glances. Nakor said, 'What about Bek?'

'He's fine with Martuch,' answered Macros. 'In some ways he is more Dasati than any Dasati Deathknight I've met. The next night and day will probably be the most fun he's had in his life. I just hope he leaves Martuch alive.'

'Why wouldn't he?' asked Pug.

'There are no allies or friends, save those arrangements made in the moment. Martuch and the other Lords of the Langradin will have safe houses and provisions put by close to the Langradin Great

House, by habit if nothing more. But for most common people tonight is a bloody game of chance, and the prize is survival. If one can survive from sunset tonight until sunset tomorrow, the usual order will return. They may be bloody rules, but they're rules.

'But for one day there will be no rules. Want something that belongs to your neighbour, take it. Want to settle an old grudge with someone who is too well protected for you to attack, now's the time. Or if you're just ambitious and the death of a few better placed individuals in your own faction, your own battle society, or even your own family would benefit you, sharpen your blades. Every death will be seen as a gift to His Darkness, and every murder a benediction.

'Bands of Deathpriests and Hierophants will be on the streets in every town and city. Anyone is fair game. Bands of ravagers will roam the countryside. Anyone with resources will hole up and barricade every door and window, or find a hole to hide in. We, on the other hand will be on the road, trying to reach a bucolic hamlet a day's ride south of the city, and it will take us most of the night and day to reach the boundary of the city.' He looked from face to face. 'I have little fear for our safety. Any one of us should have enough skill to defend ourselves from whoever we meet along the way.'

'But you fear discovery,' said Nakor.

'Yes,' said Macros. 'For if word of our existence reaches those who know what I am, or who might guess who you are, then the entire weight of the Empire, every resource of the TeKarana and the Dark God will be turned to destroying us.'

Pug said, 'Then let us go.'

Macros smiled. 'Yes, let us go. And if you have a prayer left in you after all you've seen, now would be the time to use it.'

CHAPTER 4

EMPIRE

Miranda looked defiant.

Two members of the Assembly – Alenca and a magician named Delkama – had just finished conjuring a sphere of illusion, a translucent bubble scintillating with sheets of energy which arced across its surface, sizzling patches of bright gold light and brilliant steel blue. It had slowly expanded and caused more than one usually implacable Tsurani noble to flinch visibly. It was a ward, designed to ensure that no magical scrying could spy upon the proceedings about to commence. Moreover, should anyone be attempting to view the proceedings remotely, they would only see three magicians addressing the Emperor on matters unrelated to what was really being discussed. This elaborate charade was for the benefit of Leso Varen, should he be close by and able to use his considerable power to eavesdrop on the Council.

The other members of the Assembly of Magicians who accompanied Miranda looked alarmed. Despite being among those of highest rank in the Empire, even they were tradition bound to show respect bordering on awe to the Emperor. Yet Miranda stood before the Light of Heaven with her shoulders back, her eyes fixed on the young man, and her expression one of expectation. She had just instructed – no, almost ordered – the leader of the Empire of Tsuranuanni to say nothing until the protective measure was in place.

Rarely in the history of the Empire had an outlander stood before the Emperor. The chamber of the Imperial High Council was sacrosanct, as was the entirety of Kentosani, the Holy City, and those who had been there were either ambassadors or captive leaders. Even then it was unusual for the Emperor to attend in person, for he was the divine presence, the embodiment of Heaven's bounty and a grace to the Tsurani people. Yet so terrible was the message from the Assembly to the Imperial Throne, that Sezu, First of that Name, Ruler of the Nations of Tsuranuanni, took it upon himself to grace the audience and listen in person to the alien woman's warning.

The vast hall of the High Council was filled to capacity as every ranking noble – every man and the few women who were ruling lords and ladies of the hundreds of Houses of Rank in the Empire – had attended to hear Miranda's warning. Dressed in a riot of hues, they wore robes of house colours – here one of yellow with crimson trim, there another of black trimmed with pale blue – each bedecked with beading and braids and adorned with precious stones and clasps of precious metal. They were arrayed according to Tsurani tradition in groups that constituted clans, but many who sat silently, waiting for the Emperor's reply, stole glances at confederates in other parts of the hall, at members of their own political parties. Tsurani politics were not only deadly but convoluted and intricate, an ever-shifting balancing act on the part of each ruler, weighing blood loyalty on one side against expediency and opportunity on the other.

Miranda spoke. 'Majesty, lords and ladies of the High Council, we come today with a warning, for as dire a threat as can be imagined now bears down on this world.'

Miranda had rehearsed all she would say as she and the Great Ones had awaited the gathering of the Council, and she moved quickly from the discovery of the Talnoy on her world by Kaspar of Olasko to the recent incursion of the Dasati into this world. She glossed over nothing, and she had no temptation to embellish. The unvarnished truth was frightening enough. When she had finished, she saw the Emperor sitting quietly and realized he did not look surprised by anything she had said. She glanced at Alenca who gave the slightest shake of his head indicating he didn't understand the lack of reaction either. She knew that the Light of Heaven had been kept current as to what the Assembly was doing regarding the Talnoy in their possession, but she

86

knew none of what had occurred since she had been captured had been communicated. The existence of the Dasati incursion had to have been a shock to the young Emperor, yet he sat calmly as if considering what to ask be prepared for his evening meal. Emperor Sezu had come to his office only recently, four years before, and like his father before him had ruled a relatively peaceful empire.

Miranda turned her attention from the Light of Heaven to the High Council. Once again she was astonished at the Tsurani mind, for although she had just delivered as dire a warning as could be imagined, she suspected as many as a third among the attending lords were wondering how to gain advantage from the coming chaos, and from their expressions, fully another third seemed incapable of fully understanding what it was they had just heard. It was the last third, who did understand the dangers of which she spoke, who realized they were all in peril, who showed the proper distress and who waited silently on the Light of Heaven's pleasure. The impatient shifting of silks and the nervous scuffling of leather sandals on the floor was a counterpoint to the silence as all waited for the Emperor to speak.

Beside the youthful ruler stood another black-robed magician, Finda by name, an older mage with whom Miranda had only a passing acquaintance. He was the current advisor from the Assembly to the Imperial Throne and from his

87

expression it appeared he would rather be just about anywhere else in the vast Tsurani Empire at this moment.

Miranda was not the expert on Tsurani society her husband was – he had lived among them for years – but she still understood it well enough to have a sense of what was likely to be the reaction among the ruling families. The warlike Tsurani traditions still dominated the politics of the Empire, the 'Game of the Council' as it was called, but rather than armed confrontation new means of domination and influence were employed: wealth, influence and social position. With the occasional murder, midnight raid, and abduction thrown in, Miranda thought. At times Tsurani politics reminded her of nothing so much as the criminal wars in Great Kesh; the Mockers of Krondor would have fitted right in.

Five great families – Keda, Minwanabi, Oaxatucan, Xacatecas and Anasati – still dominated the many clans and political parties that defined the governance of the Empire. Traditionally they had been the only families able to claim the title of Warlord, until the current Emperor's great grandmother seized the throne for her son. And above all others there remained one constant: the Emperor. The Light of Heaven could overrule any judgment of the High Council. He could order war or force feuding clans to put down their arms at whim. Such was his power.

All waited as the Emperor upon the golden

throne, seat of power for two thousand years in the Empire's history, pondered his response. The assembled lords of the great and lesser houses were silent to a man. No one dared speak before the Light of Heaven.

Miranda took note of the empty chair at his side, set slightly lower on the dais. It had been placed there by Sezu's great grandmother, the legendary Lady Mara of the Acoma, Mistress of the Empire, the only person in the long history of the Tsurani people to hold that title. In saving her house from bitter enemies, she had reformed a nation, freeing suffering millions from lives without hope. As a result of her acts a nation had risen that now placed as much importance on art, music and literature as it did on honour, bravery, and sacrifice in war. The Empire was not without its struggles and difficulties, but it had been reborn under the last three emperors despite attempts by traditionalists to steer the Empire back to old values and ways.

All eyes now turned to the Emperor as the Light of Heaven stirred.

Sezu, First of that Name, at last revealed his reaction: he looked deeply troubled. When his great grandmother had brought reform to the Empire she had also transformed the office of Emperor from an almost entirely ceremonial one to the ultimate seat of power within the Empire, and the weight of his responsibilities had already aged him beyond his thirty-six years. Softly he said, 'Dire words, indeed, Lady Miranda. We have been a relatively peaceful nation for more than two generations. Some difficulties with our neighbours in the Thuril Highlands and across the Sea of Blood to the south have kept some of our young men mantled in glory and heaped honours upon their houses. But we have not fought a major war since our invasion of your homeworld.'

Miranda nodded. The Emperor had Midkemian blood in him: Mara's Midkemian lover, Kevin, had been acknowledged father of Emperor Justin. And while that fact gave some vague sense of kinship, this young man was entirely Tsurani. Yet there was something else, something almost rehearsed in his next question. 'Would it not serve if this Talnoy was removed from our lands and returned to your world?'

Miranda looked at Alenca, eldest of the Great Ones, who said, 'Light of Heaven, we have considered that, and we think it pointless. It was the renegade, Leso Varen, who provided aid to the Dasati in establishing their presence here. They know now how to return, and we are sure they would do so.' He paused as if weighing his words carefully, then said, 'There is something about our world . . . Many of us think these Dasati have marked this world for a reason; we just don't know what that reason is.' He fell silent for a long moment, then added, 'We think the nations need to prepare for invasion.'

The Emperor was silent for a very long time to consider this. Then he spoke in what Miranda could only term a precise manner. She realized this young Emperor was no fool. He *knew* what she and Alenca were going to say before they said it! Her instinct that he had not been shocked was justified. But she wondered how he had known. She was also sure that he had rehearsed his reply!

'Attend me,' said the Light of Heaven formally to the assembled Council, as he stood up. The assembled lords of the Empire stood at once, for it was not permitted for any lesser being to sit in the presence of the monarch when he was not also seated. 'Our tradition is ancient, our ways time-honoured, but now we face new perils unlike any in memory. We are reminded of hallowed antiquity, of a time of myth, and the arrival of the nations over the golden bridge.

'Our lore-keepers suggest that what we fled from the Home Before Time was too monstrous a thing to even bear accounting, so no word of description, no tale or song even suggests what it was that drove us to this world. It is merely that thing from which the nations fled.' He paused for a moment, then added, 'We fear that now such a horror returns to task the nations.' He fell silent to let his words sink in. Miranda knew enough of Tsurani lore to know he had struck a chord with the lords of the High Council, for the root of Tsurani history was the Myth of Arrival. It was a tale Pug had recounted to her more than once, the image of the majestic golden bridge of light through a massive rift across which thousands of refugees flooded into Kelewan, fleeing the terrors of the Chaos Wars. It was the foundation of every Great One's training, the birth of those people who later would become the Tsurani, instilling a deep sense of community that was the heart of every magician's oath to serve the Empire.

'It is the tradition that when the nations go to war, the Warlord is given the power to conduct the business of war. That office has remained empty for years.' Miranda could see half a dozen ruling nobles looking on eagerly. One of them by rights would be granted the office, the second most powerful position in the Empire, historically at times even more important than the Golden Throne. It was the ultimate prize for any ambitious Tsurani noble. 'It is to our cousin, Tetsu of the Minwanabi, I turn.' He looked towards a grizzled noble, still powerful in bearing despite his heavy physique and grey hair. 'Will you accept this heavy burden, my lord?'

Tetsu of the Minwanabi bowed his head, barely able to contain his emotions. 'Gladly, Majesty. I live to serve: my life and honour are yours.'

The Emperor turned to the assembled lords. 'Send word to your commanders, my lords. The nations go to war. Go now and return at the second hour after sunrise tomorrow and we shall ready ourselves.' He turned to his First Advisor, an elderly man named Janain who had previously been his father's First Advisor. 'Send word to the

Priests of Jastur. I will arrive at noon tomorrow to break the Holy Seal.'

Miranda glanced at Alenca, uncertain what this particular order meant. The old magician gave a slight shake of his head. But she could tell from the attitude of every man in the room that this announcement was both important and alarming.

The Emperor continued, 'I will take the counsel with the Lady Miranda, the Great Ones with whom she arrived, and the Warlord.' He paused for a moment, then ended the assembly with the formal dismissal, 'Honours to your houses, my lords.'

He stepped down from dais and everyone in the room bowed, the common servants going to their knees. As the Emperor swept past, he glanced in Miranda's direction, and indicated that she should follow.

As the newly-appointed Warlord fell into step behind the Emperor, Alenca held Miranda back for a moment. Without preamble, he said, 'By breaking the seal on the temple of the War God, the Light of Heaven ensures all other matters become moot. No faction struggle, clan feud, or debt of blood may be undertaken until the temple door is again resealed, and that will not happen until final victory is achieved.' He glanced around as if worried about being overheard. 'You must understand the gravity of this. He has told them that not only are we preparing for the possibility of war, but that we are going to war.'

Miranda was confused. 'Isn't that what we wanted?'

Alenca said, 'It is not what I expected. Moreover, I never believed any emperor would again revive the office of Warlord. To promote a Minwanabi to that position . . .'

'What does it mean?' asked Miranda, wishing not for the first time but with more fervour than ever before that her husband were here. Pug would understand all of this.

'There is an old saying, one that I am certain you have among your people as well: keep your friends close and your enemies closer. The Minwanabi were defeated by the Acoma, the Emperor's ancestors, and rather than the usual obliteration, with every living member of that family put to the sword or sold into slavery, the great Lady of the Acoma, the Mistress of the Empire, in a gesture of mercy unimaginable to any Tsurani ruling noble, allowed the Minwanabi to survive. That made one of the original five great houses a vassal to a lesser house, an insult to our ancestors despite the generosity of the gesture.'

'I don't understand,' said Miranda.

'You would have to be Tsurani to understand fully, I fear,' said Alenca, motioning for Miranda to follow. 'A minor cousin, one of the last surviving members of the last true Minwanabi lord was made ruling lord and he later married an Acoma cousin, further binding the two houses together, but the insult to the Minwanabi by the Acoma

94

was never forgotten. I suspect that breaking the seal on the temple and putting the most dangerous man in the Empire in charge of the war is our Light of Heaven's tactic to ensure that his most bitter enemy within the High Council is otherwise occupied for the foreseeable future and not exploring the possibility of regicide.'

Miranda took a deep breath to calm herself and wondered, not for the first time, if the Tsurani were truly mad.

Miranda continued to observe the young Emperor as he oversaw the conference in his private chambers. They had met only briefly on two previous occasions, the first when he was a boy in his father's court, and the second time when he assumed the throne. The later event was so dominated by Tsurani tradition that she had been in his presence for less than five minutes, and the entire conversation had been between the young Emperor and her husband. Miranda had found it annoyingly ironic that she was soundly ignored by a tradition-bound young man who owed his position entirely to a tradition-breaking woman, his great–grandmother.

And again she was being left on the edge of the conversation while the newly-appointed Warlord and the Emperor directed the bulk of the questions to Alenca and the two other senior magicians from the Assembly. At one point in the hour-long interrogation she had verged on volunteering an

95

observation, but Alenca had shot her a warning glance and a slight shake of the head and she had remained silent. Because of her husband's affections for the old man and her previous dealings with him, she followed his lead, but wondered at what he was playing.

Despite the injury done to her pride and independent nature, Miranda was impressed by how deftly the Emperor manoeuvred the discussion in the direction in which he wished it to go, deftly controlling the flow of debate and manipulating opinion. After another hour of discussion, she was now certain that despite his youth, this Sezu of the Acoma, First of that Name, Emperor of all Tsuranuanni and Light of Heaven, was nobody's fool. When the meeting came to a close, he had fashioned a consensus without once having to appeal to his own authority.

As she rose, the Emperor said, 'Lady Miranda, a moment please.'

Alenca hesitated, then bowed slightly again to the Emperor and with an expression of curiosity indicated to Miranda that he'd wait outside for her. Once the Tsurani nobles and magicians had departed, the Emperor said, 'May I offer you something? Wine? I have several very good reds from your Kingdom of the Isles, as well as some of those that have been cultivated here, though I fear our hot climate makes for difficult vintages.'

Almost charmed, Miranda realized he was

attempting to get her to drop her guard. She said, 'Water would be fine, Majesty.'

He signalled and almost before the gesture was finished a large ceramic goblet of fresh water was presented on a tray by a servant. While she drank, the Emperor waved away the servants and pointed to two chairs placed before a massive window looking out over the central courtyard of the palace. 'Please, no formality,' he said in the King's Tongue, almost without accent.

She looked surprised.

'My guards are sworn to protect me and my life with their own,' he said, indicating the four remaining figures in the room, men clad in the traditional white-gold armour of the Emperor's personal guard. 'But they are men, and as such, likely to suffer the flaws of men. A word here, a chance remark there, and we are undone. So, while many here in Kelewan speak one or another of your homeworld's tongues, I ensured that none of these do.' He said this with humour, but his eyes were fixed upon Miranda and showed no mirth. 'So, what do you really think?'

'About what, Majesty?' replied Miranda as she sat in the proffered chair, a well-cushioned divan that faced the Emperor's. She studied his face. Like the Kingdom of the Isles and the Empire of Great Kesh on Midkemia, the Tsurani Empire was made up of diverse people, so there was no true Tsurani 'look', save that they were a short people compared to those from Midkemia. Sezu was a bit taller than average, perhaps matching Miranda's five foot nine – most Tsurani men were an inch or two shorter; some were barely taller than dwarves.

Other than that, the young man appeared the icon of Tsurani nobility, poised, calm, and almost impossible to read. If there was one thing about the Tsurani in general that annoyed Miranda it was their seemingly implacable composure. One rarely heard a raised voice or heated exchanges in public.

The Emperor sat down. 'You did well.'

'Thank you,' said Miranda, 'I think.'

The young man smiled and years fell away from him. 'I sometimes struggle to remember you're quite old, for you appear not that much more older than me, say an older sister or very young aunt.'

Miranda said, '*Very* young.'

The Emperor chuckled. 'I have been told certain things regarding your husband's whereabouts. Are those reports accurate?'

'As accurate as can be, given that he's unreachable by any means, magic or mundane,' she replied.

The Emperor leaned back, thoughtful. 'He undertakes a journey of unimaginable risk.'

Miranda's expression revealed her concern, despite her attempt to appear calm. 'As I know all too well, Majesty.'

'Then there are things I must know.'

'What would you know, Majesty?'

'The truth,' said the young monarch. 'Alenca and the others often think me still a boy – and I suspect from their vantage point of advancing age. I must be – but from your point of view they must seem as children.'

'I learned a long time ago, Majesty, age has little to do with wisdom. One can endure a lifetime's experiences in a few years or go through life blissfully unaware of the world's troubles around you. It depends on the person. Alenca possesses a calm appreciation of the situation in the midst of chaos I can only envy.'

The Emperor was silent as he considered what she said, then he spoke: 'My hallowed great-grandmother, Mara, had enough experience and wisdom for a dozen lifetimes, it seems.'

Miranda said nothing, wondering at the reference to the venerated woman.

'I believe your husband knew her.'

Miranda said, 'I'm not sure, Majesty. I know they met at least once over the years, but you must remember Pug was not always a welcome sight in these halls.'

The Emperor smiled. 'The Imperial Games. Yes, I remember the story. My great-grandmother was one of the many nobles at those games when your husband shamed the Warlord publicly and ended his power. Did you know it took almost five years to fully repair the damage Milamber did to the great stadium?'

Miranda repressed a smile. Pug, Milamber as

the Tsurani called him, was perhaps the most patient man she had ever encountered – a quality that she alternately respected and found annoying – but when he finally did lose his temper the display could be horrific. By all accounts his display at those games so many years ago could only be called heroic, even god-like. He had rained down fire, called up tornados and earthquakes, and had all of the Empire's nobility trembling at his feet in terror. At last she said, 'I had heard the damage was extensive.'

The Emperor lost his smile. 'That's not what I wished to talk about. The point I am making is that your husband and my great-grandmother caused more change in the Empire within a lifetime than had been seen for centuries previously.' He looked reflective, as if choosing his words carefully, then softly added, 'I am about to tell you something that no one outside my family knows – not our closest allies, not even cousins and uncles.'

Miranda said nothing.

'When my grandfather had been on the throne for a short while, after his father returned from your world, the great Lady Mara took Emperor Justin aside and told him a secret. He shared that secret only with his son, my father; then when I was almost a man, my father shared it with me.' The Emperor stood, but as Miranda started to rise he waved her back into her seat. 'No need for formality, Miranda: I am about to share with you the single most closely guarded secret in the history of Tsuranuanni.' He moved to a chest carved from a blond hardwood, its design intricate and ornate. It had been polished to a gleam and there was something about it that now caught Miranda's attention.

'It's magic,' she said softly.

'Yes,' said the Emperor. 'I have been told it would bring instant death to any but myself or my blood kin even to touch it – one good thing about absolute authority is that no servant has even attempted to dust it.' He paused for a brief second. 'Though it never seems to need dusting.' He reached out slowly, pausing as his fingers brushed the wood. 'Each time I open this, I must admit to a moment of concern.' Then he gripped the top and removed it. It came off easily and the Emperor put the lid to one side. He then reached in and removed a parchment.

Miranda felt a sinking sensation in her stomach. She had seen that parchment's like before.

Without a word the Emperor handed the parchment to her. She unrolled it and read it. Then she let it fall from her hands, closed her eyes and slumped down in the chair.

After a moment of silence the Emperor Sezu said, 'Apparently you understand what this means?'

She nodded. Rising she said, 'If I may, Majesty, I need to consult with a few of my colleagues on my homeworld. I must seek other wise counsel before I begin to interpret this; its true meaning may be eluding me.'

'The box has been in my family's care for over a century,' said the Emperor, ignoring formality and kneeling to pick up the fallen parchment. He rolled it up and returned it to Miranda. 'A few more days will have little bearing on what we do next. No matter what you decide this means, we must still mobilize.'

'Now I understand why you put the nations on a formal war footing.'

A look of sadness came over the young man. 'No one must suspect what we are going to attempt until I am ready to order the nations to act. That is vital. My High Council is composed of very privileged rulers who will instantly obey like any good Tsurani soldier . . . until they're given time to think. At that moment a civil war would be born.'

'Alenca and some of the Great Ones need to be alerted.'

'As few as you can, only the most trustworthy, and no one else, not until the precise moment I give the order.'

Miranda nodded. 'Very well, Majesty, but first I must return home immediately. If this is going to be your course of action, I have a great deal of preparation that must be started, as well as some very difficult people who are going to need convincing. Then I will return to speak with Alenca and the others.'

'I shall leave word that you are to be permitted

access to me at any time of the day or night, Lady Miranda. I shall provide you with whatever I may on this side of the rift.'

Miranda said, 'Farewell, Majesty and might I suggest there is one thing we can both do: pray.'

The Emperor was suddenly left looking at an empty chair, for Miranda had vanished from sight. He glanced at the four guards in the room, but they were motionless, as they always were, their eyes locked forward, unmoved by the sight of a woman vanishing before them. Sezu, First of that Name, and Ruler of All The Nations of Tsuranuanni, sat down in his chair and began to compose himself. For whatever was coming, until it arrived, he had an empire to govern.

Caleb looked up and felt an instant sense of relief at the sight of his mother. 'I was starting to worry . . .' Her expression stopped him 'What is it?'

Miranda said, 'That animal Varen got me captured by the Dasati.'

Caleb said, 'Are you . . . ?' He let the question fall away, realizing that as far as he could see his mother was unhurt and had obviously escaped.

'Only my dignity was injured. Pain, as you know, goes away.' She sat down in the other chair, a rolled parchment on her knees. 'What news?'

'Rosenvar and Joshua stand watch over the Talnoy, and Rosenvar reports that your experiments with Nakor have yielded good results. The control crystals work as well as the ring, with apparently no ill-effect.' He began to sift through a pile of parchments and papers. 'I have his report here somewhere.'

'I'll read it later.' She sighed. 'I know it's pointless to ask about your father, brother and Nakor?'

Caleb nodded. There had been some hope that Pug might devise a manner in which to send communication back to his son and wife, but everyone counted it a very slim hope.

'No word from Kaspar's expedition, either.'

'The warning from . . . what do they call themselves?'

'The Circle,' answered Caleb.

'They're interested in the Peaks of the Quor . . . that report was vague on any specific time, wasn't it?'

Caleb picked up another parchment. 'Simply that we should expect them to appear in some force down on the lee side of the peninsula before the Spring Festival.'

'That's another week, so they could be dealing with them now.' She glanced at her son. 'Are you worried?'

The dark-haired hunter pushed himself back from the table. 'Always. Especially when you and father leave me in charge.' He rose and paced around the desk. 'You know I am here only because I'm your son. There are others in the Conclave who are better suited—'

'No,' she cut him off. 'I know it is not your first

104

choice, and you'd rather be out tramping through the woods or climbing some mountain, but the fact is you've been groomed all your life to take charge should anything happen to the rest of us. You know things, thousands of tiny details that no one else, not even Nakor, knows. You just don't know you know.' She was thoughtful. 'But I think we need to find you an assistant, a magician – perhaps that young girl . . .'

'Lettie?'

'Yes, that's the one. She's not the best student we've had, but she's got an uncanny grasp of how things fit together. Yes, I'll have her sent here and you can begin to train her. I didn't realize it until now, but we have no one ready to step in should anything happen to *you*.'

'What is all this?' asked Caleb. 'You're usually not this concerned with . . . contingencies.'

Miranda looked at her younger son. She could see a hint of her husband around his mouth, and the way in which he cocked his head to one side when thoughtful. Otherwise, he resembled his mother, from the high forehead and narrow chin to the way he moved, and his tall slender build. Like many parents she was occasionally and unexpectedly struck by how much she loved her children. 'Two things, actually,' she said. 'Had that madman Varen's plan worked, I would probably still be strapped to a Dasati table being examined by their Deathpriests or I'd be dead and dissected. Many bad things besides my discomfort and ultimate demise would have occurred, the least of which was you being the only member of this family still here.'

'We knew that,' said Caleb, putting his hand on his mother's shoulder. 'There's something more. What is it?'

'This,' she said handing him the parchment she had received from the Emperor.

'Tsurani,' said Caleb. 'Father's hand.'

'Another of those damned notes!' Miranda wasn't irritated by the fact that notes kept appearing mysteriously from some future date – warning of threats, instructing them on actions to take – she was annoyed that they were always cryptic, and it was never clear as to how, exactly, to deal with the information provided. Moreover, she was truly annoyed that her husband had taken years to tell her about them, and had told Nakor before her!

Caleb read the note. There were three lines of text above his father's signature:

Listen to Miranda.
Give this to her.
Prepare to evacuate.
Milamber.

'Prepare to evacuate?' asked Caleb. 'He's telling the Emperor to prepare to evacuate . . . what? The palace? The Holy City?'

Frustrated, Miranda shook her head. She knew in the pit of her stomach that she stood a very real chance of never seeing her husband again, and with equal certainty she knew what the note meant. 'No,' she said, emotion making her voice hoarse. 'He means, prepare to evacuate the *world*. He's telling the Emperor the Tsurani will have to leave Kelewan.'

CHAPTER 5

CAPTIVES

Kaspar lay doubled over in pain.
An elf stood over him ready to strike him again if Kaspar resisted the order to move. Servan reached down to assist the General to his feet and Kaspar's look showed that he had no intention of forgetting this elf any time soon. He had tried to prolong the first break during the long march and for his trouble had received the butt end of a staff in the stomach.

The elf who had first spoken to them now approached Kaspar. 'We have no time to waste. You humans are slow. We must hurry: we still have a steep climb to Baranor.'

'Baranor?' asked Kaspar.

'Our home,' said the elf. 'We need to be there before sundown and for that reason you cannot tarry.'

Nursing his sore side, Kaspar threw one more dark look at the elf who had struck him and said, 'Your friend made that abundantly clear.'

The elf who had struck him stood glaring at Kaspar, his blue eyes fixed on the former duke.

Speaking without looking back at Kaspar, the

leader of the elves said, 'Sinda thinks you should all have been killed at the water's edge. It would make things simpler.'

Jommy muttered, 'Sorry for the inconvenience,' as he helped one of the wounded soldiers back to his feet.

'No inconvenience.' The leader said. 'We can still kill you if we must. But I have instructions that you're to be brought to Baranor to be questioned.'

'Instructions from whom?' asked Kaspar, still nursing his side where the staff butt had struck.

'Our leader.'

Kaspar said nothing, but from his expression, Jommy could tell that the General was maybe thinking of a way to escape, even though Jommy thought that an impossibility, even if they had twice the number of men. Jommy had come to the conclusion that the half-dozen or so elves with the long wooden staves were magicians or sorcerers, or whatever they called elf magic-users.

He looked behind him and saw Jim Dasher glancing around. Jommy didn't have to read minds to know what was on the thief's: he was noting hiding places and escape routes. Jommy didn't think much of the notion of fleeing – though if anyone could elude these elves in their own forest, it might be Jim; Jommy was still wondering how he had apparently arrived out of nowhere to kill that magician on the beach.

Still, if he reached the beach it would be another week before a longboat was sent to re-supply

Kaspar's forces, and if he tried to work his way around to the hidden cove to the north where Kaspar's ship lay at anchor, it would take more than a week on foot. Then there was the almost impossible swim out to where Kaspar's ships were at anchor, through rough waters and rocks, not to mention sharks and other predators. Jommy wondered if the enterprising thief was thinking of such a mad plan. And if he got there after the re-supply boat found the camp empty, he might reach the anchorage in time to watch the ships sailing away, for that would be their orders: if anything happens to Kaspar's forces, leave at once.

The captives trudged up the hillside, those able-bodied helping the wounded. As the shadows lengthened, the elves seemed to be showing hints of a rising sense of urgency. Jommy whispered to Kaspar, 'General, do the elves look a little edgy to you?'

Kaspar nodded. 'For the better part of an hour now, I'd say. I don't know how much farther we have to travel, but it's a certainty that they want to be there before nightfall.'

Soon Jommy's observation was borne out. The elves insisted that the prisoners pick up the pace, and were unforgiving to the plight of the wounded. As the sun dipped behind the western mountains pairs of able-bodied men were forced to carry those unable to keep up.

Kaspar shouted, 'What's the danger?' but was ignored as the elves began turning all their attention towards the woods rather than watching the prisoners as closely as they had been.

Suddenly, the leader shouted a warning in their language. Kaspar could see that the elven warriors and magicians were well-drilled as they spread out to counter what appeared to be some sort of attack. Kaspar shouted to his men, 'Get down!' and himself fell to the ground.

A thrumming sound filled the air and the shadows between the massive boles of the trees appeared to shift, as if darkness had achieved tangibility and could move.

'Void-darters!' the leader of the elves said to Kaspar. 'Let none touch you.'

'Then give us our weapons so we may defend ourselves!'

The elf ignored the request, his eyes fixed upon the perimeter of the column. Then a shout from up ahead alerted Kaspar that the attack was underway.

Like something from a bad dream, flashes of darkness sped through the air, shadowy forms that defied the eye. Kaspar prided himself on a hunter's vision, but he had no concept of what it was he was looking at.

Wedge-shaped, moving more like a sea skate or ray than a bird, the figures sped through the air faster than a swift, darting one way then another with impossible changes in direction. They were so flat that if they turned suddenly, they appeared to vanish for a moment, presenting an impossible target. Kaspar knew these creatures would be hard to hit with a sword, harder still with an arrow.

The elven warriors kept their swords at the ready but Kaspar already knew any contact between a steel blade and the flitting creatures was likely to be purely accidental. The only thing that gave Kaspar hope was that the creatures looked delicate, almost insubstantial, and he couldn't imagine any of them surviving a sword's blow. But how to hit them, that was the question.

Yet the flourishing of swords seemed to cause the apparitions to hesitate. Kaspar heard the voice of Jim Dasher, from a short distance away, shouting, 'Those things don't want to touch steel! Belt buckles!'

The soldiers quickly pulled loose their belts, rolling on the ground like demented rag dolls, trying to keep low while trying to free their only weapon. Some came to their knees, or into a crouch, their belts folded ready to be swung, while others wrapped the belts around their fist, buckle on top, like a hand weapon.

The swooping flyers veered off rather than be touched, but Kaspar was an experienced enough hunter to understand they were only testing their prey. 'Keep low!' he shouted. 'They're coming in . . . now!'

As if they had obeyed his command the flying creatures veered in, diving straight down at those on the trail. The elves were ready, obviously practised in dealing with these creatures, while the humans were trained fighting men, hand-picked by the Conclave for their resolve as well as their other abilities.

Kaspar spared a glance to either side and saw Jommy to his right and Servan to his left with Jim Dasher now standing slightly behind Servan's left, each man now with at least one flank covered, and then he saw black horror flying straight at him.

At the last instant Kaspar could see that the creatures had tiny eyes that looked like shimmering blue gems flecked with gold. A maw like a dagger cut opened for a second showing tiny razor-sharp teeth of brilliant carmine red.

Kaspar lashed out as hard as he could, his belt-buckle squarely striking the Void-darter under its 'chin'. He felt the shock of contact run through his hands and arms as if he had just struck an oak with his sword. The creature flew backwards, tumbling, losing its ability to fly. It struck the ground and with a flash of a metallic, grey-blue light vanished, leaving behind only an oily black smoke.

Jommy lashed out as well, striking his attacking creature slightly off-centre, sending it veering away to his right. Servan ducked and Jim Dasher lashed out with a fist wrapped with his belt-buckle on top. He grunted with pain as the shock ran straight up his arm.

In all three cases the response was the same; the creatures fled with a ghostly wail of pain.

Kaspar again stole a glance around and saw that

most of his men were unhurt. The two exceptions were on the ground, contorted as if in agony. One had a creature attached to his left leg and evil blue wisps of smoke rose from where it touched him. The other had been struck in the chest. He arched his back so severely Kaspar wondered if he'd break his own spine.

An elf slashed at the first man's leg, the point of his sword arcing across the creature's back. A tiny blue flame erupted and Kaspar for the first time saw that the elves' swords were not made of steel, but something he had never seen before. The creature released its hold on the thrashing man. The second man was not as lucky: the elf who came to stand over him drove his sword point through the attached Void-darter, straight into the prisoner. Both died instantly.

Kaspar ducked as another flyer attempted to wrap itself around his head, and as the creature grazed his scalp he felt a painful, icy tingle as if something was sucking the heat from his skin. Ice burn, he thought, remembering as a child what it was like to be hunting in the mountains with his father, and touching a dagger's blade that had grown so cold it peeled a layer of skin off as his father pulled it from his hand.

Abruptly, a huge enveloping energy surrounded the column, as the elven spell-casters responded. The Void-darters turned and fled and the leader of the elves shouted, 'Run! They will come back with their masters!'

Ignoring the dead man on the road, Kaspar yelled, 'Grab the wounded and carry them!' He picked up the man who had been struck in the leg, found him almost icy to the touch, and hoisted him across his shoulders, carrying him as he would an elk he had killed in the hunt. The man groaned weakly, but Kaspar had no intention of leaving anyone behind if he could help it. Even at the height of his madness, when under the influence of the evil magician Leso Varen, Kaspar had held to certain principles that had inspired personal loyalty of his men, and one was fundamental: on the battlefield every soldier was his brother – no living man was willingly left behind. Kaspar admitted that he might have been a murderous bastard at one time, but he was a loyal murderous bastard.

Kaspar kept his eyes fixed on the road ahead, and after running for twenty yards could see a wooden palisade ahead through a gap in the trees. The glimpse was enough to tell him that it was a fairly substantial fortification, with the battlement a good twenty feet above the foundation. The soldier in him quickly calculated the difficulty of taking such a position, uphill, while a punishing rain of arrows fell on you as you moved up to the base of the wall . . . nothing a skilled company of engineers supported by disciplined soldiers couldn't quickly deal with, but he suspected there was more to the fortification than met the eye. Even so, a couple of turtles with sappers inside could probably dig up the foundation of two or three pales in the wall within an hour. He glanced at the road as he ran and thought that a good-sized covered ram with supporting archers could probably breach the gate in half the time. Unless magic was involved . . .

On top of this hill, snug against a cliff face some hundred yards or more behind, stood a series of wooden buildings fashioned in a manner Kaspar had never seen before, and all of them were surrounded by the massive wooden wall.

As they approached, Kaspar appreciated how hundreds of trees must have been cleared to form an open killing ground. An earthen redoubt had been erected in front of the palisade. The road now fell away on both sides in a manner that would funnel attackers in front of the gate into a more confined area or have them falling off to one side or the other so that they'd end up standing below the wall, in peril of murderous bowfire from above.

To his right Kaspar could see that years of fighting had despoiled these grounds. There was something odd about it, he thought as he struggled to get his wounded soldier to safety, but he couldn't quite put a name to it. There was something different about this battlefield, something sensed more than seen.

A howling erupted behind the fleeing men and Kaspar turned around completely, to see what pursued them.

Void-darters sped in from behind, but in close

pursuit came beings that could only be described as demons out of some deep pit of hell. Cloaked in tatters of charcoal, inky black beings sat astride creatures that seemed to be the demented product of a fevered delirium.

The animals looked like elongated wolves, but had an almost feline motion. Like the flying entities, they were things made of shadow and darkness, but these creatures had pale milky white eyes.

The riders were roughly humanoid in shape, but their forms flowed around the edges, and from them a fog or smoke trailed behind them leaving grey wisps that were almost instantly lost in the evening's gloom. They howled and Kaspar saw weapons in their hands, long blades that shimmered and sparked with angry energies of the darkest red hue.

'Ban-ath protect me!' said Jim Dasher as he edged close to Kaspar.

'Run!' shouted Kaspar, for some of the men had stopped in muted horror.

Men broke in ragged formation, the elves now ignoring their role as captors, everyone trying for the safety of the walls. Kaspar expected to see archers ready to cover the retreat, but instead was greeted only by the sight of a few faces above the ramparts and none of them apparently in possession of a bow.

Burdened by the man he carried, Kaspar struggled towards the keep, again finding that will which had made him a dangerous foe before becoming a valued ally to the Conclave of Shadows. 'Where are your archers?' he shouted.

The elves' leader turned and said, 'Arrows are of no use against their masters. We must get through the gates!' He turned and fled, unconcerned apparently whether Kaspar and the prisoners reached safety before mayhem overtook them.

Kaspar laboured to keep up, for their refuge was only a hundred yards or so ahead. The first of the elves were already there and Kaspar was horrified to see that it was his men who were falling behind. 'Damn you! Help us!' he shouted.

'No one can help you!' shouted back the leader. 'You must reach the gates or you will perish.'

'I'll be damned if I'm going to be caught like a hare run down by wolves!' Kaspar turned and yelled at one of his soldiers, 'Take this man!' As easily as if tossing a dressed elk to his cook, he threw the man over the soldier's shoulders. The soldier almost collapsed under the sudden weight, but he hitched himself up and moved on as quickly as possible.

Kaspar saw that the nearest rider would be on top of him in only a few moments. He readied his belt as a weapon again, remembering with evil irony how he had stood just so a few years ago with a captive's chains as his only weapon while nomads from the hills of Novindus had ridden down on him.

From his right came a voice. 'I have an idea.'

Jim Dasher was standing at his side, holding two large rocks. Kaspar nodded, and took one.

Jim waited until the rider was almost on top of them, then pulled back his arm and threw.

His rock sped through the air and struck the rider full in the face. It passed through as if piercing smoke, but the rider flinched, pulling up with a startled cry.

'The wolf!' shouted Dasher. He picked up another rock and hurled it just as Kaspar unloaded his rock with as much strength as he could right at the creature's muzzle. The wolf-like mount snarled, a distant hollow sound, and the rock bounced off, causing it to falter.

Dasher hurled a rock at the creature's foot, causing it to stumble and collapse on the trail. The rider might have been immune to Kaspar's rock, but he seemed to abide by the same rules as any mortal rider when his mount stumbled for he flew over the creature's haunches.

Kaspar shouted, 'Run!'

He had bought those ahead of him mere seconds, but those seconds were the difference between safety and destruction. He saw Dasher scoop up one last rock, turn, throw, and then run. Realizing that the young thief was faster and not wanting to be the only one who failed to reach the gate, the former Duke of Olasko dug deep inside himself and found just enough strength to reach the threshold stride for stride with the younger man.

They leaped into the courtyard of the fortification and heard a howl of outrage from their pursuers, but while the gate was still open, the demonic creatures did not follow. The elf magicians hurried up ramps to the battlements above and when they were in place, raised their staves as one.

A thrumming sound filled the air, much as it had down on the beach when they destroyed the elemental creature, and a wave of white light pulsed from the walls. Instantly the creatures on the road retreated, their angry shouts and cries reduced to hollow echoes on the evening wind.

Kaspar's men sat on the ground, many near exhaustion. Several were now unconscious, wounded men who had succumbed to the demands of the retreat. Kaspar forced himself to remain on his feet, but even the resourceful Jim Dasher gave in to the need to sit down. Jommy and Servan looked at Kaspar expectantly, waiting for their general to tell them what was next.

As the elf leader came towards them, Kaspar said, 'Well, then, we are here. We are your prisoners. What is to be done with us?'

'You will see our leader.'

'When?'

'Now,' he said, motioning for Kaspar to follow. 'The others wait here.'

As Kaspar fell in behind the elf, 'What am I to call you?'

The elf glanced over his shoulder. 'Is that important?'

'Only if I live and have reason to address you.'

The elf smiled slightly. 'I am called Hengail.'

'Why were there no archers on the wall to cover our retreat?'

Hengail hesitated, then said, 'All our archers were with us. Only children and women were within the compound.'

As they climbed a path to a large building which dominated the community, Kaspar quickly took in his surroundings. The buildings were astonishing. There were swooping lines of wood beams supporting arching roofs, rather than the straight timbers he would have expected. Wood faces to buildings had been glazed and polished until the evening's torchlight was reflected from every flat surface as if they were mirrors. Under the glimmering reflections, Kaspar could see that the wood had been allowed to age to deep hues of many colours, mostly deep reds and browns, but with unexpected shades of grey and even a hint of blue here and there. There were more than a dozen buildings scattered around this very large plateau, but most of them appeared empty. The doorways were all open. He glanced upwards at one arching high above his head as he passed into the largest building.

The floors were also of highly polished wood, lovingly cared for from their appearance. The walls were as they were outside, magnificent in their simplicity, yet elegant as well. The building appeared to be laid out in a large cross, with a huge fire-pit of stone dominating the centre. High above, a large hole in the roof permitted smoke to exit, while a sheltering roof above it, supported by large beams at the corner, protected the hole from all but the most violent rainstorms.

Before the fire-pit sat three elves, one obviously of great age, for among the ever-seeming youth of the others, this one bore the ravages of many years: deep lines etching his face, hair white as snow, and a stoop-shouldered posture. Yet his eyes were bright and regarded Kaspar with suspicion.

Slowly he stood up. 'Who are you to come to the land of the Quor?'

'Kaspar, formerly Duke of Olasko, now in the service of the kings of Roldem and the Isles, and the Emperor of Great Kesh.'

The old elf was silent for a long moment, then he chuckled. 'Something dire must be afoot for those three vain princes to be in harmony.' He studied Kaspar, then said, 'Tell me why three mighty rulers of the human lands send soldiers to the Peaks of the Quor, and tell me true, for your lives depend on what you say.'

Kaspar looked around the room. Two other elderly elves sat nearby, watching intently, and the elf named Hengail stood silently at their right hand. Two other guards stood by the door, but otherwise the large cross-shaped hall was empty. 'What do I call you?'

'I am called Castdanur. In your tongue it means 'caretaker against the darkness'. I had a young name, once, but that was so long ago I fear I do not remember it.'

Kaspar took a moment to reply, 'Perhaps we may be of some help to you. It wouldn't do to kill out of hand those who would be your friends.' He looked the old elf directly in the eyes. 'You do appear to need friends.'

Castdanur smiled. 'Now, why do you suggest we are in need of friends?'

Kaspar said, 'Only a blind man or a fool can't see that this once was home to hundreds, and now there is only a handful. You need help. You are a dying people.'

CHAPTER 6

SLAUGHTER

Magnus dived behind the wall.

Three humans and three Lessers all crouched down behind a low wall, more of a boundary than a barrier. One of the Deathknights turned his varnin – a cross between a big lizard and a horse – and started towards their place of concealment. Pug threw himself behind the wall too, landing next to Magnus.

He risked discovery by rising just high enough to gain a clear line-of-sight to a point behind the approaching riders and cast a spell, hoping it would function here on Omadrabar as it had in his own native realm. He had spent so much time learning how to adapt magic that it was almost as much second nature to him in these alien conditions as it was at home. Most of the time he judged correctly, but occasionally he had had unexpected results.

This time things went as desired, and a sudden commotion behind the riders caused them to look around. A particularly fine illusion appeared some distance away: that of women and children fleeing in the opposite direction from where Pug and his companions hid. The Deathknights reacted in true Dasati fashion, howling their war chants and giving chase.

Pug signalled for everyone to wait until the Deathknights were safely gone. In most confrontations with a small band of armed men – or Dasati in this case – Pug had little concern for his own safety. He could easily dispose of the dozen or so riders who were now chasing the mirage. But he had no desire to take Dasati lives unnecessarily, even those bent on killing every member of his race – they were a people bent by dark forces which were beyond their power to control. And he knew that tonight was not just a circus of random slaughter, but a planet-wide ceremony, a massive ritual of blood and that death and each killing gave more power to His Darkness. Even if he could deny only half a dozen lives to the Dark God, Pug would do it.

Pug considered this deity, this supreme god of evil. From what he had studied about the nature of the gods on Midkemia over the years, he knew this was the fate that awaited his home world if the Nameless One gained ascendancy. Still, that possibility was far less immediate a worry than keeping His Darkness out of Pug's native realm. If he could aid in the destruction of this Dasati Dark God, he would be saving the Dasati as well as every human on Midkemia and Kelewan.

Pug knew they had gained only a few moments and that the Deathknights would quickly realize

the ruse and return. He wanted to avoid a confrontation if at all possible. Moreover, he desperately
wished to avoid any chance that their true nature
might be discovered. If he employed magic to
destroy the Deathknights he would have to ensure
that no one, including any hidden Lessers nearby,
could reveal their presence. He, Macros, Magnus,
and Nakor combined could hold off a veritable
army of Deathknights, killing thousands if need
be, but while each of them might be a match for
two or three Deathpriests or Hierophants, even
they couldn't withstand an assault by a score or
more determined to obliterate them and unconcerned about their own lives. His years with the
Tsurani had taught Pug all he wanted to know
about the danger of foes willing to die for their
cause.

Nakor signalled back that the way was clear and
the fugitives hurried along a path near the
roadway. They were still within the boundaries of
the great city, but in one of the miles-wide open
enclaves called a *raion*, an administrative district
devoted to agriculture within the city proper, but
under its own rule. Macros had not taken the valuable time to explain the subtle points of Dasati
civic administration, but he had left Pug with the
impression that while *raions* were less dangerous
environments than the rest of the city under
normal circumstances, these were no normal
circumstances.

Because the outer perimeter of the *raion* was

126

encompassed by the city itself, most of the usual wild animals had been hunted out years ago, but that didn't mean there were no other dangers. Night-flyers, while not common in this region, were not unheard of, and occasionally larger land predators somehow found their way inside. Moreover, tonight every Dasati who wasn't with them was their enemy. Bands of Lessers who normally wouldn't consider aggressive behaviour were roaming the byways, availing themselves of the rare opportunity to indulge in the Dasati appetite for violence. A foolish Deathknight who became separated from his society brethren could find himself dealt with harshly by those who normally lived or died at his whim. Even lords of great houses had to limit those in their presence to only their most loyal and trusted retainers.

For the demand of the Dark God during the Great Culling was that the weak must fall. Any Dasati unable to survive was by definition weak and must be given up by blood and fire to His Darkness.

They ran along a pathway just wide enough for a cart, Pug constantly checking over his shoulder to see if they were being followed. As they hurried down the narrow lane, sheltered from view for almost a mile by a tall grain crop called *sellabok*, the sky above was beginning to lighten. Pug called for a halt. 'Wait.'

The others turned and Pug softly said, 'Listen.'

The pre-dawn air was still, and only the distant

sounds of night creatures punctuated the silence. Then a distant shout from behind them signalled the location of the Deathknights they had encountered earlier. 'How far?' Pug asked Macros.

'Another two hours if we don't encounter any delays will put us outside the area known as Camlad, at which time we must either decide to circle it along the outer reaches of the city, adding several hours of journey time, or to cut through to the heart of the district. The latter is preferable, but the danger is much greater.'

'Why?' asked Nakor.

'The first spate of bloodletting will have occurred within hours of the call for the Great Culling,' said Macros. He was more out of breath than normal and Pug realized that his illness was beginning to manifest itself, probably as a result of the exertions of the previous night. 'To put it in Dasati terms, the stupid, weak, rash and foolish perish within hours. Traps will have been sprung, and skirmishes fought. Then after a lull of perhaps an hour or two, the more reckless and bold will clash with one another. That band of Deathknights we just eluded were bloodied, most likely after an encounter with another like band they vanquished.

'Those who are left are dangerous, tough-minded killers looking for prey. The blood frenzy is now at its highest and will continue that way throughout the morning. Later in the day,' he added softly, 'things will quieten down as even the most bloody-handed murderers will start to sense the coming sundown and realize that only their like remain out there, in other words those adept at killing and those equally adept at hiding.

'At that point, everyone will hunker down and wait for sunset – anyone moving through any part of the city will be an easy target for ambush. So, that means our first need is to get through Camlad and into the next *raion* before noon. Once we are out of the city again we will be mere hours from the Grove of Delmat-Ama. The White controls the Grove and most of the district around it completely; there we will be safe and there we can wait to find out just what this latest butchery signals.'

Magnus asked, 'What do you think it signals?'

Macros was silent for a moment, pondering the question. 'A beginning,' he said at last. 'His Darkness is a covetous god. He demands blood, but when he hungers greatly, it usually heralds a great change.' The Dasati who was once human sighed. 'I cannot imagine that invading a higher realm is an easy thing, even for a god. It may be that he himself intends to follow his army.' He looked from face to face. 'Come, we can discuss this in more detail once we've reached the Grove of Delmat-Ama.'

As one they and the three servants turned and hurried along the path once again as the sky in the east brightened with the approaching dawn.

The open fields of the *raion* came to an end when they reached a wide boulevard bordered on the opposite side from where they stood by a seemingly endless wall of buildings which rose up ten to twelve storeys, Macros said, 'There. Over to the right is a servants' tunnel.' He glanced around. 'Don't let the silence mislead you. There are eyes behind every window and knives concealed at every hand. Right now at least a dozen Lessers are considering how dangerous we are – are we bold and powerful, or foolish and weak – and what their chances might be at an ambush. We must proceed cautiously. Once through Camlad we will reach the Grove of Delmat-Ama.'

'Didn't you suggest we circle to the outside of this precinct?' asked Nakor.

Macros began walking. 'We've lost too much time.' Three times since midnight they had hidden, once for over an hour, to avoid confrontation with the Dasati.

Magnus asked, 'Is there much magic in use today?'

Macros hesitated. 'I'm not sure what you mean?'

'So far we have been concealing our powers to prevent detection.'

'Yes,' agreed Macros. 'We could have destroyed everyone in our path, but only Deathpriests on this world employ magic – at least only those sanctioned by His Darkness – and the presence of unknown practitioners of magic would certainly attract attention.'

'But with Deathpriests and Hierophants among the roving bands, the presence of magic itself would hardly draw notice.'

'What do you intend?' asked Pug.

Magnus's features, though Dasati, still revealed his mood to his father. Unlike his mother, Magnus was adept at holding in his feelings, even more so than his father at times, but when frustration reached a certain point, he took on a tone and a set of features that was familiar to Pug. Magnus was feeling frustrated.

'I am not suggesting we cast off our guises, and boldly walk into the canton, defying all in our path. That would be folly. But can we not use our arts to fly above this madness and hide ourselves from view?'

Macros laughed. 'The boy is wiser than both his father and grandfather. It never occurred to us to combine invisibility with flight—'

'Because no magician we know of can do both at once,' finished Nakor. He grinned, and the familiar expression, although in an alien visage, reassured everyone. 'But we have more than one magician in this party.'

'I can lift us all,' said Magnus, indicating the three other magicians and the three Lesser servants – all of whom now revealed an apparent terror at the idea of flying.

'I can shield us from scrying and other arcane detection,' said Macros.

'And I will ensure we are not seen,' said Pug.

A brief discussion of how they would manage this feat was followed by the two older magicians chanting their spells, and then Magnus began his.

Soon everyone was invisible but voices out of thin air indicated that the three servants were unable to endure the experience silently. Pug realized it must be an unnerving experience for them to feel themselves picked up by invisible forces and be suspended above the ground.

Magnus directed them to where Macros had indicated the best route lay, and they began to speed over the city. Pug found looking down exhilarating, as much for the novelty as for the view; he couldn't remember the last time he had flown without having to employ his own abilities. He didn't much care for the experience, as it always left him fatigued and with a mild headache. But this time his son was doing all the work, and he was free simply to enjoy the journey. Macros had a harder task: concentrating on discovering any scrying magic and counteracting it as quickly as possible, but with Pug's spell for rendering them invisible now in place, he had no work left to do.

The scene below again drove home to Pug just how alien the Dasati were. He had called many places on both Midkemia and Kelewan home, and had visited a dozen worlds containing intelligent beings exotic in both appearance and nature, but the strangest race he had so far encountered looked like family compared to these people.

The city stretched on for miles in all directions. Pug couldn't begin to imagine the labour required to build these . . . he couldn't call them buildings, for every single one was interconnected, all appearing to be of a piece. He was certain that sections have been added over centuries, but in such a way as to make everything appear seamless, integrated, without boundary. Completely lacking were the endless varieties of design found in even the most homogeneous culture – the Tsurani, whose city buildings were almost all uniformly painted white, indulged in a vast variety of murals and good luck symbols. But here . . . everywhere the eye travelled there were edifices of stone, dark grey blackened doorways which were almost perfectly uniformed, the only relief being a play of subtle energies throughout the stone that would have been invisible to the human eye. If you looked more closely you would find scintillating hot reds and deep vibrating purples and plays of gleaming sparkles that looked like tiny gleaming reflections of sunlight on mother-of-pearl, glimpsed for a moment, then fading. Pug thought that such touches would have been beautiful if they were not adorning such grim surroundings. Other than that, the Dasati architecture was very formalized. There were six windows set between each doorway, with a tunnel into the heart of the building every four doorways. Above the street, each storey had a landing and a balconied walkway, the design was repeated over and over. The monotony was disrupted only by vast interconnecting walls that had broad boulevards upon their spines, highways hundreds of feet above the ground upon which much of the travel and commerce of Dasati society depended.

Amongst the buildings were areas of open plaza or parkland. Each open space, be it parkland, hunting range, agricultural *raion*, or market-place, was miles long on each side. But even these, Pug could observe as they rose higher, were uniform in placement and design.

Aloud he said, 'The Dasati lack originality.'

'Not entirely,' said Macros, 'but they do have a decided tendency to stick with something once they judge it to be useful. As densely packed as the population can be towards the city centre, these arrangements of parklands and agricultural districts provide an efficient system of getting goods to market.

'The only different environment to be seen is along the shores of the oceans. The sea is far less amenable to being formed than the land, so compromises had to be made. Yet even in the coastal cities the attempt to replicate this design is evident. They have bridges and networks of vast rafts, even pilings driven deep into the sea bottom just so that they can do this.'

'Why?' asked Nakor. 'I appreciate a good design as well as any man, but one must accommodate to changing circumstances.'

'Not the Dasati,' said Magnus. 'If the design doesn't fit the circumstances they change the circumstances.'

Pug was surprised at how relaxed his son

sounded. He knew that had he been transporting everyone he would not have been so relaxed. Magnus was just coming into his power still relatively young as magicians went, and already there were things he was capable of that would be difficult for both his mother and father.

Pug's mind returned to that terrible day, so many years before, when he had stood before Lims-Kragma, after his foolish attempt to overpower the demon Jakan, and the horrifying choice he had been given. He would do what needed to be done, return to the living to finish the tasks an unkind fate and the gods had put before him, but in exchange for that respite from death he would have to pay a price. He would have to watch everyone he loved die before him.

When those of advancing age died it was hard enough. He recalled losing his first teacher, Kulgan, Father Tully, later Prince Arutha and his good friend Laurie. The untimely deaths were more difficult to accept than those lost in war to a capricious fate. But nothing had prepared him to anticipate the loss of his children before their time. He had already lost two: William, who had died on the walls of Krondor before the onslaught of the Emerald Queen's army, and his adopted daughter Gamina, lost in the same struggle with her husband, Lord James. Yet both of them had led full lives, Gamina having come to know her grandchildren.

Pug considered ruefully that he had distant

family, people he hardly knew. His great-grand-children, Jimmy and Dash, had fathered children and Pug wondered for a bitter moment if they too would be lost before him.

His reverie was broken by Nakor asking, 'What is that?'

It took only seconds for Pug to see what 'that' was. In the distance, against the rising sun, a black tower of something that resembled smoke rose up, but as they approached Pug could see that it wasn't smoke. It was an energy of some kind, and while it was wispy and smoke-like it was not rising but rather being drawn downwards.

'We must move now,' came Macros's voice.

'What is it?' Nakor asked again.

'The Temple of the Black Heart,' said Macros. 'The holiest of holies on this world. It is the entrance to the domain of the Dark God.'

'What are those energies?' asked Pug.

'Life,' said Macros. 'Given your unusual perspective in this realm, you can see it, as can I, but to the average Dasati, even to the Deathpriests and Hierophants, the air above the temple is clear. You are seeing the life essence of thousands of the dying rushing to that monstrous entity. It is feeding on them. It is growing stronger.'

'To what end?' asked Magnus.

'That we must find out,' said Macros. 'Move us to the right, in line with that flickering light to the south-east. It is a lake within the next *raion* and beyond that lies the Grove of Delmat-Ama. It is there we shall begin to gather information and assess what has occurred, and see if we can make some sense of this insanity.'

Pug remained silent, but he wondered if sense could ever be made from insanity. Thinking of that, he wondered how went the hunt for Leso Varen on Kelewan, and for a brief moment he ached to hear from Miranda and wondered if he would ever hear from her again. Pushing aside such black musings, he turned his attention to keeping them invisible from the thousands of Dasati hiding below.

They sped along in the direction Macros had indicated, until they were again over a series of parks and temples. The parks were almost always on lower rooftops, merely four or five storeys above the ground, not on top of the highest blocks of structures. If there was a single building in the centre, with high-peaked steeples and turreted towers, that would be a temple to His Darkness.

These parks had been arranged in a pattern, Pug could see from on high. The buildings formed a cross, with the parks occupying the remaining space of a vast square, the north-west, south-west, south-east, and north-east quadrants. The northernmost building was a gigantic structure, huge even by the Dasati's overblown standards. A massive foundation supported half a dozen pillars, with a centre tower rising up highest of all.

'Look at the size of that place,' observed Nakor.

'And more of the life-energy is leaving there,' Macros said, pointing.

Pug saw that thousands of tiny wisps of the black life-energy were leaking from the top of the highest tower, seeding back towards the massive intake they had observed earlier.

Macros said, 'Deep under this structure, dozens of levels below this plaza, are cavernous murder rooms. While mayhem is the word for this day, ritualized slaughter takes place on appointed holidays. His Darkness apparently needs a steady supply of Dasati life-energy to thrive, and so has bent the will of his people to this unspeakable practice.'

'How have they survived?' asked Magnus.

'In times past,' said his grandfather, 'by conquering other worlds. The Twelve Worlds were once populated by other intelligent beings, and the Dasati put every one of them to the sword or sacrificial altar and have their hearts cut from their chests.

'Over the ages, they ran out of victims, so they began to prey on one another, evolving into this culture of death and madness you see today.' Macros fell silent to let what he was saying sink in. Then he said, 'The truth of what occurred is hidden. History has been overlaid with dogma until the canon of the Dark God and history are the same thing. Only the Bloodwitch sisters have some perspective on what really occurred over the centuries, and their archives are sketchy at best.'

138

'Why is that?' asked Nakor.

'Over there,' said Macros to Pug, 'move us towards that large spire and straight on beyond. That will lead us to the Grove.' To Nakor he said, 'For centuries the Bloodwitch sisters were part of the faith of the Dark God, though it's almost certain they predated his ascension and were servants of a goddess of life or nature.

'But even though the Sisterhood finally recognized the pointless folly of a society so murderous that even its own young were at risk, they didn't come to that realization until after much of the old lore was lost. Had I longer to study . . .' His words fell away.

Pug suspected Macro's condition was more dire than he admitted. Certainly there was a sense of urgency in everything he did, and Pug couldn't escape the feeling that matters were quickly heading for a turning point.

War was coming. Either to Midkemia or Kelewan, the twin of this world, and the only things holding off the initiation of a bridgehead into the next realm were the preparations being made for the Dark God's forces. This gathering of energies must be the final preparation for such an invasion.

Pug sensed the logical need for such a war. He was only beginning to form opinions as to the root cause of this society's twisted behaviour, but it was clear to him that a brittle homeostasis existed here, social forces locked together by their own pressures: one blow from an oblique angle would cause the entire structure to collapse. How fast this society recovered from this day of whole-sale butchery would be instructive, for such a thing in Midkemia would surely bring a town, city, or even a nation to its knees.

Pug understood that in every human culture too much disruption at any level, among farmers and labourers, merchants and traders, the military or the gentry and society would descend quickly into chaos.

It had taken the Western Realm nearly twenty years to recover fully from the Serpentwar, and that was only because bright and talented men and women rose up to serve, including members of his own family.

Pug turned his attention to the parkland below. He could see a band of armed Dasati – Lessers from their attire – crouched in a shallow wash, screened from view from everywhere but above by dense shrubbery. They were bloodied, exhausted, and from what Pug could observe as he sped above them, they had finished fighting and were now trying to wait out the coming day.

As they reached the south-western boundary of the parkland, Pug thought the hiding Lessers were unlikely to survive this day, for a large contingent of heavily armed, mounted Deathknights and a pair of Deathpriests were marshalling in a square, clearly intending to conduct an organized sweep of the area. Pug wished he could intervene, but to what end? And just because in the normal course of social behaviour the Deathknights were more often the predators than the Lessers, that hardly made the latter any less bloodthirsty and murderous. He knew that given the chance they would destroy him and his companions without hesitation.

Pug realized bitterly that even though he had been able to assimilate Tsurani culture when he was a captive on Kelewan in his youth, and had become adept at navigating the cultural byways of many other alien societies, he would never fully be able to grasp the essence of the Dasati, any more than he could fathom the thinking of ants in a hill, even if he could appreciate and apprehend their social order. He then admitted to himself that he had a better chance of understanding the ants.

They continued to fly over the cityscape, seeking out potential threat amongst the uniform buildings. But the journey proved uneventful and after a long flight in relative silence they heard Macros say, 'Over there, near that open area with the small lake.'

Magnus changed their direction and took them towards their indicated goal. They descended slowly over the city to the edge of the *raion* and Macros said, 'That building over there, on that hillock.'

The building was a modest one, though like all things Dasati heavily defended. It had a stout wall with a deep trench just inside fortified with sharpened wooden stakes. 'Some local predators are quite adept fence jumpers. You'd best set us down behind those trees, Magnus. If we suddenly appear before the front door we may be filled with arrows before someone recognizes us.'

His grandson did as he was told and when they were on the ground, Pug dropped the spell of invisibility. The three Lessers were silent, as they had been the entire way, but their faces looked pale – their already-grey skin now looking ashen – and their expressions revealed relief at having their feet once again on solid ground. Macros told them, 'Go and announce our arrival, and try not to be killed before you can speak. I suggest you yell at a safe distance from the door.'

As they left he added, 'It's probably an unnecessary precaution, but one never knows. We control this entire *raion* but unless the TeKarana himself sent his personal legion into this district, our forces were most likely able to keep this area calm.

'Before we go inside, I should warn you that we have little time for planning and even less for action. Something monstrous is now underway, or this Great Culling would not have been called. History is of little interest to the average Dasati Deathknight or Lesser, but I have made it my business to ferret out as much of it as I could since I regained my human memories.

'These massive killings have only ever been

142

called for two reasons: to relieve social pressure and suppress any hint of revolution against the Dark God and his servant, the TeKarana, or to ready the people for the invasion of another world. The last world pacified by the Dasati was Kosidri, and that was over three centuries ago. There is not one indigenous form of life on that world left from the time before the Dasati found it.'

'You fear the Dasati are poised to invade our realm?' asked Magnus.

'Not quite yet, but soon. If things go as I fear they will, the Dark God will call for the Great Muster within a month, and all the battle societies will join with the armies of the Karanas and the TeKarana at an appointed place, perhaps as many as two million Deathknights and several hundred thousand Deathpriests. Another four million support Lessers will accompany them. Remember, they have six worlds to draw upon for resources.'

Pug's expression showed his shock at these numbers. 'We never faced more than twenty thousand Tsurani over the course of twelve years, Macros. And even though the Emerald Queen sent forty thousand against the Kingdom, nearly half died at sea or in the battle for Krondor. There were less than twenty thousand strung out along a hundred miles of the King's Highway. And a third of their army deserted before the battle of Nightmare Ridge.'

Nakor said, 'Two million. That's a lot.'

Pug shot his friend a quick glance, to see if he was joking and saw he wasn't. 'You know what this means?'

'It means we have to prevent them from starting the war,' said Nakor.

'Can we?' asked Magnus.

'That,' said his grandfather, 'is the question of the hour, isn't it?'

'There is only one way I can think of that might achieve that,' said Pug.

Macros nodded, as if reading his son-in-law's mind. 'Yes, kill the Dark God before the order to invade is given.'

CHAPTER 7

PURSUIT

Kaspar nodded.

Castdanur had proven an amiable enough host, for a captor, and refreshments had been provided, meagre though they were. Kaspar had eaten enough game over the years to recognize that everything provided for the evening meal had either been hunted or gathered; nothing here was grown or otherwise cultivated.

They sat opposite one another across a low table, upon furs that kept the body's heat from being stolen into the cold wooden floors. The venison was tough and gamey in flavour, but it was filling, and spiced with some wild herbs he didn't recognize. There was no wine or ale, just water, and the cooked turnips were of a variety he recognized from hunting expeditions to Great Kesh when he was a boy. They had been cooked with animal fat, not butter, and the only spice used was salt, which had a bitter, metallic edge to it, as if it had been reduced from a soda spring in the mountains rather than coming from a mine or seaside salt-flats.

The old elven leader had deftly avoided any comment on Kaspar's observation that this was a fortification occupied by a dying population, and also kept the conversation away from any revelations about his people and their history. So for the most part they had spent the evening speaking of little of importance, though each probed the other for information. Castdanur wanted to know why Kaspar and his company of men had come to the mountains as much as Kaspar wanted to know what these elves were doing here and why no Keshian ruler in history had an inkling of their occupying the mountains traditionally claimed by the Empire as their own.

As a ruler of an Eastern nation, Kaspar had had no contact with elves prior to his joining the ranks of the Conclave of Shadows, and since then only the most fleeting: one encounter with a messenger from the Elf Queen's court who had arrived at Sorcerer's Island while Kaspar had been there receiving instructions from Pug. He had had barely more than a glimpse of the envoy, and had never spoken to him.

This Castdanur was as deft a negotiator as Kaspar had ever encountered. Kaspar had no doubt that was what they were doing: negotiating for his life and that of his men. This enclave could never have remained undetected by Keshian intelligence, coastal pirates, or any number of people who might have chanced across it over the years without there being a deadly consequence for those who

146

discovered Baranor. Kaspar was certain that should any human have ventured to this enclave and lived he would only be someone they trusted implicitly. And nothing he had seen since their captivity indicated that they were inclined to trust anyone from outside.

Finally, Kaspar said, 'Are you familiar with human card games?'

'In passing. I've lived a long time without contact with your race, Duke Kaspar, but that doesn't mean over the years I've remained ignorant of your race and its . . . peculiarities. Gambling is something most elves would have trouble enjoying – our risk-taking is always about survival. These mountains can be difficult, even for those of us who've spent centuries here. Now, why do you ask?'

'There's a human expression, "it's time to put our cards on the table", which means to show what we've been hiding.'

The old elf smiled. 'I like that phrase.'

'There are powerful forces poised to strike at this world.'

'That implies those forces are not of this world.'

'Yes,' said Kaspar, appreciating that this old elf was obviously more intelligent than one might assume from his bucolic surroundings. It was a common error on the part of many nobles to make assumptions based on a person's rank or upbringing, and he had come to quickly appreciate that he had been just as guilty of that vanity before his exile and return to join the Conclave. 'There are worlds besides our own that are populated.'

'We know this,' said Castdanur. 'Word of the Tsurani war reached us – we occasionally trade with those beyond the Peaks of the Quor.'

Kaspar made a mental note to explore that remark further; if there were humans with whom these people did trade, it might be possible to get word out to those waiting for information on Kaspar's expedition and head off any unwanted trouble. Kaspar doubted at this point any of his men or himself would be travelling directly to the waiting ships with the elves' approval. The problem was that should the re-supply boat put in to the cove and find no one there, especially if there were signs of a battle, their instructions were not to investigate, but to turn tail and return as fast as possible to Roldem and seek out Conclave agents there who would in turn relay word to Sorcerer's Isle that the mission was a failure. That would eventually result in another mission being sent there to discover what had happened, depending on the other issues faced by the Conclave, which might take years, time Kaspar knew he didn't have.

'There are men with whom I am allied, men who have dedicated their lives to protecting this world. They are not well known, and I doubt word of their existence has reached you, but they are called the Conclave of Shadows.'

'A colourful name, Kaspar of Olasko. Tell me of this Conclave.'

148

'Have you heard of a man named Pug?'

'The great human sorcerer,' said Castdanur. 'Yes, word of his feats have reached us. Last we heard he humbled a prince who became King of the Isles.'

Kaspar recalled hearing that story from his own father, when he was a boy. 'In the years since then he has fashioned an organization, not of the Kingdom of the Isles, not of Kesh, but for the whole of Midkemia, for he saw during the Serpentwar that we are all of one people and we all share this world.'

'One people,' echoed the elven leader. 'Does that include us?'

'Yes,' said Kaspar. 'We are allied with the Elf Queen and her court in Elvandar.'

'Ah,' said the old man. 'Then we have a problem, it seems. For we of the Sun, we who abide here in Baranor do not serve the Elf Queen, nor her dragon-rider. We are a free people.'

Kaspar knew there was something deeper underlying this than merely not being servants. 'Neither did those who lied over the sea, in the land we humans call Novindus. And while some have come to live in the Queen's court, others have not and remain across the seas. It is all as one to Lady Aglaranna. She welcomes those who seek her out, but does not demand it.'

'Yet she makes war upon our kin to the north, is that not true?'

Kaspar regretted he knew so little of elven lore,

and only a little about those elves humans called the Brotherhood of the Dark Path. 'So I have heard, yet I have also heard it is those who we call the Brotherhood who wage war on the Queen and her people. I cannot defend that which I am ignorant of, but I will say that should those the Conclave opposes prevail, whatever differences may exist between your people and the Queen will become academic, for all life on this world will be extinguished.'

The old elf was silenced. 'Extinguished?' he said at last.

'What we have been told is that this race, the Dasati, will not come to conquer and enslave, but rather to obliterate all life on this world as it now exists, replacing it with life from their home world, from the most mightiest to the smallest. From dragons to insects to the tiniest fish in the sea, all will be pushed aside to give them a world they can fashion to their liking.'

Again Castdanur was quiet. After several long minutes, he said, 'I need to consider your words and discuss them with the others. You will go back to your men now and I trust you will rest well, despite the circumstances.'

'I'm an old soldier and hunter,' said Kaspar, rising from the low table and bowing slightly. 'I know how to sleep when the opportunity offers itself, no matter what the circumstance. I hope you'll consider what I've said seriously, and we can speak on this more.'

'Rest assured we will,' said the old elf as he rose and returned Kaspar's bow. 'Much depends on it, including the disposition of you and your men. You do believe in fate, do you not, Kaspar of Olasko?'

Kaspar said, 'I once did, when I was young and vain and believed I was fated to rule. Now I believe in opportunity, and that a man receives from life what he puts into it. It has been a lesson hard learned but it was pain deserved and I am a better man for having endured it.'

'We are a patient race,' said Castdanur. 'We are vexed by those whom you encountered on your way here, and I suspect we shall discover some relationship between those who faced you on the beaches and those who surround us every sundown, but we can speak more about this in a few days.'

'A few days?'

'I must lead the hunt,' said the old elf. 'We are, as you have noticed, facing difficult times, and we do not have stores enough to accommodate you and your men. We shall not put you to the blade merely because we are hungry, nor will we let you starve. So, a hunt must be organized. For many reasons, we can not hunt these hills or the peaks above, but must venture for a day or more to the north or south to find game. So it will be three or four days before I return, and then we shall resume our discussion. I would appreciate your word that you will cause no trouble for those left to guard you.'

'It is a soldier's duty to escape,' said Kaspar.

The old elf sighed. 'That would be foolish. Not only would we quickly hunt you down, but you would likely die before we found you. As I have said, the area around this fortification is dangerous.'

Kaspar nodded. 'I personally will remain here as a token of good faith. I can order my men to do the same, but cannot be certain all will obey.' He hesitated for a minute, unsure as to whether he needed to restate his case. 'I have said what I had needed to say, but I trust you understand that because of what I've have spoken of, it is imperative that some accommodation be reached soon; whatever brought that ship of evil men to your shores is part of a larger scheme, one involving forces that are in league with the invaders I spoke of.'

'The Dasati. Yes I know,' said Castdanur. 'We shall have an opportunity to discuss everything. We are, as I said, a patient race, and we have a different appreciation of the passing of time. We shall reach no hasty conclusions, though we will pay heed to your sense of urgency.'

'I thank you for listening.' said Kaspar.

A guard escorted Kaspar back to the long hall that was being used to confine his men. Jommy, Servan and the others looked up expectantly. Kaspar saw that they had been fed, though from the empty bowls and expressions on the men's faces, he knew that he had eaten far better than they. He ignored the silent questions in their eyes, but motioned for Jim Dasher to come with him to a far corner. He also motioned for those nearby to draw away to give them some privacy.

'Can you get out?' asked Kaspar.

'No problem,' said the thief. 'They hardly have the resources to confine a heavy-footed lout like Brix.'

Kaspar nodded. Brix was one of his stoutest warriors, a good man in a brawl, but he was the constant butt of the other men's humour because of a clumsiness that often had him tripping over his own feet. 'Can you get to the ships?'

'Ah,' said Jim softly. 'Now that's a different question. I have in my mind a route, but there's no doubt the elves know these woods a thousand times better than I. A lot of it depends on how much of a head start I get, and who they send after me. I've heard tales from others about elves' tracking skills so I doubt it would do me much good to lay false trails or that sort of thing – besides, I'm a city man mostly and my woodlore is scant. No, speed's the only edge I might possess.'

'When would you go?'

'No later than two hours from now,' said the thief from Krondor. 'It'll still be two hours from midnight and if they're expecting a breakout, they'll look for it at sunrise, I think.'

'Guards tend to be half-asleep just before sunrise,' observed Kaspar.

Jim nodded agreement. 'And there are those things out there, on the wolves. Fear of them is expected to keep us all huddled in here.' He glanced around. 'If I go in two hours, I can steal ten miles on them by sunrise. That puts me around the point and off the coast.'

'You going to try to swim to the ships?' asked Kaspar with a rueful smile. 'The sharks are impressive in these waters.'

'Do I look stupid?' asked Dasher. 'I'll build a signal fire. The Captain knows there might be one.'

'Who gave him that order?' asked Kasper.

With a wide grin, Dasher said, 'I did. I didn't think much of your original plan.'

Kaspar shook his head. 'You're a common thief, remember?'

'The Captain is one of the few on this expedition I trust – he was hand-picked for this mission by Prince Grandprey.'

'That boy's coming into his own, isn't he?'

'He's a cut above, for a youngster,' agreed Jim. Lowering his voice he said, 'Look, Kaspar, only two people here know what I really do and who I work for: you and me. We are also the only two men who can take word back to those who matter and help make some sense of it. I'll grant you an edge in wood-lore and hiding in bushes and the like, but I'm far more adept at running away than you are, I suspect. And if it comes to an in-close fight . . . well, you're a hell of a soldier, but I know more dirty tricks than you do.'

'I'm not arguing that it's you who needs to go,' said Kaspar. 'I just hope our hosts won't be too offended by your escape and take it out on us, and if they aren't and don't, then perhaps I can reason with them and your coming trials will be for naught. But if they don't . . .' He shrugged.

'Better to have me get word to our various lords and masters. Yes, I know. What do we know?'

The two men put their heads close together and began discussing the mission and the implications of the presence of the magic-user and his conjured creature, combined with what they had observed during their march up to this settlement. They continued like this for almost an hour, leaving Jommy, Servan and the other men to speculate on what the leader of this expedition and a common thief from Krondor could be plotting.

Jim Dasher waited until the men had either dozed off or fallen into low conversation so as not to disturb the wounded who were sleeping. He thought at least three of the lads would be dead by morning or mid-day at the latest unless they got proper care from a chirurgeon or healing priest. Whatever magic these elves possessed, healing didn't seem to be part of it, or perhaps they were disinclined to heal their prisoners. Either way, those lads would have a tough time of it.

Jim had weighed his options and shared a false bravado with Kaspar, who was now crossing over to speak privately with him once more. 'You ready?' he asked.

'A few more minutes,' Dasher answered. 'It might help a bit if you wandered over to where Jommy Killaroo is chatting with that old sergeant and . . . I don't know, made a quiet announcement about something. I only need a minute or so, but if you can draw attention away from the door, I can be through without anyone seeing me go.' He looked around. 'I don't know if you've noticed, but the elven guards spend a lot of time watching how we watch each other.'

Kaspar glanced at the two guards outside the door and saw how their eyes were constantly shifting from this group to that, several times lingering on Kaspar and Jim at the far end of the hall. 'Hadn't, to tell you the truth.'

'It's a good idea,' said Dasher. 'You don't know what to expect, but you reckon the prisoners do and you watch them to see who reacts in a funny way.' He glanced at the men who were sleeping or talking quietly. 'You'll have some irritated lads when you wake them to tell them to get some sleep or whatever else you do, but I'll only need a minute. There's a window above the beam – don't look up – and I'll be up there and out before anyone catches a glimpse. Wouldn't do to have the lads gawking and saying, "Oh, look! There goes Dasher!"'

'I wish you didn't have to do this, Jim.' Kaspar crossed his arms and leaned back against the wall, trying hard to look casual.

'No one else has a chance, and we both know it.'

'I almost wish I could order you to stay.'

Jim Dasher grinned, and not for the first time Kaspar was surprised how the simple change of expression made years fall away, made him look almost boyish. 'Ah, but you can't, can you?'

'No, I can't,' said Kaspar with a slowly broadening smile of his own. 'Fat lot of good being called "General" does me, right?'

Jim's grin widened. 'With me, anyway.'

Kaspar's expression became serious. He put a hand on Jim Dasher's shoulder. 'Stay alive.'

'That's my plan.'

'How many do you think they'll send after you?' asked Kaspar.

Jim shook his head slightly. 'How many do you think?'

'One, maybe two. They strike me as a pretty arrogant lot. And they don't have many to spare. Well, you've got tonight and five more days to reach the cove and signal if you're not going back to our camp.'

'Can't. It's the first place they'll look if they lose track of me.'

'An elf losing track?'

'I've a trick or two they've not seen. And if they find me, I'll deal with that. No, I need to get over the crest to the north-west, and then

157

down, somehow, to the beach where the ships are. That means we're hoisting sail on our way to Roldem in two days, not six.' He fell silent for a moment, then said, 'I hope that fellow who tried to gut you on the road is one of those coming after me.'

'Sinda?' Kaspar nodded. 'He's a real charmer. He's already burying us. If you do tangle with him, say hello for me.'

Jim nodded. 'Now, go and annoy the men.'

Kaspar did as requested and Jim glanced around. The elves had been cursory about disarming the men, knowing that one of their magicians could deal with any insurrection easily, and had taken only the obvious weapons: swords, daggers, knives, and bows and arrows. But Jim knew that a few of the men harboured knives in boots or up their sleeves and he was a walking inventory himself of unexpected weapons and tools. He reached down to his left boot as if scraping off something attached to the sole deftly, he opened a small hollow in the heel and pulled out a tiny crystal vial. He hated the thought of breaking such a precious container – the cost for having a hundred of these made in a land far enough from Krondor to not arouse suspicion had caused Lord Erik to almost – but this was just the sort of situation for which he had prepared this treasure.

He used his left thumb nail to crack the vial as Kaspar awoke those men who were dozing or asleep and let half a dozen drops of liquid wet his lips. He sucked up the tiny bit of very powerful magic and waited.

The tingling across the surface of his body told him that he was now invisible to any mortal eye. It was good to be working with powerful magicians, Jim considered, not for the first time in his life. He knew that in half an hour he'd be visible again, and he knew the potion didn't mask his tracks or other signs he might leave behind. In fact, he was counting on it.

Kaspar looked up and was startled to see that Jim Dasher was gone. He glanced around the room. One of the elves at the door looked towards him as he started speaking to the men and Kaspar quickly averted his eyes, giving the men a cursory account of his discussion with Castdanur. He then cautioned them to maintain discipline while in captivity and left them with a promise that everything would be over soon. As he crossed the floor to his pallet, he lay down and tried to sleep. He wondered if being over soon was necessarily a good outcome.

Jim Dasher had been born in the city, raised a city boy, and hated the wilderness, but he had spent months in the forests and mountains north of Krondor learning his woodcraft from a pair of very determined, very tough and unforgiving Royal Krondorian Pathfinders. He couldn't live off the land indefinitely, but he could keep from starving for a few weeks and knew better than to seek shelter in some angry cave bear's den. He was also a fair tracker – though not as adept as even Kaspar, let alone the elves – and knew how to hide a trail.

At the moment, though, he was concerned about the Void-darters and their wolf-riding masters. Jim could think in very complex fashion, a trait which had made him a most valuable asset to both the Crown of the Isles and the Conclave. While constantly assessing his situation and planning his next move, he was also reviewing the events of a very long day. He wished he had more information to take back with him, such as who the wolf-riders were. Those creatures weren't wolves, he knew, but until someone put a proper name to them, wolves would have to do. And the elves? They were a puzzle. He knew as much as any man in the Kingdom of the Isles about elves: his story about the cave and elf wizard was nonsense, but he had been to Elvandar and the trinket he wore around his neck was genuine.

He had read every document in Krondor's royal archives pertaining to the elves, from some very ancient nonsense that predated the Riftwar to every official report concerning the activities of Warleader Thomas and his wife, the Elf Queen Aglaranna. The Kingdom might have many allies, but he was certain they had none more dependable than the royal court in Elvandar.

Which led him back to not knowing what to make of this band of elves. He spoke enough of their language to have puzzled out some of what they said, but only enough to make him even more curious and frustrated.

Now, Jim Dasher paused and listened to the rhythm of the night. The breeze stirred the branches, and night birds and nocturnal animals scurried. Most went to ground as he approached, for their senses far outmatched his ability to move stealthily. But those just outside the area he disturbed in passing continued their activities, and they provided tiny clues as to how much danger lay nearby. Absolute silence was as deadly as the sound of armed men crashing through the brush behind him.

There were just the right amount of night birds' calls and the hooting that might have been an owl he had not encountered before to tell him that trouble was not hard on his heels, but he knew it would be coming soon.

He judged he had less than an hour's lead over his pursuers, and while he might have some tricks to slow them down they'd never come across, eventually they would overtake him. While keeping his attention on the task at hand, moving along the route he had mentally marked out on the way up to the elves' stronghold, he also kept looking out for likely spots to set up an ambush. There was going to be a confrontation, so it might as well be on his terms.

Jim Dasher waited. He knew that at least one, or possibly two, elves were coming fast. He didn't know how he knew, but he knew. His grandfather had spoken of his own grandfather, the legendary Jimmy the Hand, and had once mentioned his claim to possess a 'bump of trouble', an intuition that allowed him to anticipate pitfalls before actually coming upon them. Jim Dasher had no name for this gut feeling but he knew that on more than one occasion an anticipation of trouble had saved him from disaster.

'The itch', as his grandfather had called it, had begun a few minutes before, and Jim had stopped to listen. There was nothing he could hear, but somehow he had sensed a change out there, behind him, and he knew his pursuers were close.

He had no doubt he could ambush one elf and stand a fair chance – well, an unfair one, really – to best him. But a second bow or sword would almost undoubtedly mean his death or capture. Just in case there were two of them, he reached down to his belt and removed it. He had five secret pouches sewn inside it, which is why he had chosen a big rock as a weapon when facing the wolf-riders rather than use his belt as Kaspar had instructed. He deftly tore at the threads with his thumbnail, parting the fastenings used to secure two of the small compartments and set aside the vials he had secreted there. He then slid a small, thin and very lethal blade he had fashioned that was inserted into the belt just below the buckle – which also could be used as a *cestus*, a charming Quegan invention like a battle glove – and set that down next to the vials. He smiled at the image of Kaspar laying about him with his belt and thought that he should really get a special buckle made for the former Duke. Kaspar had been a thorn in the Kingdom's side for years, though he really had been more of a problem for Roldem and Great Kesh, which meant he was a threat worth enduring for the Kingdom of the Isles, but since his exile and return, he had proved to be a valuable resource for the Conclave. Besides, Jim liked him. He could be a murderous thug, just like Jim, but there was an interesting, complex man there, one who appreciated hunting, good food and wine, and the company of bad women.

He put this belt around his waist, took the blade in his right hand, picked up the first vial with his left. He coated his blade with its contents, then tossed the empty container aside. Then he picked up the second vial and waited.

The two elves were upon him without further warning. His instincts told him that it was time to move, and without thought he did, and in just the right direction.

A sword blade cut into the tree trunk where Jim had crouched just moments before and that was all the opening he needed. He broke the vial between thumb and forefinger and flicked the contents into the elf's eyes. In seconds the elf was on his knees clutching at his face and screaming in pain.

The second elf was the one called Sinda. He drew back his bow and let fly with an arrow. Jim didn't think; he reacted, moving to his left, Sinda's right, and forcing the elf to traverse his line-of-fire across his own body. That tiny adjustment saved Jim's life, for the arrow sped by his neck, close enough for the fletching to slice a shallow cut in his skin. Jim rolled forward, ignoring the rocks and twigs that cut into him, and came up hard, his shoulder driving into Sinda's stomach.

In close, the elf's bow was useless and before he could get his belt-knife unsheathed, Dasher drove him to the ground, drew back his fist and struck him hard on the point of the jaw. The elf's eyes went vacant for a fraction of a moment, but that was all the time Jim needed. He pinned the elf's left arm under his knees and reached out and grabbed the other wrist with his left hand. He pressed his small blade hard enough against Sinda's neck so that the elf could feel it and said, 'If you wish to live, do not move! There's poison on my blade and one cut will kill you swiftly.'

The elf was dazed but understood enough to go limp. After a second Jim said, 'Good. Listen. I don't have much time. Your friend has mossback venom in his eyes. You know what that means. You have perhaps an hour or two at most to get him to one of your healers. Now, you must decide what is more important, to kill me and let him die, or to save his life. You cannot do both. And killing me will not be easy. Can your people afford to lose two more warriors?'

Jim got up quickly leaving Sinda on his back, confused. 'Why didn't you kill me?' he asked.

Jim Dasher reached around his neck and pulled something off. He tossed it to Sinda and said, 'I am not your enemy. None of the men you hold is your enemy. If you let us, we will help you survive. But I need to warn my people of what we saw on the beach, for that black sorcery means more pain and death than you want to imagine is coming to these shores. No one else will try to escape. Let them help you while they wait.'

'Wait for what?' asked Sinda.

'For your leaders to decide to kill them or let them live. Now see to your friend.'

Almost as quickly as an elf, he vanished into the gloom, leaving the confused Sinda considering what he had just heard. The elf looked at the object that had been tossed to him and his eyes widened. In the faint light his elven vision easily made out the design. This was no forgery, but a genuine token given to an elf-friend by the Queen of the Elves.

Sinda helped his companion to his feet. The worst of the pain had passed, but both elves knew that the venom of the mossback lizard would

165

slowly reduce the victim to a vague and listless state, followed quickly by death. It was an effective poison, but easily cured, if one had the antidote. Sinda put his arm around his companion's waste, pulled the staggering man's arm over his shoulder and began to return to Baranor.

CHAPTER 8

THREATS

Miranda ran.

The alarm had sounded almost instantly accompanied by shouts from the hallway. She had been resting in the suite set aside for her by the Emperor, waiting for a summons to the imperial apartments within the palace for a meeting with the Light of Heaven. Dozens of servants and Imperial Guards ran to answer the clarion call. The signal was unique, for only one such rare metal trumpet existed in the Empire, and it was used to warn the Emperor when he was in danger.

Miranda didn't need to be told that dark magic was involved: she could feel it making her skin crawl and there was the illusion of a foul stench in the air as she approached the entrance to the imperial apartments. The giant wooden doors were closed, their ancient carved surfaces being hammered at futilely by a dozen guardsmen. 'Stand aside!' shouted Miranda.

Several of the soldiers hesitated, but the servants all moved away. The sight of a black robe, even if it wasn't truly black but a very dark grey, and the commanding presence of any magic-user, evoked years of conditioning, and several bowed their heads and said, 'Your will, Great One.'

The soldiers followed suit, and Miranda raised her hands. Thinking this was not a time for subtlety, she focused her mind on the great hinges and willed the stone in which they were set to become dust. Then with a shout to focus her thoughts, she extended her hand, as if pushing something away, and the air before it rippled as energy coursed through it, striking the massive doors like an invisible battering ram. They fell backwards, slamming into the stone floor of the imperial quarters with a thunderous crash. Before the echo diminished, the soldiers were through.

Miranda turned to the servants. 'Stay back. If you are needed you will be called.'

She hurried after the soldiers and had no trouble discovering their objective. A searing wave of heat washed over her as she entered the long hallway leading to the lush gardens. The soldiers before her faltered as the heat washed over them, then redoubled their efforts. She heard screams and shouts ahead as she hurried towards the conflict.

This apartment complex was the largest in the palace, a series of interconnecting rooms that allowed for the imperial family and their most loyal retainers to live apart from the rest of the administration of the Empire for long stretches.

A lavish garden rested at the entrance to the residence as you approached from the centre of the palace. It was an oasis of calm in an otherwise constantly busy and noisy community, complete with a huge pool surrounded by pavilions with hanging curtains of silk in which to evade the heat of the day. Now those precious silks were ablaze as if some wayward magical bolt of energy had ignited them.

It took Miranda only a moment to apprehend the situation. A pair of Dasati Deathpriests lay dead next to a fountain. Somehow several had materialized inside the Emperor's garden. The evidence of the carnage around them suggested that without considering their situation, they had started casting their death-spells in random directions, at any human they spied. The Tsurani magician who had been with the Emperor had answered instantly with a blazing ball of fire, probably to cover the Emperor's retreat or to forestall the Deathpriests easily locating him. Either way, the result was a conflagration that was quickly burning its way through a small fortune in silks and cushions. Miranda glanced around, her vision obscured by the smoke and dying flames. From what she could see, many servants and Imperial Guards had died a horrible, painful death. None of the bodies was garbed in imperial fashion, so the Emperor must be in another part of the complex. Miranda felt a sense of relief at the realization.

The Emperor was young, without a wife, so his life was seen as doubly precious: with no heir to crown should he die in an untimely fashion, the Empire would be without a ruler and the political chaos in such a time of great turmoil would be disastrous. As was Tsurani custom, in times of war after the formal breaking of the Red Seal on the great doors of the Temple of the War God, a herald with the imperial clarion was stationed nearby, to signal any danger to the Light of Heaven. A priest of the order of Jastur also stood watch outside the Emperor's door.

Miranda arrived just behind the first wave of Imperial Guards who were outside the family complex, and was in time to see the powerful priest of Jastur unleash his magic war-hammer. It flew through the air to strike a Deathpriest in the chest, slamming him backwards through the air. A fountain of orange blood exploded from the creature's chest as he slid half a dozen yards across the stone floor, almost to Miranda's feet.

Over the tumult, Miranda tried to be heard. 'We need the other one alive!'

She instantly knew that her cry was in vain, for Tsurani soldiers, pledged to give their life for the Emperor, swarmed over the remaining Deathpriest, bearing him down quickly under their weight and before she could reach the mass of bodies they had pierced him countless times with sword-points and daggers. Pushing aside any irritation over things she couldn't control, she turned to see an officer in the guard standing with his sword drawn, covered in orange blood. 'Where is the Light of Heaven?' she demanded.

'In his bedchamber,' answered the officer.

Miranda noticed that his skin was beginning to blister where the Dasati blood had touched it and she said, 'Wash that off before you suffer seriously, Strike Leader.'

'Your will, Great One,' he answered. Even though she had no official position within the Assembly of Magicians, because she was the wife of Milamber and confidante of the Emperor, the tradition-bound Tsurani insisted on addressing her with that honorific. She had stopped correcting people: it was a useless exercise.

She hurried past servants and guards, to where armed guards protected the entrance to the bedchamber. 'The danger is past,' she instructed them. 'I must see His Majesty.'

The senior guardsman motioned for her to stay. He moved inside the chamber and a moment later reappeared with word that the Emperor would see her. She was through the door before he had finished and found the young ruler wearing his traditional armour, all gold, holding an ancient metal sword, ready to fight. There was something about his manner and bearing that spared him any appearance of the ridiculous. He looked every inch the Tsurani warrior, despite his sheltered life.

Standing at his side was a slender magician named Manwahat, who nodded once at Miranda.

He gave her a questioning look. She returned a curt nod, and could sense that somewhere under that immobile Tsurani exterior, he must be breathing a sigh of relief. He was a young magician, as the Assembly accounted such, but Miranda knew him by reputation: he was level-headed and powerful.

Without preamble, she said, 'Majesty, you must leave the Holy City.'

The Emperor blinked as if he didn't understand her words, then his manner changed. He took a deep breath and sheathed his ceremonial sword. 'May I ask why, Miranda? I rarely receive orders.'

Miranda understood belatedly that her informality was ill-suited to any situation where they weren't alone. 'My apologies, Majesty. In my concern for your welfare, I forgot my place. It must be Varen. Disguised as Wyntakata, he has been through this palace a dozen times, and he's the only one who would know how to get those Deathpriests into your private garden.'

'Deathpriests?'

'Two Dasati Deathpriests materialized within your garden and started killing everyone in sight.' She paused for a moment, then said, 'It was a suicide attack, without a doubt. Varen wouldn't care how many Dasati die and they are fanatics in the service of their Dark God.'

'Return to the subject of why I must leave my palace,' said the Emperor.

'As Wyntakata, Varen has enough knowledge of

172

the palace to continue to attack you here. He knows that despite a fierce loyalty to the Empire, the High Council would be thrown into confusion by your death. With no obvious heir—'

'It becomes a struggle between cousins as to who next sits upon the Golden Throne,' finished Emperor Sezu. 'Yes, it makes sense. But where should I go?'

'Has Wyntakata visited any of your country estates, Majesty?'

'I cannot be certain,' said the Emperor. 'Perhaps before I took office . . .'

'Not that far back,' said Miranda. She considered how long it was since Varen's last apparent 'death' during his attack on Sorcerer's Isle. 'Just in the last year or so.'

'No, not that I'm aware,' said the Emperor. 'I will have my First Advisor consult with the house staff.' Then he brightened. 'One place I'm certain he has not visited. The ancient Acoma estates, south of Sulan-Qu. No one has lived there since my grandfather took the throne, but we have kept those lands and the buildings in the imperial house as a shrine, a site of veneration as the birthplace of the Mistress of the Empire. Yes, it is certain he has never been there.'

She nodded to Manwahat, and the young magician said, 'If the Light of Heaven pleases, I can have you and your closest retainers there in a matter of minutes.' The Emperor seemed about to object, but the magic-user added, 'Others can

173

ensure that your household follows quickly.' He nodded at Miranda.

'I'll pass word back through the Assembly and if we must we'll move the entire seat of government down there. I can issue orders from there as quickly as here if the Great Ones will aid us.'

Manwahat nodded. 'If it is your will, Majesty, it is our will.'

The Emperor turned to a servant. 'Instruct the Warlord to convene the High Council tomorrow, and I shall leave instructions on what must be done to prepare for the coming invasion.' The servant bowed and hurried off to discharge his duty.

A palace official appeared to inform the Emperor that the fires in the garden pavilion were extinguished. The Emperor dismissed everyone, but bade Miranda to linger. When they were alone with the remaining bodyguards, the Emperor's calm mask fell away and Miranda now saw a very angry young man before her. 'The war has begun, hasn't it?'

Miranda assumed a level of familiarity she wouldn't have risked even hours before. She reached out and put her hand on the Emperor's shoulder. Guards in the room shifted position slightly, ready to leap to their ruler's defence if the outland woman should attempt any harm. 'It has begun,' she said softly. 'And it will not end until the Dasati are completely repulsed from this world and this realm, or Kelewan lies in ruins at their feet. You are about to do something no other Emperor has ever been forced to do: order every house in the Empire to arms, to muster the entire armed might at your command, for never in its two-thousand-year history has the Empire stood at greater risk.'

The anger remained, but the Emperor's voice was calm. 'We will do what we must. We are Tsurani.'

Miranda hoped that would be enough. 'What of the message?' she asked.

The Emperor looked off into the distance. 'I . . . where would we go?'

Miranda knew that was the heart of the issue. The cryptic message from some future Pug to the Emperor instructing him to make ready an evacuation left a lot of room for interpretation. But taken at its worst possible meaning, to remove everyone from this world, or even just from the Empire, would be a colossal enterprise. A hundred rifts would have to be fashioned and controlled day and night, a task that would challenge the entire Assembly. Even with help from the Academy and Sorcerer's Isle, the enormity of the undertaking would be overwhelming. And during a war with the most dangerous enemies ever confronted? Miranda knew what the Emperor was thinking: it was an impossible choice.

Moreover, his question still hung in the air: where would they go?

★　★　★

Miranda saw a look of relief on her son's face as she entered the office her husband had created at the rear of their home. She wished she could smile at the look, but she knew that he was about to be disabused of any notion that she was there to relieve him from his duty.

'Mother,' he said, rising and kissing her on the cheek.

'Caleb,' she replied, 'you look as if you're ageing before my eyes.'

'I had no concept of how difficult it was to co-ordinate all the Conclave's activities as well as manage this school on a day-to-day basis.'

'Any problems?' she asked, taking the chair behind the desk he had just vacated.

'The school? None to speak of. As Father instructed, we're turning down requests to send new students, focusing our efforts on training to make our magicians ready to help in the coming fight, and everyone's co-operating.'

'And?' she asked. 'What isn't going well?'

'We've heard nothing from Kaspar's expedition to the Peaks of the Quor.'

'How overdue is contact?'

'A few days.'

'I won't start worrying until he's a week overdue,' she said. 'Remind me of the mission?'

Caleb's dark eyes narrowed. He knew that his mother had an almost perfect memory for details, when she bothered to study them and realized she must have neglected to apprise herself of the details of this mission, because it was one of the last Pug had approved prior to his departure for the Dasati realm.

'One of our agents in Freeport picked up a message between a smuggler and some unknown band of raiders whom Father suspected of either working for Leso Varen or perhaps with him.'

'For or with? He thinks they're either unwilling dupes or willing accomplices?'

'Something like that,' said Caleb. 'The west shore of the Peaks of the Quor, specifically a large cove called "Kesana Cove", along with an approximate date, was expressly mentioned in the message—'

'And your father was off and running to find out what that was all about.'

Caleb nodded. 'He also wanted to get some of the lads from different groups working together, so he asked Nakor to talk to Lord Erik about his . . . irregulars out of Krondor, and they joined with some lads from Kesh and Roldem and he put Kaspar in charge.'

'Well, your father's been curious about the Peaks of the Quor for years,' she admitted. 'We've had little luck finding out much and have both been too busy to go down there personally to poke about, so I understand his reasons.' Thinking about the coming confrontation with the Dasati, she added, 'Though his timing could have been better. Let me know if you hear anything from Kaspar. Now, go and take the rest of the day off.'

Caleb frowned. 'Only the rest of the day?'

'Yes, because you're not heading out to go hunting or whatever else you want to do. I'm sure your wife won't object to you staying at home for a few more days . . . or weeks.' Caleb's frown deepened. 'I'm not going to be here for long. I have a lot to do and I need to come up with a plan on how to accomplish it without your father and Nakor around.'

'Do what?'

Miranda sighed. 'Convince the Kings of the Isles and Roldem, as well as the Emperor of Great Kesh to accept refugees from Kelewan should it come to that.'

Caleb blinked in surprise. 'Refugees? You're thinking of contingency plans?'

Caleb saw his mother visibly wilt before his eyes. All her usual strength and vitality seemed to ebb away and she sat back in the chair with a look of resignation he had never see before. Softly she said, 'No. Not a contingency. An eventuality.'

Pug sat quietly watching the faces of those nearby, as the sun settled behind the western horizon, a portion of the city wall, so vast and so distant it looked like a remote ridge in the evening haze. He occupied a small bench where, he had been told, Lessers who farmed the grove came to eat their mid-day meal. The others were arrayed around the workers' shack, the only building in the grove, shielded from casual sight by hundreds of fruit trees. Pug considered the fruit a Dasati apple, though the colour was more of a yellowish-orange than red or green, and there was a luminous shimmer to the surface when it was freshly picked, the flesh of the fruit being a deep purple colour.

As the sun disappeared from view, Macros turned and said, 'It's done. The Great Culling is now over.' With a heavy sigh he came to sit down next to Pug. 'The killing will continue for a bit – the fights don't simply stop because the sun has set, but combatants will now withdraw rather than press the issue, and those in hiding will slowly emerge, and tonight the cleaning-up will commence.'

Nakor stood a few feet behind Pug, observing the bucolic peace that all knew to be an illusion. Safety was almost an impossibility on this world, yet for a moment, he could see in the faces of the others the same thought: once this had been a tranquil, lovely world, with industrious people whose lives in many ways resembled those on Midkemia. Softly he said, 'This is how it should be.'

'Yes,' said Pug as the sun set completely and the sky above turned into a stunning riot of colours as the western clouds reflected a spectrum no human eye could ever appreciate. 'What happened?'

'The Dark God,' said Macros. Pug could tell that his illness was taking more of a toll than usual; the exertion of the last day was bringing him to the edge of exhaustion.

Nakor said, 'No, it's more than that.'

Magnus also approached. 'What do you mean?'

'It can't just be one local god, no matter if he's this world's version of the Nameless – a Greater God – disrupting the balance. We know what happened when the Nameless One tried to take dominance during the early part of the Chaos Wars on Midkemia: the surviving Greater and Lesser Gods put aside their differences and combined to banish him to somewhere safe until order and balance could be restored. That didn't happen here. The Dark God overwhelmed the combined might of hundreds of other Dasati gods. But how?'

Macros said, 'Not hundreds. Thousands. We don't know how. The history of that era is lost.'

Pug nodded. 'Logic tells us that the Dark God could not have done it alone. He must have had allies.'

'Who?' asked Magnus. 'And what happened to them?'

'Perhaps he turned on them at a crucial moment, until he alone remained,' offered Macros.

'No,' said Nakor, again softly, as if afraid to be overheard. 'Too many things would have had to fall into place for him. It's too unlikely.' He offered a rueful smile.

Pug nodded in agreement. He weighed his words carefully, then looked at Macros. 'What do you know of the next realm?'

'The third plane of existence?'

Pug nodded.

'Nothing, really.'

'The fourth?' asked Pug.

'Again, nothing.'

'The fifth?'

Macros sighed. 'I had a few very painful but highly memorable moments in the fifth plane. When you closed the rift to the demon realm behind me, I was left in the clutches of Maarg, the Demon King. I unleashed every bit of power I possessed, stunning him for the briefest instant, and he released his hold on me. I fell to what I take it was a stone floor, in some sort of demonic palace. Merely touching it caused me great pain. I had only a few impressions, then I lost consciousness. I expect Maarg killed me moments later, for the next thing I knew I was in front of Lims-Kragma, listening to a litany of . . .' He faltered.

'What?' asked Pug.

'Until this moment, I had no memory of . . . the time between my death and my childhood here.' He paused. 'In fact, I had no memory of a childhood, really. Impressions of a mother and being in hiding, and a difficult journey to . . .' He looked from face to face. 'I really didn't live that life. My memories are . . . someone else's.'

Nakor nodded. 'Somehow Lims-Kragma put you in another's body.'

'How many years has it been since I died, Pug?'

'About forty.'

'I've been here, or at least I remember being here, thirty-three or so Midkemian years.'

'What happened to the rest?' asked Magnus.

Macros let out a slow breath. 'It's a mystery.'

Nakor said, 'Not really. What is your earliest memory, of you being you, Macros, not the Dasati you thought you were?'

'Eleven years ago, after a summer rite, I was walking home and became overcome with dizziness. I ducked out of sight, afraid that someone might see me weakened . . .' He shook his head. 'Before that, I was a Lesser, a minor fabricator of clothing.'

'A tailor,' said Magnus.

'Yes,' said Macros.

'But in only eleven years you have fashioned a planets-wide resistance to the Dark God, and have won over thousands of followers,' said Pug.

Macros closed his eyes. 'The White has been around a lot longer than me . . .'

'Who was the Gardener before you?' asked Magnus.

Macros appeared confused, uncertain. 'I . . . don't know.' His shoulders rounded as he slumped down, looking troubled. 'I awoke under a stone wall, not unlike those you see around here. I had a massive headache and I stumbled back to the hovel where I . . . where this body lived.' He looked Nakor in the eyes. 'I was not reborn, was I?'

Nakor slowly shook his head. 'I don't know, but

I think not. I think somehow the gods of our home world took your mind and put it in another body. I think that's why you're sick.'

'Dying,' corrected Macros.

'Who was the Gardener before you?' repeated Magnus.

Now Macros looked genuinely disturbed. 'I don't know,' he said again. 'I don't know who would know,' he added quietly. 'No one here is likely to know. Perhaps Martuch, Hirea, or Narueen, or they might know . . .'

'What?' asked Pug.

'The Bloodwitch Sisters. If anyone knows, it is they.'

Nakor stood, as if ready to depart. 'Then we must ask them.'

Pug said, 'Yes.'

Macros said, 'But we should . . .'

For the first time in his life, since meeting Macros the Black on Sorcerer's Island, – back when Pug was only a simple squire in Lord Borric's court at Crydee Castle – Pug saw confusion and uncertainty in Macros's face. 'Nakor is right. We are embarking on the most dangerous undertaking attempted in this, or perhaps any other, world. There is a being who calls itself the Dark God of the Dasati, who endangers not only this world, but countless others. And we are going to stop it.

'I am not going to attempt such an undertaking rashly, and waste the lives of myself and my friend and my son because someone else wants us to act the part of mindless dupes. I need to know who is truly the person responsible for all this.'

Magnus said, 'We need to know who controlled the White before you.'

'I . . .' began Macros, then he faltered. He shook his head. 'I left my home, in a quadrant of the city not too distant from here, and I took the Star Bridge to another world. Mathusia. From there I travelled to . . . a place. I don't remember where, but when I got there, they were expecting me!'

'What sort of place was it?' asked Nakor.

'A Bloodwitch enclave,' said Macros softly.

'Then we must speak with whoever is in charge of the Bloodwitch Sisterhood.'

'Lady Narueen?' asked Magnus.

'No,' said Nakor. 'She is important, but she's not in charge.'

'How do you know that?' asked Pug.

'Because whoever is in charge isn't having babies and hiding out and risking being killed by crazy Bloodknights. Whoever's in charge is somewhere very safe telling others to go out and take risks.'

'Father's in charge of the Conclave, and he certainly takes risks.'

Nakor grinned and even through his false alien visage, the smile was all his own. 'Your father, at times, is not the sanest man I know, but on our world, it's rarely the case that when you step outside the door of your home, everyone and every-thing is trying to kill you.'

'Rarely,' Pug agreed dryly.

'Where are the Bloodwitches' leaders, Macros?' asked Nakor.

'On the other side of this world, in a hidden valley in a mountain range called the Skellar-tok.'

'Then we'd better get started,' said Nakor. 'If we don't take these Lesser servants with us, we can travel faster.'

Macros laughed. 'One more night won't make a difference. I need to rest, and you do as well, though not so much as I do. Besides, I need to remain here until word of what has occurred reaches us. I may be someone else's idea of a dupe, but I am still the leader of the White and I need to know my people are safe and ready to serve.'

'One night,' agreed Pug. Looking around, he said, 'While it wouldn't be the first time I've slept outside, I don't imagine you brought us here to this grove just to sleep on the ground.'

Macros shook his head and laughed. 'No. There is a hidden entrance to an underground safe haven over there. It's a little . . . lacking in amenities, but it will serve until morning.' He led them to the workers' shed, and opened the door. Inside two Lessers stood waiting, both armed, which was unusual for those of their rank, and Macros motioned them aside. He waved his hand and Pug felt magic coalesce in the air. A trio of planks in the floor vibrated and then vanished and suddenly a flight of narrow steps led down into the gloom. With another wave of his hand, Macros caused light to appear at the bottom of the steps and down they went. Whatever the two guards left above might think about all this went unspoken, as they resumed their duties of protecting everything in this nameless shed without a word.

CHAPTER 9

DISCOVERIES

Jim ducked behind a boulder.

Not for the first time since leaving the elves, he cursed himself for a fool. Up till now, one of the things that had made him both successful and dangerous was an optimism bordering on the foolhardy, a sense there was nothing he couldn't do once he put his mind to it. Blessed with mental agility as well as a physical quickness bordering on the supernatural, he could quickly assess situations and make snap judgments that were almost always correct.

But it was those occasional moments when he wasn't correct that had nearly got him killed over the years. This time, he was certain this was going to be one of those moments if he made a wrong move.

He had considered the location of the trail taken from the beach up to the elves' stronghold, and where the ships lay at anchor on the opposite side of the peninsula and had judged a game trail up into the mountains they had passed along the way to Baranor a likely route over the crest – he had even spied a gap in the peaks in the moonlight and was feeling confident of his choice. His only concern at that time had been either other elven pursuers, which he doubted, or those wolf-riding creatures, of which there had been no sign.

Until he almost walked into their encampment.

He crouched low expecting to hear a howl of alarm at any second, but after moments passed with no outcry, he ventured to peer around the edge of the rocks.

Creatures fashioned out of nightmare sat in a large circle around a fire, or something more or less like a fire, because while it burned and gave off light and heat, it wasn't the familiar yellow-white of a bonfire, but an alien silver-red with flickering flashes of blue. Jim had only seen the wolf-riders at dusk, but now he saw them illumin-ated by this fey fire, and the sight was unnerving, even for a man who considered himself immune to any surprise. The creatures looked like humans in form, having a head, arms and legs, but they lacked features and, from what Jim could see, clothing. Their surface seemed to be an ever-changing, rippling fabric or fluid, but nothing that could rightly be called 'skin', and as he had seen before, a faint wisp of smoke or steam would coil up from the surface now and again. And the crea-tures they rode, the 'wolves' hunkered down at their side, tongues lolling, were also otherworldly. Their eyes visibly glowed, and Jim knew from the first encounter he had had with them that this wasn't the result of reflected firelight. They were eating something, though from this distance Jim couldn't tell what it was. Then one of them tossed something in an arc above the fire to a companion and Jim felt his gorge rise as he recognized what could only be an arm. The arm of a human, elf or goblin, he couldn't tell what, but it was not the limb of an animal.

Jim judged the size of the camp and tried to calculate a way around it. There were huts at a distance from the fire, fashioned from something as alien to him as was everything else he associated with these beings. They were round, with flat tops and looked as if they had been made from massive discs of some featureless stone rather than from cloth, leather or wood. There were no doors or windows he could see, but from time to time a figure would emerge directly through a wall or vanish into one.

The most disturbing thing about the entire tableau was the silence. There was no talking, no laughing, not even the sound of heavy breathing. He knew they were capable of sound, for he had heard their shrieks or battle-cries earlier that day, but now there was only an unnatural silence. However they communicated, it wasn't through what Jim thought of as normal speech.

Jim peered around trying to find the flying creatures the elves called 'Void-darters'. If they were flying around the area, he wanted to know before he tried to skirt the village.

As quietly as he could he edged around the

encampment, trying to keep sight of any movement that might betray an unsuspected trap or an unexpected encounter. After he was nearly opposite to the position at which he had begun, he saw what could only be a cage, fashioned from what appeared to be the same material as the huts. Inside it, movement revealed the whereabouts of the flying creatures. He felt a small surge of relief. These alien creatures were either supremely confident or stupid, for there was nothing like a sentry or any defences posted. If he knew what would kill them, Jim could have engineered an assault that would have them all destroyed within minutes.

He continued to edge his way around the camp until he reached a rise above it, then he hurried along the trail towards what he hoped was a pass through the peaks and down to the anchored ships.

The sky to the east was visibly lightening and Jim knew that dawn was less than an hour away. He felt a sense of relief for he had been hunkered down on the east side of the peaks unsure of which way to descend. The path he followed had cut through a gap at the ridge, but on the eastern slope had quickly narrowed until he was faced with the certain knowledge that he risked falling to his death until he could see better. He was barely above the tree-line so when he looked down all he could make out in the low light from the setting moons was a sea of tree-tops. He knew that somewhere down there must be a way to the shoreline, but at this point it was foolhardy to move without better light.

Patience was a learned skill for Jim Dasher, who by nature tended to the impetuous and rash, but over the years he had harnessed those qualities and directed them. Now he was decisive and quick to act, without thoughtlessness. And right now he needed to think.

The inheritor of a legacy of service to the Crown and to the common people of Krondor, he had discovered early in life that one doesn't often get choices as to when difficult decisions must be made. Life was rarely convenient.

James Dasher Jamison was hardly a reflective man, but there were moments when he did consider his role in a larger scheme and wondered if he would every truly realize what it was he was fated to accomplish. A boy of great promise, he was the grandson of Lord James, Duke of Rillanon, the King's most trusted advisor. He was also the grandnephew of the man in control of the largest shipping enterprise in the Bitter Sea, Dashell Jamison. Something had occurred between the two brothers: once close, they were estranged by the time Jim was born.

Jim's father, Dasher Jamison, Lord Carlstone, had been one of the finest administrators in the King's court, and his mother had been Lady Rowella Montonowksy, a daughter of Roldem's nobility and a distant cousin to their queen. In all things, Jim should have been a child of privilege and refinement.

Sent to study in Roldem, he had been quickly judged to be one of the most promising students at the university. They had waited for him to blossom as a scholar. Instead he had discovered the streets of Roldem, and the back alleys as well. His instructors at university were defeated, for while he was repeatedly absent without permission, Jim always excelled at his studies. He had a natural ability to hear or read something once and know it perfectly, a gift for logic and problem-solving that made mathematics and the natural sciences easy for him, and an ability for abstraction and logic that made even the most obtuse philosophies manageable. In short, he had been the perfect student, when he chose to be around. He was indifferent to the canings he earned for each transgression, considering the welts on his back the cost of doing what he wished. Finally, the monks who were in charge of the University judged their efforts to be futile and had sent the young man back to his family in Rillanon.

His father was determined to harness his son's reckless nature and to make a courtier out of him, so he gave him a minor position in the King's court. More often than not Jim was gone from his office, wasting time in gambling halls, inns, and brothels. He had a flair for gambling which earned him a steady income on top of his family's allowance, and a taste for women of low estate, which had got him into a fair share of brawls, landing him in the city gaol more than once. His father's position had freed him every time, though the gaoler had warned Lord Carlstone that he could not protect his wayward son much longer.

Jim's father had used every means of persuasion at his disposal to curb his son's appetite for the seedier side of life, including a threat to hand him over to the King's army for service if he couldn't stem his impulses for low living, but all to no avail. At last his grandfather had taken a hand and had sent Jim to Krondor to work for his uncle, Jonathan Jamison, son of Dashell, Jim's great-uncle.

Jim took to his new surroundings as if born to them, and quickly discovered that he had a flair for business. He also soon realized that there was a very questionable relationship between his great-uncle's many business enterprises and any number of criminal activities in and around Krondor. At first it was smuggling, then sabotage of a competitor's shipments or a well-timed fire in their warehouse. By the time he was twenty years of age, Jim was running a gang at the docks, the Backwater Boys, and collecting money from various merchants to facilitate the safe arrival of goods that somehow avoided the Royal Customs House.

Then a year later, Jim was dragged out of his

home in the dead of night by four men clad in black. He had incapacitated two of them before they had clubbed him unconscious and when he awoke, he had found himself in the dungeon in the Prince's palace.

After a cold night and long day, he was visited by Lord Erik von Darkmoor, former Knight-Marshall of the Western Realm and currently retiring Duke of Krondor. The choice given to him had been simple: learn to love a contemplative and solitary life in a very dark and damp cell without any outside windows, or work for the Prince of Krondor as an agent.

Lord Erik made it clear that his relationship to the Duke of Rillanon would not save him from the choice; his grandfather would receive a most sympathetic message from Lord Erik regretfully informing him that his grandson had gone missing, perhaps a victim of foul play. It wasn't for two more years after he started working for Erik that Jim discovered the entire thing had been his grandfather's idea and that his great-uncle was also in on the plot.

But by then Jim was fully ensconced in the intrigue and politics of the nation, an agent for the King working in the darkest alleys as well as on the roofs and in the sewers of the cities of the Western Realm. To everyone he met he was either James Dasher Jamison, only son of Lord Carlstone of Rillanon, grandson of the Duke, or he was Jim Dasher, a member of the Mockers, the apparently roughly – but in reality very well – organized criminal underground of the city.

By the time he was taken into the Conclave at the age of twenty-seven, he was a practised thief, assassin, and spy for the crown, considered their finest operative and perhaps the most dangerous man not a magician in the Kingdom. Jim cared nothing for his reputation, for most part being ignorant of it, but he did take pride in doing whatever he did well. For it was here, in the darkest hours of the night when he was alone with himself that he truly understood himself: he was the great-great-grandson of Jimmy the Hand, the most legendary thief in the history of the Mockers. One-time street urchin, servant to Prince Arutha, advisor to kings and princes, at his death he had been the most powerful Duke in the Kingdom. Jim was less clear about his own personal ambitions – he had no desire to be a duke; he loved adventure too much to be cooped up in a palace in meetings all day. He enjoyed the intrigue, murder, skulking in shadows, and being faster than the other man, that much luckier than the fellow trying to kill him, more intelligent than his opponent. He relished the constant sense of danger and the incredible sense of accomplishment he got from his missions. At the end of one, he welcomed the hot baths and clean sheets, the company of willing women, the wine and food, but after a few days he wanted nothing more to be back in the alleys, running silently across rooftops or slogging through the sewers, one hand on his knife hilt, waiting for an attack he was certain was around the next corner.

But there were moments, like the one he was experiencing now, sitting cold and alone in the dark on the top of a distant ridge of mountains, when he judged himself quite mad. To himself he muttered, 'No sane man could want this life.'

But he knew he did want it, even needed it. He had made up the Jimmyhand story as a blind, a way to make his relationship with Jimmy the Hand of Krondor a seemingly false claim, thereby heading off any possible suspicion that he was, indeed, that worthy's great-great-grandson, and therefore the son of nobility. Too many people still lived who might connect the grandson of Lord James of Rillanon with his own grandfather, the legendary former thief-turned-noble, Lord James of Krondor.

No, he admitted to himself, Jim loved this life, even the bloody-handed work, for he knew he belonged to something larger than himself, and he was certain that every man whose life he had taken had deserved it. That sense of serving something more important than his own petty desires had taken what had been little more than a collection of rash impulses, a self-indulgent desire for danger and thrills, and turned it into something useful, even noble at times, and in that, Jim had discovered a balance to his life.

Then things had changed and he experienced a set of feelings that were new to him. He had met a woman.

As he sat on top of a peak in a distant land, waiting for the sun to rise so that he could find his way safely to ships at anchor in shark-infested waters to carry word to a band of magicians about some creatures from the darkest pit of hell and a band of elves no one had ever heard of, all he could think of was would he ever see Michele again?

The sun had begun to light the eastern sky and the solid mass of darkness below him was now resolving itself into defined shapes. He pushed aside thoughts of his new love, and his constant concern that having someone to care for was perhaps the worst idea he had ever considered, and looked deep into the gloom. At first the still-impenetrable shadows confounded his eye, but after a while he began to discern a way down. What he had at first thought might be a tiny rivulet formed by ice melt or rain, looked promising, and he started moving towards it. After reaching the head of the small gully, he decided to venture slowly downwards and made a silent prayer to Ban-ath, God of Thieves, who also was considered the God of Misadventures: if there was ever an undertaking worthy of being called that, this was it, thought Jim Dasher.

It was late afternoon by the time he reached the cliffs above the agreed-upon beach. He considered the drop and again wondered how a city-bred lad such as himself could end up considering a descent that would have given a fright to a mountain goat. There was no easy way down, though there certainly was a quick one, he thought dryly.

He traversed the narrow cliff and found nothing useful, then turned and with his eyes retraced his route down to the top of the cliffs. He was likely to spend hours climbing back up to where he thought another way down might be found, and even then there was no guarantee it would provide the right descent. He would probably have to endure another night on the mountainside, and he was now both thirsty and ravenous. He recalled with bitter amusement a confidence trickster he had once encountered in a tavern in Krondor while the man waited to take ship to Elariel in Kesh. He had tried to sell Jim a 'magic cloak' which would, he claimed, allow the wearer to leap from the tallest building or wall and gently float down to the ground. A clever enough scam, for if the fool who bought it tried to use it, he'd either be dead or lying a-bed with too many broken bones to attempt hot pursuit and the trickster would be safely away in Great Kesh. But, oh, how he wished it had been true and he had such a cloak now.

He kept looking for inspiration, for he didn't relish the climb back to the other route. He decided to make one more traverse of the cliff top before he started hiking. He moved northwards until he reached an outcropping of rocks that prevented further progress, glanced down and saw waves crashing into the rocks a hundred feet below him. Not a bad dive, he thought, if the water was deep enough and there weren't rocks everywhere.

He travelled back southwards, occasionally glancing out to where the three ships waited, wishing he could somehow communicate to them that he was up here. Not that it would prove any more beneficial, unless someone on the crew had developed the ability to fly and could come fetch him to the ship, or at least fly up here with a rope.

A rope? He glanced around. If he had a rope, where would he tie it off? He walked over to a sturdy tree that had been the victim of cliff erosion. It had started leaning forward from the edge of the cliff and had then died as its roots were exposed. But the dried-out trunk was still firmly planted in the rocky soil and when he pushed hard against it he found it unyielding. It would support his weight. If only he had a rope.

He looked down and saw that the tree overhung a gap in the cliff with a ledge about twenty feet below and that the ledge also contained a small growth of trees. He wished he could gauge how high those trees were from his current vantage point. He sprinted along the cliff face, looking back several times, and finally found a bend in the cliff where he could get a good perspective. He could see the trees closest to the edge on that little ledge were in fact about thirty feet below the cliff on which he stood. He rapidly did the mathematics. He could lower himself down until he overhung the trees, and his feet should be not much more than twenty feet above the ledge and only ten feet above the trees.

Gods, he silently mused, what is desperation driving me to?

He realized that once down on the ledge, the chances of climbing back up to where he stood now were practically nil but he blocked it from his mind: he needed to be on that ship as soon as possible. He moved rapidly to where he could climb out on the dead tree, and gauged the most-likely looking tree below to try for. They were all scrubby-looking things, pines or firs of some sort – he really didn't know or care what they were – and he needed something big enough to grab on to, or at least sturdy enough to slow his fall. He didn't mind cuts and bruises, but broken bones would consign him to a slow and painful death.

He scrambled around until he was hanging directly over the chosen tree, then he let go. The fall was less than a dozen feet, but if felt like a hundred as he crashed into the top branches. As he expected, he was cut by several of the branches as they broke, but he grabbed hard onto a larger one and his fall was broken. He paused to catch his breath, then climbed down.

Once he stood at the rim of the little ledge, he wondered what madness had overtaken him. It was another thirty or more feet down, to what appeared to be mostly sand, but there were enough rocks poking through it that he couldn't be sure how deep any of it was. He looked down for anything remotely like a handhold and felt his stomach sink; the face of the cliff here was eroded by the tide and now he was on an over-hang. He considered his choices and realized he had none: he had to get down from here, no matter the risk.

He wished he had a rope. Then he corrected himself and decided if he was going to waste a wish, he'd wish to already be in Krondor – in the apartment he used as James Jamison rather than the hovel he used in his role as Jim Dasher, Mocker – bathed, rested, dressed, and entertaining Lady Michele de Frachette, daughter of the Earl of Montagren and he hoped, some day, the mother of his children.

The wind picked up and he saw the ships at anchor begin to rock slightly as the ocean chop increased. Ah, how to get there? He looked down again. He was slightly over six feet in height, so a dead hang drop from the ledge meant twenty-four feet or so to the sand. Still sufficient to break enough bones to prevent him getting to the ship. If he could just shave two yards off the distance . . .

He stripped off his boots and threw them to the sand below. Then off came his belt and trousers, then his shirt. He rapidly worked so as to get this over with before he reconsidered. He tied the belt around the tree closest to the edge of the ledge, a scant thing looking barely able to support its own weight, let alone his. Still, it only had to hold for a moment or two. He then tied one leg of his trousers to the belt, making the best knot he could, then his shirt arm to the other leg. He threw the rest of the shirt over the edge and looked down. The make-shift rope of clothing had given him the six feet he needed.

Never one to hesitate, he rolled over on his belly, ignoring the scrapes on the rock and the pain from the cuts he had already suffered from falling into the tree branches. He wiggled backwards, hoping no one from the ship was watching, given the state he was in. Then he pushed himself off and quickly went hand under hand down the fabric of his trousers and shirt. He felt a slight jerk and realized the tree was starting to fall. He went as quickly down as he could, holding at the bottom. As his momentum was halted, he heard the crack of wood above.

With a single shout he let go, flexing his knees to take the shock of hitting the ground. He hit the sand and struck the side of his head against a rock, which caused his eyes to lose focus for a moment. Then he rolled up and over and looking up, he saw the tree that was about to fall on him. Jim Dasher just continued to roll, striking more rocks as he tried to avoid being crushed by the small tree he had uprooted from the ledge above. He heard the tree fall with a crash.

Lying on the sand, aching and his head ringing from the blow, he realized suddenly – he was on the beach! He struggled to get up, and finally managed to stand despite his head throbbing and his vision being unclear. He stood motionless for a full minute trying not to fall over. His stomach knotted and he felt sick for a few moments, then he took a long, deep breath. He knew his head-blow was going to make him less than fit. He needed to start a fire to signal the captain of the *Queen of the Soldanas* to send a boat to pick him as soon as possible.

Jim Dasher found his clothes firmly buried under the bole of the tree that had almost crushed him. He cleared away sand and discovered his trousers were firmly pinned between the tree and rocks. His shirt tore as he pulled it out, and he could find nothing of his belt. He looked about and found his boots not too far away, so he went over and put them on. He stood feeling ridiculous in his torn shirt, underlinen, and boots but sighed in resignation. He needed his belt: it contained a small pouch in which was hidden a piece of flint. The buckle had a steel tongue, and together they could be used to start a fire. He could probably find a piece of flint nearby, but he knew he'd never find a piece of steel.

He looked at the three ships and suddenly they were twice as far as he had thought when he first saw them. That was because he knew he would now have to swim to them.

At least the wind would keep the surface roiling and hide him from the sight of enemies, he thought as he took off his boots. Regretfully he tossed them aside – he really liked them and it took a lot of work to make really fine new boots look old and worthless. Observing the wind and the spindrift coming off the choppy water, he wondered if that might keep the sharks away. Considering how many cuts he sported, he hoped so. Well, he thought as he waded into the surf, he'd soon find out.

Jim almost got his head removed by a belaying pin for his troubles as he clambered up the anchor rope. The sailor whom he had surprised had been warned, along with the rest of the crew, to be vigilant and wary of surprise attack.

'You never should have got that close, fella-me-lad,' he said as he helped the sailor off the deck, where he had knocked him down. 'I've a bump on my head and it's taken me off a bit.'

The sailor recognized Jim as one of the party sent ashore with General Kaspar, but he still looked ready to fight. 'Where's the Captain?' asked Jim, heading off further disputes.

'Coming,' said another sailor as the entire deck crew came to gawk at the sopping wet man wearing only a shirt and drawers.

'What's this then?' asked the first mate. 'A deserter?'

'Hardly,' said Jim, slowly adding 'sir,' as he retreated to his role of common thief. 'I have news for the captain.'

'Tell me and I'll relay it,' said the first mate.

'That won't be necessary,' said the Captain as he forced his way through the press of sailors. 'Get back to your duties!' he commanded and the sailors moved off. 'I'll take this man with me, Yost,' the Captain instructed the first mate.

Mr Yost looked unconvinced, but he nodded and just said, 'Yes sir.'

'Follow me,' said the Captain, a very experienced and loyal member of the Royal Navy of Roldem by the name of William Gregson. He, like every other sailor in this little flotilla, wore no uniform and to the casual eye appeared to be merely a commercial captain, but like every other man aboard the three ships, he was navy to the bone.

Once inside the privacy of his cabin, Gregson said, 'What news, Lord James?'

'My head is pounding,' said Jim, sitting down without waiting for leave. 'I hit a rock coming down off that cliff over there. Do you have something?'

The Captain went to his private sea chest and removed a stoppered bottle. He pulled out two small glasses and filled them both. 'Medicinal brandy,' he said, offering up a glass to Jim. 'Now, what's happened? You wouldn't be swimming with sharks if there wasn't a problem.'

'Aye,' said Jim. 'Kaspar and the rest are prisoners.'

'Who's taken them?'

'Elves, but none like any I've seen. I've got a lot to report, but as I must be on my way as soon as possible, you'll have to wait for the official word to be passed back to you.'

The Captain, his face a leathery map from years on the quarterdeck, said, 'So it's mind my own business, is it?'

'Something like that, Captain.'

'How fast is fast? The *Lady Jessie* is our fastest.'

'Not ship-fast. I need that device I asked you to keep for me.'

The Captain returned to his chest, opened it and took out a small golden sphere. 'I've been wondering what it was.'

'Something that will get me where I need to go faster than the swiftest ship in the fleet can bear me. One thing, though, before I use it.'

'What?'

'I need a pair of trousers.'

The Captain could barely keep from laughing. He went to his clothing locker and produced a pair of trousers which were slightly too large but would do. 'Boots?' he offered.

'I think yours won't fit.'

The Captain fetched another pair but they were too small. 'I'll find something along the way,' said Jim. He held up the orb and said, 'Well, goodbye, Captain,' and depressed a switch on the side of the device.

Before the Captain could reply, he was gone.

Only a slight inward surge of air marked his disappearance. Into the empty room, the Captain said, 'What do I tell the men?'

It was the dead of night on Sorcerer's Isle when Jim appeared. It was his first visit to the home of the legendary Black Sorcerer, Pug. Jim was aware that he had some sort of distant kinship with the magician, as Pug's adopted daughter Gamina had been the wife of Lord James, but Jim suspected he was hardly the first member of 'that side of the family' not to know his forebear.

He had arrived in a small room set aside for visitors, and a student had been detailed there to keep an eye on it. Even so, the student leapt a mile as Jim materialized. At last he regained his composure and said 'Wait here. I will fetch someone.'

Jim knew better than to argue for he had been given clear instructions by his great-uncle and Lord Erik that if he were ever to use the device he must do whatever he was told once he reached the island.

Jim didn't have long to wait. A regal looking woman obviously just awakened arrived with the student. She gave him a searching look. 'Who are you?'

With an only slightly mocking courtly bow, he said, 'I'm James Jamison, grandson of the Duke of Rillanon. And to whom do I have the pleasure of speaking?'

'I'm Miranda,' answered the woman. 'Come along. You wouldn't be here if the situation didn't warrant it. I've heard of you, Jim Dasher, and what I've heard is good: we need sneaky bastards on our side at a time like this.'

Jim wasn't sure if that was a compliment or not, but he decided to take it as one. Miranda led him down a long series of halls. 'Most of the faculty and students are asleep, as you'd expect. I'll warn you though, when sunrise comes, you may see some . . . people, unlike any you've encountered. Try not to gawk.'

'After what I've seen in the last two days, lady, I don't think anything will surprise me any more.'

She entered a room that was clearly an office of some sort and motioned for him to sit down in a chair opposite a desk. 'Why don't you tell me about your last two days, then?'

Jim delivered a concise and exact narrative, after which Miranda said, 'We are dealing with an enemy who is mad.' She drummed her fingers on the desktop in frustration. 'Now this.'

Jim said nothing, waiting for her to tell him what must be done next. After a moment, she said, 'What do you think we should do next, Jim Dasher?'

Jim paused, then said, 'First, I need a pair of boots and trousers that fit. Then you should do what you must with those . . . creatures, but we also need to get Kaspar and the men free of those elves. There's a certain madness to them, as well, or at least a sense of desperation. Kaspar says they're dying out, and I agree. There were perhaps only half a dozen children and only a few more women there. In total, less than a hundred in all. That fortification was home to four or five times that many at one time.'

'If my husband were here—' Miranda began. She sighed, 'But he's not.' She studied Jim and said finally, 'We're a little thin on the ground right now. My husband and two others who might easily deal with some of this are absent and I have no idea when they might return. There are other magicians here who have talent and might help to assess those creatures you saw in the mountains. 'But I'm not sure what to do about the elves who've captured Kaspar.'

'Can you get me to Elvandar?' Jim asked.

'I can get you close. No one enters Elvandar unbidden unless they have been given leave.'

'I have been there before.'

'Really?' she said, surprised. 'When?'

'A few years ago, at the behest of Lord Erik, right about the time I began to be told the truth about the Conclave.'

'I see,' said Miranda. 'Then we shall get you to the border of Elvandar.' She narrowed her gaze. 'You look as if you could use a meal.'

He nodded. 'That would be welcome. It's been a day or more since I've had anything to eat or drink.'

Miranda rose. 'I'll walk you to the kitchen.'

He followed her down the hall, into a garden, and then into another hall. He realized that these buildings were constructed like many of the villas on Queg, in large squares with a garden at the centre.

Miranda asked, 'Is this your first visit here, then?'

'Yes,' answered Jim. 'I believe you're familiar with how new recruits to the Conclave are given information.'

'In dribs and drabs as needed,' she supplied.

'On a need-to-know basis, Lord Erik called it.' He chuckled. 'I'll admit when I first learned of the Conclave I was astonished, yet now so many things make more sense to me.'

'Then you're a rare one, James Jamison – or is it Jim Dasher? For the more I know the less I understand.'

'It's Jim Dasher when I'm not in the palaces at Krondor, Rillanon or Roldem, lady. I'll grant you the advantage of wisdom, then, for it's my vanity that I can apprehend a great deal from a little information.'

'A useful trait and one of the reasons why you were recruited.'

'Ah, I thought it might be because of family.'

'Your family?' said Miranda. 'Let me tell you something of your family.'

She led him into a large kitchen where a pair of young men were preparing to bake the day's bread. Miranda motioned for Jim to go to the

210

pantry and make use of whatever he found there. He fetched out a half-finished loaf of bread from the day before, some hard cheese, a pair of apples, and a jug of some sort of ale. Then he grabbed a ladle from the side of the water bucket and drank deeply. After three such drippings, Miranda said, 'If you were so thirsty, why didn't you ask for water?'

'I've developed a knack of ignoring such things as thirst and hunger for a while, and it seemed more important to tell you what I knew.'

'Gods,' said Miranda with a laugh. 'You match your reputation, Jim Dasher. I hardly think the time to sip a cup of water would prove the end of us all. Now, eat, and let me tell you about your family.'

Jim cut bread and cheese and took a bite from both, then attacked the first apple.

'As you may know you are counted as distant kin to my husband – and no, you'd better not call me grandmother unless you have no regard for your life!' she said before he could make a comment. 'Your great, great grandfather James of Krondor died before the creation of the Conclave. Your grandfather and your father are members of a family who are steadfast in their loyalty to the Crown of the Isles, and while the Conclave's interests and the Kingdom's often overlap, sometimes they do not.

'We have an . . . accommodation with your father and grandfather, but make no mistake in this, the schism between the . . . two sides of your family is deep. It goes back to the end of the Serpentwar, when my husband refused to intercede on behalf of the Prince of Krondor when a Keshian army stood at the city's gates, and because of that the Prince, later to be King Patrick, held a deep and abiding grudge against my husband. The Conclave is dedicated to preserving this world, including its foolish rulers, but we put no one nation's needs above another.'

Jim listened while he ate. As he swallowed the last piece of apple, he said, 'Am I to believe that my loyalties are assumed else I wouldn't be here?'

'More likely you wouldn't be alive, or at the very least, you never would have been recruited.'

'Kings come and go,' said Jim. 'My grandfather has served four, and the latest is a promising young man, but that doesn't mean that when the chips are down and the last card played, he's going to make the right choices.'

'He has your grandfather at his right hand.'

'Grandfather is known to be a very wise, very shrewd, and very old man. I say this with affection, for I will miss him when he dies, but unless you can muster another miracle like the one you provided for Lord Erik, it's only a matter of months, perhaps a year at most, before he'll need to be replaced.'

'Your father?'

'No,' said Jim. 'He's a gifted administrator,

taking after his own grandfather, Arutha Jameson, Lord Vencar, by all reports, but he's not the political animal my grandfather is . . .' Jim sighed. 'Once again we face a situation that can only be called dangerous. There has been no continuity in the Western Realm since Prince Arutha died. He was the last true western lord to rule and since then there's been a series of caretaker rulers, heirs biding their time until they could return to Rillanon and take the throne, and at no time was the interest of the west seen as paramount. The Western lords are fractious and I've even heard rumours of establishing a separate nation.'

'Those rumours are not widespread,' said Miranda, 'or we would have heard.'

'Whispers,' said Jim. 'Nothing more or I would have reported it. Trust me when I say had I an inkling of any such movement being real, I would have reported it to my father, and he most certainly would have shared that information with Lord Erik.'

'Who would in turn have reported it to my husband.'

'But we have more immediate concerns than the politics of the Kingdom,' said Jim. 'Elvandar?'

Miranda nodded. 'I can take you to the river's edge, for I have yet to be granted leave to enter at will.' She said this as if it annoyed her, but Jim let the remark pass without comment. 'Stand next to me . . .'

'Ah, the boots?'

'Oh, yes,' said Miranda. She looked at his feet and added, 'And trousers that fit. I remember.'

She sent one of the students who had been baking out to fetch the desired items and the boy quickly returned with two pairs of boots, the first of which fit well and a pair of sturdy trousers that were an improvement over what the Captain had given him.

He changed and went to stand next to Miranda. She put her hand on his shoulder, and suddenly they were in a dark forest, next to a river of some size. 'This ford is swift running, but shallow,' she told him as he tried to get his bearings. This magic travel took some getting used to, he thought.

Then she was gone.

He took a deep breath and suddenly realized he was without weapons. Knowing he wouldn't be without company for long, he forded the river. On the other side he stood for a moment, listening, then called, 'I know you're there.'

Seconds later two elves appeared, seemingly out of nowhere. 'Welcome, Jim Dasher,' said one of them.

Jim took a moment in the gloom, then smiled and stepped forward. 'Thank you, Trelan. It is good to see you again.' They gripped one another's hand, and Jim said, 'I need speak with your Queen and Lord Tomas.'

To the other elf, the one called Trelan said, 'I will guide him and send back another to watch the ford with you.' Then he was off at a quick trot, leaving Dasher only a moment in which to react and catch up with him.

Jim knew from his previous visit that he was going to be running all night and most of the morning to reach the Queen's court from this part of the Elven Forest, so he let his mind relax and started thinking about keeping up with the indefatigable elf. He had only been on the trail for five minutes when he started thinking of Michele again, and cursed himself for a love-struck fool.

CHAPTER 10

SUMMONS

Bek stood covered in blood.

'Stop!' shouted Martuch, his mentor within the Sadharin battle society.

The human disguised as a Dasati Deathknight stood quivering with rage, his eyes wide and his sword poised as he sought out another enemy to kill. Martuch, Valko and half a dozen other members of the White stood in a semi-circle behind Ralan Bek, each of them also awash in gore. The Deathknights, who secretly served the enemies of the Dark One, had been swept up in the Great Culling as had every other Dasati with a sword, but no one, not even the most seasoned warrior had seen anything like what they had just witnessed.

A company of perhaps thirty-five young Deathknights had ridden down a boulevard and happened upon an enclave of Lessers who had gone to ground and risked coming out at sundown too early. As the cityscape was bathed in the orange glow of sunset, the broad street became a scene of carnage.

Before Martuch could order his group to circle

216

away from the conflict, Bek had urged his varnin forward, riding as if he had been in the saddle all his life. Before the young Deathknights had known he was upon them, six were dead. He moved like a being possessed, killing eight before the others could join in.

'They're all dead,' said Martuch.

Bek's eyes burned with an inner light that frightened even this battle-hardened Dasati. 'Let's find more!'

'No,' said Valko. 'The Culling is over.' He looked at the fifteen bodies that littered the street. 'These . . . shouldn't have died.' He looked torn between his Dasati heritage which relished the slaughter and his newfound respect for life which counted it a waste of potential. 'The Culling was over before this began.'

Martuch looked towards the others. 'Loot the bodies. Not to do so would draw unwelcome attention to us. Better to be thought brigands than heretics.'

Valko's group quickly stripped the bodies of trophies, leaving the corpses in the street for the Lessers to dispose of. As they were securing their trophies behind the saddles of their varnin, a band of riders rounded a corner a long city block away and approached. Valko's company took up position without being ordered, for while the Culling might officially be over, Bek would hardly be the only warrior caught up in the bloodletting and ready to continue killing.

As the group approached, Martuch said, 'Lower your weapons.'

The riders approaching were half a dozen temple Deathknights wearing the TeKarana's palace colours. They were escorting a pair of Hierophants, those priests given the responsibility of ensuring that everyone in the realm came to worship the Dark One. In antiquity they might have been spreaders of the word, but since His Darkness's rise to pre-eminence, no evangelical mission was required, and now they primarily served to ferret out heresy and act as spies for the TeKarana.

'Praise to His Darkness!' said the leader.

All bowed their heads for a moment and repeated the invocation. The other priest quickly took stock of the corpses on the ground. 'How many of your company lies here?'

Martuch spoke calmly. 'None.'

'Indeed?' questioned the first priest. 'I count thirty-five dead warriors and half-again as many Lessers, yet only nine of you sent them all to His Darkness?'

Valko said, 'We had the advantage of surprise.'

Without a hint of boastfulness, Bek calmly said, 'I killed six before they knew we were upon them. When they turned to face me, two more died and then my companions were upon them from another quarter. Confusion served us—'

'And these were young, barely blooded warriors,' added Hirea. 'I am Master Hirea of the Scourge, and I have taught everyone here, including Lord

218

Valko, of the Camareen. These are my most exceptional students, and these . . . *things*,' he said with contempt of the dead, 'were barely better than Lessers themselves. It was an easy killing. Little glory, really.'

'You are of the Scourge, yet you ride with the Lord of the Camareen, who is of the Sadharin if I am correct. Is this right?' asked the first priest.

'I was staying with Lord Valko when the call for the Culling came. It seemed prudent to remain with his company rather than risk returning to my own enclave.'

Looking directly at the young ruler of the Camareen, the second priest said, 'And you let him live?'

'He was my teacher,' said Valko. 'The Scourge and the Sadharin have ridden together for many years; we have not crossed swords since my grandfather's times. We have many ties.' His tone said he was finished with the topic and his defiant glare challenged the two priests to continue this line of questioning at their peril.

The politics of the societies were traditionally ignored by the Dark One's priests, but overlong alliances were often viewed with suspicion, for the art of ruling such a murderous population was in keeping factions from growing too powerful. The two priests knew as well as anyone who the potential threats to order were, and while the Scourge and the Sadharin were both venerable societies, they were not especially powerful or influential, especially on Omadrabar. They might be a power to contend with on Kosridi, but here on the capital world of the Dasati Empire, they were just another pair of provincial battle societies.

The second priest studied Bek. 'Are you Scourge or Sadharin?'

Bek glanced down and realized that the badge given to him by Martuch had been dislodged during the struggle. As he started to answer, Martuch said, 'He is my retainer. He is Sadharin.'

The first priest raised his eyebrows and his expression became one of interest. 'A student? From his demeanour and the numbers of dead at his feet I would have thought him at least a master in your ranks, if not a captain.'

'He has promise,' said Hirea dismissively. 'But among those I tutor, he is but another student.'

After a long moment of consideration, the first priest said, 'Then you will not mind if he leaves your side.' Pointing at Ralan he said, 'What are you named?'

'I am Bek,' said the human disguised as a Dasati warrior.

'Bek,' intoned the Hierophant, 'you are called!'

For the briefest second Valko and Martuch exchanged glances. Both felt the instinct to attack, to prevent the Dark One's servants from taking Bek away, but they also both knew that despite not being as powerful in their use of magic as the Deathpriests, these two Hierophants alone could tip the balance against Valko's group.

Martuch said, 'You must go with them.' Softly, so that only Bek could hear him, he added, 'Do nothing to reveal yourself. We will contact you before the end of this day. Go.'

Bek sheathed his sword and said to the priest, 'Called?'

'The TeKarana always needs prodigious warriors. The training is arduous and far more taxing than what you have endured at the hands of your old teacher—' he stressed the word 'old' in a way that would have got him killed had he not been protected by another magic-user and a dozen temple guards '—and should you survive, you will earn a place attending the Dark One's most loyal servant, his personal guard.'

'Should you achieve special merit,' said the other priest, 'you may be chosen to join his most noble order, the Talnoy.'

Bek grinned. 'Is there killing to be done?'

'Always,' answered the first priest with a grin to match Bek's. 'Today's Culling was just a taste. A banquet of death will soon be laid before the faithful.'

'Then I will come with you,' said the blood-drenched youth. He mounted his varnin and wheeled around, falling in with the guards who followed the priests.

As they rode down the boulevard and the first stirrings of normal life returned to this part of the city, Valko said to Martuch, 'What do we do now?'

'Get to the Orchard of Delmat-Ama as quickly

as we can, and speak to the Gardener,' answered Martuch. To the others he shouted, 'We ride!'

They mounted up quickly and moved at a fast pace through a city littered with the dead and dying.

The greetings were subdued. On both sides there were too many questions that needed to be asked and answered for any casual discussion.

The shelter was as Macros had described it, ample but simple. Cots were arrayed along the walls of a long room, perhaps once an underground grain storage warehouse, or even a barracks of sorts, but other than beds, a table and a stack of water jugs at the far end, the room was devoid of comfort. Two lanterns gave out a low light allowing Pug's vision to register heat once more as if it were something normally seen.

Martuch, Valko and Hirea had all joined Macros and his companions in the hiding place, while the other servants of the White stayed above to ensure that no one below was disturbed. Nakor especially seemed troubled by the news that Bek had been taken by the Hierophants. 'Why do you think he was taken?' he asked Martuch.

Martuch shrugged, one of the few very human gestures that always startled Pug when he saw it. 'For any number of reasons, but none which lead me to think they have an inkling of his real nature; had that been the case, there would not have been two clerics, but twenty, not a dozen guards, but a hundred. And there would have been no conversation.'

'They would have attacked without question,' agreed Nakor. 'Then, of those possible reasons, which do you judge to be the most reasonable?'

'Reasonable?' Again the old Dasati warrior looked very human in his expression of doubt. 'There is almost nothing left of reason in our land, Nakor. But if you ask me the most likely, it is this: Bek has grown in power since he has been here. It is no longer simply a case of him resembling a powerful young warrior.'

'Martuch is right,' Valko added. 'He exudes might. He carries himself like a nobleman born, the son of some great house, and his strength is apparent. The day I met you I would not have hesitated to cut him down where he stood had I a cause. Today, even the mightiest of our race would hesitate before challenging him. He is not just playing the part of a Dasati any more. He *is* Dasati to his core. It is daunting.'

Hirea said, 'If he were in truth my student, I would already judge him the most dangerous I had ever instructed. If I had him on the training floor, I would fear for my head.'

'Then I must go to him,' said Nakor. 'You have means?'

Martuch nodded. 'We have agents in the palace, and I know others there as well who will not think it strange that I am there. As his mentor I can bid him farewell.'

'And I, as his instructor,' added Hirea. 'But once he enters training for the TeKarana's personal guard, he will be unreachable. If we are to speak with him, it must be today.'

Nakor nodded and stood up. 'Then we must go now. For if I do not reach him and, tell him what to do, all our plans may come to naught.'

'Nakor looks the part of a Lesser,' said Pug.

'A family retainer, who comes to fetch and carry, nothing more,' answered Martuch. 'He will attract far less attention than if a third warrior appeared to bid farewell to a mere student.'

Valko said to Pug, 'I will accompany you to the Mountains of Skellar-tok.'

Pug glanced at Macros, who merely nodded. 'Sooner is better than later,' said the former human magician. He really did not look well.

As if aware of Pug's regard, he said, 'I fear I may have only a short time left.'

Hirea was visibly distressed to hear that. 'For the service we've shared and the love I bear you as my leader, I caution you never to repeat such a thing outside this room. It is taking all my will not to cut you down for showing such weakness.'

Valko was also showing signs of conflict. 'Yes, that is sage advice.'

Only Martuch seemed untroubled. 'It is too deeply in our blood, I fear. Yet I still hope we can save our progeny.'

'Then we must all be on our way,' said Pug. To Magnus he said, 'Again, you bear the burden, while I will mask us from sight. But this time we shall not merely traverse a city, but go half-way around the world, so be prepared, my son.' Magnus nodded solemnly.

Macros said, 'I shall work to keep us hidden from sight, but indeed we have a long way to go. It will not be a quick journey. I just hope we can gain the knowledge we need before the Dark One makes his intentions clear.'

'Then we must not linger,' said Pug. To Nakor he added, 'I hope to see you again, soon, old friend.'

Grinning through his mask of troubles, Nakor said, 'If the gods will it, then it will happen. Be well.'

'And you,' said Pug. He turned to Martuch. 'Go first, and we shall follow quickly behind you, but out of sight.'

Martuch nodded, and turned without further discussion, leading his companions up the wooden stairs to the surface. Pug thought to warn Valko not to be unnerved by the lack of visibility or the flying, but thought better of it. He was Dasati and if he was frightened to death he would not show such weakness, and Pug didn't have time to deal with a young lord of the Dasati who felt insulted. All he said was, 'Put your hand upon Magnus's waist and do not let go, for you will not see him.' Then Pug turned everyone in his party invisible.

They slowly made their way up the stairs after Hirea, and the Lessers remaining below to shut the trapdoor. The morning sun now climbed to the mid-heaven, and Pug felt Magnus's spell lift them all quickly upwards. Magnus's voice could be heard, 'Which way?'

'First to the west, for many hours, then when we pause to rest, I will tell you the next direction,' said Macros. 'We shall see half this world before we are done. Now, conserve your strength and let us be away as quickly as you can manage.'

Magnus turned his full will to moving them as fast as he possibly could, and soon they were speeding across the skies of Omadrabar as fast as the swiftest hawk back home. Even so, Pug knew it would be a long and arduous journey, and one he hoped was over in time to forestall whatever evil was being plotted in a deep cavern not too distant from where they flew. Not for the first time he wondered if there was even a shred of sanity in his choices, for he could not even properly call what he had done so far a plan. Rather it was a frantic attempt to respond to a horrific threat and he had to rely on his own wits, the talents of his son and Nakor, and a very disturbing young man possessed by far more than mere madness. And a series of cryptic notes from some future version of himself. Pug kept his attention fixed on maintaining their invisibility, but part of him wished he could pray. But in this alien sky, he wondered to whom should he be praying.

Nakor kept his eyes down as he had been instructed since they had first arrived in the Dasati realm. He glanced up occasionally to make sure he didn't lose track of his 'masters', Martuch and Hirea. Also, he made careful note of how this part of the Great Palace was laid out. The structure was massive. In a city on a scale that dwarfed any human construction he had seen, this palace was the crowning achievement in excess. It had taken the three companions less than an hour to reach the entrance from where they had hidden in the Grove of Delmat-Ama, but from there it had been almost a half day's ride along the streets that were within the precincts of the palace, and so far they had reached only the outer warrens. Sundown was less than an hour away. As far as they were able, the two Dasati warriors gave Nakor a narrative about this monstrous construction.

The Great Palace, home of the ruler of the Dasati Empire, occupied more space than the entire city of Kentosani on the Tsurani home world of Kelewan, and that city contained over a million people within its walls. More than two million Dasati lived within the palace precincts, five million in the central capital city. Nakor realized that the estimates of how many Deathknights the TeKarana could order into the field to invade the first realm was vastly understated. Macros had said two million Deathknights, but Nakor was convinced he was not thinking of the Dark One stripping every Dasati warrior from The Twelve Words and unleashing them . . . Something wasn't right. Once they established a bridgehead into the first realm, either on Kelewan or Midkemia or some other world, vast numbers of worlds would be in peril. But even for this god, that was a brutish and simple plan.

The wily gambler weighed every piece of evidence that he could discern, either through direct observation or from what others had said, either to him or what he had overheard when they didn't realize he was listening. He now came to an inescapable conclusion: the Dasati could not be defeated by the armies of every nation on Midkemia and Kelewan combined. At best they could be delayed. And at worst, they would sweep aside all opposition as if they were fighting children with play weapons.

Nakor resolved that whatever Pug found out about the history of this world, whatever revelations were discovered when he found the leaders of the Bloodwitch Sisterhood, no matter what the true nature of Macros – and he had serious doubts he was as he seemed to be – whatever any of them discovered, there was going to be but one solution to the coming crisis: the destruction of the Dark God.

As he considered this conclusion, Nakor weighed all the Dark One's actions in the past and something began to emerge, a sense of the true purpose behind the apparent mindless killing and destruction. There was a plan at work, a pattern of things unfolding, and he was tantalized by almost understanding what it was.

The deeper into the palace they travelled the more certain Nakor became that something profoundly evil existed at the heart of this society. Their art – what there was of it – was nothing more than a twisted celebration of their dark faith. He had been struck since entering the second realm that he had seen nothing that resembled decoration or art, except on the Dasati themselves. They had some expression of beauty – once you adjusted to their appearances, they were a very handsome race he decided – but there were no paintings or tapestries hanging on walls, no variation in colour in buildings or signs. Some of this he was convinced was due to them having a very different colour sense to humans – they could see below red and beyond violet, like certain creatures in the first realm, and they could see heat, which made them lethally dangerous fighters at night.

But it wasn't until they were inside the palace that Nakor saw anything like fine art, and here it was in the form of ghastly murals, showing murder, torture, execution and slaughter in praise of the Dark God. If there was a narrative aspect to the murals, Nakor couldn't discern it, but he did intuit that this particular section had to do with some grand conquest in ages past.

At several points along their march, as Nakor followed Martuch and Hirea, he saw what he took to be an aspect of the Dark God himself. He seemed to be shown as a shadowy presence, without features or costume. Given the vividness of the rest of the subjects in the mural, Nakor found this odd. The warriors were depicted with a stylized accuracy, heads larger than life, so as to show their ancient headgear, each with its unique style, since replaced by the badges worn on the chest-plate. The swords were different too, as were the battle flags and banners. The victims were shown piled like cordwood, after being sacrificed to His Darkness.

Other murals showed long lines of prisoners being marched towards a vast pit and cast down into it, more sacrifices for the Dark One. As they approached their destination, Nakor saw the themes of the murals turning to a more martial focus, the themes being repeated of powerful warriors in service to the Dark One, led by the TeKarana and his Karanas in triumph over a variety of alien species.

There was nothing merely triumphant in this, thought Nakor. He had visited many worlds since meeting Pug, and nearly every civilization on Midkemia, and had encountered other martial societies, even those bellicose by nature, but nowhere did he see suffering and pain celebrated as he did here. It was as Kaspar had related to them when discussing his vision at the Pavilion of the Gods, when first shown the Dasati by Kalkin, also known as Ban-ath, the God of Thieves. These people thought pain was amusing, and suffering funny. Never, from his perspective, had Nakor encountered a more twisted view of life and death.

No, he amended to himself as they reached their destination. There was a common theme. All life was suffering leading to death, and the only question was whether you were to suffer or to cause suffering. Then at the doorway that led into the Hall of Warriors, he saw one anomalous image. A Lesser, dressed as a healer, down in one corner, offering a cup of water to a suffering victim. It was odd, almost an afterthought, yet somehow significant, thought the little gambler.

As he hurried not to fall behind, one other detail caught his eye. A tiny glyph below the figure of the Lesser, almost unnoticeable if one was not examining the tableau carefully, and for a moment it made him almost stop in his tracks. It was a symbol that by any rational measure should not have existed in this universe, let alone be adorning this wall. Nakor pushed aside his astonishment, realizing that any break from the character of his adopted role could quickly end his life.

The hall they entered was large and functional, without a single decoration on any wall. Massive grey-black stones scintillated with the energies that had grown almost commonplace to Nakor, though he still had trouble finding the words to describe what he was seeing. A series of benches were arrayed in rows across the floor and a dozen young men sat waiting to be called. Around them were warriors, fathers, teachers, brothers-in-arms, all bidding their young warriors good fortune and urging them to bring honour to the houses and societies that had spawned them. There was nothing Nakor would call regret on any face, but rather uniform pride in one of their own being selected to serve the TeKarana.

Bek sat alone on a bench near the far wall, isolated enough that a short conversation would not be overheard. Nakor glanced around the room and noticed that a few of the young warriors recruited to the TeKarana's service were attended by Lessers. 'They can take a servant?' asked Nakor.

Hirea said, 'Yes, but you can't be thinking—'

'Yes,' interrupted Nakor. 'I must.'

Further debate was interrupted by the arrival of a Deathpriest, escorted by two palace guards. He said, 'I recognize the badges of the Scourge and Sadharin.' He looked down at Bek and said, 'You wear no badge. Which society do you belong to?'

Before Bek could answer, Martuch said, 'He is my retainer, by name Bek.'

'Sadharin. Which house?'

Now they were rapidly getting into murky water, for it was never considered for a moment that any of the visiting humans would undergo this level of scrutiny. Martuch said, 'Langorin.'

The Deathpriest's eyebrows rose slightly. 'Your name?'

'Martuch,' he replied, inclining his head in a deferential gesture that was so slight it bordered on insolence.

232

'You are known, even here, Martuch of the Langorin. Is this your son?'

'No,' Martuch answered quickly. 'He is from a Lesser family.'

Nakor wondered if this might be a ploy by Martuch to get Bek dismissed.

The Priest looked confused, both curious and dubious. 'How is this possible?'

Martuch looked at Bek in such a way he was clearly telling the young man to pay close attention to the story. Nakor knew that Bek at times seemed single-minded, even to the point of simplicity, but he was anything but stupid. He was murderous and bloodthirsty and he took pleasure in others' suffering, but he was no fool. A quick glance from Bek told the diminutive gambler that he would follow Martuch's lead. 'I found him during a hunt. He had been chased down by one of my youngest retainers, the son of one of my most trusted old companions, and Bek had pulled him from the saddle, taken away his sword and killed him.'

'Impressive,' said the Deathpriest, his expression changing.

'Not by half; by the time I reached the struggle, he had killed another Deathknight with his newly-acquired sword and had wounded another grievously. He stood defiant, not a hint of fear, daring me and others to come and die. I knew at that moment I needed to take him into my service, to train him for some special role. Now I understand why I was fated that day to take him in; the Dark One has marked him for a higher calling.'

'Apparently,' said the Deathpriest. He made an imperceptible motion with one hand and the guard closest to Bek moved. His hand shot down to the hilt of his sword and in a single motion he drew it, and with a looping arc, aimed it for Bek's neck. But before the blade had cleared the scabbard, Bek had moved just enough to his right to draw his own sword, reach back and drive it home. While the palace guard's blow cut through empty air, Bek drove his own blade through the man's stomach, punching through his armour and completely through his body, so that the point protruded from his back.

Martuch and Hirea stepped back to draw their own swords while Nakor moved away, ignored for the moment, but ready to defend himself and Bek with whatever 'tricks' might be needed.

But to everyone's surprise, the Deathpriest shouted, 'Hold!' The second palace guard stood ready to attack, but held his place.

Bek grinned at the Deathpriest. 'A test?'

'Impressive,' repeated the Deathpriest. He looked at Martuch. 'You would not be the first head of a family to embellish the accomplishments of a called warrior, to gain reflected glory for your house and society. I found it hardly credible, the story you told, but now . . .' He glanced to where Bek easily pulled his blade free of the man's corpse and added, 'I believe this young man, with a sword he had never wielded before that night, killed two—'

'Three,' interrupted Martuch. 'The wounded warrior died a short time after.'

'—three of your Deathknights.' He turned to Bek. 'Stand up.'

Bek did so and if he had been impressive sitting on the bench, he was now doubly so, for if anything his Dasati guise had made him even larger and more menacing than he was in human form. Martuch said, 'It was a more than fair bargain. He is the equal of a dozen men.'

'This one will rise quickly, I think,' said the Deathpriest. He glanced at Nakor. 'Is this Bek's Attender?'

'Yes,' said Martuch. 'I gave this thing to him some time ago.'

'Come with me,' said the Deathpriest to Bek, and Nakor followed the young man.

Silently, Nakor sent up a short prayer to whatever kind god might just happen to listen. He took one moment to give Martuch and Hirea a quick glance over his shoulder, then followed his strange young companion into the heart of evil.

Pug was nearly exhausted by the time they landed. One unanticipated consequence of their chosen method of travel had been a particularly vicious flying predator that had a keener perception than most. An almost disastrous attack several hundred feet above the surface of another canton of the city had nearly caused him to lose control, which would have killed them all, less than an hour into their journey. He and Macros together destroyed the flock of winged killers, while Magnus kept them from falling to their death below.

Since that first encounter, Pug had had to fine-tune his spell of invisibility to cover a range of the spectrum beyond that which the Dasati eye could see, as well as somehow defeat those creatures that hunted by heat. He had used his prodigious ability to fashion such a mystical masking, literally on the fly, but the cost had been one of near-exhaustion by the time they reached their final destination.

Valko had endured the journey with a stoicism that would have shamed a Tsurani, Pug thought. If a young Dasati warrior could be termed 'likable', then Valko was such. He only mentioned his almost uncontrollable desire to murder them twice, but the context was how difficult he judged his personal struggle with new concepts and leaving old values behind, which was as close as any Dasati came to being personally revealing, Pug decided. In a very alien way, it was admirable.

They reached a mountain stronghold that was invisible to all but the most powerful scrying magic, but Pug had no difficulty sensing it as they approached. Perhaps it was a result of the manipulation he had been controlling for almost a full day as they jumped halfway around the world.

Macros let out an audible sigh of relief when they touched the ground, and said, 'I had none of your burdens, Pug, but I fear my constitution is far less robust than what it once was.'

'Is there any danger in approaching this enclave?' asked Magnus, who seemed relatively fresh despite his efforts over the last day and more. Pug was impressed by his son's endurance.

'Most certainly,' said Macros. 'We would do well just to stand here and let them come to us.'

For nearly an hour they waited, then a last a ripple in the air around the invisible enclosure announced the arrival of a quartet of young women. Pug suspected they were either among the most puissant of the Bloodwitches, or those they could most afford to lose if Pug's group proved hostile.

'You are unbidden here,' said the leader, a striking young Dasati woman who was tall by her race's standards. She had a bearing that set her apart from the others, so Pug assumed she must be the leader here.

Valko spoke before anyone else. 'I am Valko, Lord of the Camareen, son of Narueen.'

That name provoked a response, but before the women could respond, Macros said, 'And I am the Gardener. We have much to discuss.'

The leader nodded. 'Indeed. You must all come with us.' She stared hard for a moment at Valko, then turned and walked away. The other three stepped to either side, clearly indicating that Pug and his companions were to follow the tall young Bloodwitch.

As they reached the edge of an apparently empty clearing, Pug felt the energy pulse of magic and suddenly a walled fortification appeared. He realized that they had stepped past the boundary of a massive illusion, one designed to fool any onlooker until they actually made contact with the boundary. He also suspected that there were nasty surprises for anyone who did if they were not expected by those inside.

The enclave was ancient, Pug instantly knew. It had that look of stones which had been set in place for hundreds, even thousands, of years, worn smooth and seamless by the ceaseless caress of the wind and rain. Corners once sharp were now rounded, and a rut in the stone showed where countless feet had trodden from the gate to the entrance of the main building.

This was the first Dasati construction Pug had seen that was not part of some massive urban centre. It was simply a keep. It looked similar in many respects to one that he might find in the mountains of the Kingdom of the Isles, a square stone building with a circular tower rising in the middle, commanding a view of the mountain passes below that would warn any look-out of an enemy approach hours in advance.

Inside Pug could feel the vibrancy, which suggested far more than just the bustle of women busily taking care of the day's needs, and in the distance he could hear the unmistakable sound of children. And they were laughing! The tall woman turned and said, 'You must wait here for a moment.' To Valko she said, 'And you must remove your sword and give it to her.' She pointed to another young Bloodwitch.

'Why?' asked the young Deathknight defiantly. His sword was hard won and represented much of who he was and what he had endured.

'Because there are those here who wish you to be unarmed,' answered Macros. 'Please.'

'Please,' was a word rarely used in Dasati culture, and one that usually meant a pleading for life. In this context, it was a simple request, yet a powerful one. Valko removed his belt and scabbard and handed them to the young woman.

The leader of the four Dasati women departed, leaving them alone with the three remaining escorts. The hall in which they found themselves was just what Pug would expect from a simple keep: it was a short hallway, intersecting another with two doors, one at either end, presenting a blank wall to the main entrance. In ancient days, should the main entrance be forced, invaders would have had a short route to awaiting death. Glancing upwards, Pug saw the murder gallery above, down from which would rain arrows, bolts, rocks, and boiling pitch or oil. At either end of the hallway, massive doors waited, no doubt equipped with huge bars and reinforced to withstand all but the sturdiest rams. Pug could only speculate, but he imagined this fortification had never been taken.

Unlike the other Dasati buildings in which he had been, this one had decorations hanging on the walls. Ancient banners from the look of them; possibility insignia from antiquity, emblems of houses or societies long vanished. Pug could not tell. One of them, however, looked vaguely familiar, and his eyes kept returning to it. It was simple, a red field with a white glyph in the middle. The shape of it was almost recognizable, a single vertical line, bending to the right at the top and looping down to almost close against the vertical. Below that point, a short single line crossed and below that, another, longer one. Why did he think he recognized it?

Three women returned in the wake of the young woman who had greeted Pug and his companions. The three younger women who had waited with Pug's group departed.

Pug studied the three newly arrived Bloodwitches. They were all older and gave off a strong sense of power. The eldest of them said, 'Who is the Gardener?'

Macros stepped forward. 'I am.'

The older Bloodwitch looked at him for a moment, then said, 'No, you are not. But I know who you are.'

Macros said, 'Then, who am I?'

'You are something very different, and it may take a while to explain, but you have been expected.' She glanced at his three companions. 'We did not expect them, however.' She pointed to Valko. 'Especially not him.'

Pug said, 'Lady, we have come a very long way.'

She was peering intently at him, and Pug knew that he was being regarded by more than simple eyesight, even the more powerful Dasati vision. There was magic at play. He watched her eyes widen. 'Ah, yes. Now I see. Come, we will offer you comfort and refreshment, and we shall speak of many things.'

She led Macros through the large doors on the left and Pug and Magnus followed. Magnus said, 'Father, there's something different here. Something different about these women.'

Pug nodded. 'I sense it too. They are not mad.'

The young woman who had greeted them outside moved to Valko's side and said, 'You are to come with me.'

'Where are you taking me?' he asked with a mix of suspicion and defiance.

'No harm will come to you,' she said. 'Those ahead of us must speak of many things, some of which will concern you and about which you will be told when you need to know. I will talk to you of things about which they have no need to know. It is necessary. Besides, I would like to know you better.'

'Why?' he asked, his suspicion rising.

She smiled, and it was a very different smile from those seductive and manipulative expressions he expected from young women speaking with the powerful young lord of an important family. 'Because I have heard of you since you were born, Valko. I am your sister, Luryn. Narueen is my mother, as well as yours.'

Valko was speechless as his sister led him into the heart of the Bloodwitch Sisterhood's fortress.

CHAPTER 11

ACCORD

Jim came to a halt.

It was mid-day and he was close to exhaustion when at last he reached Elvandar. His elf companion said, 'You know the way, I trust.'

'Thank you, Trelan. I can find the way.'

Jim was doubly thankful that he could slow to a reasonable walk. Trelan's idea of a slow pace through the woods was punishing to any but the most extraordinary human hunter or tracker, and Jim was neither a hunter nor tracker, let alone extraordinary. A few elves were crossing the great clearing from the edge of the Elven Forest to the heart of Elvandar. A few gave him a passing glance, but none spoke to him. They were an extremely polite people, by Jim's measure, and would speak to him only if he spoke first. And they knew any human this close to Elvandar was welcome.

Jim caught his breath as he approached the first of the giant trees that served as home for the elves of the Queen's Court. He was as amazed now as he had been the first time he visited, several years before. His sense of wonder was hardly diminished by the fact it was now daylight and the sight was even more breathtaking at night. Still, he could make out the faint glow around the trees, a light which was dramatic after sundown. And even in the light of day, the variety of colours was still stunning. Amidst the deep green foliage were trees which only grew in this forest. Most were concentrated in this grove, and they presented a feast for the eye, as leaves of crimson, gold, even white, complemented the deep emerald of the rest. One had blue leaves, and he headed for it, knowing that the ramp up the right side would take him to the Queen's Court.

He nodded a few times to elves going about their day's work – cleaning a deer skin, or fletching arrows, cooking over an open fire, or simply sitting in a circle meditating on some elvish matter or another. The elven children, while not great in number were just as boisterous and combative as human young. A pair of boys almost ran him down as they fled from an equally loud group who gave chase. Still, it was a happy noise, that laughter, a sound that barely bruised the tranquillity of the place.

Elven girls played at the feet of their mothers, and for a brief instant Jim felt a rush of envy. If there was a place more peaceful than Elvandar in this world, he could not conceive of it. As fatigued as he was, he could imagine settling down here for a long time.

He climbed the long ramp up the first tree, then transited half a dozen broad paths cut across the tops of huge branches. Some boles had been hollowed out and apartments had been created within them, complete with doors and windows. Some ancient trunks had pathways cut into their sides, winding upwards, apparently without any ill effects to the trees, which seemed to thrive under the elves' magical husbandry.

As he trudged along one of the pathways Jim glanced down and was grateful that he had no fear of heights. Scampering across slippery rooftops inured you to the fear of falling. If you were afraid, you shouldn't climb up where you can fall off, was his thinking.

Still, it was a sobering sight looking down and seeing nothing to break your fall, save some unwelcoming branches and the hard forest floor below. He took a deep breath, more from fatigue than any discomfort at being so high up and continued.

By the time he reached the entrance to the Queen's Court, word of his arrival had already reached Her Majesty. Queen Aglaranna sat on her throne, her husband, Warleader Tomas, seated at her side. She was the most regal being Jim had ever encountered, and he had met his share of human rulers. Not only was she beautiful in a slightly strange and alien way, but she held herself in the easy manner of one used to being obeyed, yet without a hint of arrogance. In fact, if anything, the inherent warmth and kindness she projected added to her aura of nobility. Her reddish-blonde hair was untouched by grey, though Jim knew she was centuries old, and her face was unlined, making her resemble a human woman of no more than thirty years or so, and her deep blue eyes were clear and direct. Her smile was heartbreaking.

The man at her side was perhaps the most daunting figure Jim had ever seen, though he had never shown anything but the utmost courtesy and friendliness when Jim had previously visited the court. Tomas was a strange being by anyone's measure, and while Jim had heard all the stories, he wasn't sure where fact ended and fancy began. The story was that Tomas had been born a human lad, in the keep at Crydee Castle, down the Far Coast. Some ancient magic had transformed him during the Riftwar into a being of astonishing power, half-human, half– . . . Jim wasn't entirely sure what. He had a somewhat elvish look to him, with pointed ears and an elf's long locks, yet his features also looked . . . different. The story went that he was the inheritor of an ancient magic, belonging to a legendary race known only as the Dragon Lords. As he had the last time he had visited, Jim was determined to find out more about these legendary beings, if only he didn't become too busy with other matters, as he had the last time he returned to Krondor.

At their side stood two elves, who looked young, though that concept had no meaning here. One was Prince Calin, the Queen's son by her first husband, the long-dead Elf King. The other was Prince Calis, her son by Tomas, and while there was a strong resemblance to their mother in both of them, Calis had inherited a robust look of strength and power from his father that his half-brother lacked. All of them smiled at Jim Dasher as he entered the court and bowed.

'Welcome, Jim Dasher,' said the Queen. 'It is good to see you again. What brings the agent of the Prince of Krondor unannounced to our court, welcome though he may be?'

'I bear grave news, and have need of your counsel, Your Majesty,' he replied.

'You look exhausted,' observed the Queen. 'Perhaps you should rest and revive yourself before we speak.'

'I welcome such an offer, but before I do, allow me to tell you the cause for my arriving unannounced.'

'Please,' said the Queen, her brow furrowed with concern.

'Agents of our enemies, an unnamed band of marauders landed . . .' Jim paused. He had lost track of time since he had been captured. Had it only been three days? 'They landed three days ago on the shores of the Peaks of the Quor.'

At mention of the location, the Queen and all her advisors stiffened, as if they sensed something dire before he spoke of it.

'With them was a magician of some power, who conjured a being the like of which I've never encountered, and it was only through the intervention of others that we were not destroyed utterly by this creature.'

247

'What others?' asked the Queen quietly.

Jim realized she already knew the answer. 'Elves, My Lady. Elves unlike any I've seen or heard of, from a refuge they called Baranor.'

Tomas nodded. 'The anoredhel. They endure.'

The Queen asked, 'How fare your companions?'

'They are taken captive. After rescuing us from the brigands, the elves took us prisoner and marched us to their stronghold.'

'How were you treated?' asked Lord Tomas.

'Well, enough, I suppose, though there was this one fellow who looked ready to cut our throats no questions asked, my lord. But these are desperate people, from the look of them, and I fear they may decide that Kaspar and my companions are more trouble to keep alive than to kill out of hand.' Jim looked around at the faces regarding him. There was something at play here, some elvish business that he was not privy to.

The Queen was silent for a long while, then said, 'Go now and rest, Jim Dasher. Eat and sleep and we shall hold council on what you have said. When you awake tomorrow, we will talk again.'

Jim had no doubt he would sleep through the evening meal once he had laid his head down, so he was not going to argue. Still, his curiosity was now fully engaged and he wanted to know what was going on. Moreover, he worried about Kaspar and the others. They might be cut-throats and brigands but these men were all loyal servants of the Crown and the Conclave, and despite their rough exteriors, all stalwart lads to their core. If he could save them, he would.

At the Queen's behest, a servant conducted him to an apartment within a bole where he found a platter of fruit and nuts and a pitcher of cool water waiting for him. With sudden pangs of hunger, he set to while the young elf who had guided him said, 'I will return with more substantial fare in a few minutes, Jim Dasher.'

'Thank you,' he said between mouthfuls. By the time the elf returned with a platter of game bird, some aged hard cheese and half a loaf of fresh grain bread, Jim lay fast asleep on the pallet on the floor of the apartment. The elf quietly put down the platter and left him in peace.

Jim awoke and devoured the rest of the food that had been left for him. After that he exited the little apartment and found the closest garderobe, in which he relieved himself and then hurried down to a deep pool where he quickly bathed. He was politely ignored by those elves also busy making their morning ablutions. As much as he admired women in their many configurations, from the willowy thin to the robustly voluptuous, he found himself admiring elven women's forms more for their beauty in an abstract fashion than with any lust. They were as beautiful as any human woman could hope to be, but there was an alien quality which robbed him of any carnal impulse in their direction. The elven men were also beautiful, in their fashion, and he admired their lithe strength. Rarely did anyone make Jim Dasher feel unfit, but every elf he saw bathing looked like an embodiment of youthful vigour, while he still felt ill-used and fatigued from his travels.

He donned his still-dirty clothing, having judged it imprudent to wash them and either wait until they dried or wear wet garb to the Queen's Court. Once he was dressed, he hurried back up to the pavilion where Aglaranna and Tomas waited.

'Good morning, Jim Dasher,' said the Queen.

He bowed and said, 'Good morning, Your Majesty.'

'Did you rest well?'

'Yes,' he replied. 'I am in your debt for my welcome respite, my lady.'

'We have conferred with our advisors on the news you brought us,' said the Queen. 'And to understand what needs to be done, you must be made aware of things few within our race know, and no one, not even our oldest friends like Pug, have been told.'

Jim raised an eyebrow at that. He had assumed that given the boyhood friendship between Pug and Tomas, Pug would be the most likely human to be told any elven lore. Still, he said nothing and waited.

Tomas spoke, 'In ancient times there was a great war between the gods. Those called Dragon Lords by humans, whom we call Valheru in the elven language . . .' He paused, as if uncomfortable speaking of these things. '. . . the Dragon Lords took a hand. In the end, they were cast out of this realm, dispersed to other universes.'

This piqued Jim's interest. A great deal of the intelligence gathered by the Conclave over the last few years consisted of references to other planes of reality. A lot of it was incomprehensible to Jim, well, most of it, actually, but he had reviewed enough of the intelligence passing through his hands on its way to Pug or Nakor or Miranda to have some sense of it: there were other places that could only be imagined by a few beings – and he wasn't one of them, but he took it on faith that they existed. Too much had happened already for him to doubt it.

Tomas continued, 'But before the last of that great struggle, one of the Dragon Lords stood apart, the one whose armour I wear when I go into battle.'

Jim had never seen Tomas don the legendary white and gold dragon armour, but he had heard of it and imagined it to be an impressive sight. Even wearing a simple robe and sandals Tomas was one of the most impressive beings he had ever met.

'He alone defied the Dragon Host,' Tomas continued, 'and his last act before the madness known as the Chaos Wars overwhelmed this world was to free all those who had been held in thrall to the Valheru.

'Most of those you know as "elves" came to

reside here, in the first court of the first king and queen, before the rise of men on this world. We call ourselves "eledhel" or "people of the light". But some did not. There are those you call the Dark Brotherhood, the "moredhel", or people of darkness. There were others, some who have since come to join us, those fleeing privation in the north, beyond the Teeth of the World, or those from across the sea.

'But one . . . tribe, if you will, were set apart and they embraced a mission. They are called "anoredhel", or "people of the sun". They have never been subject to the Queen's rule – or that of any other ruler here in Elvandar, but we have . . . an accommodation with them. They are . . . unique and their responsibility is vast.'

'Then they are in need of your aid, Majesty,' said Jim Dasher.

'How?' asked the Queen.

Jim recounted Kaspar's observation about them being a dying people. When he finished, Tomas and the Queen both looked troubled. Finally, Aglaranna said, 'For reasons you may never understand, we may not meddle in the affairs of the anoredhel. Yet we would not see them perish, for more reasons than I can tell you.' She looked at her husband and said, 'What counsel you?'

'My wife and queen, I think there is only one answer. I must go to the Peaks of the Quor and speak to their leader.'

'Castdanur,' Jim supplied. 'That's what he's called.'

'That is not a name, Jim Dasher,' said Tomas. 'It's a title. He protects the world against the Darkness.'

Unable to stop himself, Jim blurted, 'He's been lax on the job, then.' He instantly regretted what he said. 'I'm sorry, my lady, my lord. I am . . . still very tired and my better judgment is apparently missing.'

Tomas didn't smile, but his expression wasn't scolding. 'It's quite understandable.' He stood up. 'My lady, I take my leave with your permission.'

'Be swift, my husband, and return quickly.'

Jim was struck by the bond between these two, forged before he had been born yet as fresh as new lovers just discovering their passion. He indulged himself for a moment to think of Michele and wonder if it was possible for any human man and woman to discover the depth of feeling he had just glimpsed.

Tomas said to Jim Dasher, 'Where would you like to go?'

Jim longed to say, back to Krondor and a quiet supper with Michele, but instead said, 'I would return with you to see how Kaspar and my other companions fare.'

Tomas nodded. 'Then prepare yourself for a journey unlike any you've experienced so far. Stay here a while and come when I call for you.'

Jim bowed his assent. While he waited Calis

approached. 'Jim Dasher,' he said, holding out his hand to be shaken. Calis was unique, being the son of the Elf Queen and her not-quite-human consort. He had also lived among the humans the most, having served an earlier Prince of Krondor and having formed a legendary company within the Prince's army, the Crimson Eagles. That banner still held a place of honour in the great hall, though the company itself had long since been disbanded.

'Do you miss it?' asked Jim.

'Miss what?'

'The noise, the crowds, the chaos?'

Calis smiled and again Jim was reminded that he was the most like a human of any abiding in Elvandar. 'Occasionally, but here I am at peace.'

'I can imagine,' said Jim, glancing around to where the Queen's Court continued with the business of the day. 'It is soothing here.'

'Time flows differently. One of my father's oldest friends, Martin Longbow, lived as a robust man into his late nineties, and he claimed it was the time spent here that gave him health and vigour.' Calis shrugged. 'In any event, if it gets to be too big an itch, there are always tasks to do for the Conclave.'

'How are your boys?'

'Well,' said Calis. He had adopted twin sons when he married a woman from across the sea. His position in the community made him the most able to help them adapt to a life in Elvandar. 'They are out learning to hunt.'

'Learning?' said Jim. 'They've lived here for what, thirty, forty years?'

'They're still young,' said Calis with a grin.

'Barely more than children,' Jim conceded dryly.

Calis and Jim exchanged news of the commonplace variety, Calis admitting he had developed a fondness for football while living at the palace, and asking how things fared in the guild league.

Jim enquired as to how things stood along the Far Coast, for as he was painfully aware, the relationship between the King's court in Rillanon and the Western Realm was growing strained; Calis might not live in human society any more, but he was attuned to it and spent a fair amount of time around Crydee Castle.

'The young duke, Lester, is a lot like his great-great- grandfather, Martin. A good hunter.'

'Good?'

Calis nodded once. 'Very good.'

'Elf good?'

Calis grinned. 'Not that good.'

Jim said, 'Were it only that simple that the qualities of rulers could be summed up with something as basic as tracking skills.'

'Politics?'

'Always. The Western lords are growing fractious and debate in the Congress of Lords has risen to the level of open insults and threats of duels.'

Calis shook his head in regret. 'Great men once ruled the Kingdom.'

'The conDoin name is still one to be honoured,

but I fear we've not had a strong hand at the helm of the ship of state since King Borric's day.'

'I knew him, you know,' said Calis.

'Really?'

'Not well. I was much closer to his younger brother, Nicholas.'

'I've heard stories of the two of you.'

Calis sighed. 'It was a long time ago, yet sometimes it feels like yesterday. I miss Nicholas. He died a hero's death, but he died alone.' He looked over his shoulder, as if he could somehow see through the boles of trees and leaf-covered branches to where his wife laboured or his sons hunted. 'It's a bad thing to die alone, Jim Dasher.'

'I have no plan to do that, Calis,' said Jim.

Calis said, 'There's someone in your life?'

'If I have anything to say about it,' Jim answered with a widening grin.

Tomas reappeared and nothing in Jim's speculations came close to preparing him for his reaction. Tomas was resplendent in golden armour, and a white tabard and shield, both emblazoned with a golden dragon. His helm was fashioned to appear as if a dragon lay on top of his head, wings down on either side to form the cheek-guards. It also had a nose-guard to protect his face. The effect was to make his eyes even more vivid, and the already-powerful figure was now even more so in this extraordinary garb. He was a figure to inspire awe and terror in a foe.

Tomas said, 'Are you ready?'

'As ready as I can ever be,' Jim replied softly.

Calis nodded and gripped his shoulder. 'It's good to see you again, Jim Dasher. You may not be much of a hunter, but you are among the best storytellers I have met. You must come again for a visit and soon, when the reasons for your visit are less dire.'

'I look forward to that day,' said Jim honestly.

'Come with me,' Tomas said, leading him quickly away.

Despite his size, Tomas was as nimble as any elf, and Jim was hard pressed to keep up without stepping off a pathway into thin air. At last he reached the ground safely and caught up to Tomas on the edge of a great clearing. 'Prepare yourself,' was all Tomas said, then he shouted something in an alien tongue, repeating a phrase three times. Then he fell silent.

'Now what?' Jim asked.

'We wait,' Tomas answered.

Minutes went by, and soon an air of expectancy grew. Elves all around them paused lingering to see what came next. Jim had no idea, but long ago had learned there were times when it was best to simply shut up and do as he was told.

The moments passed slowly, and just as Jim was starting to feel his patience wane, a distant sound of flapping wings could be heard. At first Jim thought it was some large bird – an eagle or vulture perhaps – but the rhythm was off, the beats were too slow and the sound was growing too loud, too quickly.

Suddenly a vast shadow appeared on the ground as a massive shape loomed overhead. Jim looked upwards and felt his throat constrict, for the first time in his life feeling close to panic. The creature that was landing – and from his point of view it appeared to Jim it was going to land right on top of Tomas and himself – was a dragon. Not only was it a dragon, it was a dragon the size of a small ship!

Like most citizens of the Kingdom, Jim had heard stories of dragons all his life, but he had never believed anyone who had told him that they had seen one.

Now Jim could scarcely credit his own senses. Softly he said, 'No one will ever believe me.'

Tomas turned and smiled, the smile removing some of the awe he induced in Jim in his guise as a Dragon Lord. 'Those who know the truth will, and that's all that matters.'

A voice thundered from deep within the throat of the creature. It spoke a language Jim did not understand, and he spoke seven fluently and could puzzle out a dozen more. Tomas answered in the Common Tongue. 'I seek a boon, old friend.'

The creature was ruby in colour, with highlights sparkling in the sun of, silver, gold, crimson, and even a flash of blue. The creature had a huge crest that began between its eyes and rose up and back, descending to just above the base of the neck, the colour shifting among reds, orange, and gold, looking like iridescent flame, with silver streaks along the base, and stood tall like a cockscomb. The dragon regarded them with eyes as black as onyx.

'Speak your boon, Dragon Rider,' it said.

'To the Peaks of the Quor must we speed, to distant Baranor, for the sake and safety of all our peoples, eledhel and dragon-kin alike.'

The dragon lowered its massive head, which was easily as big as a farmer's wagon. 'Long have you been dragon friend, you who were once our master. Your word is bond and I shall carry you.'

'And my companion,' said Tomas.

Jim felt the colour drain from his cheeks. 'What?'

'There is no need to fear,' said Tomas to Jim. 'I have magic that will ensure your safety, and this is the fastest way to reach Kaspar and his men.'

'Wait!' argued Jim. 'I have this device. It will take us to Sorcerer's Island. Miranda can take us—'

Tomas smiled even more broadly and said, 'Trust me when I say, this is a better way to make an entrance.'

Jim sighed. 'Very well. If you say so.'

'I do. Follow me and step where I step. For all his size, Ryath is sensitive.'

Pushing aside an almost irrational urge to giggle, Jim followed Tomas, watching where he placed his feet, and grabbed hold as the white-clad warrior climbed up the side of the dragon's face. Tomas walked down the length of the dragon's long neck holding lightly to the large crest and when he reached the base, he sat down, wrapping his legs easily around the creature's neck, which was about the size of the barrel of a good-sized warhorse just before it met the neck. 'Sit behind me,' Tomas told him.

When he was firmly seated, Jim said, 'I'm ready.'

'Hold tight,' said Tomas, and suddenly the ground seemed to leap away below them as the dragon sprang upwards with a terrifyingly loud beat of its wings, the force of which cracked through the air like the thunderous boom of massive drums.

The ground fell away below and Jim for the first time in his life felt dizzy from the height. Then the dragon levelled off its flight and turned towards the south-east and started to accelerate.

Jim forced himself to breathe and then realized he was holding onto Tomas's waist like a baby clutching his mother. He assumed the powerful warrior wasn't discomfited for he didn't seem to notice.

Jim looked down and saw the forest below and realized they were moving at an incredible rate. He could not even begin to judge how fast they flew over the treetops – many times the speed of the fastest horse he had ever ridden – but suddenly they were out of the elven forests and into the foothills of what could only be the Grey Tower Mountains.

Higher and higher they rose and faster and faster they flew. Jim was too overcome with awe and amazement to speak, and even if he could, didn't know if Tomas could hear him.

The air turned cold, but not bitter, and given how high above the peaks they sped, Jim assumed magic was at play – this high up he should be freezing to death and unable to breathe. Still they pressed on and even faster they went, until the ground below was almost a blur of features. Then they were above a large expanse of blue water, and Jim's eyes widened as he realized they had swept out over the Bitter Sea! They had crossed the largest range of mountains in the Western Realm and over the Free Cities of Natal in minutes!

The dragon spread his wings out and soared and then levelled out its flight again, as if it had reached the limit of its speed. But even so, the velocity was staggering. Jim saw an island appear on the horizon, pass below, and vanish behind before he could recognize it as the island Kingdom of Queg. Then Krondor was below and onward they flew.

Jim's mind reeled as he tried to comprehend details in the fleeing landscape below, and his senses were confounded as the sun lowered behind them. They were flying east and soon night appeared on the horizon as they raced into darkness. Never had night fallen so fast for Jim, and he marvelled at the magnificence of a city appearing below, a thousand torch-lights flickering on the ground. The large moon rose over the eastern edge of the world, and seemed to hurdle into the sky, the small moon trailing after it like a pup following his mother.

Jim heard Tomas's voice. 'That's Malac's Cross we just passed over. We should reach the Peaks of the Quor at dawn.'

Through the night they flew and Jim found himself too enthralled by the experience to feel even a hint of fatigue or hunger. They passed over villages where only a lantern or two illuminated the streets, but which they could clearly see from on high as Middle Moon joined the other two in the sky and a cloudless night revealed the landscape below.

Jim felt the dragon turn and bank angling now towards the south-east, and he knew they must be approaching the shore of the Kingdom Sea. In the east the sky was lightening by the minute, first a faint hint of grey, then a lighter grey, then suddenly a rosy hue was quickly followed by a golden dawn. The rise of the sun as they sped downwards was breathtaking, just as the rising of the moon had been what seemed barely minutes earlier. Whatever magic made it safe to ride the back of the dragon also seemed to make it impossible to judge how quickly they were moving, Jim thought, for he knew that even at the dragon's prodigious speed it had still been a journey of hours, even if it felt as if only minutes had passed.

In the distant morning light Jim saw mountains and looking down could see the grey shapes below resolve themselves into sea and land. They were passing over the eastern coastline of the Kingdom just north of the border with Great Kesh, and the mountains in the distance could only be the Peaks of the Quor.

'Where exactly?' came Tomas's voice.

'Look for a cove a third of the way down the coast from the tip. It has a large outcropping of boulders to the north, with a high bluff rising up behind it. It's very deep and our camp was about a mile up a trail—'

'I see it.'

'Follow the trail north. You should find the elves' enclave quickly.'

The sun had crested the horizon and now day was fully upon them. The dragon slowed and now the flight was almost leisurely compared to how fast they had flown through the night. Jim tried to make sense of the landscape below, then saw the trail. 'There!'

'Yes,' said Tomas.

The dragon banked and slowed even more and they flew down to barely more than tree-top height. Then Tomas said, 'Ahead!'

A band of men, armed with bows, lay waiting in ambush, as on the other side of a large clearing elves moved down the trail in plain sight. 'I know them – those are Kaspar's men! They must have escaped and seized weapons!'

'I must stop this!' Tomas said.

He ordered Ryath to land in the middle of the clearing and with a thunderous crack of its wings, the dragon did as it was asked.

Jim didn't wait to be told to dismount when they touched the ground. He swung a leg over the dragon's neck and slid down his shoulder, landing on his feet. He took half a dozen steps towards where the ambushers crouched, shouting, 'Wait!'

The men stood up with amazed expressions and one by one walked out from their place of concealment. Jim saw Kaspar pushing forward from a position on the far side of the clearing and heard him shout, 'Jim Dasher?'

Jim looked around and saw that elves were walking into the clearing from the other side, their weapons shouldered. They looked entirely at ease. They did not look at all like guards seeking escaped prisoners.

'Don't fight!' Jim shouted. 'Lord Tomas will sort this all out!'

Kaspar came right up to Jim. 'Fight?' With a barking laugh, he said, 'What fight? You and your friend just ruined a perfectly good hunt.'

'Hunt?'

'The elves were beating the brush and driving a nice little herd of elk towards us.' Kaspar put his bow over his shoulder. 'The elk bolted when they caught sight of that dragon coming down out of the sky. They're probably half-way to the City of Kesh by now.' He put his hand on Jim's shoulder. 'Good to see you got away, and lived, and even better that you've fetched help.'

He regarded the dragon who now sat in repose on the tall grass. 'And I must say your arrival was like nothing I've ever witnessed before.'

'You should try riding one,' said Jim. 'What happened?'

'Come along,' said Kaspar and he motioned to his men. 'Start back to the enclave and we'll organize another hunt later. This one is over!' he shouted.

The men acknowledged his order and Kaspar turned back to Jim Dasher. 'Since you left, I've had a good chance to speak at length with Castdanur. He's not a bad sort once you get used to his elvish ways.' As they reached the spot where Tomas stood speaking to the elves, Kaspar said, 'Let's say we've reached an accommodation.'

'Accommodation?'

'Yes,' said Kaspar. 'We're going to help these elves survive, and they're going to help us save Midkemia.'

Jim couldn't believe that a tiny band of ragged elves could render much help to those forces already poised to defend this world, but after what he had seen in the last three days, he decided that rash judgment was a poor choice. Suddenly feeling exhausted again, he said, 'You'll have to explain it to me, Kaspar.'

Kaspar laughed. 'Willingly, but first let me meet your companion. I know him only by reputation.'

Jim grinned, then shook his head in disbelief. The last thing he had expected up to moments ago was to be standing here making social introductions.

★ ★ ★

The elves revealed more emotion when confronted with Tomas than they had shown the entire time Kaspar and the others had been confined. Castdanur and the other older elves were visibly moved by the sight of the man in the white-and-gold armour.

'Valheru,' said the old elf as Tomas walked into the central compound.

'No,' said Tomas, 'though I have his memories. I am as mortal as you, leader of the anoredhel.'

'But the old magic lives in you,' said Castdanur.

Tomas merely inclined his head, acknowledging it was so.

'Does the old knowledge also reside with you?'

Tomas said, 'Some, but there are . . . memories that are missing. Yet, I know of you and your brethren. In our complacency we assumed that hearing nothing meant you were well.' He looked around and said, 'It appears otherwise.'

'Let us take counsel,' said Castdanur. He motioned for Tomas to precede him into the central hall, then said to Kaspar and Jim, 'You should attend.'

The two men exchanged glances and Jim whispered, 'What happened here?'

Kaspar said, 'I'll give you the details later, but the heart of the matter is you did well in not killing Sinda and his friend. Had you killed those two, we would all most likely be dead by now. Sparing him and giving him that trinket convinced Castdanur that I spoke the truth about . . . certain things. I'll tell you more later.'

They entered the hall and sat in a circle, with Tomas opposite the old elven leader. Two other ancient elves sat on either side of him and Kaspar and Jim took up position on either side of Tomas.

'Know, Dragon Rider, that we are a free people, according to your own words.'

Tomas remembered the last flight of Ashen-Shugar, when the Valheru whose armour he wore had flown around the world freeing every servant of the Dragon Host, letting all know they were a free people. 'I remember,' he said, not wishing to debate the nuances at this moment.

'You know the mandate,' said Castdanur, and suddenly Tomas did remember. As in times before, memories came unbidden.

All elven-kind had been slaves of the Valheru, and while the Dragon Host rose to challenge the gods, Ashen-Shugar, the last of the living Dragon Lords flew the skies of Midkemia, freeing all the peoples once in thrall to his brethren. But the anoredhel were unique, elves given a special duty. 'You are the protectors of the Quor.'

'A task set to us in the times of our ancestors, and one we have discharged to this day. But our number has diminished and we stand at peril, and so do the Quor.'

Jim and Kaspar exchanged glances. Both had the same question: Who or what are the Quor?

'How fare those gentle beings?' asked Tomas.

'They struggle,' said the old man. 'The creatures from beyond plague us, but they are far more intent on destroying the Quor and we can only do so much. We have failed our charge.'

'No,' said Tomas with a surprisingly gentle tone of voice. 'We are here, and we shall help, and the Quor endure, imperilled though they be.'

'We are a free people,' repeated the old man. 'But we need aid.'

'Aid you shall have,' said Tomas. 'I shall ask my wife the Queen of Elvandar to send those willing to serve with you – hunters, weavers, artisans, and more: spell-weavers and warriors – so that we may once again see the Quor safely in their homes above us.'

'We thank you,' said the old man, the relief so visible on his face that he looked to be on the verge of weeping.

'It is we who thank you,' said Tomas, standing and bowing his head in respect to the three old men who sat across from him. 'I must return to Elvandar, and I will return as swiftly as I may with a few who will lend help at once. Others will come later, and we shall see Baranor reborn.'

'Children?' asked Castdanur.

Tomas smiled. 'Some will bring children, so that your young will have others to play with, and I know some of those who come will remain with you. Many of those who lived in the Northlands, who have since come to abide with us in Elvandar, will welcome coming here, for they are more like you in their ways than they are like us.' Tomas spoke of the glamredhel, the 'mad elves' who had struggled against the Brotherhood of the Dark Path for generations before coming south to Elvandar a hundred years before.

'Then I will recant our defiance, and we will swear fealty to your queen.'

Suddenly Jim realized that there must have been an ancient schism here and that Castdanur was making an enormous concession of some sort.

Tomas said, 'Only if you wish. We shall offer aid because you are blood-kin and because you bear a grave charge. We offer our help without condition and you remain as you have always been, a free people.'

Now the old man did, indeed, weep, and Tomas said, 'Soon, all will be made right.' He motioned for Kaspar and Jim to accompany him and once they were outside he said, 'There is more to explain here than time permits. Stay with these folk and help them gather food. They are at peril and the risks are far greater than anything you can imagine.' He glanced back to the entrance to the main hall and added, 'What plagues these people may be part of the other risks we face. The creatures they speak of are . . . children of the Void, creatures that should for no reason be in this world.' He smiled ruefully. 'It was one such, a minor wraith, who was responsible for me being as you see me today. I shall tell you that story some time, but for now, just know that we must ensure that these people survive. I will be back with as many warriors as Ryath can bear, and others will soon follow.'

'One thing,' said Jim.

'What?'

'What or who are the Quor?'

Kaspar said, 'I always thought it a place, a name on the map.'

Tomas inclined his head. 'They are the most ancient race of this world, and they are the heart of this world. If the creatures of the Void destroy them, then nothing can stop the Dasati. These elves, the Children of the Sun as they call themselves, have always served as the guardians of the Quor.'

'Where are they?' asked Jim.

'High above us,' answered Tomas. 'In the Peaks of—'

'The Quor,' said Kaspar and Jim together.

Tomas turned without further comment and strode out of the gates of the enclave. He moved quickly down to the meadow where the giant red dragon patiently waited to carry him home.

Jim turned to Kaspar. 'Now what?'

Kaspar said, 'We go hunting, unless you're keen to eat nuts and dried fruit for the next few days.'

Jim sighed. 'If I must. That's one thing I was never very good at.'

'You'll learn,' said Kaspar, clapping him on the shoulder. 'Come, let's go talk to our new friends about organizing another hunt, and let's pray we get some game worth cooking before Tomas returns to chase them away. There was a twelve-point stag in that group and I had my heart set on venison tonight.'

'Sorry,' said Jim, wishing with all his might that he could have convinced Tomas to drop him off along the way in Krondor. Now that would have been a sight, the a giant red dragon settling in the prince's marshalling yard. How *that* would have impressed Lady Michele de Frachette and her father, the Earl of Montagren! He sighed, wondering if he would ever see Michele again, and then he wondered if she missed him. Pushing aside that concern, he followed Kaspar back into the main hall of Baranor.

CHAPTER 12

DISCLOSURE

Miranda paced.

Alenca and the other Great Ones had gathered in an informal council. They sat patiently around a large garden in the City of Magicians, home of the Assembly. The oldest magician in the meeting, except for Miranda, Alenca watched with some amusement as she paced around, unable to remain still during the discussion. 'You should try to sit and relax,' he counselled her. 'It helps me to think clearly.'

She shook her head and kept walking. 'There's nothing wrong with the clarity of my thought. What's wrong is that we haven't yet found Leso Varen.'

Matikal, a burly magician of middle years who shaved his head, making him look more like a bruiser at an alehouse than a master of scrying magic, said, 'Every member of this Assembly, and every priest of every order, and every magician of the Lesser Path we can reach knows what to look for. Every master of detection and scrying has used every art we possess to look for any signs of necromancy. The moment we find a hint of his death magic, we shall swarm him and destroy him, no matter what the cost.'

Miranda stopped her pacing. She realized that this man was pledging his life to destroy Varen, and understood that every other member of this Assembly was also committed to dying if it meant removing the threat of the Midkemian death-magician. Miranda's position within the Assembly had always been a difficult one. Until her husband's intervention and the rise of the Mistress of the Empire, any female with the potential for magic was put to death. It was only in the last century that women who practised magic were allowed to use their talents openly, and many of the trad-itionalists still had difficulty accepting female Black Robes as 'sisters', let alone this ill-mannered wild woman from another world. It was only her marriage to Milamber, greatest of the Great Ones, that earned her their grudging regard.

The attack on the Emperor had changed all that. Now, her words were carefully listened to and every suggestion weighed thoughtfully. The single most horrendous act imaginable to a Great One had been attempted, the destruction of the Light of Heaven, and all lesser concerns were set aside in the face of that.

Alenca said, 'Perhaps he has fled back to your world.'

Miranda shook her head emphatically. 'No. My

husband is unsurpassed in the knowledge of rifts. He set safeguards before he departed on his journey. Had any rift into Midkemia been opened, it would have been detected.'

'Then he has gone to ground,' said Matikal.

Miranda said, 'Forgive my impatience. I hate being in the position of having to wait for our enemy to reveal himself.' She pointed to the north, as if she could see the distant peaks through the walls of the building. 'He's hiding somewhere, up in a mountain cave.' She pointed to the south. 'Or in some tiny hut in a secluded corner of a miserable swamp – he's endured worse over his life from what I've heard. But he'll wait as long as he must, and then he'll act, and we can only hope that when he does it's nothing worse than his last attack.'

'What,' asked Alenca, 'could be worse than an attack on the Emperor?'

Humourlessly, Miranda said, 'A successful attack on the Emperor.'

The room fell quiet. After a moment, Miranda said, 'I can do nothing more here. We have a situation on Midkemia which may be another aspect of the monstrous danger we all face here. You know how to reach me should you have need.'

Without further word she willed herself to the rift chamber, entered the rift and was back on Midkemia. A black-robed student looked up with a mildly interested expression at her sudden arrival. By agreement, the rift to the Assembly was still with the Academy on Stardock Island, not on Sorcerer's Isle. Politics aside, it was a better situation for protecting the privacy of those in the Conclave. Still, some accommodation with the Academy had to be reached. It galled Miranda that this vast university of magic that her husband had founded and built was now in others' hands, and that those others did not always agree with Pug in his judgments. Not that she always did, either, but she was his wife and she valued his thoughts even when she decided he was wrong.

She put aside her chronic annoyance at how her husband had been treated by those he raised and made a half-hearted greeting to the young student, then vanished from view. In one area of magic, Miranda was supreme: in her ability to will herself to almost any where she had ever visited. Almost every other magician on both Midkemia and Kelewan needed a device that had been calibrated to take them to a specific location, and the Tsurani artificers were the very best at building such devices. Others, like Pug, could will themselves to patterns, to complex geometric shapes set in tile on the floor of a certain place, a widespread practice on Kelewan, and in limited use on Midkemia – the religious orders had been quick to adapt the magic for use as a means of getting their clerics from one temple to another, but it did no good to outsiders unless you offered a hefty 'votive offering' or as Miranda preferred to think of it, a bribe, to utilize their patterns.

But Miranda could just see a place and go there. She didn't truly understand how she did it, which is why she had such great difficulty teaching others the knack. Magnus was her best student. Miranda thought in time he would be as adept as she was, perhaps even more so, at willing himself to a place previously visited. Still, Pug had been making progress. Nakor claimed he couldn't do it, but she was certain he lied. She found him as amusing as her husband did, but she never had and never would trust him the way Pug did. There was something about that little man, something hidden deeply within, that was just not right. Still, her husband had put his life in Nakor's hands many times and never had the little gambler failed to rise to the need of the moment, but even so she feared that some day she would lose Pug because of someone like Nakor, someone with a secret agenda of his own.

Miranda appeared in her study and found Caleb asleep behind the desk. She felt a warm maternal twinge seeing her youngest child in slumber and remembered for a brief moment when he was a baby, in her arms. She took a breath and pushed the emotion aside. 'Caleb, go to bed!'

He almost jumped out of the seat. 'Huh?'

'Go to your suite. I'm sure Marie would like to see her husband from time to time. I have work to do.'

'What time is it?'

'I have no idea,' she said, glancing out the window. 'It's night. It was mid-day when I left the Assembly about five minutes ago, so I'm not sleeping any time soon. While your father and everyone else is out saving the world, there are mundane matters to be addressed.'

'I know,' said Caleb, then he yawned. 'I've been tallying the revenues from Father's estates and holdings and reviewing some of the projects that have been waiting for weeks. And we've got to start deciding when we're taking new students again, and . . . just so many things.' He pointed to a large stack of papers and parchments, and said, 'But at least all that business is done.' He picked up a sheaf of documents and said, 'And these can wait.' Pointing to the pile he had rested his head on when he was asleep, he said, 'But these last few items need to be seen to at once.'

'Good. I'll finish and you can get back to being a hunter or whatever you want tomorrow morning. Now go.'

Caleb kissed his mother's cheek and left the room. Miranda sat in her husband's chair, still warm from her son occupying it, and wished as much as she ever had that Pug was back. She hid it deeply, but she was frightened, and what frightened her the most was the thought she'd never see her husband again.

★　　★　　★

Pug sat quietly, letting the drama before him unfold. He recognized that something momentous was taking place and was intent on understanding what he was seeing. Magnus stood behind his father, equally focused on the discussion. The three older Bloodwitches who had come to greet them were arrayed in a semi-circle of chairs. They all wore identical robes of black with orange shawl collars and broad orange belts, while the younger members of their order wore robes of white and orange.

Macros sat in a similar chair distant from them. He looked fatigued to the point of exhaustion and leaned on his staff for additional support. The centremost Bloodwitch said, 'I am Audarun, the most senior sister of our order. To my left is Sabilla, and to my right Maurin, and we three form the Triarch, who ultimately rule the Sisterhood. We are also the keepers of knowledge and defenders of life.' She looked at Macros and said, 'How did you come to be the Gardener?'

Macros was silent. He looked from face to face and then finally said, 'I don't know. One day I was walking home from my place of business and I had a . . . seizure of some sort. I got dizzy and fell down behind a wall so as to not reveal weakness to anyone. Then I had memories of my last life and . . . I knew I was . . .' His voice faltered. 'I went home and felt . . . ill. I had dreams. I had a family. They were frightened. When I awoke my mate begged me to be strong, not to be taken and killed, but to return to work and keep them safe.' He lowered his head. 'I left that home and have never seen them again.'

'Go on,' said Audarun. 'Where did you go?'

'I walked a very long way. I don't remember very much, save that I hid some times, and other times I merely walked down very busy streets as if I were on an errand. I stole food when no one was looking, and . . .' He closed his eyes, as if it would help him remember. 'I came to a place.'

'What place?'

'I don't remember.' Macros opened his eyes. 'It was like the Grove of Delmat-Ama, but it wasn't there. It was another place.'

'What happened?' asked Audarun, in a gently reassuring tone.

'I met someone.'

'Who?'

'He said his name was . . .' Again Macros closed his eyes. 'He said his name was Dathamay.'

The three women exchanged glances.

'You know that name.'

'Yes,' said Audarun. 'It is a false name, from a very old fable. What did he say to you?'

Macros kept his eyes closed. 'He said he had expected me . . . no, he said I was expected. Then he . . .' He opened his eyes. 'He put his hands on my head, almost like a benediction, and . . . my pain was gone, my memory . . . clear. I remembered much of my previous life and my current life, in proper order.'

'As I thought,' said Audarun. 'What sort of man was this? A Lesser? A Deathpriest?'

'I can't remember . . .' said Macros. He slumped down in his chair.

The attending Bloodwitches looked disturbed, but rather than the sort of conflicted self-control Pug had witnessed by members of the White when evidence of weakness was apparent, this was a genuine concern.

'What is the matter with him?' asked Audarun, rising from her chair.

Pug stood as well. 'He told me he is gravely ill, dying.'

She looked puzzled. 'I should have heard of this.' She went to Macros's side and knelt down. She examined him and then gave instructions to one of the younger Bloodwitches. The woman left the room to retrieve the items requested. 'Bring him with us,' she said to Pug and Magnus.

They picked Macros up between them and carried him out of the room, down a series of halls, and into a sleeping room, barely more than a cell. Pug had seen many such in temples throughout Midkemia and Kelewan. A pallet, a small table and a chair were the only furniture. A simple burning wick in a bowl of oil on the table was the sole source of light.

They put Macros on the pallet and Audarun continued to examine him. The young Bloodwitch arrived with a large basket with vials, jars, and waxed paper packages and a second young woman followed bearing a steaming pot of water. Audarun quickly prepared a strongly-scented drink and when it was ready, motioned for Pug and Magnus to prop up Macros and put the draught to his lips.

Macros revived enough to sip the drink and after a few minutes he regained a semblance of alertness. 'Did I faint?' he asked.

'Yes,' said Audarun. 'Or, rather, you lost the ability to remain conscious.'

'I'm dying,' said Macros.

'Who told you this?' asked Audarun. She pulled the small chair next to the pallet and sat down.

'An Attender. A healer . . .' He looked confused. 'I don't remember where. My memories are fading. I have more difficulty with every passing day recalling things that I knew without pause just weeks ago.' He glanced at Pug. 'I knew much of what I remembered from my human life was lost, but now I'm losing my memories of this life as well.' He looked at her. 'I fear I have little time left.'

She stared down at him. 'You have no time left, whoever you were. For you are not dying, my friend; you are already dead.'

Pug and Magnus stood motionless and stunned. Finally, Macros softly said, 'Yes, that would make perfect sense.'

Pug said, 'It makes no sense to me.'

Audarun looked at Pug. 'For you to be here, in

that guise, so perfectly achieved and maintained, I can only assume you to be a magician or priest of most puissant ability. Illusion is not something we do well, we Dasati. There is no need. We are a people who prize strength and force above all else.

'But while the Deathpriests may understand necromancy in all its subtle and dark aspects, we of the Bloodwitch Sisterhood understand life in all its subtle and bright aspects.' She paused, then said, 'This vessel does not contain true life.' Looking Macros in the eyes, she said, 'You are a simulacrum, false life resembling the living.'

She looked over her shoulder at the young attendant and asked for a few more items, and the young woman left. Returning her gaze to Pug, Magnus, then Macros again, she said, 'The magic used to create you is vast, alien to me, and of a design I can barely begin to understand. No mortal being could fashion such as you, and that leaves only one alternative.'

'A god,' said Pug.

'Of your world,' she added quickly. 'Some agency in your universe judged it vital to pierce the barrier between our realms, in anticipation of some act by the Dark One, in order to aid the White. I am no theologian, but the Sisterhood has more untainted lore than anywhere else in this realm; for the Dark One's Hierophants have destroyed everything except approved doctrine everywhere else. I shall see if I can find any reference to any such act before, but this much I know: rules have been violated, rules as binding upon the higher power as the need for air and water are upon we mortals. Whoever did this thing, whoever sent this . . . creature here, did so knowing that the consequences of such an act could be as disastrous as that which he was trying to prevent.'

'"Desperate times call for desperate measures" is an old saying among our people,' said Magnus.

'Perhaps,' said the old Bloodwitch. 'But while it is sometimes wise to set a backfire to stop a wild-fire from spreading, if the backfire gets out of control—'

'It becomes a bigger wildfire,' said Pug. He fell silent.

After a moment the creature called Macros said, 'If I am not who or what I think I am, why am I here?'

'I cannot tell you,' said Audarun. 'When we received word that someone calling himself the Gardener had appeared, more than ten years ago, we waited and watched. We knew there were powerful forces behind you, for you merely had to appear before our followers and they would do your bidding, as if you had been leading the White for years. Martuch is one of our oldest, most loyal allies, and he was asked by Lady Narueen to seek out this Gardener and ascertain his purpose.

'We were certain it was a ploy by His Darkness's servants, but there were too many . . . oddities.

Martuch not only did not discover anything nefarious in this Gardener, but like so many others he fell easily into taking instructions from him, and assigning to him the role of leadership in the White that he claimed. So we kept watching.

'After many months, it was clear that this creature had a mission, and as far as we could discern, that mission was in concert with our own. Moreover, he provided a strong focus and a clear mission we had lacked. Until then, the White had been little more than an association of Bloodwitches and a few sympathizers who shared information and occasionally saved bands of women and children from marauding Deathknights. We had enclaves, such as this one, scattered throughout the Dasati realm. The presence of this leader, this Gardener, provided a much-needed focus for our activities. We've recruited powerful allies, like young Valko, and we've established a far more effective presence throughout the Empire, and so we are stronger.

'Thus, we have benefited from his appearance, but since the start we've known something about all this to be false, to be fabricated, for in the Dasati it is unheard-of for a humble Lesser suddenly to rise up and become a leader of power. And using magic unknown in the history of the Sisterhood? Impossible.' She stared for a long moment at Macros. 'What is your purpose, strange creature? That is what we wish to know.'

The thing that was Macros stared back weakly

at the old woman. 'I . . . only know I have been driven to lead the White, to get it ready.'

'Ready for what?' asked Audarun.

'I don't know.'

Suddenly Pug said, 'I know.'

All eyes turned to the magician. Pug looked at Macros. 'You have a message, somewhere in your memory, that someone was desperate to relay to us, but not until we had been here a while and seen with our own eyes the circumstances we are confronting.'

Macros said, 'But nothing stirs. Nothing is apparent.'

Magnus looked at the creature who had claimed to be his grandfather's spirit in a Dasati body and with a detached interest said, 'How do you feel?'

'The potion has restored some of my strength and I feel . . . otherwise, I feel empty.'

'The false life given you is draining away,' said Audarun. 'Your remaining time is short. At some point you will close your eyes and cease to be. There will be no pain.'

Macros lay back and stared at the ceiling. He said, 'I feel I should be angry, or frightened, or something. Instead I am merely concerned that I fulfil whatever mission I was created for, to bring you that message, Pug, if that's what I am to do.' He fell silent and then took a deep breath. 'It's so very strange to have these memories, yet to be told they are not my own.'

'What about this Dasati body?' Magnus asked Audarun.

'I suspect it was meant to die at that moment of faintness, when those false memories came, perhaps from a weakness of the heart or some other malady. But something – someone – seized that instant to instil the false human memories and keep the Dasati mind intact.' She shook her head slightly. 'It is an admirable feat, as subtle a magic as any I've encountered, yet at the same time it's extremely powerful necromancy.' She let out an audible sigh. 'I wish I knew who did this.'

'Ban-ath,' Pug said.

'Who?' asked the old witch.

'Ban-ath,'

Magnus said, 'The God of Thieves?'

Macros nodded. 'Kalkin.'

'Who is this being?' asked Audarun.

Pug said, 'In our realm we have many gods, though from what I have learned, not as many as you had before the rise of the Dark One.'

She smiled. 'How can one realm have more gods than another?'

Pug said, 'I'll leave theology to the clerics, but it may be that we merely find convenient labels for common elements so that we can better understand them; in short, fifty of your gods may in reality be only fifty aspects of a single god we worship under a single name.'

'Tell us of this Ban-ath.'

'Ban-ath, also called Kalkin, Aderios, Jashamish,

and many other names by people of other nations. His simple soubriquet is "The Trickster", but he is more than this. He is the God of Thieves, but also the God of Lost Causes and Hopeless Quests, a rule-breaker and a master of misdirection.'

She laughed bitterly. 'Olapangi! Also known as the Deceiver to our people. I have long been a student of the old lore, and among the ten thousand gods he was always a favourite of mine. There are many old stories of the Deceiver, how he played pranks on the other gods and mortals alike. The name Dathamay, the man who this creature said came to him and made all things clear, that name is from an ancient myth: Dathamay was a tool of Olapangi, a dupe who went among the people telling them one thing, while Olapangi did another. The Deceiver was our most colourful, and often most dangerous god.

'He could be gentle or vicious, compassionate or ruthless, often at whim, but always with a purpose. We have an old saying, though few among the Dasati would recognize it as originating with the stories of Olapangi: "by whatever means necessary."'

'The ends justify the means,' said Magnus.

'Ah, you have similar wisdom,' she acknowledged.

'I don't know how much wisdom there is in absolutes, but it is often the case that if the ends are vital enough, means that would otherwise be unthinkable . . .' Pug's eyes widened. 'I am such a fool,' he said softly.

'Father?' said Magnus.

'I . . . we, have all been used.'

'By Ban-ath?'

'Yes,' answered Pug. He went over to Macros, leaned down and looked him in the eyes, as if trying to see something within. 'You have been most ill-used of all, for whoever you were in this world, your time came prematurely and you were not even granted the dignity of being found at the roadside and given the rites of your people.'

Macros said, 'Now I remember.'

'What?' asked Pug.

The Dasati with Macros's features looked up and smiled. 'I have a memory of you, Pug. When you and Tomas and the dragon Ryath came for me in the Garden . . .' He laughed. 'The Gardener! Kalkin's an evil bastard at times, but he does have a sense of humour.' He paused and Pug could see he was now in pain. With shining eyes, Macros said, 'We stood in the Garden that hovers at the edge of the City Forever and spoke of the dangers we thought we faced, the return of the Dragon Lords to Midkemia. You asked, "Then, why haven't the gods acted?" Do you remember how I answered?'

Pug nodded. 'Yes. You said, "They have. What do you think we're doing here? That is the game. And we are the pieces."'

'Nothing has changed, Pug. That's the message. This is still a Game of Gods, and we are the pawns they use to win or lose. Kalkin can break rules like no other, for it is his nature, but even he has limits to what he does directly. And there is more. It is not Kalkin acting alone. He could not affect this realm without the consent of other gods.' His voice grew weak. 'I . . . Macros . . . was always the god's creature and he prepared the way. You are their creature, too, but you have a destiny beyond mine . . . his.' He closed his eyes, and Pug could see that the end was fast approaching. 'You must find Nakor. He has the answers.'

Pug nodded. 'I will.' He put his hand over Macros's eyes and said, 'We have no more need of you.'

The Dasati who had the memories of the ancient human magician slumped down. To the Blood-witches, Pug said, 'Do with this empty vessel as you see fit.'

Audarun said, 'There were more questions —'

'And this creature had no answers,' finished Pug. 'It had accomplished its task.'

'And was that?' asked the old matriarch.

'We must return to the heart of the city, for somewhere there is a being of incredible danger, and a little gambler who is my friend, who is trying to control that being. And my friend, I have just been told, has the answers.'

'What being does your friend control?' asked Audarun, motioning for her attendant to take away the dead body that had been host to Macros's memories.

'A strange young man who is far more than

289

merely a man. His name is Ralan Bek and he is here to save two universes. Your prophecies name him the Godkiller.'

The three old Bloodwitches sat in silence, weighing Pug's words. 'How do you know of the Prophecy?' asked Audarun after a time.

'Martuch,' Pug replied. 'He has said things in passing, and I have pieced together some sense of them. I do not yet fully understand our role in this matter, but it is as this lifeless creature said – what Macros the Black, my wife's father, said to me lifetimes ago – that this is a Game of Gods and we are only pieces on the board.

'But we are also beings of will and intelligence and I will not see any of us squandered in a foolish gambit.' Pug turned to look at Magnus. 'We have a long journey.'

'I think I can take us straight away to the Grove, Father.'

Pug looked surprised. 'Really?'

Looking on as four young women came to pick up the dead Dasati and carry him away, Magnus said, 'Mother's been teaching me and I'm sure I can do it. I can transport us there without a device.'

'We need to collect Valko and go,' said Pug.

Audarun held up her hand. 'Young Valko will not travel with you.'

Pug looked warily at the old woman. Whatever else these Bloodwitches were, they were Dasati and capable of instant and extreme violence. This enclave of women might lack the aura of insanity of the rest of this race, but that made them no less potentially dangerous. 'Why?'

'He has a role to play, which is as critical in its own fashion as yours, of that I'm certain.' She rose slowly. 'If the Dark One vanished this instant, the slaughter in his name would not. There are too many, from the TeKarana down to his lowest servitor, who have a vested interest in seeing things remain here as they are.

'The society we live in has at its heart an evil that infects every aspect of our lives. Even if that heart dies now, the infection will continue for centuries. Too many would continue as if nothing had changed.

'There must be a wholesale reordering of our culture,' said the oldest of the Triarch. 'Not only must the Dark God be destroyed, but the TeKarana and the Karanas, as well as the topmost leadership of the Dark One's temple, all must be removed, and once that has occurred, we will still have to endure decades of unrest.'

'As powerful lords rush to seize power,' said Magnus. 'You speak of chaos.'

'It is better for there to be chaos,' answered Audarun, 'than an order that calcifies a race, stagnates it until it becomes a thing despicable, a culture of death and horror. It would be better to become the animals we devour, for at least they care for their young.' She fixed Magnus with a steady gaze. 'Let the strong survive, but

291

we shall teach them, eventually, to care for the weak.'

Pug said, 'You choose a harsh path.'

'It was chosen for us long ago, magician.' Audarun rose. 'We are not your allies, but we do share common interests. We have no desire to see your realm invaded or your world subjugated. Our race can survive only through expansion, for we will turn on ourselves if we cease to look outwards. So, we must force that inward turning, create a civil war that will last generations and end the horror that is what we have become. We must cut off our own hand before it does even graver injury.'

Pug nodded. 'Harsh indeed. But many will attempt to seize power in the name of the Dark One, even if he is somehow vanquished, and they will use the existing social order to crush opposition.'

'We are the only opposition,' she said. 'In our hallowed history we were more than you see now, and we had many gods, human. We served them with joy and they guided us. But now we have no rallying point save to oppose the Dark One. If somehow they were to return to us, perhaps we might find a less terrible fate, but that is the stuff of dreams.' She indicated the direction Valko had been taken. 'He is our beacon, he will stand in opposition to the horror that our leadership has embraced.

'Valko has been chosen, along with several others of noble rank and honoured lineage, to be the next generation of leaders for our race. With good fortune, he may even be the next TeKarana.

'You have no concept of how remarkable it is that he could learn the truth and assimilate it as rapidly as he has; most young warriors would have flown into a killing frenzy at a suggestion of the things he has calmly embraced. Most would have killed you by now for the mere fact of your existence.

'We, the Triarch, have lived here in this refuge our entire lives, spared the constant madness emanating from the pit wherein lies the Dark One. His poison seeps out of there and reaches across the stars and damns every last Dasati. We are among the few who have escaped that touch, yet even to us your presence is a . . . trial.'

'Then, lady,' said Pug, 'we shall remove ourselves as quickly as we can, and be on our way. Know that while the survival of our race is our paramount concern, I also hope we will be helping yours and we wish you well.'

'Then you are a better race,' said Audarun. 'But one day perhaps we shall equal you.'

Pug turned to Magnus. 'Let us go now.'

Magnus came to stand next to his father and put his hand on Pug's shoulder. He closed his eyes for the briefest second, recalling the secret room below ground in the Grove, and instantly they were there.

Two Lessers leaped away in terror until they saw the faces of the two who had mysteriously

appeared before them. Pug made a gesture of re-
assurance, as he glanced around to find themselves alone, then said to Magnus, 'Let us rest and
see if Martuch and Hirea return this night. Else
it is just the two of us in an alien place and we
have a difficult task ahead.'

'To find Nakor?'

'To find Nakor.'

CHAPTER 13

SECRETS

Bek lashed out with his sword.

The trainer barely leaped aside quickly enough to survive, and received a glancing blow off his left shoulder. It rocked him and he staggered a step back, which saved him from losing his head as Bek halted the travel of his sword to his left, and reverse-cut to his right, a backhand blow that was all but impossible for any but the strongest, fastest swordsmen in the Dasati Empire. For a novice Deathknight, it should have been impossible.

'Hold!' came the command from above.

The trainer and Bek both looked up to see who had shouted the command. A man resplendent in black armour edged with gold peered down from the gallery overlooking the arena. Every instructor and trainee in the massive arena halted at his command. The black armour he wore was of the TeKarana's personal guard, and he sported decorative pauldrons which made his shoulders impossibly wide and came to an upswept point ending in a wicked-looking golden barb. His helm was topped by a high metal crest fronted by a stylized serpent twining around a tree. The crest ended in a fall that dropped at the back between his shoulders. He exuded power.

Pointing at Bek, he shouted, 'Who trained you?'

Bek laughed, and shouted back, 'I trained myself.'

Nakor stood to one side, eyes down. He winced at the arrogance.

But the man above returned the laugh. 'Can I believe it? I must, for no sane warrior would teach a move such as that. Wait on the sand.'

It took only a minute for the observer to leave the balcony and work his way to the training floor, but in that brief respite, Nakor came to Bek's side, offered him water, and whispered, 'Remember, you are the protégé of Martuch and you were trained by Hirea. Remember!'

The large warrior in the decorative armour strode across the yard and came to stand before Bek, the only person on the floor who was taller. All eyes turned to witness the exchange. The warrior said, 'Attack me.'

Without hesitation Bek unleashed a furious combination of blows, feints and thrusts that had all the onlookers gaping. But the warrior in the black armour was obviously no novice to combat, for he moved out of Bek's line of attack with a nimbleness of foot that was unexpected in someone so large, let alone burdened by heavy armour.

Then he countered and let loose a blow that

296

came close to crushing the side of Bek's skull. Bek merely twisted his wrists and brought his blade up to block, and the shock of the blow reverberated across the sand.

Back and forth the two men duelled, Bek's ferocity and power matched and countered by the other man's speed and experience. The onlookers began to form a circle around them because it was becoming clear that something unusual and amazing was taking place, and that should either warrior err, someone would die suddenly.

Back and forth they moved, exchanging blows and parries, until finally the warrior in black stepped away and shouted, 'Hold! Enough!'

Bek hesitated, then put his sword down.

The warrior in black said, 'Again, who trained you?'

This time Bek looked him in the eye and said, 'Hirea of the Scourge.'

'I know him. Scourge, small society . . . but respected, old house, good man. One of the best on Kosridi.' He removed his helm, and Bek saw a battle-scarred face, an older Dasati warrior, but one still in the height of his power. 'I am Marlan, Imperado of the Justicants, First Order of the TeKarana's guards. I have never seen anyone like you, Bek.'

Bek was dripping with perspiration. He said, 'You're fast. Strong, too. You are very hard to kill.'

The older warrior grinned. 'I will mention your name. We shall need replacements, and we shall need them soon. Who knows? You may be the one to take my head some day if I don't die on some cursed alien world.'

'I'll make it quick and salute you,' said Bek, returning the grin.

With a slap on the shoulder, Marlan turned and departed.

The instructor said, 'You have been honoured, young Bek.'

Nakor was dying to ask questions, but he knew that here, more than most anywhere in the Dasati realm, not acting the part of a Lesser would get him killed in seconds. The instructor turned to him and said, 'Clean up this mess. We are done.' To Bek he said, 'Retire to the barracks and wait for the mid-day meal call. You have earned some extra rest.'

Nakor hurriedly picked up the items belonging to Bek, and turned to see the large warrior grinning at him. 'What?' he whispered.

Bek said, 'He got tired and was afraid I was going to kill him.'

'Who, Marlan?' asked Nakor softly as he bent over to pick up a large, dirty cloth of some wool-like material Bek had been using as a towel.

Bek laughed. 'Him, too. No, I mean the instructor. He was getting tired.'

'How do you feel?'

'I feel wonderful, Nakor.'

Nakor said quietly, 'Good. I am pleased you feel well. Now, let us return to the barracks and wait.'

'I like to fight.'

'I know, but we must do as we are told a little while longer.'

'Yes, Nakor.'

They hurried out of the training arena, down a vast corridor that led to the recruits' barracks. A pair of young warriors was there, resting after their arduous training that morning. One sported a huge welt on the side of his face where the instructor had unceremoniously demonstrated why he needed to keep his guard high, and the other had a slight cut to the thigh that was bandaged. Nakor observed the Dasati constantly, and was astonished that the culture managed to survive, given their murderous ways. Had either of those young warriors sustained a serious wound, they would have been left to die, their lingering agony the source of amusement to the others on the training floor. Since coming to the training floor the day before, Nakor had witnessed one such incident. The jeering Dasati considered watching such a death an entertainment, a respite from training.

Nakor had travelled throughout the Empire of Great Kesh and down into the client states south of the vast mountains called the Girdle of Kesh – he had been born in the foothills of those great peaks. He had seen many strange things, but nothing as alien and difficult to fathom as the Dasati. He had encountered a travelling troupe of players once, in a small city called Ahar, and remembered a remark made by the company's leader, the man responsible for writing the skits and songs as well as staging them. Nakor had asked what the key was to making the audience laugh, for while he knew little of performance, he realized that the more the audience laughed, the more money the players earned.

The two of them had been playing at cards and Nakor hadn't seriously begun to cheat, so the head of the company of players was winning. He was in a good mood and paused to answer the question. 'It's all about pain, Nakor,' he had said. 'If you care for our hero and feel his pain, that's tragedy. If you laugh at him, that's comedy. Comedy is other people's pain.'

The Dasati carried the concept to an insane length. Since reaching this realm he had seen a number of people in pain or dying, and the general reaction was to laugh at them. Only some of the Lessers seemed inclined to help, and they were despised for it. Empathy was weakness to the Dasati.

As they reached their place in the barracks – a heavy bunk for Bek and a mat on the stone floor for Nakor – a bell's deep peal reverberated throughout the building so loud that it felt as though the stones beneath their feet shook. Nakor looked at the two resting young warriors and saw they were as uncertain what to do as he and Bek were.

A moment later a warrior in black armour strode

through the far entrance and shouted, 'Stay where you are! That was the muster call for the Palace Guard. You will wait and attend the mid-day meal when called.'

The massive bell sounded again, and a third time, then fell silent. From a short distance away, Nakor could hear the sound of running feet, and knew that hundreds of Lessers were scurrying around in anticipation of whatever was required of the Guard by that call. Nakor's curiosity was piqued, but he knew there was no way he would risk his usual indulgence of that curiosity. Had he been alone, he might have risked being killed out of hand for being in the wrong place – for over the years he had become very adept at staying alive – but he did not dare to leave Bek alone for even a minute.

They waited and a few minutes before the mid-day meal, a dozen recruits entered the barracks, stripped off dripping tunics and trousers, bathed quickly, and donned clean clothing, while their Lessers ran about, trying to anticipate their masters' needs. Nakor sat quietly on the floor at Bek's feet, watching the almost reflexive manner the young warriors kicked or cuffed their Lessers when annoyed. He sighed. He had always been a vagabond, and thought of no place as home, even the village of his birth, but for the first time in his life he felt homesick, wishing he was back on Midkemia, anywhere on Midkemia. The searing heart of the Jal-Pur desert looked attractive to him right now.

Bek rose without saying anything, and Nakor took a second to realize he was moving to the serving hall where the mid-day meal would be provided. Nakor and the other Lessers would wait until the warriors had departed, then after a frenzy of cleaning up the barracks, they would scurry off to the room where their food was provided, eat quickly then hurry back to be here waiting for their masters. In so many little ways, it was an existence without joy.

Nakor grabbed a bowl of something resembling stew and a hunk of coarse-grain bread – he discovered that even with the successful translation to Dasati form the food here was disagreeable: it was one of the many examples he could cite as to what a joyless society the Dasati were. Food was regarded as a necessity and sometimes the excuse for social events, but it was never considered an art form. He remembered with longing a meal he had had at Talwin Hawkins' River House in Olasko, and wondered if he'd ever have a meal like that one again.

He heard voices through a door that led to the Imperial Guards' marshalling yard. Glancing around to see if he was observed, Nakor slipped down the hallway and hung back, just out of sight. A commander stood on a dais and addressed his warriors. '— this night! We muster at once, and depart at dawn! Worlds to conquer await! Each of you has found favour in His Darkness's sight and your willingness to serve His will until the last has gained you a special place in his regard. Rejoice in this, for we shall begin a campaign of conquest unmatched in the annals of the Dasati Empire! For the Dark One!'

'His Darkness!' shouted the gathered guards, and Nakor quickly turned and fled back to the room where the other Lessers waited. He darted around the corner and sat down before he was noticed then stood up as if he had finished, put down his dish and returned to the barracks to wait for Bek. Something important was underway and it began tonight. It could not be the invasion Pug feared, for there were not enough Deathknights gathered, but this mustering of the Imperial Guard was a prelude to something vital.

He wished he could have heard more.

Jommy turned to Kaspar and the others. 'Now that's something you don't see every day. And here we are seeing it for the second time.'

Kaspar nodded. Captain Stefan said, 'But I wager it's something we're never going to see again.' The four of them were standing a short distance away from the welcoming elves, Servan hunkered down while Jommy, Stefan, and Kaspar leaned back against the wall of the long hall.

The massive dragon had been astonishing enough when it had carried Tomas and Jim Dasher into the compound the day before, but now it landed with a party of three on its back. A pair of women, both dressed in long dark dresses, was sitting close behind the white-and-gold-clad figure. They dismounted nimbly and came to where Castdanur and his two advisors waited.

Tomas announced, 'Castdanur, this is Miranda of Sorcerer's Isle and her student Lettie.'

The girl with Miranda was young and slender with an upright posture that was almost rigid. She looked from face to face with a calm mask, and nodded. Miranda said, 'I am going now,' and vanished.

Castdanur said, 'What is this—?'

Suddenly Miranda appeared again, this time surrounded by a band of elves, dressed in leather of a similar cut to the clothes worn by the Sun Elves. This band of newcomers wore necklaces of stones and rough gems, and two had eagle-feathers hanging behind their ears, tied into locks of their hair.

Jommy glanced at Kaspar who said, 'Those are the elves from north of the Teeth of the World.' He dropped his voice. 'They're called something like "the Mad Ones" by the other elves, because of something back in history. You don't have to be told they're different: you see them in Elvandar and they stand out. Baranor looks more like their kind of place.'

The leader of the band with Miranda walked straight up to Castdanur and said, 'Brother, we hear of your need. We answer it. I am Talandel.'

The old elf stood with shining eyes, and said, 'We welcome our brothers and sisters. ' He looked to where Miranda stood and saw that four of those with her were children. 'You return life and hope to us, brother.'

The children stood rooted in astonishment, staring up at the huge red dragon who now crouched peacefully in the courtyard. Miranda shooed them away and vanished. Less than a minute later she appeared with another small band of elves, who crossed to stand with the first. This process continued until more than a hundred elves from Elvandar had been transported to Baranor.

Within minutes the courtyard was filled with the sound of voices, and Jim Dasher turned to Kaspar and said, 'I never heard it quite this lively in Elvandar.'

Kaspar shrugged. 'I doubt we've ever seen that many happy elves before.' He pointed to where the children who lived in Baranor were already starting to play with those who had newly arrived.

Castdanur spoke loudly, so that all might hear. 'Our new brothers and sisters, there are halls and rooms enough for all! Pick those that you will, for this is your new home. Tonight we feast!'

Tomas approached Kaspar. 'How are your men doing?'

'The wounded will live. We've been helping the elves hunt since Jim vanished to fetch you. All in all, for a band of prisoners we've been treated more like guests.'

Tomas dropped his voice. 'Castdanur is like many of the old spellweavers in Elvandar. He adheres to tradition, which can be a trap.' He glanced over. 'I remember enough of my human heritage to recall when the elves' sense of time seemed far more leisurely than good sense dictated. But in this case, it almost lost us something far too dear.'

'The Sun Elves?' asked Jommy.

'The Quor,' answered Tomas.

Kaspar introduced the Captain and the two youngsters to the dragon-rider, and Tomas said, 'You're Caleb's fosterling.'

Jommy said, 'In a manner of speaking. He and Marie welcomed me like another son.' He grinned. 'They're as good as people can be.'

Tomas returned the smile and the alien aspect of his heritage dropped away for a minute. 'His father was like a brother to me when we were boys; he was my parents' fosterling.' He looked over at the gathering of elves and said, 'I must stay for a while longer, to preside at the feast tonight.' He lowered his voice and said to Kaspar, 'This is a far better situation for those who have come here today; they are the most restless among the glamredhel, and they have found kindred spirits among the anoredhel.'

Miranda came over and nodded to them, 'Kaspar, Jommy.' Kaspar introduced his Captain and Servan, and Miranda said, 'Where's Jim Dasher?'

Kaspar glanced around. 'He vanishes like a mist in the morning sun. I have no idea.'

Tomas said, 'He was very concerned over that enclave of creatures he saw up to the north. You don't think he headed back that way to investigate?'

'I don't know him that well—' Kaspar began.

'You know him better than anyone else here,' interrupted Miranda. 'Do you think he's out playing hero?'

Kaspar shook his head. 'He's a lot of things, but he'd never accept being called that. But he can be duty-bound, and that might be cause enough.'

Tomas looked around. 'We've got a few hours of light left. It shouldn't be too hard to pick up his trail if he's heading in the direction.'

Jommy said, 'I'm bored. I'll go.'

'If what Jim said is close to accurate, you'll need me along. Let me settle Lettie in here and then we'll be off,' Miranda announced.

Servan and Captain Stefan volunteered as well, but Kaspar declined. 'We're going to be noisy enough with this lot along.' He looked to where Miranda was talking to the young female magician and said, 'I have no idea what her woodcraft is like.'

Jommy grinned. 'You don't know her like I do. If those creatures hear her coming and are at all smart, they'll clear out and head back to where they came from.'

Kaspar said, 'Tomas, it might be better for all of us if you mentioned to Castdanur that we're going to poke around up north. He and I have come to an . . . understanding, but trust is still a little thin.'

Tomas inclined his head in agreement and moved away.

'I thought you and the chief were thick as thieves,' said Jommy to Kaspar.

'Remember what Tomas said about elves' sense of time being "leisurely"?'

'Yes.'

'For five hundred years they've only encountered brigands, pirates, smugglers, and every other stripe of outlaw up here. Their view of humanity is less than positive, you could say. It's going to take a while before they'll trust any of us, but,' he gestured at the animated conversations taking place among the various elves, 'this will go a long way towards convincing them we can be trusted.'

Jommy recalled what he had heard about Kaspar since he had come to serve the Conclave and found it ironic that he should be talking about trust. Yet he had proven himself as a reliable agent since his return from exile.

Tomas returned with Miranda. 'If we're to find where Jim Dasher went, we should leave now.'

Kaspar shouldered a bow he had been using since Castdanur had let them hunt and said, 'With you two,' —he indicated Miranda and Tomas— 'along I doubt I'll need this, but I find it reassuring to have some sort of weapon.'

Jommy just patted the hilt of a large hunting knife at his belt as if to echo Kaspar's sentiment.

Tomas waved a farewell to Ryath who, with a snap of its massive wings loud enough to sound like thunder, took to the sky. The elves watched silently as the massive creature vanished into the heavens.

They trotted out of the gate and followed the main trail to the south-west, then turned north, following a game path where obvious footprints had been left in the east. A quarter of a mile up the trail, Tomas pointed to a broken branch, still green and dripping sap. 'He's making it easy.'

Kaspar said, 'Knowing Jim Dasher, he's doing it intentionally.'

As the afternoon lengthened, they moved purposefully up the trail and after travelling for two hours they found another broken branch indicating that Jim had turned northeast, climbing towards a gap in the ridgeline above. As they reached the lower lip of a plateau, they could see a figure kneeling behind sheltering rocks, observing something on the other side.

Crouching low, the four approached until Kaspar stood at Jim's shoulder. Quietly, Jim Dasher said, 'What took you so long?'

'Social niceties.' said Kaspar.

Tomas slowly drew his sword. 'Where are they?'

'Just over this rise,' said Jim. 'They appear to be resting. From what I've seen, they are most active at sundown, then are awake all night.' He glanced at the sun, low in the western sky. 'They'll start whatever they're going to do, hunt or feast, in about an hour.'

'Castdanur says these wolf-riders suck life from bodies.'

'Eat them, too, from what I saw,' whispered Jim.

Tomas inched past Jim. Then the other four saw him rise up without hesitation and charge. 'Stay here!' he shouted.

'Well,' said Jim, 'I guess that means the sneaky quiet part is over.'

Miranda hurried past the three men. Jim looked at Jommy and Kaspar and said, 'I guess that means the "stay here" part of things is over, too.' He stood up, drew his two belt-knives and started after Miranda.

Kaspar reached out, grabbed Jim Dasher by the collar and pulled him backwards, almost yanking him off his feet.

'What?'

'I don't worry about her,' Kaspar said. 'But when a man who can command dragons tells me to wait, I'm inclined to wait.'

Jim looked at Jommy whose expression indicated that he couldn't believe Jim had even thought about going up there after Tomas had told him to wait.

Tomas strode into the clearing and saw the first creature. It was one of the large 'wolves' lying across the threshold of a hut and as soon as it saw Tomas it leapt to its feet, took a bounding jump and with a ghostly howl attacked him. Tomas's golden blade arced through the air and when it struck the creature there was an explosion of sparks, energy so bright that Jim, Kaspar and Jommy were forced to look away. A smoking gash where the blade struck erupted into tiny flames of silver and the creature staggered, then fell over on its side. With a gasp it went limp, then suddenly its entire form was engulfed in silver flames.

The commotion caused the human-like 'riders' and their creatures to erupt from the huts. Tomas lay about him with his sword, his speed and power astonishing. Miranda stood with hands outstretched and lances of dazzling blue energy skewered any creature that attacked her. Where her spells struck, the creatures were thrown backwards, crashing into the huts or sliding across the ground.

The howl of rage and pain was the strangest sound any of the three onlookers had ever heard, a distant empty hooting and grunting that echoed as if from the depths of some distant canyon. Miranda changed her attack and a booming sphere of white light exploded from around her. It passed through Tomas with apparently no ill effect, but when it struck any of the dark and smoky forms, they fell writhing and their echoing cries grew louder.

Tomas moved with stunning speed, wheeling his sword to left and right, and each time he struck a creature fell. With no defence due to Miranda's spell, the remaining creatures fell to him as if he were a farmer scything down wheat.

He moved to the stone cage where the Void-darters were thrashing around, trying to batter their way to freedom. 'Miranda, can you destroy those things without opening the door?'

'What kills them?'

He held out his blade. 'This contains magic which was ancient before man came to this world. As long as I have held it, I do not know exactly what went into its fashioning. But those things are feeders on life and so is this blade.'

Miranda said, 'I think I know something I can try.' She waved her hands in a quick, intricate pattern, and a pulsing globe of purple light sprang into being before her. With a wave of her hand she sent it crashing into the cage and as soon as it touched the creatures they began to thrash about even more violently. Still they did not die.

Miranda tried another approach and a wash of fire appeared from the palms of her outstretched hands. The flames burned bright orange and when they struck the creatures seemed to go rigid and fall to the ground. Tomas instantly threw up the latch, opened the door and was in the cage slashing with his sword until every darter was nothing more than smoking black char.

Miranda said, 'Those things are very hard to kill.'

Jommy, Kaspar and Jim came to stand next to Tomas. Kaspar had been given a vision of the Dasati world by the god Kalkin and had been the one to carry the warning of the Dasati incursion into Midkemia to the Conclave, but even he had never seen their like before. He said as much. 'Are they some sort of Dasati I don't recognize?'

Miranda said, 'They're nothing like the Deathpriests.'

Tomas looked grim. 'They are not of the Dasati.' He looked deeply troubled. 'They are worse, far worse.'

Jim looked at Kaspar and Jommy. 'Worse?'

'There is a crack in the face of reality, a tear in the universe, and what you see here is seepage from the Void. That is why the huts and fire are so alien. This place is now an anchor for that rift. More of those things can find their way here unless we—' He looked completely around, and then asked Miranda, 'Can you destroy everything here?'

'Everything?' she asked.

'To the soil beneath our feet, to a depth of —' he calculated. 'Twenty feet. Everything. There must be nothing but a large hole in the ground here when you've finished.'

Moving away from the centre of the village, Miranda said, 'Blowing things up was more Magnus's predilection when he was young, but if you just want things destroyed, I can do it.' To the four men she said, 'You'd better move down the trail.'

They did as she requested and after a moment they saw her climb onto a low boulder, affording her a view of the village. She began a long and complicated enchantment and suddenly the ground beneath their feet shook and the trees nearby swayed. It felt as if a massive earthquake had been unleashed. But rather than rolling, it became a series of sharp shifts, as if someone were shaking the ground by hand in staccato jerks. Then a low sound, not the usual rumbling of an earthquake, but rather a deep, grinding howl started and grew in intensity. When it reached a volume that caused Jommy, Kaspar and Jim to cover their ears, a deafening eruption blew a massive tower of earth, rock and trees into the sky. It was as if a pair of vast, invisible hands had scooped up the soil beneath the village and everything on it, ground it all into dust and rocks and tossed the mass high into the sky.

Miranda hurried down to the four men and said, 'We should get down the trail quickly. It's about to start raining rocks.'

The five of them ran down the trail and as she had predicted, a pelting fall of stones and soil began to rain over them. Fortunately, they were near the edge of it when it began and quickly left the cascade of earth and rocks behind them.

Tomas said, 'Without any aspect of their realm here, it may take them some time to rediscover a way back here.'

'Who?' asked Miranda. 'What were those creatures?'

Tomas halted. 'Whatever else may be occurring

with your mad magician,' he said to Miranda, 'or with the coming war with the Dasati,' he said to everyone, 'nothing is as dangerous as what we have just encountered.'

'What were those creatures?' Miranda repeated, this time her tone more emphatic.

'Children of the Void. When Jim first told me of them, I did not realize what manner of creature was here. I thought a lesser spectre or a wraith, perhaps even a lesser manifestation of the dark agents. But those beings were Dreadlings, minor Dread, but Dread nevertheless. The things they ride have no name I know, though the Valheru called them 'dreadmounts'. The flying creatures are also nameless, but like hawks and falcons, they are raptors who flush "game" for the Dread.'

'The elves called them Void-darters,' said Kaspar.

'As good a name as any,' said Tomas. 'They are dangerous, but nothing like those they serve, the Dread.'

'What are the Dread?' asked Jommy as Tomas turned and ran down the hillside.

'Beings so alien they make the Dasati seem like brothers to humanity. They are drinkers of life and stealers of souls, and they have somehow found their way into our realm.'

Hurrying to keep up with the human-turned-Dragon Lord, Kaspar shouted, 'Could this be part of the Dasati plot?'

'No!' answered Tomas emphatically. 'This is something far more dire.' He stopped and turned to Miranda. 'Whoever you have whom you trust, magician or priest, call a convocation of the most powerful, and I will come to you in three days. I must return to Elvandar and speak with the oldest spellweavers and lorekeepers. Castdanur had no idea who these creatures were and that shows how far the anoredhel have fallen. They have elders, but no Lorekeepers.' He shook his head in frustration. 'I must also speak with the Quor.'

'Who are the Quor?' demanded Kaspar and Miranda at almost the same instant.

Tomas kept walking as he spoke. 'They are the heart of Midkemia, beings ancient and benign. Even the Valheru left them untroubled, for they knew the Quor were linked inexplicably to the very centre of all life here. Should they perish, it is said in legend that the world would perish with them.'

They stopped and looked at one another.

'Those creatures we just destroyed are . . . youngsters. They were no more than children out on a picnic, playing,' Tomas continued.

Miranda's face went pale. 'I couldn't kill them, Tomas. I could only incapacitate them.'

'It is impossible to kill that which is not alive. They are children of the void, and no living creature can understand them. Of all the foes the Valheru faced, mightiest of them all were the Dread.

316

We invaded their realm and many of the Valheru fell. We returned, keeping them at bay, and told ourselves how mighty we were.

'Pug and I faced a Dreadmaster when we searched for Macros, many years ago. We bested it by guile and power, and it took two of us. As far as I know, this sword,' he patted the pommel of his weapon, 'is the only thing on this world that can destroy one at a touch. There may be other artefacts of which I am ignorant which can also harm them; this is why we must convene and speak with every artificer and priest we can trust.

'If the Dread have found a way into this world . . .' He stopped and pointed up the mountain. 'Those children may have blundered into our realm without understanding what they had found. But had their lords and masters found that passage, this entire continent would soon be in ashes. The princes of the Dread are beings of vast power, perhaps as great as that of the gods, and if they have a hand in any of this . . .' He took a deep breath. 'I wish Pug were here.'

Miranda said, 'I wish that every day.'

Tomas resumed walking. 'I will call Ryath and get quickly to Elvandar, then return with spellweavers. We must speak to the Quor and investigate that site you just destroyed, Miranda. If there is still some weakness in the fabric of the universe up there that brings us closer to the Void, we must know about it. Explain this to Castdanur, Kaspar.' He leaped high onto a boulder, a jump no human could duplicate and held his hand aloft. 'Ryath! I summon thee!'

Within a minute a thunderous explosion above them signalled the arrival of the dragon. 'I come, Dragon Rider.'

'I need your assistance, once more, old friend,' said Tomas to the giant red dragon. 'Our world stands in peril and we must seek to save it.'

Tomas didn't wait for the dragon to land, but leaped from the boulder onto its back. The dragon turned and with a single snap of its massive wings shot up into the sky, leaving the four humans staring in awe.

Miranda turned and faced downhill, her shoulders hunched in barely contained anger. The others hardly heard her as she said, 'Where *is* my husband?'

Pug welcomed the sight of Martuch and Hirea. 'What of Nakor and Bek?' he asked.

The two old fighters said, 'They were well, last we saw of them.' Glancing around, Martuch said, 'Where is Lord Valko?'

Pug said, 'With his sister and the other Bloodwitches. They said he needs to remain with them for a while.' He looked down a moment, as if considering his next words. 'I sense something is converging. Enough was said to lead me to believe that the White is positioning itself, getting ready to move if the opportunity presents itself.'

'Ah,' said Hirea. 'Then the Gardener remained as well.'

Pug said, 'I have much to tell you, some of which may be difficult to understand, but before I do, what of the muster?'

'No one has passed word to the leaders of the battle societies or any of the great houses. A great muster is coming, that we know, but we do not know when. There has been a calling of the Imperial Guard, which is unusual. We judge it to be a prelude.'

'A prelude to what?' asked Magnus. 'Is there no one in the palace who might be able to shed light on this?'

Martuch said, 'Our alliances are twisted, at times, and there are many factions even within the White. The Gardener forged a strong, single purpose, but before that . . .'

Pug said, 'I have some sense of it. Before that it was chasing alliances and a great deal of talk.'

Martuch bridled and Hirea looked ready to draw his sword. 'Many died so that we might have alliances and talk, human,' said the old instructor. 'Valko's father willingly gave his life so that his son could assume the mantle of House Camareen. We are a race of fighters; plots and planning do not come easily to us, and above all else, we chafe at waiting.'

'I think you will not have to wait much longer,' said Magnus. 'Father, tell them about the White, the Bloodwitches, and the Gardener. And most of all, tell them about Ban-ath.'

Pug nodded. 'Listen, my friends, and realize that what I am about to tell you may strain your credulity, but every word I say to you now is true.' Pug then began to tell them the tale of Macros the Black and the Trickster God.

CHAPTER 14

DISASTER

The Council was in an uproar.

Several factions loyal to the Emperor had banded together to block what they felt was the blatant attempt by the Warlord to re-establish a predominance not seen since before the time of the Mistress of the Empire. Tetsu of the Minwanabi, Warlord of the Nations of Tsuranuanni, by grace of his cousin the Emperor, stood and held up his hands. 'Silence!' he commanded.

The office of Warlord was supreme, in the absence of the Emperor, but he faced a generation of ruling lords and ladies who had never before been confronted by anyone wearing that mantle. They were far less inclined to heed his commands than their ancestors might have been. Even so, Tetsu was a charismatic leader and he carried the majesty of office, as well as a dozen Imperial Guards who now moved around the vast hall urging the raucous rulers of the Empire to calm.

'Heed me!' shouted Tetsu.

Tetsu of the Minwanabi was torn. He had been raised unlike any other heir to the mantle of power in the Empire. House Minwanabi was one of the five great houses of the Empire, and his place among the ruling elite of the nations had been secured before his birth. But history had conspired always to place the Minwanabi in a subsidiary role to their cousins the Acoma, the Emperor's house. For as long as he could remember, Tetsu of the Minwanabi had plotted and schemed to rise to the highest position possible in the High Council, and whatever murderous fantasy he might imagine that would put him on the golden throne he had kept to himself, for he was, at the last, Tsurani. But today he was shaken to the fibre of his being, for today was his first day ruling the High Council in the Emperor's name, and today he had left the Emperor's retreat on the old Acoma estates, where over a long breakfast the Light of Heaven had told him things no sane man could hear without being shaken. He had been given a mandate by the Emperor and no matter what fantasies of ambition had filled his nights, he put them aside in the light of day, for he was, at the last, Tsurani.

'Heed me!' he bellowed and at last the room fell silent. He looked from face to face of the rulers, many of whom were friends or political enemies, and he said, 'This day I spoke with the Light of Heaven. By the arts of a Great One I was transported from his side to this very palace. My first duty is to relay his wishes that all here are well and prosperous.' He paused for effect. 'My second duty is to remind you of the unthinkable attack on his person in this very palace less than a week ago.'

Now the room fell dead silent, for to a man or woman, the ruling elite of the Empire could not imagine a more horrific event than an assault on the person of the Emperor. In their tradition, the Emperor was a beacon of hope for the Tsurani, placed on Kelewan by the gods, to show their pleasure with the nations. He was a benediction.

'Hark to the words of the Light of Heaven!' shouted Tetsu. 'The armies have been called! The Red Seal of War on the door to the Temple of Jastur has been broken! The light of day now shines on the symbols of war! The Empire of Tsuranuanni now goes to war with a race known as the Dasati!'

Azulos of the Kechendawa shouted, 'Where are these Dasagi? I have never heard of these people!'

'Dasati,' corrected the Warlord. 'And as to where they abide . . . heed the words of the Great One, Alenca, speaking for the Assembly and for the Light of Heaven.'

The old magician had been standing close to the Warlord's throne, waiting for his moment to speak. He slowly walked to the centre of the hall and looked around, seemingly identifying every face in the chamber.

'Let me speak of the Dasati,' began the old magician. For nearly an hour he repeated every detail so far discovered about the would-be invaders, building upon the earlier warning given to the

Emperor and High Council by Miranda. Those rulers who had been in attendance the first time were subdued and looked gravely concerned, and those lords who had not been in attendance the first time appeared confused or incredulous. At first there were many whispered questions but by the end of Alenca's narrative the leaders of the Empire were silent and convinced. For the first time in the history of the Empire a terrible danger was upon them, an enemy more powerful, more ruthless, as determined and with a far vaster army than the Tsurani.

The Warlord rose. 'I thank the Great One Alenca for his calm reciting of the facts. Now, I speak for the Empire!'

That formal declaration caused every ruling lord and ruling lady in the High Council to focus their undivided attention on the Warlord, for those words signalled that what came next was in no way said for personal glory, house-honour or gain, but would be solely for the good of the nations.

'We all are bound by our pledge to the Empire, and to the Light of Heaven, and I have been given the great burden of conducting this war. I will issue edicts today. Each of twenty-five houses, whose rulers will be contacted at the end of this meeting, will be given to the command of a regional—'

A shattering sound accompanied a blast of air which knocked Alenca across the hall as if a giant hand had swatted him. The old magician struck the floor hard and slid for a dozen yards, his body as limp as a rag.

A purple oval of energy hung above the floor of the great hall of the High Council, and through it erupted a stream of warriors in black, with gold trim at the points and edges of their armour, shouting incomprehensible words as they ran straight at the first Tsurani noble they spied.

Ceremonial swords and robes of silk were batted aside effortlessly as the nobility of Tsuranuanni was slaughtered with frightening efficiency. The Imperial Guards in the great hall died defending the rulers of the Empire, for despite being among the most dedicated warriors in the Empire, the Palace Guard were soon overmatched and overwhelmed. Within half a minute, fully a quarter of those in the hall were dead or dying.

As Dasati warriors flooded into the palace, a figure emerged from the shadows of a remote hallway, one rarely used by functionaries shuttling documents from the great hall to an administrative wing of the palace. He moved to where Alenca lay stunned to insensibility, perhaps dying from internal wounds. He looked down and with an expression of mock regret, lifted his foot and crushed the old man's windpipe with the heel of his sandal, ensuring that the first of many Great Ones of the Empire was dead this day.

The sharp downward step threw him off-balance and he barely avoided falling over. The body of Wyntakata, now host to Leso Varen, was troubled

325

by a lameness that the magician found annoying. But until he could establish a safe location where he could begin to fashion his dark and murderous magic and create the means to possess another body, he was confined to this one. He smiled at the screaming and carnage. He smiled to see valiant Tsurani rulers die like so many children as the Dasati guards of the TeKarana killed every human they saw. He waved his hand slightly and employed a spell of seeming, so that no Dasati would mistake him for a target. He was certain that no matter his arrangement with the Deathpriests he had contacted on Omadrabar it was unlikely that any of these warriors had been told, 'Oh, by the way, don't kill the slightly decrepit, lame fellow in the black robe'.

As often as death was his chosen means to power and the heart of his black arts, Varen was certainly no stranger to blood and pain, but he found this wholesale murder far less entertaining than would have been the case had humans invaded the Tsurani palace. The alarm had sounded and more Imperial Guards, among the finest warriors in the Empire, came rushing in to die like kittens attacking a lion. It just wasn't fair, Varen thought. In this realm the Dasati were simply too powerful. Yet, he noticed with interest, some of the first to arrive were already showing signs of that odd intoxication he had noticed the first time he had encountered the little simulacrum who had been their first explorer into this realm. That delightful little creature had burst into flames after being in the sunlight of this world too long. He wondered if he would ever understand that aspect of the realms, the different levels of life and heat and light, the heart of energy-magic that so many of these Great Ones delighted in learning. That type of magic had never interested him very much, except for the life aspect, and that only when he was taking it in order to capture the dying energies. He paused for a moment to consider how useful fanatics could be. The Tsurani would, to a man or woman, die to defend the Emperor who, he assumed, was somewhere far from here. And the Dasati, personal guards of the TeKarana, were already doomed to die for the Dark God and their master, for those who survived this slaughter would succumb to the excess of energy in this world. He wondered if they would just fall over and die, or if they would burst into flames like that little creature did. Too bad he couldn't linger to observe.

Varen looked around the hall, now reduced to an abattoir with blood bathing every stone. He noted with amusement that some of the blood was orange, so despite their decided advantage in strength and power, it seemed the Dasati were taking some damage as they destroyed the leadership of the Tsurani Empire.

Imperial soldiers were still flooding into the room, and Varen was getting bored with watching other people killing one another, so he turned and

ambled back down the hallway to the administrative wing of the palace. As he passed the first
door into a suite of offices used by functionaries
who worked on behalf of the Imperial First
Advisor, he glanced inside to admire the scene of
his own handiwork. A dozen officers of the court
lay in contorted poses, several clawing at their own
faces from the pain that had killed them mere
minutes before. Now that, he thought, was death
as art!

He whistled a meaningless ditty as he strolled
down the hall, past another half a dozen offices
littered with bodies. Grinning, he thought that
killing off the leaders of every great house was
amusing and would certainly cause the Tsurani a
lot of problems, but it would be hard for the boy
emperor to try and run his Empire without a
bureaucracy!

Martuch hurried down the ladder to the hideout
and said, 'Word has reached the palace of the
TeKarana, and we now know what the muster
yesterday was about.'

Pug, Magnus and Hirea sat on cots and all
looked at the old warrior.

'At the Dark One's bidding, the TeKarana sent
two legions, the Third and Fifth, ten thousand
warriors, through what they are calling portals,
into your realm.' He spoke to Pug and Magnus.

'Where?' asked Pug.

'The Tsurani world. I do not know the details,

but the rumour is that each warrior was told to prepare his death legacy.'

'Death legacy?' asked Magnus.

Hirea said, 'Each warrior in the service of the TeKarana or one of the Karanas has a box within which he places any items he might wish to have passed back to his house or society. It can be personal items, messages to fathers or mentors, or anything the warrior wishes to leave as a legacy.'

'It means,' Martuch added, 'that every warrior was being sent to his death. This was both a murder raid and a suicide raid. The warriors were being told they were to die for His Darkness.'

Hirea shook his head in disbelief. 'Two legions,' he said softly. To Martuch he said, 'You know Astamon of the Hingalara's oldest son served with the Fifth.'

'I liked Astamon, even though House Hingalara were Salmodi.' He looked at Pug and Magnus. 'The Salmodi and Sadharin almost always end up on opposite sides of any dispute. But there are some good men in every society.'

'What does this mean?' asked Pug. 'Why the suicide raid?'

'It means a lot of Tsurani are now dead, and the Dark One doesn't care how many of us he kills accomplishing that end.' Martuch sighed. 'So much of what I have come to reject is accepted as normal among my people, but even the most die-hard of us would have trouble accepting the loss of ten thousand lives merely to bloody a foe.

We are conquerors,' he added, 'not *chattak* to be slaughtered at a whim!'

Magnus said, 'I don't understand.'

Pug said, 'Cattle.'

Hirea said, 'It is a matter of personal pride for any Dasati warrior that what we take, we keep. Six worlds have been conquered since the rise of the Dark One, and in every case we have never surrendered a jot of what we have taken. For a Dasati to die is one thing, for we all expect that, but we die so our people may expand their territory. We do not die just to die. It is not the Dasati way.'

Martuch saw that the explanation wasn't entirely clear to Pug and Magnus, for he had lived among the beings of the first realm and knew more about their ways. 'We are not a philosophical people, like the Ipiliac. They understand things we can not imagine. They imagine things we can not comprehend. We are a violent race which judges conquest as the highest manifestation of successful violence, for violence without purpose is—'

'Comedy,' said Pug softly. 'Other people's pain.'

'And that is offensive,' said Martuch. 'It makes a mockery of what ten thousand Dasati warriors, the best of us, were born to do: conquer!'

'To laugh with contempt at the pain of others, that is one thing. But to see waste like this . . .' Hirea's words trailed off.

Magnus said, 'It depends on what they were chosen to do, why they were used.'

330

'What do you mean?' asked Martuch.

Magnus looked at the old warrior thoughtfully. 'If the TeKarana wanted merely to overwhelm Kelewan, he could have ordered millions of you into the field.'

Martuch and Hirea both nodded in agreement.

'The Tsurani are valiant warriors, and to a man they will die defending their homeland, but they could not withstand such an attack.'

'So there must be a compelling reason to sacrifice ten thousand of his personal guards, rather than launch a full-scale invasion of Kelewan,' said Pug. 'I do not know for a fact, but I suspect it will take as much adjustment for the Dasati warriors to exist on my plane as it did for us to exist here.'

Martuch said, 'Absolutely. I can travel to Delecordia without much discomfort. The Ipiliac are as much like me as Hirea is, but they live in a world caught half way between this realm and yours. But it must have taken centuries for them to have grown accustomed to the energies of that world.' He paused. 'Without preparation it would be difficult for any of us to live there for more than a week or two. Some might adapt, but others would sicken and die. But Delecordia is not in the first realm. It would be impossible without much the same preparation as you endured for any Dasati to exist in your world for more than a few hours, perhaps a day or so at the most.'

Pug recalled just how arduous the conditioning

he, Nakor, Bek, and Magnus had endured had been. 'How can they hope to prepare an army of non-magicians to invade?' he asked quietly.

'They don't,' said Martuch. 'We Dasati do not change to exist in the new world; we change the world to our liking.'

'How?' asked Magnus.

'By magic,' said Hirea, as if it was an obvious answer to the question.

'But,' said Pug, 'magic on that scale . . .' He fell silent. 'The Dark One does not need so many lives merely to open rifts to the first plane of reality, or to move armies through them; he needs millions of lives so that he has enough power to remake worlds!' Pug fell silent. Magnus looked down at his father and saw a man nearly overwhelmed by the enormity of what confronted them. 'Father?'

'This attack today, it's not to conquer, but to confuse.'

'What do you mean, human?' asked Martuch.

'Your TeKarana has an ally, an insane necromancer by the name of Leso Varen. He's a body stealer, and is somewhere within the Empire of Tsuranuanni. My wife and others are trying to track him down, but he could have taken the body of anyone. They're looking for signs of his death-magic, but until he reveals himself . . .'

'How do you know they are in league?' asked Hirea.

'Because they have similar goals: wholesale destruction and death on Kelewan.'

'Why would any human desire that?'

'He's mad,' said Magnus.

'But he's not stupid,' said Pug. 'If he sees a gain by throwing open the gateway to Kelewan to your people, he will. And no Dasati would ever understand what he must have told them.' Martuch and Hirea both were paying rapt attention. 'He knows enough of the Tsurani to realize that if the Dark One's agents attempt to establish a foothold to begin changing that world, the Emperor could order a million warriors to swarm the position, each willing to die for the Empire. And the combined might of the Assembly of Magicians and every magic at the disposal of every temple would also be unleashed on the invaders. It might wreak havoc on the Tsurani, but they would shut down any foothold on their world as soon as it was detected.' Pug fell silent for a moment, considering what he had just said. 'The Dark One needs time to establish a large enough presence on Kelewan so that the entire might of Tsuranuanni, a million warriors, thousands of magicians and priests, all together, can't stop him.'

'That means chaos,' said Magnus.

'Yes,' agreed Pug. 'He needs to plunge the Empire into chaos so that they cannot respond to his incursion.'

'How?' asked Martuch.

'By killing the Emperor,' said Magnus.

'Or obliterating the Assembly,' said Pug. 'Varen cannot dislodge the temples, they're too scattered and it would take too long. So it must be the Emperor or the Assembly.'

'Or the High Council,' suggested Magnus.

'Yes, that could be his . . .' Pug stood up and looked at Martuch and Hirea. 'I must speak to Nakor, tonight.'

'Impossible,' said the old fighter. 'We already said our official farewells as mentor and trainer. You can't go alone. There is no reason for anyone, let alone two Lessers, to come requesting a meeting with the Lesser of a recruit to the Imperial Guard.'

'Is there a way of keeping track of what the recruits are doing, in case an opportunity presents itself?' Pug asked.

'It's possible,' said Martuch. 'Members of the White are gathering in key locations throughout the Empire, but especially around the palace of the Karanas, the TeKarana, and the Dark One's Temple. We have not told anyone of what you have revealed about the Gardener and the Bloodwitches. For the time being let everyone believe we are under the guidance of a single, wise intelligence.' He sounded tired as he added, 'We must do what we must: there are no options, and we cannot choose our time. If we are to strike soon, then it will be soon.'

'Ready or not,' said Magnus.

'If I can reach Nakor, perhaps I can at least contribute to your being more ready than not.'

'I'll see what I can do,' said Martuch, standing up. He moved towards the ladder leading up to the surface. 'Rest for now. I fear that in a short time we may either have no time to rest, or be resting for eternity.'

Hirea waited until his friend had departed, then said, 'What you told us about the Gardener weighs heavy upon him. The Gardener was the one we believe was going to deliver us from the Dark One's madness.'

Pug considered his next words carefully. At last he said, 'You may still be right.' When Hirea looked at Pug with a curious expression, he added, 'Before he left us, the intelligence that was Macros, that tiny bit of him which had been placed in the Dasati body led me to believe that Nakor is the key to this. "Find Nakor", he said, and I believe that is the key. Nakor and Bek.'

'Bek,' said Hirea, almost as if it were a question. 'I have trained many warriors, human, some among the greatest of my lifetime, but that one is not a natural being. From what I know of your race, no human should be able to do what he does, and now, no Dasati can do what he does.' He looked at Pug. 'What is he, really?'

'I think he's a weapon,' said Pug. 'But only Nakor knows for certain.'

Hirea removed his sword-belt and laid it on an empty bunk. He stretched out on another. 'Then we must wait.'

Pug said, 'But not for long.' To Magnus he said, 'No matter what Martuch finds out, tonight we must find Nakor.'

★   ★   ★

335

Miranda was nearly frantic at the reports coming through the rift from Kelewan. A massive assault was underway in the Holy City. Despite the estrangement between her husband and the leader-ship at Stardock, many of those at the Academy were still friends or agents.

From all reports, a wave of thousands of Dasati had literally erupted through a rift in the chamber of the High Council. No Tsurani in that room or within half a mile of it had survived. The Imperial Guard, except for those around the Emperor at the old Acoma estates, had given their lives defending the Tsurani nobles. Alenca and half a dozen Tsurani Great Ones had died within minutes of the start of the assault. Others had arrived in response to the alarm and most had been killed as well. Most magic appeared to have no effect on the Dasati, though one enterprising magician who survived managed to do so by the expedient method of dropping a massive stone statue on two Deathknights. Thinking back to her own encounter with the lesser Dread up near the Peaks of the Quor, Miranda wondered why she hadn't thought to use her powers to pick up a boulder and drop it on one. It might have worked.

Miranda sat back in the chair usually occupied by Pug, feeling overwhelmed. Caleb entered a few minutes later.

'More word from Kelewan.'

'What?'

He handed her the message. 'The last Dasati

died less than two hours ago. Some were weakened, apparently, by exposure to the Tsurani sun or because of something in the air that sickened them. Whatever the cause, the last Deathknight was overwhelmed in a market square by a dozen merchants who tore it apart using tools and kitchen implements.'

'It's nice to know they can die,' said Miranda bitterly. 'What else do we know?'

'There are as many as fifty thousand dead or wounded.'

'Gods!' she exclaimed. 'That many?'

'It's estimated that ten thousand Dasati came into the city in three locations, two in the Imperial palace – one right in the heart of the High Council's meeting chamber, while they were in session, one in the centre of the administrative suite where all the palace functionaries work, and the third in the richest merchants' quarter in the Holy City.'

Miranda had already read a report which indicated that the High Council had been sitting when the attack came. She still had no word on the sum of the damage, but given the number of dead and wounded Caleb relayed, she was certain the damage had been appalling. 'Varen.'

'How do you know?'

'The Dasati could not have known how to do this much harm in so focused a way. Varen had to have told them. In a single attack they've decapitated the Empire of Tsuranuanni.'

337

'There's still the Emperor,' said Caleb.

'But who is there to command?' Miranda stood and began to pace as was her wont when under stress. 'Eldest sons? Daughters? Wives? The leadership of every house in the Empire has been disrupted, which means every political party and every clan as well. Right now the balance of power in the Empire is completely overturned, and for every house that has an eldest son groomed to rule and step in to his father's place, there are a score who are torn by grief and without effective leadership.

'This is a far worse disaster than had the Emperor been slain.'

Caleb said, 'At least he lives.'

'Yes, and that gives the Tsurani a single advantage.'

Caleb asked, 'What is that?'

Miranda turned and said, 'Blind obedience.'

Caleb's expression turned doubtful. 'How does that become an advantage if there's no effective leadership?'

'The Tsurani need generals. We can give them generals. They just have to be ordered to obey foreigners—'

'And if the Emperor orders them to obey generals from Midkemia, they will,' finished Caleb.

Miranda said, 'Now, how is that meeting Tomas asked for coming along?'

'Everyone who is willing to come will be here by sundown.'

'Good, I don't know exactly what Tomas will say to everyone, but I have a pretty good idea. I've only met him a few times, but from what your father has said about him, he's hardly a man to panic, but I think he's worried, Caleb.'

'Did Father ever speak to you about the Dread?' He sat down in a chair in the corner. Miranda sighed. 'There are lots of things your father doesn't talk about, mostly from the early days. I think it has to do with a lot of different things.'

'Such as?'

Caleb was not the sort to probe idly, so his mother knew him to be genuinely interested. She realized once again how different he was from Magnus and his parents. As the only member of the family without the ability to practise magic he was always somehow detached from their shared experiences, no matter how much they tried to include him in their lives and how much they loved him.

Miranda said, 'I don't have much time before Tomas's meeting, but I can speculate a little.' She closed her eyes as if remembering something, then said, 'I also haven't talked a great deal about my youth, and I am older than your father.'

He grinned. 'You've told us not to remind you.'

She returned the smile, for while she was truly not vain, she played the role as a way of nettling her husband and children. It was one of her failings, but a tiny one. 'What you remember, it's real. It doesn't matter how accurate your memory of

339

something is, it is real to you. What you perceive as reality *is* reality.'

'I'm not sure I understand,' said Caleb.

'I have no doubt, because of all of us, you most of all live in a real world, Caleb. You don't deal in the abstracted concepts of magic. You live a life of things you can touch, see, smell. You are out in the forests hunting, tracking—' She interrupted herself. 'If you see bear tracks, let us say. Artfully fashioned, created by some manner of boot-maker, it's a pair of boots worn by a man to make it look as if a bear had passed.'

Caleb shook his head. 'The depth would be wrong, because a bear weighs—'

Miranda raised her hands. 'That's not the point. Let us suppose I use magic to create perfect bear prints and you encounter them. What do you think?'

'Perfect?' he asked, not sure that was possible. Shrugging, he said, 'Fine, I find these perfect bear tracks. I think you're a bear.'

'Exactly. You follow them expecting a bear and until the moment you discover I was making the tracks, you think "bear, bear, bear". And then when you discover it wasn't a bear, what happens?'

'I don't know. I'm supposed to laugh at the joke?'

She almost rolled her eyes, but resisted the temptation. 'Until the moment you discover I made the tracks, if your brother showed up and asked you what you were doing, you would say you were tracking a bear. But from the moment you discover

I made the tracks, you think "Mother made the tracks". She looked him in the eyes. 'Do you understand?'

'I'm not entirely sure I do.'

'Your perception changed. From that moment onward, whenever you think of that set of tracks or tell the story to someone else, it's "Mother made those tracks". You might even tell someone, "I thought it was a bear", but in your mind there was no bear.'

'There was no bear,' said Caleb, now looking more confused.

Miranda laughed. 'If I hadn't given birth to you, I'd wonder who your parents really were.'

'I'm not stupid, Mother.'

'I know,' she said, laughing harder. 'It's just that you like only in the real world of things you can touch, feel, and smell.' Her humour vanished. 'Your father lives in a world of the mind, more than anyone I know, including myself or your grandfather. He may some day be eclipsed by your brother, but Magnus has a lifetime of experience to go through to catch up to your father. Your father is like others, though, in that his life experiences are real to him, and his perceptions of those experiences may have changed, *but not his feelings about them.*'

Caleb suddenly understood. 'So I can remember how I felt when I thought I was tracking the bear, even if now I have stopped thinking of it as a bear!'

'Yes! Your father went through a great deal of pain and suffering in his youth, and he's endured much since then, but the tribulations he faces now are being faced by a man with a lifetime of experience and hard-earned lessons.

'But the feelings of his youth, muted they may be, are still the feelings of his youth, and are remembered the way he felt at the time he lived them. Did he ever tell you of Princess Carline?'

'Not that I can recall.'

'She was the daughter of Lord Borric, and by adoption Pug's "cousin" of sorts, but when he was a lad in the kitchen at Crydee Castle, he thought himself in love with her. Fate conspired to give him the opportunity to press his suit, and then took it away from him, when he was captured by the Tsurani. She eventually wed a friend of his and became Duchess of Salador, and she died. But somewhere within your father is a tiny memory, a distantly recalled echo of a boy's love for an unobtainable princess.' She paused. 'He misses his wife,' she added calmly.

Caleb took a second then said, 'Katala.'

'I know your father loves me, and in many ways I am his perfect match, as he is mine, but to be as powerful as your father is, and to stand helplessly by and watch the woman you love die of a wasting disease . . .' She sighed. 'More than once I have tried to imagine what that must have felt like, and I can't. And he misses his children.'

Caleb nodded. William and Gamina had both

died in the battle for Krondor, at the end of the Serpentwar, years before Caleb's birth. 'It is easy to forget that I had a brother and sister who died before I was born.'

'But your father loved them desperately. And he never forgave himself for his estrangement from William at the time of William's death. It's one of the reasons he has never tried to tell you which path in life you should take.'

Caleb shrugged. 'I thought Father let me go wandering around, hunting, fishing, and trapping because I was useless at magic.'

Miranda smiled gently. 'If Magnus had wanted to wander around, hunting, fishing, and trapping, your father would have let him. That was the lesson he learned from William.'

'So Father doesn't talk much about the past.'

'No, mostly because he doesn't need to dredge up the painful memories; he has enough pain right now to deal with.'

'So you're saying Father never talked about the Dread.'

'Only a little, and I suspect he'd say much the same that Tomas has and will say.' She stood up. 'We must go. I really didn't mean to talk so much about your father, but the question you asked put me in mind of something that has long since been a struggle for me, the part of my husband I cannot touch: his memories and feelings for his first family.'

They fell silent, and at last Caleb said, 'I worry about him, too, Mother.'

Miranda's eyes welled up and she blinked. 'You'd think after all we've been through I'd get used to—' She cut herself off and stood up. 'We need to go and speak to our guests.'

Caleb followed his mother through the long halls of the villa until they reached a clearing to the west of the largest building on the island, save for the empty castle on the distant bluffs over-looking the sea. A series of benches had been erected, forming a semi-circle. Miranda had called together forty of the most powerful magicians not in the Conclave, an equal number of clerics of the various orders – most of whom had already reached an agreement with the Conclave, or who were more or less favourably disposed to them, and four of the most senior members of the island community. Many of these gathered folk greeted Miranda and Caleb, others were intent upon their own conversations. She ignored the preening representative of the faction known as the Hands of Korsh at the Academy. Keshian traditionalists only slightly less hidebound and reactionary than the other faction, the Wand of Watoomb, they were too caught up in their own self-importance to be of any political use. The good thing was that they had isolated themselves from social conflict and national politics so effectively that neither the Kingdom nor the Empire viewed them as a threat. Had either monarchy possessed a hint of just how much magical ability existed on the Island of Stardock, she was certain their reactions would be quite different. She also liked the fact that Stardock drew attention away from Sorcerer's Isle. To the rest of the world a mad magic-user, 'the Black Sorcerer', lived here alone. Over the years that guise had included her father, her husband, Nakor, and any number of students adept enough to scare off pirates or more innocent vessels that had wandered off course. A little blue light sparking in a tower window of the old castle, some horrible noises, and if necessary a hideous illusion or two on the beach below, and they gave this place a wide berth.

Now Sorcerer's Isle resembled a spring garden party at the royal palace at Roldem, save that there were few beautiful ladies and no dashing young courtiers present.

Miranda said, 'Thank you all for coming,' and all conversation stopped. 'Tomas of Elvandar should be here in a while. But before he arrives here, I wish to say something.

'Each of you is known to the others, if not by sight, then by reputation. Each of you is here because you are acknowledged as both a master of your arts and an influential member of your particular orders or societies. I can do no more than beg you to believe that what you are about to hear from Lord Tomas, as fantastic as it may sound, is the truth.' She heard the dragon approach before she turned and saw it. Those sitting in the semi-circle in front of her looked up in astonishment.

Caleb walked over to stand next to his mother and whispered, 'Gold is better.'

The dragon Tomas rode now dwarfed the red one he had ridden earlier. This majestic creature had a head the size of a freight wagon, and its wingspan could have covered the entire width of the main building on the island, with the tips touching the ground. The massive dragon touched down as lightly as a leaf fluttering from a tree and Tomas leaped down from its shoulders, more of a drop than jumping from a rooftop. He thanked the dragon and it sprang into the air, spiralling away in a steep climb into the evening air.

Without preamble, Tomas said, 'That you are here means that Miranda and Pug have confidence in you, and confidence will be required. I bring you a warning, and it is most dire.

'I am named Tomas, Consort to the most radiant queen, Aglaranna, ruler of Elvandar. I am by her appointment and the consent of her subjects Warleader of Elvandar. I wear the mantle of Ashen-Shugar, Ruler of the Eagles' Reaches, and carry his alien memories, though I am as mortal as any here. I have been allotted a longer life span than other humans, but I know that eventually death awaits me.

'I have travelled beyond the stars and into the Halls of Death herself, and have spoken with gods and demons. I tell you this so that you may know something of what I am, and what I have seen, for now I must speak of the Dread.

'Some of you may know the name from your ancient lore, others may have never heard it, but in the end, it is all the same, for you know nothing of them. I am the only mortal being on this world who knows of the Dread, save one, and he has travelled a long distance hence. So, put aside any preconceptions you may have and listen.'

Caleb whispered, 'He just told us all to forget about the bear, didn't he?'

His mother nodded.

Tomas began his tale.

When he had finished, the word that best described the assembled magicians and priests was 'shaken'. Without embellishment or dramatics, Tomas had told them the tale of the Valheru's first and only encounter with the Dread, in a realm called 'the Boundary' by the Dragon Lords. It was a place between the realms and the Void and, like the Hall of Worlds, the City Forever and the Garden, a place that defied rational description.

Tomas said, 'There is a place, the Peaks of the Quor, in that part of Great Kesh closest to the Island Kingdom of Roldem. It is there we discovered a leak in the barriers of reality, a place where this world and the Boundary co-existed. Somehow children of the Dread – beings almost benign by the standards of the Void – found their way into the Boundary and then from there into this world. They were playing: yet that play was deadly. Miranda and I excised their existence from this world and I hope that ended the risk, but I asked for you all to be here today to warn you that there is a possibility the risk is not over. For if the Dread ever find their way into our realm, we shall have almost no time to respond.'

'How can we respond in any rational fashion to a threat such as the one you describe?' asked the High Priest of the Order of Dala in Krondor. The elderly cleric wore his simple white robes today rather than the richly embroidered raiment of his office.

'That is why I asked Miranda to call this meeting now,' said Tomas. 'It may be that the need will never arise, but it's far better for us to be prepared for something that never comes than to be unprepared when there is need.'

'What can you tell us of these beings?' asked a magician named Komis from Stardock. Unlike most who affected the dark robes originally worn by Pug when he founded the Academy, Komis had chosen richly ornamented robes of dark plum, edged with white cord at the collar, cuffs, and hem. His youthful features belied his position in the Academy where he was a senior instructor in what was being called shadow magic, the study of energies linked to the other realms. His studies lay at the heart of most of the questions Tomas raised.

'Little, save that their very touch can draw out life-energy and wither flesh in moments if you have no means to protect yourself. The more powerful they are, the more intelligent. Those we destroyed yesterday were little more than mindless youngsters, unable to speak – or at least unable to speak in any fashion we can apprehend – but eager to experience the hunt and taste flesh in our realm.

'The more powerful among them can be understood: I have spoken to one and know where one is imprisoned.'

'We must examine it!' exclaimed the High Priest of the Order of Ishap in Rillanon. The Ishapians were the oldest order extant, the only public order to serve one of the greater gods, and while each temple was autonomous, the Ishapians wielded great influence: more than one inter-temple war had been prevented by both sides appealing to the servants of Ishap for guidance.

Tomas shook his head. 'The journey is arduous and the destination is almost impossible to access.' He thought for a moment, then said, 'Let me consider such an expedition, for by combining arts . . .' He looked at Miranda who made a noncommittal gesture. She knew what he was speaking of. A Dreadmaster had been trapped by Pug and Tomas in the deepest bowels of a black citadel in the heart of the City Forever, a place only bordering on reality.

One of the magicians said, 'If we know its nature, we might fashion a spell of binding!'

'And banishment!' added a priest. 'If it is not of this realm, it can be sent away with the proper exorcisms.'

That triggered an animated discussion among those in attendance. Tomas motioned to Miranda to step aside and when they were out of earshot of the others, he said, 'We're off to a good start.'

'I hope so,' she answered. 'You did a masterful job of underplaying the menace at just the right time, so as to make them look even more dire.' Her features darkened. 'Though I really don't know how much more dire things can be.'

'The Dread can not be truly killed. The Dreadmaster Pug and I captured in the City Forever is almost certainly still alive, if someone hasn't freed him.' Tomas glanced over at the discussions. 'There will be many questions for me to answer tonight. May I stay here?'

'Of course. You never have to ask. You are family.'

'More than ever, I wish Pug were here. His knowledge of what we face might be better than my own.'

She said, 'I know one thing: you can't wish him back any more ardently than I do.'

'Of course.'

She said, 'In all of this, I can't escape the feeling that somehow everything is interconnected. The arrival of those creatures near the Quor, and the Dasati. Can it be possible that before he fled Varen was also trying to fetch creatures from the Void to this world?'

'Anything is possible. Varen is by any measure insane. But he is a servant of the Nameless, and while the Nameless is often content to inflame his servants and send them out to cause mayhem, he would never be so foolish as to think the Dread in this realm could serve him. The gods above all others are foe to the Dread, for the gods represent the essence of our reality and the Dread are as far removed from our reality as anything in the universe.'

'When you go to study that Dread you have locked away,' said Miranda, 'I want to come with you. I need to know if there's a way I can kill one, or at least get rid of it.'

Tomas agreed. 'Now,' he added. 'I should talk to some of these men of power and influence.'

'When do you seek the Quor?' she asked.

'Soon, in a matter of days. Why?'

'Because I would like to go with you.'

'We'll see,' he answered as he turned away. 'There are things it is sometimes better not to know.'

She could only nod in agreement. How well she knew that.

CHAPTER 15

INVESTIGATION

Pug vanished.

Martuch had been expecting it but still he went wide-eyed when Pug cast his spells. The decision to seek out Nakor and Bek had already been made when more reports of what had occurred on Kelewan reached them. Agents of the White passed along snatches of information throughout the afternoon, and into the evening. Alone, each of these snippets provided a glimpse of the situation, but when put together, the result was horrific.

Three columns of attackers had been inserted into Kelewan by Dasati Deathpriests creating a rift-like 'portal' that allowed dozens of Deathknights to pass through each minute. Three locations in the Holy City had been targeted: the council chamber in the palace, the wing set aside for the First Advisor and all other ministers and their aides, and the heart of the merchants' district.

Pug knew instantly that the Dasati had derived their intelligence from Leso Varen. The Dasati would have seen the wisdom in destroying the leadership and surrounding bureaucracy but the assault on the merchants would have been beyond their imagination. There was nothing remotely resembling a merchant class in this realm, and the concept of disrupting the financial underpinnings of the Empire would be so alien to them that it could only have come from Varen.

Pug's mind was spinning. If he could discover who was in touch with Varen here, then perhaps when he returned, if he returned, he might be able to find the malignant butcher.

Martuch said, 'This is madness.'

Pug laughed. He found himself suddenly unable to stop laughing. Hirea and the two Lessers who served the White stood in obvious shock at the sound coming from the seemingly empty air. The effect was doubly troubling, for not only was the source of the sound not apparent but, to the Dasati mind, laughter was closely linked to pain and death.

'Father, what is it?' asked Magnus, and Pug's laughter stopped.

'I'm sorry,' said Pug. He took a deep breath and let it out slowly. 'I was suddenly struck by the enormity of what we have to do and then to have Martuch call it madness . . . everything we have encountered since the advent of Leso Varen has been wholesale madness. So I was overcome by a sense of how mad must it be for what we're doing now to be singled out as madness in the midst of all this other insanity. I don't know why it struck me as funny, but it did.'

Magnus said, 'You're just tired, Father.'

'We all are.'

Hirea said, 'I see no humour here.' He stood up from where he had been sitting quietly. 'If you must do this thing to reach your friends, it is best we do it soon. There is a very small amount of time left before our presence anywhere near the Palace Guards' enclave will be noticed.' Without another word he climbed the ladder to the trapdoor. He lifted the door and peered about, making sure no one was in that part of the grove before continuing up.

Pug and Magnus followed, Magnus telling Martuch when he was clear of the ladder. The warrior and the two Lessers followed, and when all were above ground, the trapdoor was replaced.

It was evening, but enough was going on in the city that two warriors riding as if on urgent business would hardly be noticed. Martuch had been adamant about the need to be into the palace and out again before dawn. He had given Pug explicit instructions on how to reach the most likely location to find Nakor and Bek: the recruits' barracks.

Pug and Magnus mounted behind the two warriors and held tightly as the war-trained varnin were unsettled by the additional weight on their backs. Martuch and Hirea moved off at a brisk pace, for two riders in the middle of a supposedly empty orchard at this time of day might arouse interest.

They rapidly made their way to the first tunnel

into the city proper and if anyone took note of their passing, it was not apparent. Quickly they moved down busy boulevards, though they were less crowded than would be usual. The recent Great Culling had taken its toll. While death was a constant in Dasati life, there was a hint of anticipation and anxiety in the air, that somehow the Culling was but a foreshadowing of more troubles approaching.

When they had first come to this realm, Pug had noticed that many Deathknights would venture into the evening without benefit of armour, preferring comfortable robes and riding on less temperamental mounts than war-varnin. And many more ladies of the Dasati thronged the streets, moving freely from one location to another, from those places designated for food and beverage, akin to the Midkemian inn or restaurant, and places reserved for Lessers of particular skill groups, the closest thing the Dasati had to shops; but tonight there were hardly any women in sight and no man was abroad who wasn't wearing armour, save for Lessers following Deathknights.

Of Deathpriests and Hierophants he saw none. All were busy and that was another sign that something important was underway. Pug didn't know if it meant preparation for the invasion of Kelewan – though he thought the leaders of the great houses and the societies would be given some warning to muster – or perhaps another Culling, should the

Dark One need more death-magic to create more portals.

As they reached the precinct whose entrance was closest to the quarters likely to house Bek and Nakor, Martuch and Hirea reined in their varnin. Martuch spoke without looking back. 'We will take backstreets and circle the precinct. We will return here at sunrise. If you are able to, be visible and we will stop as if you belong to us and have you follow behind. If not, we will pause. Speak to us if you can and let us know what you need. If we do not find you . . .' He let the thought go unfinished. Pug knew what he meant.

'If we don't find you,' he said softly. 'We will find our own way back to the Grove.'

Hirea said, 'Good fortune.'

'And you,' answered Pug.

When the two riders had departed, Pug said, 'Magnus?'

'Here, Father,' came a voice to his right. Magnus reached out and made contact.

'We need to stay close to the wall. One touch by even a Lesser and we are undone.'

They hurried into the tunnel, past a series of closed doors and curtained windows.

'Everyone seems to be keeping out of sight,' said Magnus softly.

'That's to our benefit,' answered his father.

Down the long hallway they scurried. The corridor was wide enough for half a dozen riders to pass shoulder to shoulder, but it was deserted.

Pug worried that it was so quiet someone might hear the sound of their passing, but he pressed on. There were no guards anywhere to be seen which seemed very strange, but then Pug remembered he was not dealing with human rulers here. Even the Emperors of Tsuranuanni or Great Kesh had over the ages been confronted by ambitious nobles and threats from within as well as by enemies across their borders. But here, the TeKarana commanded almost universal obedience – the only exception being the White – such a minority as to be no more than a myth to the masses of the Dasati Empire. When the vast majority of males in the population are under arms and loyal to the point of fanaticism, security becomes an afterthought.

Martuch had given him precise instructions on how to find the new recruits' barracks and they soon reached the first dormitory. But once through the door they realized the enormity of the task, for arrayed on each side of the aisle in which they found themselves were hundreds of bunks, in which sleeping Dasati youths rested. How to find Bek?

Lessers were scattered around the room on sleeping mats on the floor, making any attempt to walk between the sleeping cots very risky. But they could walk the perimeter of the room, and this they did, moving quickly and quietly through the first room, but seeing no one who resembled the huge young warrior or Nakor.

They passed into a second room, and a third, and there was still no sign of either Bek or Nakor. Several times sleeping young Deathknights would stir, but Pug found it remarkable that the Dasati didn't snore, nor did they seem to move much when sleeping; to a man they all slept on their backs and while there was some variation in position, none of them slept on their sides or stomachs. Pug wondered if it was some sort of survival trait: not moving while you're asleep lessens the chance of a predator finding you, or perhaps it allowed the sleeper a quicker response time if attacked. He didn't know, but he found the almost uniform sleeping pose oddly disturbing.

But when they reached the fourth chamber, their fortunes changed. In a far corner they found Bek sitting up on his bunk. Nakor sat on the floor, speaking to him in a very low voice. As they neared, Pug could hear him saying, 'Soon things will change and you will have a great deal to do in a very short time.'

Bek whispered, 'Yes, Nakor. I understand.'

'Good,' Nakor whispered in return. 'I may not always be with you so I must be certain you know exactly what it is you're supposed to do if I'm not there.'

'I understand,' repeated the young warrior.

'Good. Now, go to sleep. I must speak with Pug and Magnus.'

Bek lay back in the same position as all the other Dasati warriors, and Nakor turned, looking right at Pug and Magnus. 'I was wondering when you'd find me.'

Still invisible, Pug asked, 'How?'

'Later,' said Nakor, standing up. 'Make me invisible, too. If they find me wandering around, I'll be killed. There's something I must show you.'

Soon Nakor was as invisible as Pug and Magnus. He whispered, 'We must go through that door on the left over there,' — it was clear which door he indicated — 'and then down the corridor to the right. I'll tell you where next when we reach an intersection.'

He moved silently out of the barracks and when they passed through the door, Pug could see that they had left the last of the recruits' barracks. Nakor's whisper carried well enough that they didn't have to strain to hear, for this corridor, like the others, was empty. 'Something big is going to happen, soon, Pug. Everyone is terrified. Even the Deathknights. I don't know why. I've never seen fear in a Dasati before. I mean, I've seen cringing Lessers, but that is as much a part of their role as true fear – any Lesser who thought he had an opportunity to kill a Deathknight or Deathpriest and win status would do so without hesitation – but even Deathknights can barely conceal their trepidation.'

'I can feel it,' answered Magnus. 'Something is making them afraid.'

Pug let out a long sigh. 'I have been battling disquiet, too, since we left the Grove.'

'We all have strong minds,' answered Nakor. 'Think how it must be to these people, who don't know fear.'

'Where's it coming from?' asked Pug.

'That's what I want to show you.' They reached the junction and Nakor said, 'Now we go to the left, and it's a long way. I'm going to run and I suggest you do the same. When you reach the end, you'll know where to stop.'

'Wait,' said Magnus. 'I can still fly us if we stay low.'

They rose off the ground again, and sped along the corridor. Pug hoped his son's control was as precise as it needed to be, for he had no doubt magical skills would be of little aid if they went bouncing off a stone wall.

The corridor went on for what must have been miles; unlike the others it was unlit. Pug now had to completely rely on the illumination from the stones, invisible to the human eye, but providing a low residue of shapes and textures to the Dasati eye. He would miss this ability, he thought, when he got home . . . and felt a sudden stab of pain, an anxiety he had not experienced.

He knew he would somehow get home. He had been promised that by no less than the Goddess of Death, for she had foretold his fate, and he was doomed to live until he had served the gods' purpose and that fate also included watching everyone he loved die before him. He would get home, but he had no way of knowing if Magnus or Nakor would.

'You can slow down now,' said Nakor. 'We're coming to the end.'

They reached the end of the very long corridor, Pug calculating they must have flown more than two miles. 'I almost got caught here, last time,' said Nakor. 'I wasn't invisible. It's a trick you'd think I'd have learned by now. I talked my way out of getting killed.'

Pug was amused, and wished he could have heard that exchange, for he had no doubt the Dasati who had been here had been as confused as any human once Nakor got through with one of his confidence tricks. 'You'll have to tell me about it some time.'

'We can get visible now,' said Nakor.

Pug ended the spell of invisibility.

'Where are we?'

'This is a most clever and useful thing,' said Nakor. They stood on a platform and Pug could feel a vibration through his feet and heard a deep and distant thrumming noise. 'Soon a thing like a wagon is going to come by and we are going to get on it. Move quickly because it doesn't slow down.'

'What—?' began Magnus, just as the device Nakor had described appeared.

It was like a wagon, in so far as it had a flat bed and what would have been a driver's bench, except there were no animals drawing it. And rather than a cargo bed in the back, there were more benches. 'Jump!' Nakor shouted.

They did, and all three arrived within one bench of one another.

'It takes some practice, I guess,' said Nakor.

'What is it?'

'I don't know what they call it here, but I think of it as a really big tram.'

'Tram?' asked Magnus.

'Miners use them,' said his father. 'Dolgan the dwarf king in the Grey Towers told me about them. We were travelling through an ancient mine and I saw an abandoned tram off in a side tunnel.'

Nakor said, 'I've seen them down in Kesh, in the copper and tin mines. They have big wheels so they can be pulled by mules. They load them up with ore and haul it out of the mine. They use little ones they push by hand to fill the big ones. Sometimes they lay roadways of wood.'

'How does this thing work?'

'There's some massive contrivance, an engine of some sort, perhaps water-driven or by some other means, that moves along on a giant tether in a big loop. If you ride it long enough, you end up back where you got on.' He paused. 'Hang on, there's a place ahead where we—' Before he could finish there was a hard jolt and suddenly the tram picked up speed. 'I think there's a device that moves it from a slow tether to a fast one. There's another jolt when we slow down at the other end.'

'Who built it?' The Dasati?' asked Magnus. Pug

understood his son's question. The constructions on this world and Kosridi were massive, beyond the abilities of people on Midkemia or Kelewan who had built some impressive structures by human standards. But the scale of the building and engineering in this world required such things as they had observed: massive doors beyond any known means of moving; arching bridges that spanned miles and defied the imagination. Nothing they had seen of the Dasati indicated that this was a significant population with the talents and abilities to build such things, nor was there a hint of any new construction or projects. To all appearances, it was a society stagnant to the point of necrosis.

'Where does this take us?' asked Pug.

'Into the heart of madness,' replied Nakor as the tram sped along into a vast tunnel leading to the darkness.

The tunnel seemed endless. Pug lost track of time, though he was certain they had been moving for less than half an hour. Still, at the rate of speed they were travelling, they must be at least ten or more miles from where they boarded. 'How much longer?'

'We're about half way. That's why I said we had to hurry. And we cannot linger at our destination. Or at least I can't. You and Magnus can decide what to do when I show you what you need to see. I have to get back before they rouse the recruits lest Bek does something . . . well, something that Bek might do.'

Pug noticed that since coming to the second realm, Nakor's usually cheery spirits were all but absent. He was subdued, and Pug could understand why: not only were the Dasati a grim and bloody people by human standards, but their concept of humour was almost exclusively limited to pain and suffering. There was more. Over the last few weeks, there had been a growing sense of despair and fear, and the attitudes and habits of the population in the city had been changing. Fewer ventured out after dark, and markets that had been thronging when Pug had first arrived on Omadrabar were all but deserted. Groups of Lessers scurried in the shadows and cringed visibly as Deathknights rode past. Deathpriests and Hierophants were all but absent from public view, being locked away in the black heart of the Dark One's temple, involved in preparations for the Dark One's next horror.

Martuch and Hirea were even more stoic than usual, barely speaking unless asked direction questions. Pug was left with the impression that there was usually a sense of relief after a Great Culling, a sense of survival and relative calm. But this time something was different. Rumours abounded in the city, but no one really knew what was coming next, for nothing like this had ever occurred before. The loss of two of the TeKarana's legions was a sacrifice unprecedented in Dasati history.

The tram jerked and slowed and Nakor said, 'We get off in a moment.'

They stood up, and when the tram moved along-side a long platform, they all stepped off. 'This way,' said the little gambler.

They hurried down another long corridor and then Nakor stopped them. 'From here I got lost, and the only reason I wasn't killed was because Bek behaved himself back at the training barracks so no one noticed his Lesser was not there for a day. I wandered around and found this thing I must show you. But now that you're here we can get there fast.' To Pug he said, 'You need to make us invisible again.' To Magnus he said, 'You need to fly us, straight up there.' He pointed up into the gloom above them. 'It goes very far up. Then you'll need to fly us straight that way,' he pointed straight ahead, 'and then we'll need to go down, very far down, into a very dark place. Are you ready?'

Pug said, 'Yes,' and wove his enchantment, rendering all three of them invisible.

'Hold on,' said Magnus and Pug gripped Nakor with one hand, and his son with the other. They rose straight up into the air, rising rapidly until there was nothing but gloom above and below.

'How far up does this go?' asked Pug.

'Seventy-five flights of stairs, but I lost count so it may be seventy-six or seven.'

They reached the topmost floor and Nakor said, 'A bit more, over the rooftops.'

Magnus took them up until they were higher than the highest roof. The sky above was still lost in darkness. 'How big is this place?' asked Magnus.

'Really big,' answered Nakor. 'I used a couple of tricks and the best I can tell is that the roof is another two thousand feet above us.'

'Who could build such a thing?' asked Pug.

'And how?' said Magnus.

'Only the gods, I think,' replied Nakor. 'Only the old gods of the Dasati.'

Remembering the Necropolis of the Gods in Novindus, Pug said, 'Perhaps. Certainly I can't imagine any mortal being building this.'

'Neither can I,' said Nakor. 'And I can imagine a lot of things.'

They flew above the huge set of rooms below them, and at last came to a vast cavern. 'How big, do you think?' asked Pug.

'Miles,' said Nakor. 'They have a lifting device I found a distance from here, and it took a long time for me to get where we are going. But no matter where I was, or what sort of tricks I used, I couldn't see the far side. It was like standing on the edge of a great bay where you can see coasts curving to your right and left, but vanishing into the mist, and you can't see beyond the horizon.'

'Where are we?' asked Magnus.

'Ah,' said Nakor. 'I thought you'd have deduced it; we're in the Temple of the Dark One himself.' Softly, he added, 'He's down there.'

★   ★   ★

Downward they sped, through a murk unmatched by anything Pug had ever encountered, for not only was it devoid of light, it was as if life itself had been leached out of the very fabric of reality. Soon they saw a light below them, an angry red-orange glow with a tiny fringe of green at the edges. 'The god is down there,' said Nakor, softly, as if fearful of being heard.

'But won't we be seen?' asked Magnus.

'It seems occupied with its own concerns,' said Nakor. 'At least the last time I was here, it didn't pay attention to me.'

They continued down, until a shape emerged in the middle of the red-orange glow. At this distance it was a large featureless black mass, but as they approached they could see it was undulating around the edges. 'What is that?' whispered Magnus.

Nakor said, 'That is the Dark God.'

Pug looked astonished. He had interacted with the gods on Midkemia but they had always presented themselves in roughly human form. This being, however, looked nothing remotely like a human or even a Dasati.

It was enormous, easily hundreds of yards across and its shape was difficult to apprehend, because the edges kept moving, flowing and undulating, as if a supple bag of some material had been filled with oil or water, yet it moved with a slower motion than liquid. Pug was reminded of silk flowing slowly in a breeze. There was no colour on the surface of the being, yet it could not properly be called black. The sensation was that of a void of colour and light, without the accompanying energies visible to the Dasati eye. Evil, was how Pug thought of it, yet even that was attributing too much vibrancy and dimension to it. It was devoid of anything he could recall . . . save for one time! He pushed aside a stab of fear bordering on panic.

The head of the creature was massive, but dwarfed by the enormity of the rest of its body, rising up at least four feet above the torso, on some semblance of a neck.

'Somewhere out there,' said Pug, 'there are arms and legs.' There was a tone in his voice Magnus and Nakor had never heard before.

'What is it, Father?'

Pug looked more closely at the creature's head, at the two searing red slashes of glowing orange light in the black mask. Around the head, like a crown, floated flickering tiny red flames. 'I know it,' he said.

'What?' asked Nakor. 'What do you mean, you know it?'

'It is no god, Nakor, or at least not as we understand such things.'

Magnus said, 'What is it then?'

'The Dark God of the Dasati is not of this realm, or of any other we comprehend. The Dark God of the Dasati is a creature of the void. We are looking at a Dreadlord.'

'What?' asked Magnus, steering them away from

the Dreadlord towards the edge of the vast pit. Little was known of the dread, but he had heard enough to understand why his father's voice was forced to calm; his father was frightened, and Magnus had never experienced that before. 'What is it doing here?' he asked, his own calm barely maintained.

'Ah,' said Nakor. 'That explains much.' He sounded surprisingly unfazed by the revelation. Magnus glanced at Nakor and saw the little gambler had his eyes fixed on the Dreadlord, studying it as they moved across the pit.

They could feel a strange heat rising, a heat that was both unnatural and troubling. The red-orange light from below seemed to liquefy, as if the Dreadlord was squatting in a huge lake. Pug had a worrying idea. 'See that green flame dancing across the surface of the liquid?'

'Yes,' answered Nakor. 'Life trying to escape.'

Magnus said, 'We can see life?'

'I've seen it once before, when your mother and I helped Calis destroy the Lifestone and set free all the trapped souls within.'

'Like so many things we can't see as humans, we can see with Dasati eyes,' answered Nakor. 'This monstrous entity is living in a sea of captured life. It is bloated to a massive . . . thing, huge beyond its original capacity. It has become engorged, like a glutton at a feast that never ends, swollen like a monstrous tick endlessly sucking blood from a dog. Look!'

As they approached the edge of the vast pit, they could see that there was a ceremony underway. A dozen Deathpriests stood arrayed in two rows, behind which stood armed Deathknights wearing orange armour. Pug assumed they were temple guards. A long line of shuffling Lessers came inching towards the edge of the pit, and when each reached the edge, a priest would give a quick benediction and they would be pushed over the edge. The Lessers fell into the roiling surface of the liquid, which Pug now understood was mostly blood, and sank from view.

Those who hesitated were picked up and thrown in by Deathknights. Most wept or had a shocked look of resignation on their faces, but a few revealed wide-eyed panic and some tried to bolt. Those who did were cut down by the Deathknights standing behind the priests, and their bodies were rolled into the mass.

'Over there!' said Nakor, and Pug looked to where he pointed. A small raised dais, perhaps used by some high-ranking official, perhaps even the TeKarana himself, had been erected here from which to observe the endless sacrifice.

Nakor said, 'Magnus, can you remember this place well enough to bring us back here in a hurry if you need to?'

'I think getting us *out* of here in a hurry would be a better idea.'

'That too,' whispered Nakor. He added, 'Some-times the creature seems to sleep but I wouldn't want to try to sneak in that way again. Last time I was with a bunch of those poor souls who are being fed to that monster so I was unnoticed when I walked in.'

'How did you get out?' asked Pug.

'I used some tricks,' Nakor said. 'Come, we need to start back: I don't want to leave Bek un-attended.'

'Nakor, is Bek the Godkiller?'

'Maybe, maybe not,' answered the little gambler as Magnus lifted himself and his two companions into the air. 'But he has a role to play. When I'm sure it's safe to leave him, there are some places I must visit.'

'Where?' asked Pug.

'There are rooms all over this temple, many containing scrolls and things that no one looks at any more. These were once a great people, Pug. Magnificent even, and I think it *was* the Dasati who built these amazing places. That meant they were like the Ipiliac. Much of their creative great-ness was drained away by the need to survive between the realms. Here, the Dasati turned all their energies to build, to create, to investigate. They must have had great scholars, poets, artists, musicians, healers, and engineers living here. They must have been almost gods themselves when this horror came to them.'

'There is so much we may never know,' said Pug. 'How a creature of the void came to live at the heart of this world . . .'

'Better go faster, Magnus,' said Nakor. 'Time is fleeting.'

Magnus used more speed in leaving than he did in approaching, so they rapidly reached the top of the enormous pit. As they descended down to the tunnel leading to the tram, Nakor said, 'Whatever Bek's role may be, I believe he needs to try to kill it.'

'But you said you didn't know if he was the Godkiller,' said Magnus.

'Yes, he may not be, but he needs to try.'

'How do you know, Nakor?' asked Pug.

The little gambler emerged from his invisibility. 'I don't know how I know, Pug. I know a lot of things and I don't know how I know them. I just do. Now, we had better move along.'

Pug and Magnus became visible too and Nakor turned to hurry down the tunnel towards the tram. The father and son exchanged a silent question. Both knew that Pug had not removed the invisibility from Nakor. Nakor had done it himself.

Pug hurried along after the strange little man wondering if he would ever learn the truth about him.

CHAPTER 16

SUN-ELVES

Miranda screamed.

Unable to contain her frustration, she threw the message across the floor. She swore, then said, 'The King won't see me.'

Caleb said, 'It's understandable, Mother. Father hasn't been on good terms with the Crown of the Isles for many years. In fact, he hasn't been on good terms with any nobles save those working with the Conclave.'

'I'm your mother! I don't expect you to be reasonable. I expect you to agree with me.'

Caleb was motionless for a moment, then he started to laugh. 'I see. I'm sorry.'

'I'm losing my sanity,' said Miranda as she began to pace in her husband's study. 'I fear I'll never see your father again, despite his reassurances that he will return. I fear for Magnus and even Nakor.' Softly she added, 'I really don't know what to do next, Caleb.'

Caleb had never seen his mother so distraught. She even sounded helpless as she admitted her uncertainty. His mother was many things, but never in her life had helpless been one of them.

There had to be a reason for this lack of decisiveness. 'What is it?'

She sat down in her husband's chair. 'I'm agonizing over what your father would do in this situation. Would he simply appear in the King's private chambers and threaten him?'

'Hardly,' said Caleb. With a wry smile he added, 'You might, perhaps, but not Father.'

She glared at him a moment, then was forced to smile. 'Yes, you're right.'

'I think he'd find those nobles of influence who are most favourably disposed towards us and speak with them.'

'That's either old Lord James or Lord Erik.'

'James is, by some convolution, a cousin,' said Caleb. 'That might have some weight in persuading him to intercede with the King. Erik, on the other hand, is an old companion of Nakor, and he's seen at first hand what enemies like the Dasati can do. He stood at Nightmare Ridge.'

That one statement spoke volumes. Miranda knew that those who had suffered and fought through the Serpentwar would understand the price of not preparing, not standing staunchly against the coming insanity. If the Dasati were not stopped in Kelewan, there was nothing to prevent them from invading Midkemia next. The problem was that few who had stood at Nightmare Ridge, or who had fought in any fashion against the Emerald Queen's army during the Serpentwar, were still alive. And even those who were still living were in their seventies or eighties. Those few nobles who hadn't retired to their estates were outnumbered by younger men, to whom the Serpentwar was just a fight their fathers or even grandfathers talked about. Like the Riftwar, or the War of Jon the Pretender, or so many struggles with Great Kesh, it was just another bit of history, and it couldn't be like that now, could it?

Miranda weighed her son's words silently. Outside, a bird called and she glanced out to see that it was a beautiful morning on the island, and the was sun burning off the pre-dawn mist. 'You're right. We need men on our side who understand what is at risk. I'll send a message to Lord Erik.' She thought for a moment, then said, 'But I will not give up on Lord James. I think, though, I'll need an intermediary.'

'Who?'

'Jim Dasher, his grandson. He's apparently more in touch with what it is we're facing, since he found those creatures of the void. I will see him soon, and ask him to intercede with the Duke of Rillanon.'

'When are you going to see him?'

'This afternoon,' said Miranda, 'which is in about an hour given how far east of here the Peaks of the Quor are.'

'I'll be interested in what you find there.'

Miranda stood and went to her son's side. Putting her hand on his shoulder, she said, 'I know you chafe at being in charge here, and I've stolen

Lettie from you for a while, so you don't even have the assistant I promised you. But if she's going to take over for you some day, I need her to be aware of every significant issue facing the Conclave.'

'Take over for me?'

'You don't think I'm not aware of how difficult it is for you to be a leader, Caleb? You've always been a loner, in so many ways. I don't know if not being a magician caused it, or if you would have been this way in any event. I was thrilled when you found Marie and brought her and the boys here, for I despaired that you would ever find a mate – I wouldn't have minded some grand-children who were really yours, because Magnus certainly hasn't shown any signs of giving me any.'

Caleb laughed, genuinely touched by his mother's concern. 'I'm a man full grown, as they say in Yabon, Mother. I've made many choices beyond those set for me by you and Father. I wouldn't be your son if I hadn't come to the same conclusions you had: we serve because we must.'

'Thank you,' she whispered.

Caleb added, 'And I wouldn't worry about Magnus. He has been in love . . . once.'

She nodded. Magnus's very young, foray into romance had broken his heart, and he had retreated from matters of intimacy, save with his family. She worried as mothers do, but she often reminded herself that she hadn't married and started a family until well past two hundred years of age. 'Now, I must go. I'm anxious to meet these Quor. I am amazed that there is no mention of them anywhere in your father's library. Between what he inherited from your grandfather and what he's added since then . . .' She took a slow, deep breath. 'It's strange.'

'Before you go, regarding the coming war, what of Kesh and the other Kingdoms?'

'The Eastern Kingdoms are of little matter; we have some allies, but they are low on resources. Kesh feels a debt since we saved the Empire from Varen. She'll answer the call. But what I fear most is what will happen when I ask for the next favour.'

'Refugees?'

'Yes. There are going to be millions of them. Potentially more than the entire population of Kesh and the Kingdom combined. No ruler is going to welcome that many aliens with loyalties to other rulers over their borders. No, we need another solution.'

'Wynet?'

'The plains above the great escarpment would be perfect, if your father hadn't already settled the Saaur survivors up there. We've remained cordial with them all these years largely by ignoring one another. If we put a hundred thousand Tsurani warriors next to them, they might become irritable.'

'There are a lot of islands to the west.'

Miranda said, 'The Sunsets and the archipelagos beyond? Fine if you care to live in a hut and fish for all your meals, but if you want to revive a displaced society . . .' She sighed. 'What we need is an empty world.'

'Is there one?'

'Your father would know,' she said with scantly hidden bitterness.

Caleb kept silent. His parents loved each other deeply, but as with many married couples each had qualities that annoyed the other. For his father, Caleb knew it was Miranda's insistence on having her own plans and ideas irrespective of what the consensus of the Conclave was; she even had agents of her own who were not part of his father's larger organization. As for his mother, Caleb knew that she envied, perhaps even resented Pug's vast knowledge of worlds beyond Midkemia. For all her powers, Kelewan and the Hall were the only two realms beyond Midkemia that she had explored, and she would never have experienced either of them had it not been for Pug.

'I'll be leaving for the Sun Elves' enclave in a little while. Go and get a bite to eat and then come back.'

Caleb nodded and yawned. 'Sorry. Been up since before dawn.'

She smiled. She knew well that Caleb was always up well before dawn. She watched her son depart and then sat back, looking at the communications on the desk in front of her. She found it almost impossible to concentrate.

She missed her husband more than she could

ever have imagined before this mad venture into the Dasati realm had begun. They had been separated before, but they had always been confident that they would see each other again. This time she was not so certain. Her husband had a secret, something she had been aware of since meeting him during the war against the Emerald Queen's army. There was something he refused to talk about, something he wouldn't even hint at, but she knew him well, and from time to time she would catch him looking at his sons in a certain way or, when he didn't realize she noticed, her. It was as if he were trying to burn their features into his memory, as if he feared each time he left he'd never see them again.

She pushed herself away from the desk. She couldn't continue sitting there. She knew Caleb would understand when he returned and found her gone. Closing her eyes for a second, she recalled exactly where in the Sun Elves' compound she wished to be, then willed herself there.

Tomas turned as she appeared. 'Miranda! I thought you might not be coming.'

'I wouldn't miss it,' she said with a brave smile. Whatever trepidation she might feel about her husband's absence, she would never show anyone her concern. Firstly, because she hated showing weakness, and secondly because the Conclave required the confidence of its allies, and these Sun Elves were still too suspicious of humans to be counted allies yet. So she knew her continued participation here was needed to build that necessary trust.

Castdanur nodded to her in greeting, and his manner seemed genuinely warm. She did not have a strong sense of this place prior to her first visit with Tomas, but she could feel that somehow things had changed. The old leader of the Sun Elves was almost aglow with happiness. 'Lady Miranda—' he began.

'Just Miranda, please.'

'Miranda,' he started over. 'My people are in your debt. Lord Tomas told us of your part in destroying the Void beings' encampment. We have been plagued by them on and off for years and they have cost us dearly.'

Miranda shot a glance at Tomas, whose subtle expression suggested that some things were best left unsaid, such as why the Sun Elves had not petitioned for help from the other elven people when the Dread had first appeared. Debates over independence, stubbornness, and foolhardy choices would be put off for a more relaxed, contemplative time. Right now there was a more pressing concern. 'It was my pleasure,' she said. 'Tomas actually rid us of them, I merely obliterated the residue of their trespass.'

'It was necessary,' said Tomas. 'Had you not, it might have been easier for them to return. Now I think we need only concern ourselves with the original weakness in the fabric of our world that let them slip through in the first place.'

She bit her tongue, trying not to blurt out that the one person best able to discover that leak in the barriers between the real universe and the Void was on another world, in another plane of reality! Instead, she nodded, and said, 'With Castdanur's permission, I'll have some of our most gifted magicians work with your spell-weavers, Tomas, on that problem.'

Tomas nodded. To Castdanur, he said, 'We are ready.'

'Then follow me, please,' said the old elf. He motioned for two other elves to accompany them.

Tomas said, 'I don't think we need an escort, Castdanur.'

The old elf inclined his head in acquiescence, and waved the two away. As they left the compound, Miranda looked around and saw that the new arrivals were already hard at work rebuilding portions of the community that had been neglected. 'It looks as if the newcomers are making themselves right at home.'

'They are our brothers and sisters. They return what was lost to us, and you have rid us of the plague that had weakened us. Before I depart on my journey beyond, I will see Baranor reborn.'

'That is a good thing,' Miranda said. Then she realized something was different. 'Where are Kaspar and his men?'

'With the return of our brethren, and because of their good works on our behalf, we judged it safe to release them. Kaspar and the one you call

Jim Dasher have proven to be elf-friends indeed.'
To Tomas he said, 'I returned to Jim Dasher the
talisman given to him in Elvandar, and to Kaspar
of Olasko, I gave another. Both are welcome here
whenever they care to return.'

Miranda sighed, 'Ah, I need to speak with Jim
Dasher.'

'By evening tide, they will be at sea.'

Tomas said, 'We can search for them when we're
finished here.'

'No need,' said Miranda as they began trudging
up a long trail that circled around the stronghold
and wended its way high into the mountains. 'I
can catch up with Dasher in Roldem.'

They walked quickly up the pathway and Miranda
realized after half an hour that she was with two
exceptionally good hikers, a elf and a being with
the powers of a Dragon Lord. In fact, Tomas
despite his heavy armour, appeared to be lingering
to allow Castdanur and Miranda to keep up with
him. Feeling annoyed at her fatigue, Miranda
employed a little magic to make herself light on
her feet, a small spell of levitation so that it felt
as if she were strolling along rather than trudging
uphill.

For the better part of two hours they hiked an
unremarkable trail until they came to a large
meadow. Castdanur stopped and said, 'Here we
enter the true realm of the Quor.'

Tomas said, 'I remember.' Miranda shot him a
sidelong glance. and he went on, 'There are times

when Ashen-Shugar's memories come to me unbidden; things that I did not know until something causes me to remember.' He stood silently for a long moment, fists on his hips, apparently taking in sensations, identifying feelings. At last he said, 'I remember . . .'

Ashen-Shugar sped across the skies, and to those who had been held in thrall, he declared, 'Do now as you will, for you are a free people!'

Those known as elves – *edhel* or 'the people' in their own language – bowed their heads as one in respect to their former ruler. The others of the Dragon Host had risen against the new gods and as the Chaos Wars raged across the heavens, this one Valheru, the Ruler of the Eagles' Reaches, had taken their destiny and placed it in their own hands.

Other races were also freed, and new races were arriving through great tears in the fabric of space and time. 'A great struggle is approaching,' Ashen-Shugar shouted and by the magic of the Valheru, all those below heard his words. 'Take this world and make it your own!'

The people chose various different paths. Those who followed the light of reason, those given the guardianship of lore and wisdom – the *eldar* – led their followers to a sylvan glade and began fashioning a wondrous home, becoming one with the woodlands that would one day be Elvandar. Those who followed and served were called the Elves of

Light, the *eledhel*, and from their ranks rose wise rulers, the first kings and queens.

Others chose to emulate the thirst for power of the Dragon Host, those who wished to rise to the power of the Valheru. Those seekers of darkness were known as the Elves of Darkness, the *moredhel*.

Others were driven mad with fear, terrified of being left without their masters, like domesticated dogs turned loose in the wild, running in packs so fearsome that even the wolves grew to fear them. They were called the Mad Elves, or *glamredhel*.

Others dispersed, travelling across land and sea, living with other races, humans and dwarves, some with goblins and trolls. They forgot their very nature and became as aliens. These were the Elves From Across the Sea, the *ocedhel*.

And high in the Peaks of the Quor, Ashen-Shugar confronted the beings so profoundly ensconced in the heart of Midkemia that even the Valheru would not trouble them. For amongst these peaks, in an isolated enclave, lived a race which was connected to the very fabric of every life on this world. A harmless, gentle race which lived in a way unfathomable to even the most powerful of Valheru or the wisest of the eledhel. Their purpose was incomprehensible and their nature equally confounding, yet even the most violent of the Dragon Host could sense within themselves some profound meaning. It was not something that could be explained;

it was something that could only be understood intuitively.

And there were guardians, sun-burned elves who hunted and lived below the Peaks of the Quor, whose only task was to keep this extraordinary place well and untroubled. The Valheru dubbed them 'Guardian Elves', or *tirithedhel* in their tongue. They called themselves the *anoredhel*, or Elves of the Sun.

To them Ashen-Sugar said, 'You are now a free people, but you are held to your charge, for should any harm befall the Quor, so perishes the world.' And with that he flew away . . .

Tomas blinked. 'I remember.'

'Remember what?' asked Miranda.

He shook his head. 'Many things. We should continue.'

Castdanur indicated the direction he intended to lead them, then turned and walked away across the meadow. At the far edge he entered a narrow pathway. Tomas followed, with Miranda taking up the rear; but when she stepped onto the trail, she faltered then stopped. Everything had changed. The very nature of the air was different. Colours were more vivid, sounds had a new harmony to them, and tantalizing hints of exotic fragrances were carried on a breeze that caressed her cheek like a lover. Miranda found herself repressing a shudder of pleasure, for it was as if every good thing imaginable was happening at the same moment.

Miranda had travelled to many places, not as many as her husband, but still enough that she was not easily astonished, but this was a place to bring the most jaded traveller to his knees in wonder. She felt tears welling up at the sheer beauty of it all. She could not put a name to what she beheld, for to the casual observer nothing would look remarkable compared to the mountain-side just a few paces below, yet there was something amazing here. She could see life! She could see energies that coursed through the very fabric of every living thing before her. The trees glowed with a soft illumination and each bird was a sparkling, darting presence above. The very insects flitting through the air were tiny gems of colour, green, blue, golden, moving here and there. A column of ants wending its way up the side of a tree to gather sap from a chip in the bark were a line of diamonds moving up, emeralds moving down.

'What is happening?' she asked softly.

'This is the Quor,' said Tomas. 'Come.'

She took a deep breath, gathered her wits, and followed as the old elf and human-turned-Dragon-Lord continued up the pathway. Tomas was like a mote of sun, blinding to look at if her eyes lingered too long upon him. There was a power in him Miranda could barely stand to behold, and Castdanur was like a warm old fire, the embers beginning to fade, but still giving warmth to any nearby.

As they approached a grove in a deep vale, Tomas said, 'The Quor appeared at the advent of the Chaos Wars, or rather Ashen-Shugar has no memory of their existence before then. The War was protracted . . . I no idea whether it lasted days, weeks, decades, or epochs. The very nature of existence changed; and by the time the Valheru became aware of the Quor, they realized instantly that there was something here not even they dared to question.

Miranda stopped at the edge of the grove.

Giant trees, alien and graceful, with leaves that sang in the breeze and soft hues that had no place on this world rose upward like dancers caught in an instant of time as they leapt into the air. Crystal shards floated amongst the branches, refracting light in a rainbow spectrum. The air bore hints of spices and floral notes, tantalizingly familiar suggestions of some alien aroma.

And everywhere there was music, odd harmonies played on strange and wonderful instruments, heartbreakingly beautiful, but so faint as to linger at the edge of perception, a suggestion of tone and resonance hidden behind the rustling of leaves, the splash of falling water, the soft tread of feet upon the soil.

'What is this place?' Miranda whispered, as if afraid that to speak loudly might break some incredible enchantment.

'The realm of the Quor,' answered Castdanur.

'Here resides one of the true wonders of our

world,' said Tomas. He pointed up the hill and Miranda saw figures slowly approaching. They were green in colour, human in shape, but with elongated heads without hair, their jaws pointed. Their ears looked like ridged crescents and they walked in a loose jointed fashion on long, narrow feet. Each wore a tunic to the mid-thigh, fashioned from some brown material, caught in at the waist by a leather belt. On their feet were sandals woven from something that looked like reeds. They had black eyes and tiny noses, and their mouths seemed continually set in a round expression of surprise. Each carried a long pole of wood, either a staff, or a sharpened stake.

Behind them came illuminated beings.

Miranda could put not other words to them. They were pillars of crystal, or light, or energy, but somehow she recognized instantly they were intelligent beings. They were the source of those wonders around her, she felt sure for the hint of music in the air appeared to emanate from them, and the soft glow that surrounded them gave the distinctive colour to the area. She thought the strange and wonderful aromas in the air probably came from them as well.

Castdanur turned to Tomas. 'Dragon Rider, you must stay here. They cannot abide the touch of your cold metals. Lady, if you would come with me?'

She followed, still overcome with wonder.

When he reached the first of the green beings,

Castdanur bowed his head for a moment in greeting and reverence. 'These are the Quor, Miranda.' To the first of the Quor he spoke in a language unlike anything she had encountered, very tonal, almost like singing.

The Quor replied in the same tongue, but his voice was the trilling sound of reed pipes. The Quor bowed its head slightly and Miranda was struck by the notion that it had very little mobility in its neck. Up close, the creature's skin resembled nothing so much as the skin of a green plant.

Then Castdanur indicated the pillars of light. 'And these are those the Quor serve, the Sven-ga'ri.'

Miranda could barely speak. There was such a feeling of beauty surrounding these beings of light. 'Castdanur,' Miranda said, finding herself whispering, 'what are the Sven-ga'ri?'

Castdanur said, 'I don't know, lady. They are something miraculous that has existed here since the time before memory.'

'I've never heard of either the Quor or the Sven-ga'ri, and I've lived on this world for a very long time,' she softly said. 'I was around when your father was a boy, and I have never seen their like.'

'Few have,' said Tomas from a short distance behind.

Suddenly she was certain of something. 'They are not of this world.'

'No,' said Tomas. 'But they are now a part of it.'

'How can that be?' said Miranda, hardly able to

take her eyes from the beauty of the crystal beings. Each of them rose ten or twelve feet into the air, with their lower extremes floating a foot or so above the soil. They were tapered at both the top and bottom, and they had a large bulge in the middle. There was a considerable variation among them, some being taller, others rounder. But all of them had a ruff of crystal or light which extended completely around them. Lights circled around their heads in complex patterns, in different colours for each of them. Some had green and gold, others silver and blue, red and white, or other combinations. In all it was quite dazzling.

Tomas said, 'No one knows.' He took a deep breath, as if drinking in the intoxicating quality of the surroundings. 'If there is good in this world, Miranda, it is here. These beings are something unique, and I do not know how I know, but I can feel it in my bones that should anything evil befall them, the injury done to this world might be irreparable.'

'Can they understand me?'

Castdanur said, 'The Quor understand them, but they choose not to, or cannot, use human speech.' He pointed to the Sven-ga'ri. 'The Quor speak for them, and to them.'

Miranda nodded. To Tomas she said, 'So this is why you were so adamant about our meeting with the priests and other magicians, and so alarmed by the appearance of the Dread.'

'Yes,' Tomas said. 'That the children of the

Dread appear anywhere on this world is cause for the gravest concern, but so close to here, that is alarming.'

'What would happen—?' Miranda began.

'They would consume everything here,' said Tomas. 'And the world as we know it would change . . . or worse.'

'Worse?'

'Castdanur, tell her.'

'We believe, as did the Valheru, that these beings are tied to the living heart of Midkemia, and should any harm befall them, the heart of the world would be injured, or even die.'

Suddenly Miranda felt a flood of feelings so profound that tears welled up in her eyes. 'What?'

Castdanur looked at her and said, 'The Svenga'ri are speaking to you.'

Tomas said, 'Ashen-Shugar and the other Valheru were not given to introspection but these were the only beings besides themselves they respected, perhaps even cared for; at least they never attempted to subjugate them or in any way harm them, which for the Valheru was unique. The Valheru might not have understood these beings, but that did not make them immune from wonder. It was, perhaps, the only time in their existence they knew wonder.' Tomas paused for a moment considering something, then said, 'I think the Sven-ga'ri speak with feelings, Miranda.'

'Yes,' she said, her eyes wide, brimming with tears, and her voice choked with emotion. 'Already, I would lay down my life for them.'

Castdanur said, 'So it is with all who meet them.'

Tomas said, 'We must go.'

Miranda could barely tear herself away from the warm glow of standing near these amazing beings, but at last she turned and slowly walked away. When they were a short distance off, the feelings of overwhelming love she had encountered began to fade, and when they reached the edge of what she had come to think of as the Glade of the Quor and stepped back into the forest, and the world returned to normal, she took a breath and shook her head, as if to clear it.

'Do you think this is how they protect themselves?' she asked.

Castdanur said, 'If it were so, then why would they need the Quor, or the Quor need us? The Valheru,' he added, looking at Tomas, 'made us guardians for a reason.'

Tomas shrugged. 'My memories of the Dragon Lords are incomplete. But there is some wisdom in what you say. I for one am unwilling to place the fate of this world in the Sven-ga'ri's hands or take the chance that the Dasati or the Dread would react as we do to their wondrous songs.'

'I agree,' said Miranda. Before leaving Sorcerer's Isle she had been almost overwhelmed by despair, but now she felt renewed and vowed that no harm would befall these strange and wonderful beings, nor any other creature on this world.

She walked down the trail as the sun set over the western peaks across the bay, feeling reinvigorated with a new sense of purpose. Terrible things were coming, but she would not be cowering in some dark corner waiting for those horrors to seek her out after having destroyed all she loved in this world. She would meet those horrors head on, defiant and willing to give everything she had to the last moment, to preserve all she loved in this world.

CHAPTER 17

PRELUDE

Valko struck hard.

The Deathknight he faced was practised and wary and avoided the slash, but he left himself open for a circling move, which Valko finished by impaling him on the point of his sword. He spun quickly to find another opponent and was almost struck by a vicious blow from above. He raised his sword and blocked it then, grabbing the hilt of his sword with both hands, dropped low and cut hard at the back of his second opponent's legs, causing him to collapse. Valko flipped his sword and plunged it down into his opponent's throat, then looked up, ready for the next confrontation.

His side was barely holding their own against the seemingly endless waves of the TeKarana's Deathknights. How they had finally discovered the stronghold of the Bloodwitch Sisterhood and the virtual leadership of the White was a question that would have to wait; perhaps it had been a traitor, or one of their own loyal servants had been tortured into revealing this location, but either way the damage was done. Even if they were victorious for the moment – and the outcome was still in doubt – everyone here would be forced to flee and the leadership of the White would be disrupted for weeks to come.

Valko signalled for two other Deathknights serving the White to rush to support the fight over on the right hand side and took a breath while surveying the scene. They were in the large court-yard where he had first entered after breaching the illusion that surrounded the home of the Bloodwitch Sisterhood. The magic-users were embroiled in a confrontation with half a dozen Deathpriests who had been accompanied by the palace Deathknights.

The red-and-black-armoured Deathknights were easy targets for Valko and his silver-clad warriors, but there were too many of them for him to find a tactical advantage. His warriors were more talented and might be able to win through attrition. But that faint hope was growing dimmer by the minute, for if the Deathpriests overcame the Bloodwitches any magic turned against Valko's men would end this struggle quickly.

Suddenly a howl of madness cut through the sounds of battle and abruptly there was something unimaginable in the midst of the struggle. A being nearly double the height of the tallest warrior in the fray had appeared. There was a mantle of smoke around its shoulders. Its skin seemed to be of a scintillating white-blue crystal material and it radiated a pulsing energy that Valko could feel across the grounds of the compound. It made the hair stand up on his arms and neck, and he could see it having the same effect on combatants on both sides of the battle.

The creature lashed out with a long, powerful arm, its heavy black nails leaving smoking wounds wherever they struck. The first victim of the attack was one of Valko's Deathknights, but the second was a Deathpriest who had come too close to the edge of the fray after killing a Bloodwitch, his neck snapped by a crushing grip from the monster's massive hand.

Valko shouted, 'Back!'

He had seen there were more foes close to the monster than his own men, and instantly recognized the opportunity to let the creature do his fighting for him while he ascertained the best way to deal with the monster. He used hand-signals to organize the defenders and they moved to the positions he indicated, leaving the palace's Deathknights to defend themselves from the monster. Valko saw that the Bloodwitch Sisters were being bested by the Deathpriests, so he gestured for four of his fighters to attack the Deathpriests from behind.

They did as he commanded and he watched.

Valko had been given neither command nor rank by the Bloodwitch Sisters, but when the onslaught by the forces of the Dark One had begun less than fifteen minutes earlier, he had just naturally taken charge and no one had questioned his instructions. He was Lord of the Camareen, and while not the most experienced warrior present, he was the highest ranking noble. And he proved to have been an adept student of Hirea. He had kept a catastrophe from befalling the Sisterhood, and now it looked as if there might be a chance for them to survive the assault.

If he could contrive a way to best this monster.

Retreat never occurred to Valko. It was not in the Dasati nature. You won or you died; it was that simple. But he was not stupid enough to throw away his life or the lives of his warriors needlessly. He saw with satisfaction that the warriors he had sent to attack the Deathpriests had made quick work of them while they were occupied with their arcane battles with the Sisterhood, and now they had gained a slight respite while the remaining palace Deathknights were engaged with the monster. Valko ran to where Audarun stood exhausted, the old Bloodwitch having spent all her energy in the fight with the Deathpriests. 'Do you know what this creature is?' he asked.

'I can only speculate, I have never come across such a thing in life or in lore. I'm not even certain who conjured it here, for it appears to be as much a shock to the Deathpriests as it does to us.'

Valko signalled his remaining Deathknights to regroup and in moments, they stood ready to defend the Bloodwitches from the monster. A handful of palace Deathknights were still struggling to find a way to kill the conjured horror, and Valko watched closely, looking for any hint of weakness in the creature. Behind him, half a dozen Blood-witches were also chanting quietly, some with their eyes closed, trying to sense something of the creature's nature or power.

As Audarun began an enchantment, Valko returned his attention to the creature as it was confronted by the last of the palace Deathknights. He wished every one of them dead, but they were dying with courage, and he saluted that.

Soon there remained a single Deathknight, and he began to retreat, taking the creature farther away from where Valko and the others waited. Valko swore in frustration as some of his companion Deathknights began to laugh at the palace knight's cowardice. 'Enough!' he shouted. 'As amusing as it is to see the coward die painfully, we have more important things to think about, such as killing that monstrosity.'

'I see no weakness in the creature,' said a voice from behind him, and Valko turned to find Luryn standing at his shoulder.

'You should not be here,' he said. He had found the idea of having a sister difficult at first, but as he had spent time with her he had begun to see her resemblance to their mother and felt a drawing towards her, a sense of connection, which both pleased and troubled him. Sisters were to be sent off to mate with sons of powerful families, and bear them sons, to forge alliances; they were not people you grew to care about.

So much of what he had been taught as a youth by his mother was now coalescing into a new and troubling perspective. Valko found himself caring about those in the room, so that instead of just wanting to be victorious against the monster, he also wanted to protect his sister and the other Bloodwitches, as well as those Deathknights serving the White. He hated the conflict that came with those feelings when all he should wish to do was to kill whatever stood in his way.

Then suddenly Martuch, Hirea, another four Deathknights and two of the humans disguised as Lessers appeared in the courtyard. The human known as Pug moved fast: before the others could react he had already begun to cast a spell. As the monster killed the last palace Deathknight, a canopy of energy formed around it, and it looked back towards Pug as a pattern of crystals appeared on the surface of the canopy. Each crystal emitted a bright yellow line of energy, connecting to another crystal, and abruptly the creature found itself trapped in a latticework of energy.

It charged and upon contact with the lattice an explosion of smoke and flame erupted from its hand and shoulder. It howled in pain and rage, an echoing sound that once more caused Valko's hair to stand up on his neck and arms.

Mindlessly, the monster lashed out, but each contact with the energy lattice caused it more injury and pain.

Valko watched with a fascination bordering on revulsion as the frenzy of the monster grew with every passing second. Finally it was flailing around inside the trap, its body a mass of smoking, flaming wounds as it continued to throw itself against the latticework in a futile attempt to escape.

Pug said something to Magnus who stepped forward and incanted another spell. A pulse of force left the palms of his outstretched hands and struck the confined creature. It howled one last time and then exploded in a blinding silver-and-red flash, its destruction filling the courtyard with a stench of char and decay.

It had taken less than a minute for the two human magic-users to vanquish the creature. Martuch and Hirea both stood as if stunned: their years of battle-training had done nothing to prepare them for this.

Valko hurried to where Pug and Magnus waited, both looking exhausted. Pug and Magnus had left Nakor with Bek and hurried back to the rendezvous only to discover they had missed Martuch and Hirea. It was dawn and the city had been frantic; bells were pealing and the call was going out to muster the societies. All Deathknights and their followers were to be ready to receive orders from the TeKarana on behalf of His Darkness at noon the following day.

Magnus had used his ability to transport himself without a device to return them to the grove, where they had arrived just minutes before Martuch and Hirea rode in. A quick discussion resulted in them deciding to find Valko, for the absence of the young Lord of the Camareen would be noticed at the following day's muster. Pug had had the time to inform the two Deathknights of what he had discovered in the heart of the Dark One's temple.

Martuch now surveyed the carnage around the courtyard and said, 'Everyone must leave, now.'

Audarun clapped her hands once, and called out, 'Prepare to evacuate.' She looked at Martuch and Valko, then nodded once in agreement. 'We have contingency plans. We knew it was likely that the Dark One's followers or the TeKarana's agents would discover this sanctuary eventually.'

Those Bloodwitch Sisters who were uninjured hurried to gather up the essentials they needed, while the five who were too injured to help rested wherever fate had placed them. Martuch inclined his head towards them and Audarun nodded once.

The old warrior swiftly drew his sword and quickly went from one wounded witch to the next, dispatching them in turn with a clean blow. Each witch closed her eyes and stoically waited for her death.

'Why?' Pug, asked, appalled.

'The journey is arduous,' said Audarun. 'If we left them behind, the Dark One's priests could extract knowledge from them, despite their devotion. All of us know this risk; all of us accept death willingly rather than becoming the instrument of betrayal.'

Hirea said, 'Betrayal, yes. Somewhere in the White we have a traitor, for this attack was too co-ordinated, too well conceived to be by chance, and it coincides too neatly with the coming invasion of the human realm. The Dark One wishes no enemies at his back when he launches his onslaught into the human world.'

Pug looked a Audarun. 'Can you find the traitor?'

She nodded. 'We have means, now we understand there is one to find.' She signalled to a young woman standing a short distance away who came and listened as she gave instructions. The young Bloodwitch nodded once and hurried off. 'It is done. If the traitor has not fled or been killed in the attack, we shall find him.'

'Him?' asked Magnus.

'The Sisters undergo years of training, young human. No, the traitor must be a male Lesser. No female Lessers abide here.'

Pug nodded as Valko moved to stand at his side. 'What was that thing?' he asked.

'A creature of the Void,' replied Pug. He glanced around at the slaughter. 'What happened here?'

Valko said, 'At dawn a scout reported a party of the TeKarana's palace guards and some Death-priests were approaching along a seldom-used trail to the south. Audarun said to remain calm, for such groups have come close from time to time without piercing the illusion that hides this sanctuary.

'I suggested the Deathknights here should stand ready, anyway.'

'A wise precaution,' said Hirea, obviously pleased that his student had shown more patience than the average young Deathknight. Most young Dasati warriors would have been inclined to attack at once, without waiting to see if it was necessary.

Pug said, 'Obviously, they knew where to look.'

Magnus said, 'Everything we've seen tells us there have been preparations in place for a very long time.'

'Yes,' said Audarun. 'We grew complacent, thinking we had remained hidden for so many years. But it may be simply that we were not enough of a threat to warrant attention until now.'

Martuch returned from dispatching the wounded. 'You are required for the Great Muster,' he said to Valko.

'The Lord of the Camareen must appear in the Great Hall of the Sadharin. I will go with you. Hirea will have to join the Scourge.'

'No,' said Valko.

Martuch frowned. 'No?'

'It is time.'

'What do you mean?' asked Hirea.

'There will never be a time when so many Deathknights – from the societies, from the palace guards, from the temple – will be absent from the city. They will be off-world, on the other side of the portal,' said Valko. He turned to Pug and Magnus. 'You have brought the weapon to destroy the Dark One, and I am fated to kill the TeKarana. If more of his men come and find this place deserted he will assume that the Blood-witches and the White have gone to ground, are hiding in the thickets like so many mothers and children. Instead, we will summon all our forces out of their musters, and marshal inside the precinct of the Great Palace, and when the TeKarana is at his most confident, when his armies have marched off to conquer another world, then we will strike.

'The chancellors of the Orders may notice that one or two Deathknights from the societies are absent at the muster but they will almost certainly conclude that they were killed or injured during the Great Culling. When this raiding party doesn't return, they will conclude some of those missing from the muster were here, and were servants of the White, dead or in hiding.' Valko's eyes were almost alight with passion. 'It is time! Send word that I am dead,

Martuch, in a battle last night. Then muster our forces at the agreed place, and impress on our men the need for stealth and cunning. We will wait, like children in hiding, until the army has departed, and when the TeKarana is most certain of his invincibility, we shall strike!'

Those Deathknights who stood nearby raised a cheer of approval, even Hirea and Martuch. Pug realized that no matter how reasonable these men were compared to others of their race, they were still at heart Dasati and only a short step between being rational beings to becoming murderous warriors lacking any shred of compassion. But he also knew that there was some sort of prophecy involved that made it likely Valko would plunge ahead despite any advice anyone might give.

He turned to his son. 'We can do nothing more here. We can only hope that your mother and those allied with her have prepared the Tsurani for what is to come, and that she has found and destroyed Leso Varen.'

Despite his respect for his mother and her single-minded ability to pursue a goal until it was achieved, Magnus had grave doubts that she would be able to find the necromancer and deal with him.

The cheering died down and Valko said, 'What will you choose to do, human?'

Pug considered. He was becoming certain his time on this world was growing short. 'If you are moving against the TeKarana, then Nakor must decide quickly what to do with Bek.' Pug was not convinced that Bek was the prophesied Godkiller, but he knew there were many things he didn't yet understand, including the reasons why they were all in this realm. He didn't know if Nakor could shed any light on these mysteries. He would not leave Nakor behind if he could avoid it, and if Bek was not fated to die here, then that strange young man as well had to be returned to Midkemia.

'I hope you will be victorious against the TeKarana and unseat him and that the Dark One's power is blunted, but I must return to my own realm for there will be many of your warriors over-running a world that I once called home. I will go back with you.'

Valko weighed Pug's words and nodded once. 'Can you move us all by your magic?'

Pug looked to Magnus who said, 'If you wish to return to the Grove, I can move perhaps four or five of us at a time. It will take several trips.'

Valko said, 'One trip will be enough. You only need take your father, Martuch, Hirea, and myself.' To the remaining Deathknights he shouted, 'Accompany the Sisterhood to their new place of hiding. Protect them! If we fail, you are the seeds of the new White.'

The Deathknights who served the White saluted the young lord and departed, and Valko said, 'Let us be away, for there is much to do and scant time.'

Pug nodded. Magnus motioned for the three Dasati to come close, bade them to take hold of one another, and suddenly they were gone.

Miranda asked, 'Have I made it clear enough for you, Lord Erik?'

Erik von Darkmoor settled into the large chair in his private quarters and let out a long sigh. 'Yes, Miranda, you have. Even if you hadn't, Nakor wouldn't have gone to the trouble of keeping me alive this long if he hadn't judged the situation grave, and that alone would have convinced me that any warning from the Conclave should be treated with the utmost gravity.' He shifted his weight and grimaced.

'Are you all right?'

'No, I'm dying . . . again.' He looked out of the window of the palace, his favourite view, to watch the sun set over the harbour in Krondor. 'I don't mind being dead; it's the getting there that's aggravating.' He motioned towards a large wooden chest at the foot of his bed. 'Would you do me a favour, please, and fetch a small vial from that chest? It's in a pouch of black velvet.'

Miranda opened the chest and fetched him the pouch. Erik carefully unknotted the two cords that kept it closed, and took out the vial. He pulled out a tiny stopper and tipped the contents of the vial to his mouth. Then he tossed the empty vial on to the table next to where he sat. 'There. That's the last of it. I've nursed along that elixir Nakor gave me and it's kept me fairly fit . . . for a man pushing a hundred years old.'

'I thought closer to ninety,' said Miranda.

'Well, never let the truth get in the way of a dramatic point,' Erik countered with a smile. As she watched she could see lines beginning to fade from his face and the colour return.

'How much time do you have?'

'I don't know. A few months perhaps.' He sat back. 'I'm tired. Down to the core of my bones tired, Miranda. I've served the Crown for the last seventy years, and I deserve a rest.'

'We all do,' she replied. She chose not to delve into the fact that she and her husband had been fighting against the forces of madness since long before Erik was born. Still, he had served with distinction and fought his share of battles. He had never wed and fathered children, and she realized how much starker that must have made his life compared to her own. And while he had lived a long time, he had aged, while she seemed forever a woman in her late thirties or early forties in terms of appearance and vigour.

Erik slapped his hands on the arms of the chair. 'As to your first need, I can do nothing. The King is adamant. He has no love for your husband and less love for the Tsurani.'

'Why?' she asked. 'The Empire and Kingdom have been at peace since the end of the Riftwar. The Tsurani aided the Kingdom during the Battle of Sethanon. You've had more trouble with Kesh in the last ten years than you've had with Tsurani since the peace treaty was signed.'

'You're not talking about a few hundred or even a few thousand refugees, Miranda. You're talking about millions. More Tsurani than the entire populations of Kesh and the Kingdom combined. There's not one duke who would want them in his duchy. Who would feed them?'

'They can work. They are artisans and farmers and carters . . .'

'They are aliens. Not even the Earl of LaMut would welcome them and he's of Tsurani blood! They're too big a threat.'

Miranda knew that would be the answer, but she had hoped for better. 'How many would you take?'

'Me?' asked the Duke. He laughed and again she saw the vigour returning to his features. 'I'd look the other way if you settled a few thousand up in Yabon and Crydee. If you sneaked a few thousand more into the villages along the Teeth of the World for the border lords to worry about, I wouldn't care. But I could not fulfil my oath of office if I didn't follow my liege lord's orders, Miranda. I simply could not.'

Miranda said, 'Any ideas?'

'Novindus would be my suggestion. It's still recovering from the ravages of the Emerald Queen and might be able to absorb a lot of Tsurani. Hells, they could conquer the entire continent and no one up here would care.'

'Kaspar is down there now, talking to a friend of his.'

'Well, I'll bet he has better luck than you, because you haven't had any.' He sighed again, this time more from emotion than fatigue. 'And I'll guarantee Jim Dasher Jamison is having even less than you. His grandfather is a cunning and dangerous man, just like his own grandfather – and he was one sneaky bastard – but he's as steadfast and loyal to the Crown as you are to your cause. Jim won't move his grandfather – and that means he won't move the King – to settle one Tsurani farmer in the Eastern Realm.'

'What about my other favour?'

Erik grinned. 'That is another story.' He stood up and stretched and Miranda could see the years falling away again. Now Erik looked like a vigorous man of fifty or sixty years of age, still fit and dangerous. 'I've got a mess here in the Western Realm, but it's time my staff earned their keep and they can keep an eye on it for me.'

'What are you suggesting?'

'Well, you'll want generals for the Tsurani army, and I'm a general. Or at least a Knight-Marshal, which means I order generals around.'

'The Prince would give you leave?'

'The Prince would wear green paint and dance in the city square if I told him it was a good idea.'

Miranda laughed at the image.

'Edmund's a good enough fellow, but everyone this side of a stone statue knows he's a caretaker prince, sent out here because he's so ineffective no one back east will worry about him becoming ambitious.' Erik's mood turned serious. 'We may have a civil war brewing when I get back – if I get back. I swear you to an oath of secrecy, but the King is not a well man.'

Miranda was alarmed. The King was young and had no male heir. 'What is it?'

'No one knows, but I suspect it's something dire. Every priest that could be trusted has been in to see him, and I may even ask you or the Conclave for help if I can persuade the King to trust you. He's been growing slightly less hale every year, and he and the Queen have had no male children, and the Princess is only seven years old. We've had a string of royal cousins on the throne of Krondor for the last ten years and the King keeps moving them around lest they grow ambitious.'

'Erik, if the King died tomorrow, what would happen?'

'Prince Edmund and a dozen other royals would return to Rillanon and appear before the Congress of Lords, all of them claiming the throne. And there would be a dozen royals standing right beside him claiming the crown. We'd have a kingdom brokered like my old friend Roo used to broker wheat and barley – and he told me enough stories about trade for me to think it's every bit as nasty a business as war. If no claimant to the throne gained consensus in the Congress, we'd have factions, and that could lead to open strife.'

'Civil war,' said Miranda.

'Yes, and we haven't had one of those in a very long time.'

'Who's the closest conDoin male?'

Eric said, 'That's the difficult part. Lord Henry of Crydee is. Harry's a grand fellow, but his ancestor, King Lyam's brother Lord Martin, swore an oath on his own and his descendants' behalf never to claim the crown. I'm sure it seemed like a good idea at the time, but right now I wish he'd kept his big mouth shut.' Erik's frustration was evident. 'Harry would have the unconditional support of the Western Nobles, and not a few of the Eastern rulers as well. But without a legitimate claim, many who would have supported him will oppose him because of that oath. So, the one fellow who could keep the kingdom from civil war is the one most likely to cause it should anyone press his claim.'

Miranda said, 'I don't envy you.'

'The only other conDoin male right now is a child, Prince Oliver, the son of the King's dead brother, Richard. He's six.'

Miranda turned towards the window. Night was falling. 'I will leave you, Lord Erik. When can you come to aid the Tsurani?'

'I have put my affairs in order and my successor will be here tomorrow. Lord John deVres of Bas-Tyra will arrive sometime before noon by hard ride from Salador. I will be forced to endure one of Edmund's receptions and tomorrow will be the formal investiture and my retirement from office. The Prince will insist on giving me titles to lands I'll never have time to see, and from which I'll get income I will never have time to spend. In short, I'll be ready to join you in three days' time.'

Miranda said, 'I will come myself to take you to the rift.' She paused. 'A suggestion?'

'Yes?'

'If the King does not survive, it might be politic for Prince Edmund to go to Rillanon and propose himself as—'

'Prince Oliver's regent,' said Erik with a grin. 'I've already discussed it with Lord James of Rillanon.'

Miranda said, 'Nakor told me you were very clever for a blacksmith.'

Erik looked regretful. 'There are days, and tomorrow is shaping up to be one of them, when I wish I had never left the forge.'

'I understand. Three days, then.'

'Three days.'

Miranda vanished and Erik sat down to think.

Kaspar moved his knight. 'Check.'

General Prakesh Alenburga sighed. 'I concede.' He sat back. 'You're still the best opponent I've faced in years, Kaspar.'

'I got lucky,' said Kaspar. 'And you're distracted, General.'

'True. I've spoken to the Maharajah about your . . . suggestion.'

Kaspar had been waiting to hear the Maharajah's response. He had arrived two days earlier and found the capital of the new, vigorous Kingdom of Muboya enjoying a period of prosperity. A new palace was being constructed on a bluff over-looking the city, replacing an ancient citadel that reminded Kaspar a little of his own home in Olasko. It seemed centuries since he had lived there.

'What was his reaction?' Kaspar asked.

Alenburga sat back, his craggy features set in a thoughtful expression. 'Given that you have never even met our beloved ruler, you certainly know how to gauge a man.'

'Comes from years of trying to keep your neigh-bours from crushing you while trying to crush them in return,' said Kaspar dryly.

Alenburga laughed. 'Very well put. As you suggested, last time we met, the Maharajah married off his youngest sister to the second son of the King of Okanala and secured our southern border.

'But as it happens, the new Princess of Okanala can't abide the Prince's touch – and he apparently isn't all that interested in touching her in any event, preferring to go whoring with his chums, gambling his father's kingdom away, or sailing boats that are built for racing – if you can imagine such a waste of gold – and so our ruler is not happy with the circumstances as they stand.

'Your suggestion that we take in an army willing

to swear fealty to him – and the prospect of settling such an army down south, very close to the Okanala border – is very appealing to the Maharajah, but it is counterbalanced by the concern over where the loyalty of such soldiers may lie – to their own leaders or to the Maharajah?' He spread his hands in a gesture of uncertainty.

Kaspar shrugged. The reaction was much as he had expected. 'I don't suppose the word of an outlander would count for much? They are the most oath-bound bunch I've ever encountered. If they swear fealty to the Maharajah, they'd cut off their own thumbs at his order.'

'I believe you, Kaspar. In our brief encounters I have come to judge you accurately, I think. You were once a very proud man who was humbled, and you are a more than capable military man. A ruler, too, I think at one time, or someone placed very high by birth.'

'You read me well,' said Kaspar.

'You have never lied to me, though you probably never had cause: if you had, you'd no doubt lie as convincingly as a young whore seeking to persuade a rich old man she's in love with him.'

Kaspar laughed. 'I have been known to avoid the truth when it served me to do so.'

'So, what do you propose?'

'Come with me. There are some things I cannot tell you yet, but there are things you should know. If I judge *you* accurately, you are a man loyal not only to his ruler but also to his nation and people.

415

I think you realize that your young Maharajah is looking for an excuse to finish what he started, his conquest of everything down to and including the City of the Serpent River. He wants to finish building his empire. You know the risks. While you're resting and rebuilding, so are your enemies, including Okanala.'

Alenburga ran his hand back through his grey hair. 'Ah, Kaspar. Why can't you take service with me? I'd make you my adjutant, second-in-command of all the armies of Muboya.'

'I lost interest in conquest some time back,' said Kaspar. 'I know what it's like, and I also know what it feels like to be on the other side.'

'Well, go take service with Okanala, then,' said Alenburga with a laugh. 'Facing you in the field would be more fun than those jesters the King employs. The only reason we didn't win was we ran out of time and gold.'

'And men,' said Kaspar, remembering the dead bodies of Bandamin, his wife Jojanna, and the boy Jorgan lying by the roadside, while the Master of the Luggage wept over them. 'You ran out of men.'

'Which is why you thought we'd welcome a few thousand seasoned warriors?'

'Something like that. Though it's more than a few thousand.'

'How many more?'

'How many would you like?'

Alenburga sat back, regarding Kaspar with a

focused attention. Then he said, 'I suspect you have more than I want.'

'More, I think, than any reasonable man would want.'

'How many?'

Kaspar could feel all hope draining away. 'General, with all candour, from what I know of the situation facing the Tsurani, they may not have much of an army left by the time they deal with the threat to their world. But if they're smart, they'll pull up stakes and run. That would mean a million warriors, and three times that in women, children, and other non-combatants.'

'Four million?' said the General, a look of genuine astonishment on his face. 'Our entire population is less than a million, Kaspar.'

'I know. I doubt there are four million souls living in the Eastlands in all the kingdoms and city states.'

'Just how many Tsurani are there?'

'I don't know exactly, but they have an imperial census they use for taxes, and I have been told that the last one – seven years ago – accounted for twenty million citizens and slaves in their empire.'

'You hear things, Kaspar, and sometimes you judge them to be rumours and stories, tales told by those given to exaggeration. When I was a boy and heard stories of the Riftwar, it was something of legend. Here in the Eastlands we'd see the occasional trader from your continent up north. We knew you were up there, but we never had much contact. The Riftwar was this amazing tale of aliens from another world who used magic to invade the Kingdom of the Isles. A ten-year struggle and a climactic battle. Very much the stuff of sagas, but in all of that, we never heard a jot of information about the order of battle, the disposition of resources, or provisioning the troops – the stock and trade of the working soldier, Kaspar. To us, it was all a fantasy.'

'Not for those dying up there, General. As difficult as it may be to believe, I have met some people who lived through that war, and the one that devastated this continent afterwards, and I can tell you it was no fantasy to them.'

'But millions of Tsurani . . .'

'I will tell you everything you need to know, but time is short.'

'Kaspar, you know I would probably recommend to His Majesty that we accept your Tsurani refugees, or at least some of them, if I could guarantee their good behaviour.'

'Then you should meet them,' said Kaspar with a dark grin.

'Really?' Alenburga sat back in his chair and looked at Kaspar across the chessboard. 'How do you suppose I can do that?'

'Well, I have arranged for you and your general staff to take part in a first-hand demonstration of the Tsuranis' ability to fight.'

'Kaspar, now you're being glib.'

Kaspar smiled. 'Yes, I am. Let me tell you of the Dasati.' Speaking quietly and calmly he told the General everything he knew of the situation on Kelewan and the minutes soon turned into hours. When the General's batman came to see if Alenburga needed anything, he was waved away. By the time Kaspar had finished the story, evening had become night and the palace in Muboya was silent.

The General let out a long, slow breath. 'Kaspar, that is a remarkable story.'

'It is true, every word, I swear.'

'An army of millions with no effective leadership?'

'I need you, General,' said Kaspar. 'The Tsurani need you. I have officers waiting, but not enough of them. I have one experienced commander who has led men in the field and can conduct brilliant tactics and who has a brilliant grasp of logistics: Erik von Darkmoor. I am not being vain when I tell you I am his equal. But I need a strategist. If you can come to Kelewan and help them mount a defence, you'll understand what type of soldier you'll find ready to do your bidding. They are tough, loyal and fearless. But I need a high command and I need a full staff in place. And I need it soon.'

'How soon?'

Something in Kaspar's belt pouch buzzed, and Kaspar pulled it out rapidly. It was a signalling device given to him by an artificer on Sorcerer's

Island, at Miranda's instruction. Every member with military training had one, from Kaspar down to the boys serving with him, Servan, Jommy, and the others. Key officers in Roldem, Rillanon, Krondor and other cities would have their devices buzzing. It meant that word had reached Miranda that the Dasati had begun their invasion of Kelewan.

Kaspar looked steadily at the General. 'I need you now.'

CHAPTER 18

INVASION

The woman screamed.

'Help me!' she cried, clutching her baby to her chest. She was covered in blood and spattered with an orange fluid unrecognizable to the scouts.

Their horses pawed the ground nervously as the woman neared. One scout dismounted and halted the wide-eyed woman and looked at her baby. With a single shake of his head he indicated to his companion the child was not sleeping, but dead.

With an equally curt gesture the still-mounted rider indicated he would move away and leave his companion to direct the woman to the south, where the army was mustering. There were healing priests there who would do what they could for the woman. Others would say a prayer for the baby.

The dismounted rider tried to calm the woman and the other moved his steed up the northern road. The report that a small village in the foothills of the mountains had been razed had reached them two days ago. Word had been sent south by fast rider and then by magical means to the Holy City. In a few hours, the order to muster had been given, and warriors from every house and clan in the north had answered the call. The gathering point was a small outpost closest to the reported incursion, a small fort housing cavalry from House Ambucar. The small cavalry detachment, some of the finest horsemen in the Empire, had the duty to patrol the foothills to the north.

The outpost's primary duty over the centuries had been to prevent raids by the migratory Thūn to the north, so they were in a good position to respond to the Dasati incursion. The rider pushed his horse up a steep rise to a crest and looked to the north. Part of his normal patrol area, this road and the village that had nestled in a vale below were as familiar to him as his own son's face. Most buildings were intact, though two were burning at the far side of the village square, erected around the common well. The scout surmised the fires had been the result of overturned cook fires, perhaps, else the other buildings in the village would also be ablaze.

The woman he had met on the road was the only proof this village had been occupied. One hundred twenty or more men, women, and children, all serving House Ambucar were gone. An experienced tracker, the scout quickly ascertained what had just happened.

The village had been struck by a raiding party

of mounted men . . . if that's what they were, he considered, for the tracks in the dust were made by no animal he had seen before; neither horse or needra or Thūn warrior made those marks in the dirt. He ranged around the village a few more minutes, then saw drag marks. For a moment he was confused, then he realized the villagers had been trussed up in large nets and dragged away.

He was too old and experienced a scout to doubt his own eyes, but nothing of this made sense. As a young soldier he had served a tour in a garrison across the Sea of Blood and had fought against slavers from the lost tribes of Tsubar, those malignant dwarves who used human as slave labour. You wouldn't drag valuable slaves, risking injury and death; you'd truss them up in a coffle or herd them aboard waiting wagons.

The village that had been the site of the first alarm was but a half-hour's fast ride up the road. If he hurried, he might overtake the raiders, burdened as they were by their captives. There was only one way for them to travel, for on the right the river Gagajin flowed down a series of rapids and cut gaps, at times falling a hundred feet below the roadway, and on the right a series of steep hillsides vaulted upward, giving little room for more than a trio of riders or a heavy wagon to pass.

A short time later he saw by dust on the road ahead he was catching up with the raiders, and none too soon, if he could tell from the splatters of blood along the trail. If the villagers were netted as he suspected, many would be dead, crushed under the weight of their companions or from the repeated pounding as they bounced along the ground.

There was dust over a rise, a position from which he should be able to see the next village. He hurried his now tiring horse up the steep road, and when he came to crest, he reined in.

Galloping down the road were men – if that was what they were – mounted on creatures unlike anything he had ever seen, from this world or the world of Midkemia. They dragged large nets behind them, in which a dozen or more bodies were confined. Weak cries told the scout a few wretches endured within the masses of the dead. But what commanded his attention was what he saw as their destination.

A sphere without feature rose up above what should have been the village of Tastiano. It rose easily three hundred feet, and from the rider's vantage, appeared to be half a ball buried in the soil. Which would mean a six hundred foot diameter. More than a quarter mile across! He realized it must be some Dasati magic as he saw the first rider vanish through the wall as if passing through a sheet of smoke.

Two Dasati riders were turning and the scout realized he had been observed. Their alien looking mounts were quickly at a gallop and the scout turned his horse about. He put heels to the mount's barrel and urged him to a gallop. His horse was tried, but bred for endurance as well as speed and he just hoped it was faster than those monsters coming after him. He had to carry a warning, for at the last instant, just before he lost sight of the murky sphere, he had seen it expand. It was now bigger than it had been moments before.

The magician cast a spell. A pair of Dasati Death-priests erected a protective barrier but not before one of them was struck by a flaming globe of fire. Tomataka, the Tsurani Great One who had cast the fireball was knocked backwards by the concussion of the following explosion. The Deathpriest standing next to the one who had been struck was thrown sideways almost thirty yards and slammed against a rock-face hard enough to break his bones.

The battle had raged all morning, with thousands of Tsurani warriors streaming into a pass that led into the small valley. They were south of the village Tastiano in the northern mountain range that bordered the Empire, The High Wall, or where that village had rested before being devoured by the black sphere. The river Gagajin had one of its two sources in the mountains high above this valley and what was called the Greater Gagajin flowed through heart of the valley.

The Dasati had chosen well in establishing this

beachhead, for there was only one access point – a narrow pass a few hundred feet above the river. The Gagajin flowed too quickly and the pass was too constricted for boats to be used to ferry soldiers upstream. To the south of the valley the invaders could move directly into Hokani province, threatening old Minwanabi estates now belonging to the Emperor's family. From there it would be down to the city of Jamar, then on to the City of the Plains, off Battle Bay, where the great rift which had enabled the original invasion site of Midkemia still existed. Or they could swing south-west, and attack the city of Silmani, the northernmost population centre on the River Gagajin, then cut down through what was left of the Holy City of Kentosani, on to Sulan-Qu and down to the ancient Acoma estates, where the Emperor was hidden away.

Tomataka was one of a dozen magicians who had volunteered to accompany the massive response to the reports of invasion that had been communicated to the Assembly the day before. The Empire was in turmoil, although some order had been restored by the simple means of the Emperor issuing edicts and every house in the north of Hokani obeying. Tens of thousands of warriors were on the march, although many were still days away, but the first few hundred accompanied by the Great Ones had entered the valley pass this morning at dawn.

The Great One picked himself up off the ground, his ears still ringing from the impact. He could see dozens of Dasati warriors pouring out of the Black Mount. It was the size of a small mountain and as black as soot at midnight, hence the name. No light came from within and there were no apparent doors or windows, yet the Dasati warriors and priests seemed to pass through with ease.

Hundreds of Tsurani warriors were hurrying up the trail above the river and were essentially throwing their lives away to halt the Dasati advance. The Great One's head was pounding and he was unable to focus enough to conjure any spell that would help, so he retreated slowly from the advancing front to gather himself. But when he looked towards the Black Mount he noticed with alarm that it was larger than when he had first arrived: there had been a lightning-struck tree and an odd rock formation at the far edge of the growing black sphere; now they were gone from sight. He calculated and judged that the sphere must have grown a dozen or more yards on that side in less than an hour.

Still feeling wobbly, he turned and staggered down the trail from the line of advancing Tsurani footmen. He knew that somewhere down the trail Tsurani cavalry would be waiting. Horses were still a rarity on Kelewan, but every major house now had a number, and they would not waste them trying to force them through on a narrow footpath, but would keep them in reserve for a counter-offensive should the Dasati reach the bottom of the trail and the great plains below.

The magician knew that the Dasati would succeed in doing this. He had seen their Deathknights fight and he had seen his countrymen die, and he had no doubt. The Tsurani Empire, and this entire world, could not stand on the strength of Tsurani bravery and dedication alone.

Newly-appointed Supreme Commander Prakesh Alenburga looked around the room. In ancient days this had been the court of Lord Sezu of the Acoma and his daughter, the legendary Lady Mara, later known as the Mistress of the Empire. Alenburga did not understand the gravity of history those names represented, but he had quickly come to appreciate the weight of Tsurani history. Everything he had seen since coming to this world spoke of ancient times, and a tradition that was deep and rich. These were a great people and he felt a strong attraction to them, perhaps because his own nation was young and had none of the trappings of history these people exhibited at every hand.

Alenburga bowed before the Emperor, his head still aching from the spell used by the priest Miranda had summoned to teach them all the Tsurani language, in an hour. That had been yesterday evening, but by the end of that hour he could understand and be understood, and that had been worth the pain. 'I pledge my life to discharge the great responsibility you have placed in my hands, Your Majesty,' he said solemnly.

Emperor Sezu, named for the last man to rule this very house, inclined his head, 'It is we who thank you, Commander.' He looked around the room. Beside Alenburga stood Kaspar of Olasko and Erik von Darkmoor, and behind them stood their makeshift staff. Jommy, Servan, Tad, and Zane stood to the right of Alenburga's headquarters staff, which consisted of a score of officers from Kesh, the Kingdoms of Roldem and the Isles, and the Eastern Kingdoms. Two of the boys would serve with Erik as aides-de-camp, and the others would serve in the same capacity with Kaspar. The Emperor nodded in the direction of this team and added, 'As we thank all of you who have come to our world to fight on our behalf.'

The Emperor now looked towards the assembled Tsurani nobles who clustered on the other side of the audience hall; it had once served well for a ruling lord of a single house, but for those gathered at the Emperor's command, it was decidedly cramped. 'You, the surviving rulers of the great houses of the Empire, you have our thanks, as well, for understanding how dire our situation is. In these outworlders, we have placed the care of our Empire. It is our edict that you shall obey them as you do us in the conduct of this war. Now, go and marshal your soldiers, for we are in grave peril.

'For the Empire!'

'For the Empire!' answered the Tsurani rulers and no matter what their personal feelings were about taking commands from the new Supreme Commander, they would keep those feelings in check and do as they were ordered.

'See to your commands, my lords, and be ready to march at once. You are dismissed,' said the General.

There was a slight intake of breath by several leaders, and to a man they looked at the Emperor.

Alenburga turned to see the Light of Heaven standing erect and calm to all outward appearances, save for a tell-tale whitening of the knuckles where he gripped the edge of the throne. The General realized the severity of his breach of protocol and bowed his head. 'If the Light of Heaven permits?'

The Emperor was motionless for the briefest of moments, then he nodded his approval. 'We will assemble here again in one hour by which time I would ask that the latest intelligence we have on the invaders be made ready for our consideration. All warriors in the Empire must be ready to march as soon as possible and all provisions and other logistical support must be made ready with the utmost haste. We must move swiftly and decisively.'

That order was something the Tsurani lords

could understand. As one they bowed, turned and left the room. Alenburga turned to the other Midkemians. 'We need a few minutes to discuss how we're going to do this. Kaspar, Erik and General Shavaugn from my staff are, in that order, the chain of command. Should anything happen to me, Kaspar will assume command of the armies.' He let out an audible sigh of relief.

He turned to face the young ruler of the Empire and with genuine apology in his tone said, 'Your Majesty, please forgive any future breach of decorum for we are outlanders, and we need to be about our business. If you'll permit me?'

The Emperor said, 'We understand. We shall attend and observe and remain silent.'

Kasper nodded slightly, indicating the General should continue. Between them, they had quickly contrived the title of Supreme Commander to two ends: first to convey in as unambiguous a fashion as possible Alenburga's position and rank, and secondly to avoid any suspicion that the office of Warlord had been given to a non-Tsurani, an act that could bring more tradition-bound nobles to rebellion, even in the face of an invasion.

Word of the assault on the Holy City and the destruction of the High Council had only just reached the general population, and news of the invasion was still days away. Alenburga looked around the room and said, 'We need an order of battle, and before we can do that, I need to have

431

an understanding of our resources and their deployment.' He looked at his sub-commanders. 'What do we know?'

Kaspar pointed to the map. 'The incursion is here, in a small valley about twenty-five miles upriver from the foothills. About ten thousand Tsurani warriors are strung out along two lines of march, here and here.' He pointed at the river and the plains to the east. 'If the Dasati break containment and move in strength, they can strike in almost any direction. Their best course, in my opinion, would be to come south and move along this road that follows the river. Once they get south of the gorges and rapids they could then use the river. If they either bring or make boats, that will give them the ability to move swiftly and bring significant supplies with them.'

Erik said, 'I don't think so.'

'Why?' asked Alenburga.

'They'd have to establish another beach-head, somewhere downriver, and that would put them at risk of a severe beating – they may be better individual soldiers but we outnumber them down there right now with more coming fast. Also, if they move along the riverside, they can be flanked and find themselves with the river at their back. I think their best course would be to take the river road, then turn west,' his fingers stabbed at a large area of plains to the west of the river road, 'then turn south, coming straight at Silmani from the north. There's nothing there but farms and pastureland.'

Alenburga squinted as if visualizing the terrain on the map. 'I'd try for here,' he said, pointing to a spot north-east of the city of Silmani. 'If I read this map right, there are half a dozen fords within a mile each way, and a large forest to the south giving them timber for siege engines. That way they don't have to worry about which side of the river they are on should we counter-attack.'

Jommy started to fidget and after being ignored for a few more moments cleared his throat. Without looking back, Alenburga said, 'Something you care to add, Captain?' The four young men had been given that rank as a way for the Tsurani to accept they were empowered to carry orders on behalf of the generals.

'No disrespect, General, but aren't you . . . we, overlooking something?'

'What would that be?'

'These Dasati, well, they're not human, are they?'

'And your point?' said the General impatiently.

'Well, our Tsurani friends here, for all their differences, are still human like us, and we can expect them to think largely like us, but these Dasati, well, sir, they're something else. What if they don't care about losses in taking a bridgehead or the need for lumber for siege machines, or swimming across the ocean . . . ah, sir?'

433

Alenburga stood motionless for a moment, then said, 'The boy's right. This is not a human army we face.' He looked at the Emperor. 'Majesty, is there any way for your magicians to get us close enough to the front so that we can observe them?'

'I will request it, at once, General,' the Emperor answered.

Looking from face to face, Alenburga said, 'Well, then, let us wait, and while we wait, let's have something to drink. My head is still pounding like an anvil.'

Erik grinned. 'I know what you mean.'

Chairs were brought by servants and refreshments appeared swiftly. While they waited for the summoned magician, the ad-hoc military leadership of the Tsurani Empire – foreigners all – started to get to know one another.

Kaspar pointed. 'Look over there!'

It was the morning after they had taken command of the Tsurani forces, and General Alenburga and his staff were on top of a hill overlooking a widening of the trail above the River Gagajin. Alenburga looked to where his second-in-command pointed and saw that a new stream of Dasati Deathknights was joining the fray.

Miranda, at Kaspar's left hand, said, 'They must have opened another portal within the sphere.'

The Black Mount now occupied a large portion of the north end of the valley, and now rose higher than any of the surrounding hills. It was clearly growing in size as Miranda had predicted the night before after arriving from Midkemia. She and a score of Tsurani Great Ones had attempted every type of mystical assault on the structure of the sphere, to no apparent effect. What Miranda had encountered while escaping the first sphere seemed to have proved to be of no benefit in trying to assault this larger sphere. The Deathpriests had – it seemed – learned to counter human magic.

After a few minutes, Alenburga said, 'Damn.'

'What?' asked Erik.

'What do you make the rate of casualties to be, von Darkmoor?' asked the Supreme Commander.

Erik said, 'Twenty to one.'

'Closer to thirty to one,' said Kaspar.

'The Tsurani are easily the most fearless warriors I have ever seen,' said the old General from Muboya. 'I am honoured to have been given command over them.' He took a moment and inclined his head in respect to Lord Jeurin of the Anasati, who was barely more than a boy, but ruling lord of one of the most important houses in the Empire. It had been a political decision to place him on the staff, but Kasper had come to recognize that he was a quick study, and had appointed him as a third aide, along with Tad and Zane. The young lord acknowledged his General's praise of his soldiers.

Alenburga said, 'But I dislike wasting their lives to no good purpose.' He turned to Kaspar. 'Take a position south of the hills, where the river empties into the plains. I want you far enough away that the Dasati must charge you, but close enough that you can cut them off if they try to flank you to the south-west or south-east. These Dasati may not be human, but I know what warriors in armour look like; I haven't seen any cavalry or siege engines yet, so expect an infantry charge.' Miranda and the Great Ones had speculated to the General that the Deathpriests had used some enchantment to keep the Deathknights alive long enough to wreak havoc on the Tsurani, but were either reluctant or unable to use that same magic on the Deathknights' mounts or machines from the Dasati plane. Miranda had tried to explain why the Dasati needed to stay within the sphere to survive, or needed a magic to adapt them to Kelewan's atmosphere and energy state, but the General waved away the details once he understood the basic concept: once outside the sphere, the Dasati became overwhelmed by the energy of this level of existence and started to die after a few hours.

Kaspar nodded. 'Unless they come at us mounted on flying rugs, we'll be ready.'

'Now, here's the tricky part. I need you to come up with a battle plan to slow them down. I want them to take three days to cross territory that should only take one. Can you do that?'

Kaspar nodded. 'I already have an idea.'

'Good. Get one of these magicians to get you down south and start scouting the terrain.'

After Kaspar did as he was instructed, Alenburga

stood silent for a while, watching the conflict below. He measured each confrontation and watched with stunned admiration the heroism of the Tsurani warriors. He spoke just loudly enough for Erik and Miranda to hear him. 'Had I had ten thousand of these valiant men with me, I would have conquered from the whole of Novindus. What astonishing bravery.'

Erik said, 'They'll die to a man to save this world.'

Lowering his voice even more, Alenburga said, 'They can't.'

Erik looked at his new commander, a man whom he had quickly come to judge as being perhaps the best strategic thinker he had ever encountered, as worthy of friendship as he was obedience. So as not to be overheard by those nearby, Erik said, 'Why?'

Turning to look at Miranda, Alenburga asked, 'As the Black Mount expands, the Dasati create new portals, yes?'

She could only nod.

All the colour drained from Erik's face. 'The rate of their attack will only increase . . .' he almost whispered.

'And while I was never the student of mathematics I should have been as a boy, the area of that sphere doubles and redoubles all the time, correct?' the General asked.

Again, Miranda nodded. 'It is exponential.'

'So where there may be four gates by the end

of today, in a few days there may be eight, then sixteen in a week, or sixty-four in a month?'

Miranda said, 'Instead of dozens of Dasati rushing into this world each minute, there'll be thousands.'

Alenburga nodded, as if this confirmed his worst fears. 'We need to regroup. Men are dying need-lessly down there.' He saw a brilliant flash of light near the edge of the sphere and said, 'And not only soldiers. Get the magicians out of there, Miranda.'

Miranda, not used to military protocol did not immediately leap to do his bidding but said, 'Why? They are doing the most harm to the Dasati.'

Patiently, the General explained. 'True, but when they are tired from killing Deathknights, they become easy prey for the Deathpriests. I'm guessing the Dasati have a great many more Deathpriests to spend than we have magicians. Besides, I have a better use for our magicians than throwing huge balls of fire around.'

'What?' persisted Miranda, as the General turned and began walking down the hill.

He turned. 'I rarely have to explain myself,' he said, 'but you are no soldier, and I need you to be clear about what I propose, so that you can make these Tsurani Great Ones understand. More than anything else, the one advantage we possess is the terrain. I may not know it well, but Lord Jeurin and the other Tsurani field commanders do, and we must use that advantage. The second benefit you're about to gain us is something any field commander would sell his soul for: rapid communications. If the Tsurani magicians don't find it beneath their dignity, they can rapidly carry commands and intelligence between the battle-field and my headquarters, and we will profit immeasurably. Battle plans and tactics rarely survive the first hour of a fight, and the general who can adapt the quickest, who can order his troops to the best position available fastest, will win the day, even if his forces are outnumbered.'

'So you think we can defeat the Dasati?' asked Miranda.

'No. It's going to be impossible. We're losing thirty soldiers to each of theirs, and while we have an advantage in the power of the magicians, they are mortal and will fatigue. Eventually enough of them will fall that that seemingly endless flood of Deathpriests will overwhelm whoever's left. No, all we can do is slow them down, and the more time we gain, the more time you have.'

'For what?' she asked.

'To get as many people through the rift and off this world as you can. We will fail. Barring some intervention by the gods, we cannot hold this world. We must evacuate.'

Miranda was silent for a moment, then she said, 'I understand. I will get to the Assembly with all haste and begin to prepare a way for us to evacuate as many as we can.'

439

'I don't know where you're going to put them,' said the old general from Muboya, 'but anyone you can't get though the rifts will die here.'

As Miranda vanished, Alenburga saw Erik von Darkmoor looking at him quizzically. 'What?'

Erik said, 'You're going to stay, aren't you?'

'And you?'

'I'm a lot older than you, my newfound friend. If anyone should stay to the last, it should be me.'

Alenburga smiled. 'And I, my newfound friend, think it would be impossible to go back to sitting around a table with my lord ruler, listening to political chat and social gossip, knowing I quit this struggle too soon. I have no wish to die, but if I'm going to survive, I'll be the last one through the rift, and if I die, let it be saving as many lives as I can save.'

Erik nodded, smiled, and put his hand on the General's shoulder. 'I wish we could have met sooner.'

'I wish it as well. I'm tired of Kaspar beating me at chess, and I hear you're not particularly good at the game.'

Erik laughed, despite the carnage below. But after a moment, the mirth died as he turned his thoughts to the bloody business ahead.

Martuch, Hirea, Valko and Magnus watched as Pug closed his eyes. He said, 'I have only done this a few times on my world, and never here, so I do not know how likely I am to succeed.'

440

Pug was attempting to use mystic sight to peer above the hidden room in the Grove of Delmat-Ama and see what the sudden eruption of noise was. It sounded as if thousands of people were racing through the orchard above, making far more noise than had been heard even during the height of the Great Culling.

Pug's vision rose through the darkness that was the solid soil beneath the grove, and suddenly he could see. He had never been rigorous in practising this particular spell and wasn't especially gifted at it. But within a moment he had no doubt as to what was occurring up there.

He opened his eyes. 'They're killing everyone.'

'Who?' asked Martuch.

'Everyone,' Pug repeated. 'The TeKarana's legion is herding everyone towards the Black Temple. It's as if they're beating the brush to drive vermin from a field or herding game animals towards hunters.'

Martuch and Hirea looked at one another, then Hirea said, 'Never in the history of our people has there been anything like this . . .' He shook his head. 'We must do something.'

Pug sat back, tired from his exertions. 'We must wait a little longer, I think.'

'Why?' asked Martuch. He stood up, obviously ready to climb the ladder and see for himself what was going on.

'If you were conducting such a massive operation,' said Pug, his tone revealing his impatience at having to explain, 'and you knew that some of the Lessers you sought out were very adept at hiding, what would you do?'

Hirea looked at Martuch and even to Pug and Magnus his expression was easy to read. 'You'd leave behind Deathknights to follow after at some long interval to catch those coming up for air, you fool.'

Martuch looked as if he might draw his sword and turn on his old companion, but after a moment of a silent inward struggle he let his hand slip from the hilt of his weapon and then he sat down in his chair, frustration on his face. 'This is obscene,' he said softly.

Hirea agreed. 'This is why we do what we must.'

'What do you suggest?' asked Martuch of Pug.

'We wait. We will soon hear the second wave of those driving the stragglers before them, I am certain.'

'What then?'

'We find Valko and the others, then see if there's any remote possibility we can locate Nakor and Bek. But we will indeed have to move soon, for the Dark One has made his commitment; he's using tens of thousands of lives to expand his invasion of Kelewan, and I am certain he will use every life on this world if he must to take it.'

'Every life?' asked Hirea, for even though he understood much of what Pug had told him of the Dread and the creature known as the Dark God of the Dasati, he still couldn't quite grasp the enormity of the concept.

'Why not?' said Magnus. 'He has eleven other worlds. There are many more millions of Dasati to kill on Kosridi if he runs out here. And when Kosridi is barren, he'll start on another after that.'

'How did we become like this?' asked the old trainer.

'Generations of lies and manipulation,' said Magnus.

Pug nodded his agreement. 'Let me tell you of what I know of the Chaos Wars.' He began to tell the two old fighters about the visions he had on the Tower of Testing in Kelewan and other stories and tales, woven together in a long narrative about the fall of the Two Blind Gods of the Beginning and the rise of the Valheru on Midkemia, the banishment of the Dragon Lords, and the Battle of Sethanon after the Riftwar. He told the story without embellishment, and when he had finished, both of the old Deathknights sat silently.

Finally Martuch said, 'Do you think that war extended here?'

Pug said, 'I think that war existed in every aspect of reality. I think from the Chaos War down to the struggle we face today, the fight is all the same: the balance of the universe has been distorted and we are caught up in the conflict to restore it.

'It never made any logical sense to me that this was only some internal struggle between those forces we call good and evil; for even evil exists within a paradigm that requires a balance with good, or if all is evil the term loses meaning.

'There is nowhere in my plane of existence where evil pre-dominates as it does in the Dasati Empire, yet here you are, and with other agents of the White, you seek to restore the balance. Because evil cannot exist without good to contrast with and to balance it.'

'I don't understand,' admitted Hirea. 'Yet I will accept your explanation.'

'It's not simple,' said Magnus. 'But somewhere before history, a breach was made between what is our collective, real universe, including all the planes of existence, and the Void. It is from the Void that the thing you call the Dark One came. He distorted the balance of this universe so much, disrupted the normal give and take between opposing forces so severely, that he was able to supplant the Dasati deity of evil and grew in power after seizing his place and driving out all the original Dasati gods.'

Knowing that Pug had mentioned the Talnoy on Midkemia, Magnus added, 'We may never know who gave the Dasati gods safe haven on my world, but there they remain, and perhaps if they were to return . . . perhaps the balance in this realm would return that much faster.' He let out a slow breath. 'But for that to happen, the Dark One needs to be destroyed, I think.'

A sound from above caused everyone to fall silent. Feet were pounding on the ground above, followed by others in close pursuit. Pug said, 'Soon. We can move soon.'

'I hope Valko and his knights are safe,' said Magnus.

'They are safe or we are all lost,' said Hirea.

'Where are they?' asked Pug.

'We have one place, prepared against this day, that has never been used before. It is very close to an ancient entrance into the palace that will lead us to the heart of the TeKarana's private apartments. It is our plan to burst into those apartments from below, to kill the TeKarana before his Talnoy guards overwhelm us and claim the throne.'

'Claim the throne?' asked Pug. 'How is that possible?'

Martuch and Hirea exchanged glances, then Martuch said, 'It is easy to forget that despite your appearance and your ease with our language, you lack fundamental knowledge of our culture, human.' He pointed to his friend. 'Should I kill my friend in battle, that is one thing. I gain honour for my house and society, and can take what I will from his body as the spoils of battle, on the field. But should I kill my father, I become ruling lord of my house, as Valko did when he killed Aruke. And if I kill my liege lord, overpower him and take his head, then I am entitled to keep all that which was his.'

Hirea finished: 'If Valko kills the TeKarana, he *becomes* the TeKarana. Why do you think the TeKarana keeps an army of fanatically loyal Talnoy with him at all times?'

Magnus said, 'But that means . . .'

'Someone must kill the Dark God,' finished Pug. 'Or Valko's reign as the TeKarana will be a very short one.'

'What do you propose?' asked Alenburga.

Kaspar said, 'The Tsurani are as brave as any soldiers I've ever seen, but they lack a sense of organization above the company level. Co-ordinating this could prove difficult.' He looked towards young Jeurin of the Anasati. 'My friend, I have a very difficult task for you.'

'Whatever I must do, Lord.'

The entire Tsurani command structure was now located in a makeshift pavilion erected on a hillock near the river, less than half a mile from where the river emptied into the plains. They could easily see the dust raised from the fighting a short distance upriver and soon they'd be able to hear the sounds of battle. The Tsurani were being slowly rolled back, and Kaspar was seeking a plan to thwart the Dasati advance as Alenburga had requested. Miranda and a half-dozen magicians had just arrived after beginning the evacuation and were standing off to the side, ready to do whatever the General bid them.

The General looked at Kaspar who spoke to the young Tsurani lord. 'I need you to take the vanguard, there'—Kaspar pointed to a position half-way between their current location and the first rolling hills on either side of the river— 'and I want two detachments of as many soldiers as we can muster on either side. Lord Jeurin, you must retreat, very slowly, drawing in the Dasati. We will surround them and press in.'

The young noble saluted and hurried out of the tent, shouting orders to his retainers.

Kaspar said, 'What of those behind the vanguard?'

Alenburga turned to Miranda. 'Can you keep them busy for as long as an hour?'

She sighed, 'We can try.'

'How goes the evacuation?' Alenburga asked.

'Badly,' she answered. 'A second rift is being fashioned as we speak, one that will empty into Novindus, but it will take some time, perhaps another day. The one that stands open now is in a small chamber in the Assembly, and we can only send through dozens of refugees at a time. And even then they're going to be on an island in the Sea of Dreams in disputed lands between Kesh and the Kingdom. The only good news is that thousands of Tsurani are on their way to the rift-sites, so when they are ready to open, they will be able to travel through at once.'

'Thousands,' said Erik von Darkmoor quietly, leaving unsaid what everyone knew: millions of Tsurani would be left to die if something miraculous didn't occur.

At three hours after noon, the order was given to retreat and what was left of the Tsurani forces fighting in the gaps of the river canyon fell back.

The Dasati pushed forward, but halted when they saw the army arrayed on the plains less than half a mile away.

Thirty thousand Tsurani soldiers stood in fixed ranks, in three squads of ten thousand each. Clouds of dust from the rear spoke of thousands more soldiers on the march, and the commander of the TeKarana's Deathknights realized that at last they faced a formidable foe. Until now, the slaughter had been immense, the Deathknights killing Tsurani soldiers at a whim, but adjusting to the Kelewan climate and the energies of this level of existence was starting to take its toll. For every Deathknight killed by Tsurani weapons, two were falling ill and having to return to the Black Mount, where Deathpriests would see to them, or kill those too weak to recover.

However, more Deathknights were coming through the portals every hour, and the Mount was expanding. Kaspar reckoned that a full head-quarters was now probably housed inside it, and his opinion was shared by the rest of the staff.

From what Miranda had reported about her captivity by the Deathknights, he knew that this probably wasn't merely an invasion site, but the point at which they would begin to transform the world, to turn this entire planet into a habit-able world for the Dasati. And every Midkemian present knew that it was literally only one step away from Kelewan to reach their own home-world.

'Soon,' said Erik. They were far enough behind the lines that they would face Deathknights only if their plan failed totally, but Erik drew his sword out of habit. He had stood in the line in too many battles over the years not to feel the need to have it in his hand.

Miranda and the Tsurani Great Ones had removed themselves to a position on a high hill to the west of the invaders, from which vantage point Miranda could make out most of what occurred. They were waiting until an agreed-upon signal to attack the rear of the Dasati column and inflict as much damage as possible on the Deathknights and Deathpriests. Opposite them, in a small vale hidden from sight, waited the Tsurani cavalry, six thousand horsemen ready to strike from behind when ordered.

Alenburga said, 'They're coming!'

The Dasati began to move forward, but rather than their previous mad charges, they moved in lock step.

'Good,' said Erik. 'They're accepting the gambit.'

Alenburga said, 'Let's hope none of them plays chess.'

Kaspar grinned, 'Let's hope our young Tsurani lord can keep his forces from acting like Tsurani and they play their part.'

Slowly the Dasati advanced towards the waiting Tsurani.

'Archers!' shouted the Supreme Commander, wishing he had a host of catapults and trebuchets here as well.

A flag was waved and a company of Lashiki bowmen responded, launching a volley of arrows high into the air. It was as if the Dasati were ignorant of archery as an element of war. The arrows rained down and hundreds of Deathknights faltered, impaled by shafts. Those behind merely shoved the wounded aside, or stepped on the backs of the fallen. Onward they marched.

'Wait,' said Kaspar as Alenburga was about to give another order.

The Supreme Commander looked at him. 'How long?'

'Another minute.' Kaspar paused and at last said, 'Now!'

Alenburga signalled to Jommy, who waited on a horse at the base of the hill. Jommy nodded once, then turned and put his heels to the barrel of the animal and raced to the rear of the waiting Tsurani. He had one job and he knew exactly what it was to be, yet that didn't diminish his concern. Where he was going was about to become very dangerous.

Another flight of arrows rained down on the Dasati as Jommy reined in next to Lord Jeurin. 'Orders from the Supreme Commander, my lord! Now's the time!'

The young ruler of the Anasati shouted. 'Advance in order! Advance!'

The Tsurani had been given detailed instructions as to their role in this battle. They knew that those in the centre of the line were the most likely to die today, but to a man they stepped forward briskly and marched head-on towards an enemy more powerful and harder to kill than any foe they had ever faced; an enemy, moreover, determined to kill every living thing on this world.

From his vantage point on the hill behind the lines, Kaspar turned to his companions. 'Now it begins,' he said softly.

CHAPTER 19

COUNTERSTRIKE

Pug signalled.

He had used his ability to send his sight upward one more time: the way ahead was clear and without any apparent traps. 'It's time,' he said to Valko. It was now or never.

Martuch, Magnus, Hirea and Pug had made the dangerous journey from their hideout in the Grove of Delmat-Ama to Valko's staging area, a vast chamber, easily able to contain the thousand or more Deathknights of the White who had gathered there. Even now as they prepared to launch their assault on the TeKarana, dozens of stragglers were finding their way into the chamber.

Their orders had been simple, but for those Dasati who served the White they had been hard to accept. They had been told that when word came they had to go to ground, not to fight, but to hide. As if they were children or females, they were to hunker down and wait until they were told otherwise.

Trusted Lessers who served the White had been given the critical task of spreading the word. And despite all the years of preparation it had almost been too late. Half a dozen key messengers had been swept up in the massive drive to bring sacrifices to the Black Temple and were assumed to be lost. Another hundred or more Deathknights had died fighting the TeKarana's palace guards. They had been given no choice, for any Deathknight found in the city after the call to muster was presumed to be of the White; all others were many miles away awaiting their orders to invade Kelewan. The only warriors in the city not the TeKarana's men or Temple Deathknights were enemies.

Valko now drew his sword and ordered his men to be both cautious and silent. Pug marvelled at the discipline shown by the Deathknights of the White, for caution and quiet were hardly hallmarks of the Dasati warrior.

A lever was tripped and a massive stone wall now slid sideways, revealing a gaping black tunnel leading upwards. Valko moved forward and Pug found himself amazed once more by the acuity of Dasati vision and their lack of need for torches as long as there was the merest hint of light or heat.

They moved into the darkness.

Kaspar signalled to Servan, who turned his horse and rode as if a thousand devils were chasing him. He had his sword drawn, ready to fight if need be, but his mission was to carry a message to a sorely beleaguered Anasati command bearing the brunt of the Dasati assault. He got close enough to Lord Jeurin, to shout, 'Now! My lord, now!'

The Tsurani noble had been barely seventeen years of age when word of his father's death had reached him. Despite losing his father, along with the family's First Advisor, Force Commander, and all senior leaders attending the High Council, he had shown a remarkable intelligence and resolve. He had stood ready to defend himself, but willed himself to not fight until given permission. Now he had been told to put his soldiers in harm's way, and to fight a delaying retreat, but no longer would he let his soldiers die protecting him. He saluted Servan, then shouted, 'Withdraw in order! Withdraw!'

Servan saw him push forward, past retreating Anasati warriors, who were doing their best to delay hundreds of Dasati Deathknights while hundreds more pushed in from behind. The young ruler was afire with rage, venting the pent-up fury he had held in check since the death of his father. He leaped past one of his falling men to strike downward, hamstringing a Dasati Deathknight, who reached for him with an outstretched mail gauntlet, missing the young Tsurani warrior by mere inches. 'Back!' shouted Jeurin. 'Retreat slowly!'

Another Dasati Deathknight leaped forward, but the two Anasati warriors flanking Jeurin intercepted him. Individually, the Tsurani were no match for the Deathknights, but these soldiers had trained together for years, and they were protecting the life of their young ruling lord. One took a shield-shattering blow that drove him to his knees, but the other took advantage of a slight opening and drove his sword into the exposed area under the arm of the Deathknight's armour. Orange blood spurted out in a fountain as he yanked loose his blade, and the three fell back another step.

The Deathknight tried to raise his sword arm, but couldn't. The weapon fell from fingers unable to grip, and he went to his knees. One of the Tsurani warriors was about to step forward to deliver a killing blow, but Jeurin grabbed him by the armour at the back of his neck and yanked hard. 'No!' he shouted. 'Back! Fall back slowly!' Then to himself as much as the others, he said in wide-eyed wonder, 'It's working. The outworlder's plan is working.'

On all sides, the Tsurani were pressing in, save the middle, where Jeurin was withdrawing. This forced the Dasati to press forward in a large circle, with those Deathknights caught in the middle unable to reach the Tsurani. Suddenly the majority of the Dasati were forced to watch helplessly as the surrounding Tsurani cut and hacked down every Deathknight before them. Now, if they pushed forward, all they achieved was to shove their own men into the waiting Tsurani line.

The most senior Deathknight in the centre looked around, helpless, uncertain of his next move; an experience no Dasati had ever encountered before.

Alenburga watched all this in admiration. 'That

young man is worthy of any honour the Emperor wants to give him,' he said to Kaspar and Erik.

'They all are,' said Erik.

The Dasati were now forced together in an even tighter cluster, and Alenburga waited to see a break between those now surrounded by the Tsurani and those still streaming down the trail from the Black Mount. When a break occurred, he said, 'Signal Miranda it is time!'

A Tsurani soldier standing nearby picked up a very tall post upon which a banner of bright green hung, and began waving it back and forth.

On a distant hill, Miranda saw the signal and shouted, 'Now!'

As co-ordinated as court dancers, a dozen Great Ones of the Empire of Tsuranuanni rose up as if being carried by a giant invisible hand. Reaching down with their magic, they raised two additional magicians each, so that thirty-six of the most powerful magicians on this world floated high in the sky, giving them an unobstructed view of the gap between the river trail and the plains beyond the foothills. As she had expected, Miranda saw the lines of Dasati were broken, and those in the gap were slowing, waiting to see what was occurring in the battle less than half a mile ahead of them, while their commanders decided what to do next. She was no student of military tactics, but she had witnessed enough battles to realize that the Dasati were even worse than the Tsurani at co-ordinating large number of warriors. She was not certain exactly what Kaspar's plan was in every detail, but she understood enough of it to realize it was working.

'Forward!' she cried and signalled them to move on.

In formation, thirty-seven magic-users of enormous power swept down to a position high above the invading Dasati, and from there began to rain death on the invaders.

Jommy turned to Tad and Zane as Servan raced back from the battle to join them. 'Look at that!' he shouted. In the distance, above and behind the battle was a great display of lights and energies, towers of flame and pillars of smoke rising up, almost blinding the onlookers.

Tad grinned at his companions. 'Don't get Miranda mad.'

'Come on,' said Zane, pointing to the command position. 'We need to get back.'

The four youngsters, together for the first time in months, were enjoying their new role as leaders of men while still testing their capabilities. Jommy was by far the most confident, being the eldest and most experienced, but right now they were inexperienced youngsters being given a huge amount of responsibility.

The Tsurani command structure was in tatters, as every ruling lord save a handful, had been obliterated by the Dasati raid on the High Council. Those left alive were in key positions around the

Empire, but at this particular battle no seasoned veteran leader was present. Worse, most of the houses of the Empire had lost their First Advisors, Force Commanders, Force Leaders, and others in the dead lords' retinues who would have been valuable assets in this struggle.

Now tens of thousands of Tsurani soldiers awaited commands from foreigners, relayed by other foreigners, to inexperienced leaders, aided by soldiers roughly of the rank of corporal or minor sergeant in Midkemian terms. The few Strike Leaders and Force Leaders who were still alive had been placed in critical positions and were desperately trying to co-ordinate those soldiers under their command.

'So far it seems to be working,' said Zane, pointing to where the Dasati were being drawn into a tighter group.

The four rode back to the command position, in time to hear General Alenburga shout, 'Archers! Pick your targets!'

The word was relayed, and the Lashiki archers – the finest in the Empire – shot high into the air so that the arrows fell straight down into the middle of the Dasatis' congested position. They were helpless to defend themselves against such an attack.

Jommy drew up his mount, jumped down and tossed the reins to a lackey. Rushing to where the general staff was arrayed, he saluted the officers and said, 'Orders have been relayed, General. They wait your signal.'

'Not yet,' said the crafty old soldier from Novindus.

Kaspar looked from Erik to Alenburga and saw in their expressions the same murderous satisfaction he felt at trapping a large force of Dasati and destroying them, without incurring worse casualties.

More and more arrows rained down on the centre of the Dasati formation and Erik said, 'I find it impossible to believe they don't have shields.'

'I don't begin to guess how these creatures think,' answered Alenburga. 'All their swords look like hand-and-a-half. Maybe they've become so tradition bound, variation isn't encouraged, or even allowed.'

Kaspar said, 'If the vision I had is real – and so far nothing shows me it wasn't – they are a strange and twisted people who gave up innovation centuries ago.'

'Or maybe they just think they're invincible?' suggested Erik.

In the distance they could see the flying magicians were continuously pounding away at the contained force of Dasati hemmed in along the river above the plain.

Kaspar's laugh was a bitter sound. 'Another hour of magic raining down from above and they'll lose that vanity.'

'Perhaps,' said Alenburga, 'but what I want to know is where are their Deathpriests and why aren't they answering the magicians' attack?'

★　★　★

Miranda was tiring but she was still energized by her chance to lash out at the enemy. Not since the war against the Emerald Queen's army had she felt this outraged or so focused in her anger. Down there were those who had put her husband and her eldest son at risk, captured her and subjected her to insult and indignity; she was more than happy to be the architect of their chastisement.

But she found that focus was becoming increasingly difficult with each passing moment, as fatigue began to rob her of much-needed energy. She took a moment to glance first to one side, then the other, and saw that some of her fellow magicians were also beginning to show signs of exhaustion.

Gathering as much energy as she could muster, Miranda cast down a huge ball of crimson energy. This served two purposes. Firstly, it was causing serious harm to a large number of Dasati now held up in the river pass, with their way downward stalled by the immobile forces in front of them, and their way back to the Black Mount jammed by those following behind. And secondly, it signalled to Alenburga that it was time to unleash the cavalry.

The massive red flash was also seen by the Lord of the Tolkadeska, a sixteen-year-old lad who had never been in a serious fight in his life, let alone a battle. He tried to keep his voice from breaking as he raised his sword and shouted, 'Forward!'

A thousand horsemen hidden in an arroyo west of and just to the rear of where the Dasati line of march had been severed moved out in orderly fashion. The boy leading them might be without experience, but the riders of the four houses that followed him were not. They were veteran horsemen all. Horses had come to Kelewan during the Riftwar, Kingdom mounts taken as prizes. Kasumi of the Shinzawai had been the first noble to understand the value of cavalry and House Shinzawai had been the first to breed horses on Kelewan.

Like Kasumi, many Tsurani nobles quickly became mad for horses across the Empire, and in the decades since then, more horses had come through the rift from Midkemia via trading. Now the Tsurani prided themselves on having light cavalry the equal of any on Midkemia, including the legendary Ashunta horsemen of the Empire of Great Kesh.

Every rider was as anxious to answer this insult to their nation's sovereignty as those on foot. They were eager to join the battle and drive out the invaders. As the first thousand moved out, two other companies took up position, ready to re-inforce when ordered.

Young Lord Harumi of the Tolkadeska made a prayer to Chochocan, the Good God, asking not to shame his ancestors by failing in his mission. He raised his sword and shouted, 'Charge!' and none of those nearby noticed that his voice broke.

Hooves slammed the soil like thousands of hammers at a forge, and the ground shook. Dasati Deathknights on their right flank felt the vibration before they could hear the sound because of the havoc raining down from above as the magicians in the air kept throwing every evil spell of destruction they could conjure at them.

The Tsurani cavalry slammed into the left flank of the Dasati, turning a slow retreat into a roiling mass of confusion. On foot each Dasati was the match of dozens of Tsurani, but when they were confronted by cavalry, the odds of their attackers were significantly improved. Dasati Deathknights were bowled over and sent flying into the mass of their own forces retreating up the trail. The fury of the onslaught drove dozens of Deathknights off the trail and down the steep embankment, landing many in the river, where they were pulled under by the weight of their armour.

Lord Harumi of the Tolkadeska lashed out with his sword and was easily blocked by an experienced Deathknight, who then quickly reached up and grabbed his leg, pulling him from the saddle. Slammed hard to the ground, the young ruler of his house didn't have time to raise his sword in defence as the Deathknight drove the point of his sword through the traditional laminated hide armour of a Tsurani ruler, ending a line of Tolkadeska lords going back over a thousand years. Those around him took note that the boy brought no shame to his lineage and when he died, his voice didn't break.

Alenburga said, 'Good. They're retreating.' He turned to Zane. 'Ride to the front and remind our eager Tsurani captains that they are not to enter the last valley at the river's head – if they get that far.' As Zane saluted and turned to run to his horse, the old general added, 'And try not to get killed.'

'Sir!' Zane snapped a salute as he left the make-shift command post.

Erik said, 'That went well.'

'Yes,' said Kaspar. 'But it was just one battle.'

'And unless the Dasati are total idiots,' added Alenburga, 'they won't let themselves be drawn into a cluster like that again. I won't guess how they think, but if I was their commander, I'd be plotting how to get my own cavalry into the fight.' He let out a sigh. 'It's been a long day.' As the sun lowered in the west, he asked, 'Do we know if they fight at night?'

'We have no intelligence on that,' answered Kaspar.

'Your young Jommy is right. We cannot make assumptions about how these creatures think and act.' Alenburga turned to those officers waiting behind the three senior leaders of the Empire's army and said, 'I want the field cleared of the wounded as quickly as possible, and I want defensive positions erected even faster.

We will act as if we know another attack is coming after sundown.'

Another attack came after sundown.

In the vast tunnel, Pug held up his hand and they waited, listening. He had given himself the responsibility of moving ahead of the vanguard as an advanced scout, because he was, except for Magnus, the most powerful single being in this invasion force. Magnus had been stationed next to Valko and told to protect him at all costs.

There had been a constant background sound as they entered the tunnel, and it had got increasingly loud as they passed near tunnels that Martuch said led from the palace complex to the Black Temple, in a rough latticework fashion. It was hard to put the name to the sound, but it caused Pug's skin to crawl.

Pug motioned for the force behind him to move along, and over a thousand Deathknights loyal to the White came forward, moving with deliberate haste. No one knew for certain exactly how long the palace guards would be occupied with the slaughter of the city's vast population, but this attack had to be conducted before any significant number of them returned from this mission of death.

Pug detected movement ahead, and felt his pulse race as he anticipated, at long last, a direct confrontation with the Deathpriests who protected the TeKarana. While preparing for this raid, Pug

464

had asked Valko and the others for as much information as they could provide about what they might encounter. It proved to be sketchy at best. Little was known beyond this old, abandoned sub-basement complex attached to the closest access to the TeKarana's private complex within the Great Palace. The TeKarana was served by a thousand dedicated Talnoy – Pug didn't feel the need to share his knowledge of the real Talnoy still hidden on Midkemia, or that these were merely men in armour that looked like the ancient captured gods of the Dasati. He lived in a community almost completely isolated from the rest of the beings on this planet. He had his own staff who were separate from the larger palace staff of Effectors, Facilitators, Interlocutors, and other minor Lessers, and a harem of females chosen from the better houses in the Empire. There had never been any record of his acknowledging a son. Moreover, it was unclear when this TeKarana had taken over from his predecessor and how. Rumours abounded, but no one knew the truth of it. It was suspected that one of the planetary Karanas would be selected to replace the ultimate leader when it was time, but no one outside the innermost society of rulers on this world knew exactly how the system worked.

Pug reached what appeared to be a dead end, a blank wall of the ubiquitous black-grey stone used as the primary building material in the Empire. He motioned for Valko to approach and said, 'Is there a way in or do I have to break it down?'

Valko seemed impressed, for the first time since meeting Pug. 'You can break this down?'

'Not quietly.'

Valko actually smiled, the first time Pug had seen him do so. 'No, there is a way.'

Martuch and Hirea came forward and the three of them spread out and placed their hands on the wall, feeling for something that Pug could not see, no matter what aspect of his magic-enhanced sight he used. After a few minutes, Hirea reached low and triggered a mechanism. There was a deep but surprisingly soft rumble and the massive wall rolled into a pocket on the right, revealing another passage leading up.

'This way,' Valko said, and Pug and Magnus entered the passageway, towards the palace.

Nakor held Bek back. Bek was dressed in the strangely disturbing armour of the Talnoy, a look very familiar to Nakor from the time he had examined ten thousand of the things hidden in a vast cavern on Midkemia, an experience bordering on the mystical. But there was nothing remotely mystic about these Talnoy, for each was simply a fanatic, loyal to the TeKarana, wearing ancient armour. The red-trimmed black armour of the palace guards was far less ornate than the gold-trimmed monstrosity now worn by Bek, and both were far gaudier than the real Talnoy armour

Nakor had seen. It was as if the Dark One's servants had felt the need to be more impressive in appearance than those they had replaced.

Nakor had heard the summons to the palace before Bek could respond, and had simply ushered his young companion into an alcove off a storage room, as hundreds of Talnoy guards hurried to answer the call. Bek had not questioned Nakor's instructions, but Nakor could tell he was getting restless after sitting silently in this tiny room for hours. Softly Nakor said, 'Soon. They'll be here soon.'

'Who will be here, Nakor?' asked the hulking young man.

'Pug and the others.'

'Then what will we do, Nakor? I want to do something.'

'You will be able to do something soon, my friend,' whispered Nakor. 'It will be something you like a lot.'

Miranda could feel the fatigue threatening to overwhelm her, yet she forced herself to cast one more spell of scrying. Then her eyes opened wide and her head jerked back as if someone had slapped her.

'What is it?' asked General Alenburga. His eyes narrowed in his sunburned face as he studied her.

'That hurt.'

'What hurt?' asked Kaspar of Olasko.

'They've erected some sort of . . . barrier against scrying inside that thing.'

Two dozen additional magicians had gathered since the end of the first phase of the battle, just before sunset, and they were a welcome sight when the Dasati started their second assault an hour after sundown. The Tsurani had used a different tactic this time, convinced that the Dasati would not err again and try to charge a fixed position where the Tsurani could surround them.

Alenburga had ordered a company of Tsurani engineers who had arrived towards the end of the battle to erect as many barriers as they could across the opening where the river trail emptied into the plain. The Dasati could still come through, but not in numbers unless they first stopped to remove the barriers, or tried to swim downriver.

Then a dozen heavy ballista and a pair of trebuchets were unloaded from the wagons and erected, just as the Dasati again advanced down the trail. As their vanguard reached the end of the trail, Tsurani archers high in the hills overhead fired down on them, every fifth arrow being aflame, while those operating the trebuchets hurled huge barrels of flammable oil into the pass. The barrels each held fifty gallons of oil, and they were designed to disintegrate on impact, spreading the oil in every direction. It took a few minutes for the fire to begin in earnest, but after it caught hold, it quickly erupted into an inferno that forced many Deathknights into the river where they were pulled under the fast-moving water by the weight of their own armour, or helped to their death by Tsurani spearmen who used their long pole-arms to hold the Dasati underwater as they attempted to reach either riverbank.

After an hour of this, the Dasati beat a hasty retreat up the path.

Now they were attempting to anticipate the Dasati's next move, hence Miranda's attempted scrying. 'I was never very good at that sort of thing, anyway,' she said.

The four young captains were waiting nearby, all of them showing evidence of fatigue. Zane was nearly asleep on his feet and Tad had to nudge him a few times to keep him alert. General Alenburga noticed and said, 'Pass the word to stand down. Set pickets at the edge of the hills, a mile in each direction, and we'll wait. Find whatever comfort you may and get some rest.'

The four young officers hurried off to discharge their duty and take a break.

Alenburga said to Miranda, 'I don't have any idea how you do what it is you do, but you look as if you could sleep for a month. Go. I have a tent set up a mile or so to the rear. There's food and a sleeping pallet there.' He detailed a soldier to escort her, and added, 'My thanks to you and the other magicians. I doubt we'd be standing here if it wasn't for your amazing skills.'

Miranda gave him a wan smile. 'Thank you. If you send for me, I can be here in minutes.'

Alenburga cast his gaze in the direction of the

Black Mount. 'I doubt we'll be hearing from our new friends before dawn. They may see in the dark like cats, but we've given them a lot to think about.' As he watched Miranda departing with the escort, Alenburga said to Erik and Kaspar. 'That's what I'm the most worried about.'

'What they're thinking?'

'Yes,' said the General.

Erik said, 'Something occurred to me during this last struggle.'

'Out with it then,' said Alenburga. 'You don't strike me as the shy type.'

Erik smiled. 'I didn't want to speculate until I saw if they were going to come at us a third time.'

'What is it?' asked Kaspar.

'Why make the second attack? All they have to do is hold us outside the river pass, keep us some distance back, and eventually that sphere is going to encompass this area and they can strike out in any direction. More to the point, why go to the trouble of creating all that slaughter in the first place? Why not just keep expanding the sphere?'

Alenburga ran his hand over his face. 'My eyes feel like I've got a desert's worth of grit in them.' He looked at Erik first, then Kaspar. 'There are a lot of questions I have no answers to.' He paused, then said, 'How did the Kingdom defeat the Tsurani in the first place, is one.'

Erik said, 'I've studied every record of that war, and the best answer I can come up with is, because the Tsurani weren't serious about it.'

470

'A twelve-year war and they weren't serious?'

'Seems it was merely a side ploy in some big political game they were playing here.'

'I'd hate to see what would have happened if they had been serious,' said Kaspar.

'We'd all be speaking Tsurani from birth, I think,' observed Alenburga. He took a deep breath. 'But none of the descendants of the Tsurani will be left to speak Dasati if we don't prevail.'

'What next?' asked Kaspar.

'We wait.' The General looked around for a likely place to sit and found a large rock where he could lean back. He sat down and said, 'The really bad thing is that I have no idea what to expect next from those monsters in the dome. The good thing is that come early morning tomorrow, we'll have three times the soldiers to throw at them.'

'Something tells me,' said Erik, sitting down nearby, 'we'll need them.'

Kaspar remained standing and looked towards the sphere as if he could somehow see it in the dark. Softly he asked, 'But will that be enough?'

Joachim of Ran was nervous. He was nervous every time it was his turn to watch the ten thousand motionless Talnoy. He was also nervous because the only other magician from Sorcerer's Isle who was on duty was no older than he was – barely twenty-six years of age – and he had even less experience as a magician, and was sound asleep outside.

The Conclave had been taking care of these . . . things, for some time now, Joachim assumed. He didn't really know much beyond his instructions, which were to watch them in shifts with other magicians who came and went from Sorcerer's Isle, do nothing, but make sure someone knew if anything untoward occurred in this vast cavern.

Joachim was not entirely sure what 'untoward' meant exactly, but he was entirely sure he wouldn't like it if he knew. He couldn't help how he felt; these motionless things in the vast cavern below were unnerving, standing row upon row like monstrous toy warriors, each in identical armour, each as unmoving as the rocks surrounding—

He blinked. Did one of them move? He felt his heart pound and his skin puckered with goose-flesh. He looked hard, but he could see no sign. It must have been some trick of the night, a game of the mind, he decided, yet still his heart raced.

Should he call Milton, the other magician? Taking a deep breath to calm himself, Joachim thought he would only be mocked if he did. He applied himself to needlessly adjusting the single torch stuck in the make-shift sconce above him, and decided it was the flickering of the light that had caused the illusion. No wonder the mind played tricks. He was once more astonished at how far the illumination carried in this otherwise pitch-black hole in the ground. He took another deep, calming breath, and turned his attention back to the tome in his lap. After his first stint of guard duty here he had decided to at least keep current on his studies. He was not the finest scholar in the Conclave and needed to refresh his memory on the more convoluted cantrips, and he had particular trouble with the ones written in Keshian, as he was not a very good student of languages.

He turned his attention to the page and after a while became lost in trying to master an especially odd phrasing. Then out of the corner of his eye, he saw another flicker of movement and his head jerked up. In the front row of the long line of Talnoy . . .

He had to get hold of his imagination. Everything was exactly as it had been moments before . . . or was it? Heart thumping, unsure of what to do, Joachim waited, watching for any other movement.

The first of the TeKarana's guards to spot Valko's forces died before his mind could register what it was he saw. Pug had decided against subtlety at this point and simply used a very basic spell of physical control to throw the man as hard as he could against a distant stone wall. It had the same impact as if he had fallen five hundred feet onto hard rock. The sound of it, certainly, was bound to alert others down the hallway to the fact that something was amiss. The splatter of orange blood covered yards in every direction.

'Impressive,' said Martuch to Magnus. 'I must remember not to annoy your father.'

'Good decision,' said the younger magician, a little surprised at the Dasati's dry humour in this situation. Of course, compared to the other Dasati they had encountered, Martuch was almost human in his outlook. But Magnus was equally surprised at his father's outburst, and realized that Pug must have been concealing a profound amount of anxiety since they arrived in this realm. And since he knew that Pug never worried about himself, he must be anxious about Magnus, Nakor, and even that very strange young man, Ralan Bek.

Magnus knew there were things going on that his father had not confided in him, and that Nakor and Bek were playing some role that he could not anticipate, but he had come to trust his father implicitly over the years. A prodigious talent even as a child, Magnus had always been given the opportunity to master his craft at his own pace, challenged, but never overburdened, and that training, despite his mother's often impressive lack of patience, had given him a graceful approach to a very difficult practice. Magnus knew some day he might surpass his parents in ability, but that was still decades away, and right now there was a very real question if he would live minutes, let alone decades.

Pug turned a corner leading into a vast gallery, in which a company of Talnoy guards lounged, apparently a reserve squad detailed to go wherever they were needed at a moment's notice, for the chamber had a dozen large passages leading out of it like spokes. A few had their helms off, chatting while they waited, and once again Pug realized how much of their advantage came from the illusion these armoured figures were the Talnoy of myth, the nearly impossible killing machines feared by all.

Pug didn't hesitate. He raised one hand above his head, and a massive display of blue energy – a huge pale globe in which lightning danced – appeared above that hand. He hurled the globe into the midst of the Talnoy Deathknights. Sparks of energy shot out first one way, then another, dancing from target to target, stunning each warrior they touched and throwing them into a momentary seizure. Some fell over twitching while others stood upright as if locked in paralysis: fully a third of those in the company were incapacitated by Pug's spell.

Valko and his men charged.

Taken by surprise, the two hundred Talnoy were unable to respond in any organized fashion. More than half the Talnoy were executed as they lay twitching on the floor or while attempting to rise, and those who had managed to put up some resistance were quickly overcome. Two or three warriors of the White assaulted each Talnoy still standing and suddenly it was over. Pug did a quick inventory and saw two of Valko's Deathknights were dead and dozens had minor wounds, while the Talnoy lay dead to the last man.

Pug looked from tunnel to tunnel, wondering which way to move, and examined the markings above each entrance. In Dasati fashion, energy glyphs designating the tunnel's use were inscribed within the stone, visible only to Dasati eyes, their equivalent to a road sign with destinations on it. Pug quickly scanned each and then he saw it, an energy glyph much larger than the others. It must be the mark of the TeKarana.

As if hearing Pug's unanswered question, Valko pointed to that very glyph and said, 'That way.'

Pug looked down the long tunnel. They were one long dash from the TeKarana's apartment. He said, 'Magnus should come up between us, for we haven't seen a Deathpriest yet, and when we do, we may see quite a few of them.'

Valko said, 'Your magic is impressive, human. If it can be used in a more selective fashion, that would be useful; it may be some of them are agents for the White. We have a few placed high within the palace, and they might have contrived a plausible reason to not be involved in the murder at the Black Temple. I trust some of them are still here in the palace, for as soon as we attack, they will join us.'

'One can only hope,' Pug whispered. 'Still, we'll assume none of them are until we know otherwise.' He motioned for his son to move ahead of Valko. 'Keep me in sight but fall back to protect Lord Valko if you see the need.'

Magnus said nothing as his father hurried ahead. He waited for a moment, then set out after him.

Nakor waited, listening, and then he heard it. 'Come along, Bek. We are going to go find you a fight.'

'Good, Nakor. I was very tired of standing still,' said the large young man.

They hurried along, half-running, half-trotting, towards the sound of battle.

'When we get there,' said Nakor. 'Can you kill all those wearing armour like yours and leave the others alone, please?'

'Yes, Nakor.'

'Oh, and you might want to take your helmet off so that Pug and the others know who you are.'

'Yes, Nakor,' said Bek, immediately taking off his helm and casting it aside.

As they neared the sounds of fighting, Nakor said, 'Remember what I said?'

'Yes, Nakor. Can I go now?'

'Yes, go,' said the spry little gambler.

They rounded the hallway and at the far end could see a vast courtyard opening up to the heavens. Even from where they stood they could see that a fairly impressive fight was in progress. From the blinding flashes of energy and deafening sounds reverberating down the hall, Nakor judged that Pug and Magnus must be there, which was as he wanted things to be. He sensed that the time was fast approaching when all of his plans, plans that had been years in the making, were at last about to come together.

The only concern he had left was, would Ralan

Bek, a total madman, play his part? Everything Nakor needed to have happen, the fate of three worlds, and the lives of everyone he had come to care about over the last hundred years, would come to nothing if Leso Varen did not do as Nakor expected him to do. There were times, thought Nakor, when being a gambler was not necessarily a good thing.

CHAPTER 20

RETURN

Pug cast his spell.

An explosion of brilliant illuminations confounded the Deathpriests for a moment, which was all the time Magnus needed to lash out with another enchantment. Sparkling lights exploded from the palm of his outstretched hand as if he had cast ten thousand minute gems – diamonds, emeralds, rubies, and sapphires. But the beauty of the spell was in stark contrast to its effect, for it shot through the Dasati Deathpriests like minuscule razors. Orange spots of blood appeared first on their faces and exposed arms, but such superficial signs were irrelevant, for to a man their eyes went vacant as dozens of tiny holes were ripped through their brains.

Half a dozen more Deathpriests now hurried into the room. They paused, cautious, and then as one began an assault on the rear of the Talnoy guard. Pug noticed that each man wore a white sash that had hastily been tied around his waist.

Valko turned as another figure raced into the room: a massive Talnoy guard, but this one was not wearing any helmet.

'Wait!' shouted Pug. 'That's Bek!'

Valko hesitated for an instant, then stepped back as Bek hurried past him, an expression of demented glee on his face as he raised his massive sword and swung it like a woodsman chopping timber. A Talnoy who had been aiding another in pressing back two of Valko's Deathknights was sundered from shoulder to crotch and the two halves of his body fell apart in an explosion of orange blood. Bek grabbed another Deathknight by the back of the neck, as if he were a fractious puppy and turned rapidly, in almost a dancer's pirouette, throwing him hard against a third warrior half-way across the room. With a sudden reversal of his spin, he completely cut through another Talnoy, his blade sundering the warrior's armour with the shrieking sound of tearing metal and a shower of sparks from the blow.

Pug stood back, awed. Bek was now a force of nature, something worse even than the most terrible warrior Pug had ever seen. Pug had heard from Tomas what a challenge Bek had been when they had first encountered one another, but now Pug wondered if even the legatee of the Dragon Lord armour would survive an onslaught of this war god incarnate. Certainly there was more to Bek than he had ever suspected, for it seemed that whatever was hidden inside him was now coming to fruition.

Valko circled around to where Pug stood and said, 'No mortal can do this. What is he?'

'I don't know,' Pug said. He could see that the situation was rapidly approaching victory, as the knights of the White were disposing of those Talnoy guards who were not throwing themselves at Bek to protect the TeKarana. Taking a deep breath, he continued, 'When we first found him, he seemed a strange young man, possessed by some . . . agency, and we thought perhaps we understood his nature, but since coming here . . . I don't know. It's as if he's a Dasati soul in a human body.'

'He's terrifying,' said Valko, completely unaware of making the most profoundly alien admission possible for a Dasati Deathknight to utter.

Pug looked back and saw the others in the White company were also watching as Bek weighed into the fray, laying about with his sword as if he were a giant among mere men. He took wounds, but ignored them, and each time he struck a Talnoy guard fell. Quickly the Talnoy began to do something unthinkable a moment earlier, turning to flee. Bek crippled two from behind before they could take a step, then set off in pursuit of the handful that were trying to organize a stand on the far side of the room. In a half-dozen strides, Bek was upon them and with the efficiency of a butcher in an abattoir he finished them off in moments. Then the room fell silent. Deathknights of the White stood in mute astonishment at what they had just witnessed.

Valko said, 'This will not last long. No matter

how much confusion exists in the palace and the city beyond, as soon as we pass through that door into the TeKarana's inner chambers, every loyal Talnoy guard and palace Deathknight will come as quickly as they can. We must move decisively and without hesitation.' He turned to his company, many of whom were barely able to stand, and said, 'No one beyond that door is our friend.'

Valko looked at the Deathpriests who had joined them and saw Father Juwon, one of the first to begin his training to serve the White. He was as highly placed in the Brotherhood of the Dark One as any serving the White, and a powerful practitioner of magic. He hurried over and said, 'Your mother and sister are well.' He spoke rapidly. 'We located the traitor, a Lesser who served in the kitchen. He revealed himself to be a Deathpriest and did not die easily. Everyone you left behind is safe and the Bloodwitch Sisterhood is intact, and ready to serve when needed.'

'How go things elsewhere in the city?' asked Pug, ignoring the odd expression on the face of the High Priest when a Lesser spoke up without permission.

'This is the human magician, Pug,' said Valko. 'And that Lesser there is also a human magician.' He indicated Magnus.

A voice from behind the priests said, 'And I am, too.'

They looked around, and there was Nakor. The

little man said, 'I mean, I'm human; I'm not a magician. I'm a gambler. But I know a few tricks.'

The Deathpriests did not seem to know what to make of Nakor.

Pug said, 'We haven't much time. How are things?'

'Madness, beyond anything we have ever encountered, or even heard about; what is happening now to the people of this planet makes the Great Culling we recently endured look like nothing more than ridding a tiny bush of pests. Now there is wholesale murder around the world, Valko.' Juwon closed his eyes for an instant, a gesture Pug found very human, then he looked at the young Deathknight. 'While the great muster waits patiently to go to the human realm and die on another world for the glory of the Dark One, tens of thousand of Lessers are being slaughtered everywhere.'

'Everywhere,' said another Deathpriest. 'It's as if no living thing on Omadrabar is safe.'

'Nothing is,' said Pug. 'I know more of the nature of rifts and magic portals than any man living on my world or on the Tsurani world. This thing that tethers this world and Kelewan is like nothing I've sensed before. I can't be certain until I get closer to it, but the only thing I have seen that is remotely like it was the death rift used by a mad human magician to leave Midkemia for Kelewan.'

'What are these rifts you speak of?' asked Valko.

Nakor said, 'Be brief; we have little time left.'

'Rifts are portals, if you will, between worlds. Those I understand are fashioned with magic that is both powerful and subtle. But this one, used between our two realms, is a thing of death-magic, necromancy of a power beyond my capacity to contemplate. It is more like a vast tunnel, allowing travel in both directions, and it is fuelled by the deaths of your people. I think there must be a way to close it, to save my realm from the Dark One, but I won't know until I reach it.

'The Dark One is a bloated creature of the Void, near-mindless in his hunger for life. The next realm, my home, is far richer in life. That is why he seeks to rise into my realm, rather than extend his reach beyond the Twelve Worlds.' Almost to himself he added, 'The only mystery is how he found the means to reach our plane from yours.' Pug paused, then continued, 'The Dreadlord is seeking a way into my realm using the deaths of your people as a means. He has been devouring your people for ages, building up his strength and readying himself for this migration to my realm. He's now using this wholesale murder to fuel the rift between our worlds, and doesn't care if he kills every living thing on this world or the other eleven ruled by the Karanas in his name.

'He will destroy the entire Dasati race if needed to reach the next plane of reality. There is nothing that can change the fate of the Twelve Worlds unless we conspire to destroy the Dark One.'

Valko looked to where Bek waited, his body covered in orange blood, his eyes fixed on the doorway leading into the inner sanctum of the TeKarana. 'Is he the Godkiller?'

'If he isn't, I don't know who is,' said Pug.

'No,' said Nakor. 'He is not the Godkiller.'

All eyes turned to Nakor.

In amazement Pug said, 'What did you say?'

'I said he's not the Godkiller. Bek is here to allow the Godkiller to destroy the Dark One, but he is not the Godkiller.'

'I don't und—' began Pug.

'There's no time,' said Nakor. 'Bek, open that door!'

Ralan Bek reached out and took a huge handle in his left hand, his right holding his sword as he prepared to visit mayhem on whoever waited on the other side.

Pug could hear the sound of metal bars screaming as they bent in protest, yet the fasteners that had locked them out now broke free beneath Bek's powerful pull as easily as if they had not been there, and with far less protest than had any siege device or engine been used. Pug wasn't sure that his magic could have accomplished the task so easily.

A dozen men in Talnoy armour waited on the other side of the door: as one they launched themselves at Bek. Two died before they could take a full step; and a third as his second foot touched the ground.

Now, Valko and the other Deathknights of the White attacked.

Pug turned around and around, trying to ascertain where the next attack might come from. The chaos at the door blocked his view for a moment, as he dodged through the carnage while Bek slaughtered everyone in front of him, and Valko's men surged on either side, streaming into the room, their battle cries ringing off the vaulted stone ceiling.

Pug knew here he would encounter the most powerful of the Dark One's Deathpriests, for they would be ready to defend the TeKarana. The throne room was vast, a long oval with a door at one end through which they had just entered, a dozen massive stone pillars rising on either side and down at the far end, a mass of waiting men.

As Pug and Magnus hurried forward, they saw the Deathpriests who were gathered at the far end of the room, surrounding a powerful-looking figure arrayed in orange armour: the TeKarana. And between the TeKarana and the attackers stood a veritable army of defenders. Pug said to Magnus, 'We don't have time for this.'

Magnus said, 'I understand,' and rose into the air, above the battle.

As with everything else in this dark and twisted world, the TeKarana's personal quarters were vast. He sat upon a throne on a circular dais situated on twelve concentric rings of stone, rising from the centre of the floor. Like every other room in

486

the palace, the walls were bare of anything resembling human art, but here they sported trophies: the skeletal remains of hundreds of warriors, each still wearing their armour: a mute testimony to the power of the ruler of the Twelve Worlds.

Beyond the throne lay the entrance into the TeKarana's personal quarters, where terrified Lessers and women of the harem dressed in seductive raiment peered through the door. Seeing Magnus rise into the air, many of these turned and fled.

If the sight of a Lesser flying caused any of the combatants to hesitate, they paid for that pause with their lives. Magnus sent lances of searing energy that burned everything they touched save the stones of the floor and wall. Flames erupted from the clothing and flesh of any Deathpriest too slow in erecting a protective barrier from the soaring magician.

Magnus had a mystical protective barrier in place, when the Deathpriests unleashed a wave of magic. Noxious-smelling tendrils reached out from their hands, long flowing ribbons of death spreading throughout the room. The Deathpriests were indiscriminate, killing defenders as well as attackers, for they knew that the defenders were not going to save the TeKarana, but that killing everyone else in the room until reinforcements arrived would.

Pug lashed out with a blinding silver-white flash that withered each tendril as it extended across the room and the Deathpriests shook as if in pain, some crying out as their spells were sundered, then turned their attention to the two magicians. Those able to respond sent forward a swirling cloud of black motes, as much like a swarm of flies as anything else Pug could put a name to, and he erected his own shield before Magnus and himself. While Pug defended, his son unleashed another withering attack on the Deathpriests and two more fell screaming as they erupted into flames.

Bek cut his way through the defenders like a farmer scything through wheat and the Death-knights of the White behind him spread out to engage the Talnoy. Valko moved to stand on Bek's left, ready to leap forward and confront the TeKarana.

Pug and Magnus together were more than enough of a match for the Deathknights and father and son worked in concert like two beings with the same mind. Magnus seemed to know without being told when he needed to defend against the Deathknights, and Pug's counterattacks quickly left them dead or disabled. Quickly, all magic threats in the room were blunted.

Within minutes only a handful of bloodied defenders stood protecting the TeKarana, a tall, massively-built warrior, of the same stature as Ralan Bek. He held a sword almost identical to the one Bek carried, save that it was decorated with precious metals along the blade and with gems on the hilt.

'Your corpse will receive a position of honour above my throne!' he shouted at Bek, as he rose from his throne, descending the steps to the floor opposite the hulking young warrior. Pointing at Bek in challenge, he shouted, 'Never has any warrior challenged me within my own demesne!'

Pug used his arts to pick up the last two Deathpriests and fling them across the room, ending their magical threat. He saw Magnus return to stand on the stone floor, untouched, though he like everyone else in the room was smeared and spattered with orange blood.

Bek saw the TeKarana's challenge, and swept aside those remaining guards between himself and the ruler of the Twelve Worlds. He was unrelenting, coming straight at the TeKarana. Valko and the remaining Deathknights of the White finished off the remnants of the TeKarana's Talnoy guards on the flanks, and as Bek lashed out and the clash of swords rang out through the hall, all eyes turned to the struggle. Two terrible figures of power now battled.

Pug raised a hand to add his magic to the attack on the TeKarana, but Martuch reached out and yanked him by the shoulder. 'No! You must not interfere!'

Pug saw that none of the other Deathknights, including Valko, were rushing forward to help but instead were all watching with rapt attention as the two titanic figures battled. Each blow was answered and the sound of it was as if a mad god of blacksmiths worked steel on a massive anvil.

For minutes Bek and the TeKarana struck back and forth, evenly matched, as each blow was received and answered, each thrust met with a block or riposte, and no injury was given or taken. For what seemed a long time to Pug, the room was silent except for the sound of the two combatants, as metal rang upon metal and grunts of exertion punctuated gasping intakes of breath.

Then the balanced shifted. Bek was in rapture as he fought, each strike seeming to empower him and make him stronger, while by contrast the TeKarana's breath became more laboured and he began to slow. The first sign of the inevitable was a strike to the TeKarana's upper left arm as Bek's sword cut through his orange armour as if it were paper.

'Impossible!' said Hirea.

'No,' said Nakor, quietly. 'Watch and you will see something remarkable.'

Valko stood beside Pug, holding his sword and Pug could see the conflict in the young Dasati lord's face. Pug realized that Valko had assumed that he was the prophesied one, the warrior destined to destroy the TeKarana and prepare the way for the Godkiller, not this human warrior in the guise of a Dasati.

Now the TeKarana swung wildly and over-extended himself, and Bek levelled him with a back-handed blow, the metal clad gauntlet of his

490

left hand striking him squarely on the side of the head. The TeKarana's helm went flying and this was the first time that any who were not of his inner circle had seen his face since he gained the throne.

He looked . . . ordinary. His build was massive and powerful, but there was nothing in the face of the Ruler of the Twelve Worlds that spoke of any special quality. His expression was dazed from the blow to his head, his nose ran orange blood and he blinked furiously, as if trying to will his vision into focus as he held himself up on all fours, defenceless. Bek took one step forward and kicked the Dasati full in the face, sending broken teeth and more blood flying to splatter the floor.

The TeKarana was stunned, but not incapacitated: he rolled away from danger, then came to his feet with a belt-knife in his hand. He made a menacing feint with it and reached for his sword with his free hand, and Bek swung down hard, causing sparks to fly when his blade struck the stone. The TeKarana barely withdrew his hand back in time.

'It's over,' said Martuch.

'Not yet,' said Nakor.

Bek laughed, and it was a harsh, chilling sound that filled those listening with the madness of battle. Even Pug felt the desire to grab a weapon and join the struggle, as alien a feeling as he had ever experienced. He looked at Magnus and saw that his son felt the same way. He nodded to him once and both magicians incanted a quick spell which freed their minds of intruding thoughts and emotions.

Bek stepped back, indicating to the TeKarana that he could pick up his sword. This small measure of fair play was a gesture so alien to the Dasati that it took a few seconds for comprehension to dawn on the TeKarana. But once he saw he was not being taunted, he reached out with surprising speed and picked up his blade. He kept it moving in a looping circle and suddenly swung it down towards Bek's head. Bek blocked it easily, holding his long sword easily in one hand, then struck the TeKarana hard on the point of the jaw with his free hand. The battered warrior's knees went wobbly but he held tightly to his sword. His legs trembled and he began to fall to his knees, but Bek reached out with his left hand, seizing the TeKarana's right wrist and prevented his collapse. Bek crushed the TeKarana's wrist and the sword fell from fingers gone suddenly limp. Slowly Bek let him down, until he knelt, defenceless, before the large warrior.

Bek released his hold and the defeated warrior fell backward, his right hand useless. The pain had made his eyes go vacant for an instant. Instead of stepping forward and killing the TeKarana, Bek turned his back, and walked towards Valko.

The TeKarana shook his head, regaining his wits. He looked at the retreating back of the huge warrior, frowned, then reached down to retrieve his weapon with his uninjured hand. Gripping his sword tightly, he struggled to his feet, his target the exposed back and neck of his opponent.

Bek stood motionless, then looked down at Valko and said, 'Kill him.'

The TeKarana raised his sword and just as the blade came fully upright, Valko stepped past Bek and ran his sword-point into the TeKarana's throat. With a wrenching twist that almost decapitated the Ruler of the Twelve Worlds, he yanked free his blade.

'What just happened?' asked Magnus.

Hirea said, 'Bek just gave Valko an empire.'

Valko looked at those in the room, his expression indicating that he was just as confused as everyone else as to what had happened and why, but he understood the gravity of the moment. He stopped, picked up the fallen TeKarana's ornamental sword and walked slowly to the throne.

Less than a minute later a company of Talnoy guards raced into the chamber to find hundreds of Deathknights of the White kneeling before the throne, upon which sat a young Dasati lord. At his feet lay the prone body of the former TeKarana.

As the first Talnoy hesitated, Juwon, in the robes of a high priest of the Brotherhood of His Darkness, cried out, 'Valko! TeKarana!'

Such was the Dasati way that the Talnoy instantly bent a knee in the presence of their new ruler. No question was asked, and no protest was sounded, for in the order of Dasati life he who kills his liege becomes ruler. Valko was now supreme ruler of the Twelve Worlds.

Pug softly asked Martuch, 'How long will this last?'

The old Deathknight shrugged. 'Who can say? If it is as you suggested, and the Dark One cares no more for this realm as he flees, then as long as Valko can keep his head on his shoulders. Many will see him as a youth, ripe for killing, and many will die to keep him on that throne.' He indicated the general direction of the Dark Temple and said, 'But if the Dark One needs a pet ruler on the throne, then it will last only for as long as the Dark One is busy. Once word reaches him that a rogue Deathknight has deposed his favourite, every Temple Deathknight in the Empire will be heading here to kill him. They will obey the Dark One's Deathpriests before they obey the TeKarana. Even if we can defeat the Dark One, we may have a civil war; the only question is will it be a long one or a short one.'

'Short one?' asked Pug.

'The only friendly Deathknights not at the great muster and invading the human world are those of us here. If the Dark One orders his forces to attack us here, it's a very short civil war.'

Pug reckoned there were roughly a thousand Deathknights, including the newly-arrived Talnoy guards in the chamber.

'There are perhaps a few more palace guards scattered around who would bend a knee to Valko,

494

but the Dark One still has perhaps twenty thousand Deathknights in the city and another five thousand at the Black Temple,' Martuch finished.

Magnus looked at Bek, who stood almost motionless, his expression rapt and distant, as if seeing something in the air. Then he turned to Nakor and said, 'What has happened to him?'

'He's come home,' said Nakor. The little gambler looked around the chamber as Deathknights of the White and the TeKarana's Talnoy guard stood uneasily side by side, awaiting the first command from their new ruler. He then looked to where Valko sat, also looking uncertain, and said, 'Valko's young, but he will start a change here that may take centuries. Eventually these people will find their way back to where they should have been had the Dark One not come to this realm.'

Pug said, 'Nakor, you have knowledge we lack, obviously. We shall soon face an army of Deathknights loyal to the Dark One and our forces are exhausted.' Pug looked his old friend in the eyes. 'There have been times over the years when I knew you were holding back, not telling me everything, and I merely thought it was your way, but now, for the sake of all we've sacrificed and all we've hoped to gain, we need to know what you know.'

Nakor laughed. 'That, Pug, is impossible. But you do deserve the truth.' To Magnus he said, 'Can you take us to the Dark One?'

'Yes,' said Magnus. 'I remember that overlook, where the TeKarana and his court watch the ceremonies.'

To Valko, Nakor said, 'Ruler of the Twelve Worlds, my time here is almost at an end. You must endure and lead your people into a new era.' He pointed to Bek. 'He will remain with you a while longer, but soon he must go about his own business.' Now he moved to stand before Bek. 'Goodbye, Ralan Bek,' he said quietly.

'Goodbye, Nakor.'

'You know what you must do?'

'I do,' said the massive youngster. With a grin as wide as Nakor's he said, 'I finally know what it is I am supposed to know.' He looked down at his diminutive companion and asked, 'And you know what you must do?'

'Yes,' said Nakor. He reached up and standing on tiptoes he put his hand over Bek's eyes. The young man stood motionless for a moment, then his head jerked back as if he had been struck and he stood blinking for a moment. Then he smiled. 'Thank you, little human,' he said with obvious joy. He looked around. 'I will protect this boy until the others get here.'

'Good,' said Nakor. 'Fare you well, Ralan Bek.'

'And fare you well, Nakor the Isalani.'

Nakor said, 'Martuch, Hirea: guide the lad.'

'Others?' asked Pug.

'You will see, soon enough,' he said to Pug. To Magnus, Nakor said, 'Come, the three of us have much to do and little time. Let us go to the Dark One's pit.'

Magnus obliged and Pug and Nakor felt the sense of dislocation, almost a faint jerking feeling as they left one place and arrived at another. Suddenly the three of them were standing before the TeKarana's throne on the observation platform witnessing a scene of madness beyond their experience.

Thousands of Dasati were falling from above, some bouncing off the rock-face, others falling directly into the burning sea of orange energy and green flame. Others landed on the bloated thing that was the Dark God and a few pitiful wretches were still living when they landed. One or another was picked up by the Dark One's magic and carried screaming towards his massive maw. The featureless head was without distinction, yet the two burning red eyes regarded its next victim. While no mouth could be seen, the victim would vanish into the face of the Dark One, who would swallow the Dasati whole.

'This is unnecessary,' said Nakor. 'The creature can suck life energy with a touch. The eating is . . . theatrics.'

'Terror is a tool of the Dread,' said Pug. Turning to look at Nakor, he said, 'Why are we here? We may be noticed at any moment, and even the three of us can not best a thousand Deathpriests, or that thing in the pit if it reaches out to us.'

The gallery beyond where they stood and the

rim of the pit above as well as a dozen openings at various levels of the cavern were thronged with Deathpriests and temple Deathknights.

'We're waiting,' said Nakor. 'We're waiting for the Godkiller, and when he arrives, we must each carry out our appointed tasks.'

'Nakor,' asked Magnus softly, 'what are you not saying?'

The little gambler sat. 'I'm tired, Magnus. Your father has understood for quite a long time that I am not entirely what I seem, but he's had the consummate good grace to let me play the fool when it served my purpose and not ask too many questions.'

'You've always been a good friend and staunch ally,' said Pug.

Nakor let out a sigh. 'My time is almost over, here, and it is fitting that you should know the truth.' He looked from Pug to Magnus. 'You will inherit a burden from your father, and it is a heavy one, but I think you will be equal to that task. Now, I need a moment of time with your father, alone if you don't mind.'

Magnus nodded and moved away to give them some privacy.

To Pug, Nakor said, 'You must make good your promise and suffer your trials, my friend, but if you are resolute, all will come to pass as it must. You will, in the end, save our world and help restore a much-needed balance.'

Pug looked hard at Nakor. 'Do you speak of—'

'No one knows of your arrangement with the Death Goddess, Pug, except she and you.'

'But you do,' Pug whispered. 'How is that possible? Even Miranda doesn't know.'

'Nor can she, or any other mortal,' said Nakor.

'Who *are* you?' Pug asked.

'That,' said Nakor, 'is a very long story.' Then he grinned his familiar grin and said, 'All in good time. Now we must wait.' Looking over at the horrific scene in the heart of the pit, he said, 'I hope our wait is short. This place is no fun.'

Men screamed in pain and shock as the Black Mount suddenly expanded in a single gigantic spasm. Where it had been half a mile away one moment, the next it loomed over the command centre, mere yards from Alenburga's headquarters. Miranda managed to get a defensive shield up but it was already too late.

The screaming stopped as abruptly as it had started. The men who had been positioned before the commander's observation point on the ground below the hill had, it appeared, been bisected by the arrival of the sphere. Blood and body parts rimmed the edge of the sphere.

Miranda cried, 'We must pull back!'

Stunned by the sight of the Black Mount, General Alenburga now ordered, 'Withdraw!' To the four young captains who waited to carry out his instructions he said, 'Head south. There's a knoll near a stream that feeds into the river. Grab as many maps as you can carry and take them there.' To Kaspar and Erik he said, 'Gentlemen, it's time to go.' To Miranda he said, 'Madam, if you and your magical friends can shed any light on this development, sooner is better than later.'

The commanders of the Tsurani army made an orderly, but hurried, departure.

Miranda felt confident that the sphere wouldn't expand again for a while, but her curiosity was piqued. She closed her eyes while others around her beat a hasty retreat, and sent her mind forward.

She encountered the mystic anti-scrying magic she had been repulsed by previously, and sought once more to neutralize it. She had discussed this problem with several other magicians while they were resting, and had got several useful suggestions. She realized one point made was possibly the most cogent: it wasn't a barrier, but rather a counter-spell, one designed to harm, injure, or kill should intrusion be pressed. If that was the case, she could counter it, as long as she was willing to endure some discomfort.

She forced her mind to conjure up the strength of will to push her mystic sight through the barrier and felt a sharp stab of pain as she did so. She battled the pain and erected defensive spells of her own to counter the attack on her mind, and then she looked at what was occurring inside the sphere. The revulsion she felt as her mind registered the scene before her caused her to recoil instinctively. She almost fainted as she tore her mind back to this side of the barrier.

An unknowable time later, she found Erik von Darkmoor standing over her and Miranda realized she was lying on the ground. 'Are you all right?' he asked calmly in the midst of the organized chaos.

'I saw . . .' she said weakly as the old warrior extended his hand to help her to her feet.

'What did you see?' he encouraged, supporting her by one arm.

'We must . . .'

'What?'

Her eyes were unfocused and her thoughts were cloudy. She said, 'We must leave.'

'We are leaving,' he said. 'We're pulling back to regroup.'

'No,' she said. 'We must leave . . . this world.'

'Miranda,' he said calmly as he walked her down the hill to where a lackey held his mount, 'what are you saying?'

He saw her wits return and despite her obvious exhaustion, her eyes were wide and her features became animated. 'Erik! They've opened . . . I don't know what to call it. It's not a rift as I know it, but rather . . . a tunnel! It's some sort of passage between the two realms, and it's occupying almost the entire inside of that sphere!' She looked back at the monstrous Black Mount that rose up into the late afternoon sky like terrible dark boil on the surface of the planet. 'The mouth of the tunnel is this vast pit, only a hundred or so yards inside the edge of the sphere. It must expand as the sphere expands.' She squeezed her eyes shut, and took a deep breath. 'Most of your troops . . . they must have fallen into that void . . . tunnel, whatever it is.'

'Gods,' he said softly.

'Erik,' she said, looking around and realizing that Alenburga and Kaspar had already departed. 'You have to tell them. Everyone . . . we must evacuate as many people as we can. There are Deathpriests inside that thing, stunning those who fell inside, your men, and they had Deathknights throwing them into the opening of the tunnel . . .' She closed her eyes as if willing herself to remember. 'Erik, they're feeding it. They're using your soldiers to make it stronger, make it bigger.'

Erik's face drained of colour. 'And when it gets strong enough, it'll jump again?'

'Yes,' said Miranda, almost unable to frame the word. 'The sphere will get bigger . . . and bigger . . .' Her voice grew softer and she started to wobble on her feet. 'Until it covers this whole world . . .'

'But it can't keep growing . . . forever.'

Miranda's face was ashen. 'No, it only needs to get big enough to let something come through from the other side . . .'

'What?'

'The Dark God of the Dasati,' she whispered. Miranda went limp and only Erik's firm grip kept her from falling to the ground.

'You!' he shouted to a nearby soldier. 'Get a litter! Bear her to the Supreme Commander!'

'Yes, sir,' said the Tsurani Strike Leader he had addressed.

Erik looked at the sphere as he waited. Against the armies of the Emerald Queen at Nightmare Ridge he had survived with what he had. This time, however, he felt a sense of helplessness. This time maybe no one would survive.

Pug and Magnus covered their ears to protect them from the shrieking sound. Nakor was knocked to the floor.

The entirety of the cavern shook and vibrated and many of those near the rim of the cavern fell over, screaming as they fell to their death. Nakor sat up and pointed. 'Look!'

A circular column of air was swirling down from above, like a giant wind funnel, and through it fell more bodies. Flashes like lightning cracked through the gloom, illuminating the vast cavern with a blinding silver light. Above a giant hole appeared at the top of the funnel, and more bodies started falling through it.

'They're Tsurani!' shouted Magnus.

There was no mistaking the armour and the human forms as thousands of men cascaded down through the hole. Suddenly the giant form of the Dreadlord shook and he began to shimmer and flow like silk in the wind.

Then from the surface of the malignant being

tendrils of foul-smelling smoke rose up, and flowed into the funnel, combining with it, and seeming somehow to add to its volume.

'What is happening?' Pug shouted to Nakor.

'The Dreadlord has opened a passage between this world and Kelewan,' shouted the small man. 'It is not like your rifts, Pug, or even the portals used to gain a foothold. Now this world and Kelewan are linked, and as the Dreadlord gains strength, he'll push the area of his control outward. The greater the surface of Kelewan he covers, the more people under the dome of his control will die. The larger the number who die, the bigger the dome. Kelewan is to be his next home. He is using his own being, the energy he has stored inside himself from thousands of years of death, and he's using it to pull himself through to Kelewan. Somewhere in this process, and soon I fear, he will begin his journey through that tunnel to Kelewan.'

'What of the Dasati?' asked Magnus.

'They are dupes on an unimaginable scale.' He looked at Pug. 'Your father has already come to understand the truth about the Dark One. He is using them as a means to gain access to the next highest plane: the idea that he is opening up a new realm for the Dasati is a lie. He will abandon this world and move on, but not before he drains this one of all life.

'Once he's established himself on Kelewan, he'll erect a Dark Temple, like this one, then return the planet to its former state, and whatever remnants of humanity exist on it will be allowed to breed and repopulate and form new societies while the Dreadlord sleeps. He will sleep for centuries, but his dreams will hold sway over the emerging tribes of mankind. He will make Kelewan a mockery of its former greatness, turning the Tsurani into murdering death-worshippers like the Dasati and start them moving upward to the next highest realm.'

'How do you know all this?' asked Pug.

'Because it's happened before, Pug,' answered Nakor. 'In other places and here, on this world.' Nakor signalled for them to make their way to the relative shelter of the dais behind the TeKarana's throne. He crawled around behind it on all fours, and they staggered against the wind and crouched down next to him. He said, 'It's that long story I mentioned.'

'Is it time to tell us?' asked Pug.

'Yes,' said Nakor. 'It is time for the truth.' He held up his hand and suddenly time stopped.

'That's a very good trick, Nakor,' said Magnus, true awe in his tone.

'Yes, it is,' said Pug.

'I can't hold this for very long, but at least we'll have a bit of quiet,' said the little gambler. He sat down on the stones. 'I'm very tired, Pug. I should have died a long time ago, I think, but as you know better than anyone else, sometimes the gods don't care what you think should or should not be happening.'

'What is this truth you're going to tell, Nakor?' Pug pressed.

'There are some things I don't know, and some things that are still in doubt and can't be fore-told. And even a few things I'm forbidden to tell you.'

Pug looked at his long-time friend and said nothing.

After a moment, Nakor said, 'I have something inside me, Pug. As does Bek, but what he carries and what I carry are not the same. Inside Bek is a sliver of something very powerful.'

'You said you thought he might have a sliver of the Nameless within him,' said Magnus.

Nakor grinned and shook his head. 'No, I lied. That's not it. When he was a boy I think he was just a bad boy, a lout, a thug or killer waiting to get hanged or have his throat cut . . . but somehow he became entangled in this thing we do, this struggle to restore a long-lost balance in . . . well, in everything.'

'Go on,' said Pug.

'The first night he stayed with me, outside the cave with all the Talnoy hidden inside, he was curious, as I expected him to be, and he sneaked inside to look. I pretended to be asleep. I knew then I'd either have to kill him or use him. So, I did something to him.'

'What?'

'I reached inside him and there I found a strange and marvellous power. It was familiar and I had a dream.' Nakor smiled. 'More of a vision, maybe. Anyway, time stopped then, or I had hours of thoughts in seconds, but suddenly I knew . . . everything. Bek came to me because it was pre-ordained that he should. The thing that moved him was the same as what moved me, when I was young. Both of us were tools of the gods, but with a different purpose. I was to be his guide, and he was to be the vessel to bring something back to Omadrabar that had been lost. So, I made him a vessel.'

'A vessel?' asked Magnus. 'For what?'

'For what was inside one of the Talnoy in the cave.'

Pug was speechless. What the Dasati with Macros's memory had told him was that each of the Talnoy housed the soul of a lost Dasati god. 'You put a god inside him?'

'Only a tiny little bit, but enough.'

'Enough for what?' asked Magnus.

'Enough to make sure the TeKarana died, even if Valko didn't kill him, and that something of critical importance would come back here.'

'What?' asked Pug, now totally confused by the little man's convolutions.

'The gods, Pug. Remember, all the gods on all the realms are just aspects of the same fundamental powers, and all the gods of our realm and those above and below are locked in a struggle with the creatures of the Void. When the Dark One rose to power, a mad plot was put in place, one that caused the ten thousand gods of the Dasati to hide in plain sight.'

'The Talnoy.'

'Yes. The Dark One is powerful, but there is nothing intelligent about the Dreadlords. I don't even know if they can be said to think the way we do. They exist, they act, they have purpose, but . . . they are beyond our understanding. So, the Dreadlord first subverted the worshippers of the God of Death, Bakal, and began the Dark Temple. When the Chaos War raged here, the Dasati gods were given haven.'

'On Midkemia,' said Magnus.

'Yes, in that cave, where they have stayed for . . . more years than I can count.'

'What of the one Kaspar found?'

'That was put there by Macros, at the bidding of . . . well, the one who is really behind all of what we've been struggling with. Macros was only another agent of the gods. So, Bek is the first of the ancient Dasati gods to return home. To these people, he is Kantas-Barat. On our world he would be Onan-ka.'

'The God of Battle,' said Pug.

'It seemed right for these people. The Happy Warrior has come home. Bek will remain for a while, but his mortal days are over. He has been consumed by the god that is within him. Bek as we knew him when he first appeared is no more.

508

He has been dead since before we came to this realm, really.'

'How did you put . . . a tiny bit of a god into Bek, Nakor?' asked Magnus.

'That's the hard part to explain,' said Nakor. He pointed to his own chest. 'I have something here, and sometimes it . . . takes over. Sometimes I remember it doing things, tricks I don't know, and other times . . . it's just blanks. I go to sleep one place, wake up another, and sometimes people are very angry with me, or sometimes I have things I didn't have before in my sack.'

'Do you know who's doing this?' asked Pug.

'Oh, yes,' said Nakor with a grin. 'And you need to know, because you need to take him back.'

'Take who back?' asked Magnus.

'Ban-ath.'

Pug sat down next to Nakor. 'The God of Thieves?'

'The Midkemian god of thieves,' confirmed Nakor. 'He cannot stay without a protective vessel,' — Nakor pointed to his own chest— 'or he will perish – well, he won't perish, but the tiny part of him I carry within will – and what he has learned here must go back. You must be his vessel for a little while, until you get home.'

'But why don't you take him back?' asked Magnus.

Nakor grinned. 'Because I'm not going back. This is my time.' He looked around at the vast cavern and said, 'It's an odd place to die, don't you think? At least I'll have a lot of company, human as well as Dasati.'

'Why do you need to stay, Nakor?'

'Because something very big, and very important, needs to happen, and I need to be here to see that it does. I will have just enough tricks left to ensure that this thing goes as it should, and then I will . . . end.' He stood up slowly. Pug also stood up. Nakor touched his own chest with his hand and said, 'He may answer some questions; perhaps he will think he owes you that much. Perhaps not.' He moved his hand from his chest suddenly and put it against Pug's, and instantly Pug could feel something flow from Nakor's hand into Pug's body.

'What—?'

'I'm going to rest now,' said Nakor. 'You have something you must do, and soon.'

'What?' asked Pug.

'You must go to the cave in Novindus and tell something to the Talnoy there, with that crystal I fashioned, or the ring, either will do.'

'What must I tell them, Nakor?' asked Pug as he helped his friend sit down again.

His eyes suddenly tired and his face lined with age, the tiny gambler looked at his friend and said, 'You must open a rift to Kelewan, near the Dasati invasion site. Then tell them one thing: tell them to go home.'

Magnus said, 'We must find Martuch and have him send us back.'

'No need,' said Nakor. 'He would tell you what I am telling you: stop trying so hard.'

'What?' asked Magnus.

Grinning even more, Nakor said, 'Your father understands.'

Magnus looked at Pug who started to laugh. 'It's all a joke, isn't it, Ban-ath?'

A voice inside his head said, 'Sometimes.'

Pug reached out and took his son's hand. 'With all those things taught to us by Martuch on Delecordia, we began a process of trying to be here. Now, to go home, all we must do is—'

'Stop trying,' finished Magnus.

Pug gripped his son's hand tightly. 'Just let go, Magnus.' He looked down at his old friend and said, 'I will miss you, gambler.'

'I will miss you as well, magician.' Nakor yawned. 'The end comes quickly as it must. That is good, for I am very tired and need to rest. The God of Thieves gave me a far longer allotment than most men have, so I do not feel cheated it ends now.' He rested his back against the rear of the throne. 'I'm going to start time again, so it will get noisy and unpleasant. You might want to leave now.' He held up his hand and suddenly the wind and noise returned.

Pug said to his son once more. 'Let go, Magnus.'

Magnus closed his eyes and tried to relax. 'Father, it's as if I've clenched my fist for a year. I can't unfold my fingers.'

'Slowly. Let go slowly.'

Pug and Magnus stood motionless, concentrating the part of themselves that had been controlling the magic that allowed them to stay in the second realm, and suddenly, there was a wrenching pain, as if fire burned across their minds. Then their lungs burned and their skin felt as if lightning danced across it.

Both men fell to their knees and then lay prostrate on the ground. When the pain ebbed away and they at last could open their eyes, they found they were no longer in the deep cavern. Instead they were in a crater littered with stones and rubble. The noise and stench of the deep pit was gone.

Pug felt his lungs almost collapse from the pain of breathing, but with each breath the pain lessened. After a moment he sat up and saw his son, looking as he always had. Magnus groaned and then started to cough and finally managed also to sit up. Pug saw that his son's illusion was gone and that he looked human once more.

'Where are we?' Magnus asked his father.

Pug stood on unsteady legs and looked around. 'I recognize this! We are in a sub-basement—'

'But there's nothing above us,' interrupted his son.

'I know, but once this was the lowest level of the great arena in the Holy City.'

'We're back on Kelewan?'

'Apparently,' said Pug as he looked around. 'Given the congruency of the two worlds, it makes sense that if we changed the realm in which we resided, we wouldn't have any reason to change location.' He pointed to the rubble surrounding them. 'The Dasati raid . . . it was more like utter destruction.'

A pain erupted inside Pug's chest and head, and he doubled over, only staying upright with his son's help.

'What is it, Father?'

'Ban-ath,' said Pug. 'He's reminding me I need to get back to Midkemia.'

'Can you conjure a rift home, or should I fly us to the Assembly?'

'I can make a rift and take us where we need to go,' said Pug, though he was almost at the point of total exhaustion.

He closed his eyes and Magnus looked around the crater that had at one time been the bottom of the great arena in Kentosani. The stones around them still reeked of conflict magic and Magnus detected other energies. A great battle had been waged here, as both magicians and priests from the various orders fought against the raiding Dasati. If the reports that had reached Valko were true – and apparently they were – the Dasati had destroyed a large part of the population after killing everyone in the Tsurani High Council and the Tsurani response had been slow; early estimates had put the dead at fifty thousand Tsurani, warriors and common people. But looking at the devastation around him, Magnus could easily believe more than that number had perished, for this was the result of Tsurani magic, not the deathmagic practised by the Dasati. Some group of magicians and priests had literally torn this arena down around the ears of the Dasati. While his father worked, Magnus used his own arts to rise into the air, gaining a better look.

Once he could see over the rubble that had been the shell of the great arena, he wished he hadn't. The entire heart of the Holy City was in ruins. Fires still burned in sections abandoned by those who lived there and nowhere close by could Magnus detect any sign of life. There was still a faint stench of decay on the wind as bodies left unburied lay where they had fallen. Scavengers had finished most of the work days earlier, but just enough death lingered on the stones to suggest to Magnus this was now a dead city.

He felt overwhelmed, even after all they had been through. Could they really stop the Dark Lord from reaching this world?

He lowered himself down just as his father finished casting his rift-spell, and a doorway-sized grey oval appeared in the air. Without saying anything to his son, Pug stepped through and Magnus followed him.

Caleb stood in shock as his father and brother walked through a rift into his father's office and then he raced forward as his father collapsed to the floor. Magnus also could barely stand and had to put his hand to the wall to steady himself.

'Mother will be overjoyed to see you,' Caleb said, as he knelt beside Pug, 'if you have the good grace not to die on me before she returns.'

Magnus smiled. He enjoyed Caleb's dry sense of humour. 'It's good to see you, too, little brother.'

Half-conscious now, Pug required the help of both his sons to regain his feet. Once he had stood up, he said 'I feel sick. The transition.'

Magnus felt as ill as he had when they had first transited to Delecordia.

'Get a healer,' said Pug to Caleb. 'We do not have the luxury of time. We cannot afford to lie abed for days.'

'I'll send for one,' said Caleb, 'but until he arrives, to bed with both of you.'

Caleb called for help and a pair of students came to take Magnus back to his quarters, while Caleb helped his father to his own.

As soon as Caleb left his father to await the healer, Pug felt a searing pain across his forehead and he arched his back in agony. Then the pain vanished.

A man stood next to the bed. 'Sorry,' he said. He was a familiar figure, short and bandy-legged and wearing a tattered orange robe. He had a rucksack hanging from one shoulder and held a staff in the other hand. He waved his hand and Pug's pain and fatigue lessened.

'Nakor?' asked Pug in wonder.

'Not really, but I thought you'd prefer this appearance to the others I've used over the years,' answered the figure. 'And should anyone chance upon us, it'll save a lot of questions.'

'Ban-ath?'

Bowing, the figure said, 'At your service, Pug. Or rather, you've been at mine. And you're not done yet, but we are getting close to the end.'

Pug sat up, feeling as if he had rested for days. 'What have you done?'

'Well, if all goes according to plan, I've saved the world and everyone in it, as well as a sizeable piece of this entire universe,' said the god in Nakor's form. 'You're looking a mess, magician, and you have much left to do, so clean up while I tell you some things.'

'More lies and manipulations?'

'Oh, almost certainly, eventually, but for now I'm content to limit myself to the truth, for right now, that will serve me best.'

'The truth?'

'Yes, magician, this time you hear the truth.'

CHAPTER 21

TRUTH

Pug listened.

'There's little to be gained by rushing, but time does press. Still, after what you've endured over the years—'

'Over the years?' Pug interrupted.

The god who looked like Nakor held up his hand. 'Do you remember the story Nakor told you, the parable of the scorpion and the frog?'

'The scorpion kills the frog who is helping it cross the river and when asked why answers, "because it is my nature". Yes, I remember it.'

'Good,' said Ban-ath. 'Because it is my nature to lie, to manipulate, to steal, cheat, and ignore laws and rules at every hand. It was I who put you where Macros could find you, Pug. I who guided him to Crydee and let him think watching over you was his idea. It was I who manipulated every step of Macros's way, making him think he was serving the lost God of Magic.' He betrayed a moment of reflection in his expression as he gazed out into space and said, 'It will come to pass that Sarig returns, just as the others returned, as the Dasati gods returned to their realm . . . if we survive long enough, but Macros was not Sarig's servant. He was mine. His vanity was my biggest ally; he never once conceived that anything he did might not be the product of his own genius.

'I manipulated his magic to infuse the ancient armour found by Tomas in the dragon's cave, so that my magic could bridge time and space, and convey Tomas's thoughts back to Ashen-Shugar, manipulating one of the enemies of the gods, so a war we were losing could become a war postponed.'

'What?' Pug was incredulous.

'What you call the Chaos Wars is only a small part of a much vaster conflict, one about which you are now learning, one which has been raging since before the rise of humanity and even the creation of the gods. At the advent of a new epoch, when we who are your gods rose and deploy those forces you think of as the Two Blind Gods of the Beginning, as the Valheru rose against us, all of that . . . well, to put it bluntly, at that time we . . . or more to the point, *I* was on the losing side.'

Pug could only stare at the likeness of Nakor.

'So I cheated.'

Pug suddenly started to laugh. He could not help himself, but in that instant he realized that no matter how vast and deep this conflict was, no matter how dire the results were for millions of intelligent beings, to this entity, this 'god', it was just a game, no more worthy of respect than a game of lin-lan in the back room of an ale-house in Krondor.

Nakor's face grinned. 'Ah, you do appreciate a good joke, don't you?'

'Joke?' said Pug, sobering. 'I'm laughing at the sheer madness of this all. I'm laughing to stop myself from reaching out to strangle you.'

'I wouldn't recommend your trying, Pug,' said Ban-ath, suddenly solemn. 'Understand, I am the scorpion, and I can no more change my nature than you can become a frog.'

Pug waved away the remark. There was a knock at the door, and suddenly the figure of Nakor was gone. The door opened and Caleb appeared with a young woman behind him, a healer named Mianee.

Pug said to them, 'I'm fine, really. Bring me some food if you don't mind, and some ale. Actually, I'm famished.'

Mianee was a no-nonsense type who refused to be put off, so Pug endured a quick examination, after which she pronounced him fit. She left and Caleb returned with food and ale. When the tray was on the table at the bedside, Pug said, 'I would like some time alone, son. I'll call you if I need something.'

Caleb appeared about to ask a question, thought better of it, then left, closing the door behind him. Pug looked from the door back to the tray and found a stranger standing next to it, picking up a piece of cheese. He was of slight build and had curly brown hair and Pug took a moment to recognize him. 'Jimmy?'

'Of course not,' said the figure, nibbling at the cheese. He was now the twin of young Lord James, Jimmy the Hand, when he had first come into Prince Arutha's service as a squire. 'This is very good.'

'Ban-ath,' said Pug.

'Of if you prefer Kalkin, Antrhen, Isodur, or any number of other names humanity inflicts on me – Coyote is one of my favourites – but no matter the name, I am myself.' He gave a theatrical bow which very much reminded Pug of the former thief who had grown up to marry his daughter and become one of the legendary figures of Kingdom history.

Pug sat back and started to eat. After a moment of silence, Ban-ath said, 'As I was saying: we were losing the war with the ancient powers and the Valheru were doing us no good. Of a hundred lesser aspects and the dozen greater aspects of the godforce only a dozen lesser and four greater endured.

'You must understand I am giving you a limited perspective, a glimpse of a far greater whole, but a whole which is beyond even your not inconsiderable intellect's ability to grasp. Yours is, perhaps, the greatest mind in the history of the human race on Midkemia, Pug.' Pug began to object, but Ban-ath cut him off. 'Save your modesty, for although it may be considered a pleasant quality by most people, I don't see it that way. Vain people like Macros are easy to manipulate. There is an axiom, "you can't cheat an honest man", and an honest man admits his own shortcomings. With you I must approach certain tasks in a different fashion than I did with Macros; I could easily convince him he was the genius behind all his plots and intrigues;. You, on the other hand, are more effective working on behalf of something you believe in, and while telling you the truth is less fun, it is more efficient. Still, I'm willing to be honest – occasionally – since I am a creature of hard facts and probabilities. Best of all, you know what you don't know and long to learn, which is why you're a great deal more intelligent than most people.' Ban-ath waved him out of the bed. 'Get dressed.'

With a snap of the god's fingers, Pug was suddenly wearing a clean, fresh robe.

'The food?'

Another finger snap and Pug was no longer hungry. 'With rank comes privilege. We can talk while we travel. We have a lot to see.'

Another finger snap and they were somewhere else.

It was a void, but not like the one he had experienced when he had destroyed the original Tsurani rift at the end of the Riftwar. This felt different. Rather than the absence of anything, this place felt as if they were surrounded by everything, but in a fine powder, compared to which the finest mote of dust was grotesquely large and coarse. 'Where are we?' Pug asked.

'We are in the fourth realm below, or what your poets, dramatists, and not a few clergy called the Fourth Level of Hell.'

Thinking of what he had glimpsed through the portal to the fifth circle when Macros had battled the Demon King Maarg, and what he had seen of the second plane – the Dasati plane – he said, 'This is not what I expected.'

'Nor is it what you would have encountered millennia ago, had you cause to visit.' Pug detected an odd tone in the god's voice, a note of regret. 'This was to the Dasati world what their world is to yours. There were beings living here, Pug, a little more civilized by your standards than the demons, but not by that much. Still, they had a society, or rather a great many of them, for they were spread far and wide throughout this universe, much as humanity is spread throughout our realm.'

'What happened?'

'The Dark One,' said Ban-ath shortly.

'What do you mean?'

'No one knows, or at least no one I know does, and I know a lot of people . . . billions in fact.'

Pug glanced at the source of the voice, expecting to see Nakor again, but there was nothing but void all around him. 'What am I seeing?'

'A plane of reality so devoid of life that it has been reduced to a fine primordial grit, a place where every single bit of reality has been equally distributed across the entire volume of this reality.'

'How is that possible?'

'In an infinite universe, anything you can imagine is possible somewhere, probable, even.'

'Then this entire realm is completely devoid of anything beyond this . . . fine dust?'

'Well, nothing is eternal, or at least we'll never know. Even the gods as you think of us have limits on their perceptions and existence. It may be that for some reason or another two motes will bump into one another and bind, and eventually a third will join them, and that attraction will continue as it pulls more matter into a sphere. Eventually all that is here will be pulled in and when it reaches a certain level of density—'

'It explodes,' said Pug. 'And a new universe is created. It's what Macros showed us—'

'In the Garden by the City Forever, when the Pantathians trapped you, Macros, and Tomas was there with that dragon, yes, I remember.'

'You remember?'

Laughing, the God of Thieves said, 'I orchestrated it!' His tone turning serious, Ban-ath added, 'You may never fully understand, nor may you ever forgive me – about which I care nothing – but many of the pains you've suffered and the wonders you've observed have been part of a much larger plan, one that has been preparing you for what you must do now.

'Seeing that image of how your universe began was merely your first lesson in appreciating just how vast things are, and how important what you're about to do is. For you must do something that you would have been unable to until now. You had to see a universe born, watch people die including those you've loved, travel the Hall of Worlds, and do so many other improbable things, Pug, because you must undertake even more arduous and challenging tasks and make decisions no mortal should ever have to make.'

'What decisions?'

'In time. Right now you must learn more.'

'We're not really here, are we?'

'No. We're still in your room, actually, and you're sitting quietly on your bed staring into space, but for the sake of what comes next, think of yourself as being on an amazing journey.'

Ban-ath snapped his fingers.

There was a flash and suddenly they were in a different reality, one in which massive chunks of rock and debris sped past at great speed. This time Pug saw a sky that was more akin to what he might expect of the Dasati universe, a place of colours and energies vivid to the eye, but beyond human senses. But here there were vast curtains of colours with massive flows of energy pulsing across their surfaces, and he knew he was witnessing something incredibly distant. Sheets of scintillating colours, red, purple, violet, and indigo shimmered impossible distances away, covering incalculable areas in the heavens. A giant rock the size of a mountain tumbled past, energy dancing across its face, sending jets of magma erupting into space. A vast distance away, stars illuminated the vault of the sky, though there were far fewer than in the night skies at home.

'Where are we?' asked Pug.

'This is the third realm, most recently occupied by the Dark One. As you see, he left enough big pieces behind this so that level of reality has a chance to reform a little more rapidly than the realm we just left. There are corners of this universe where life still exists, a few minor civilizations in fact. They may even endure long enough to reach out to other worlds.'

'Why is there less destruction here?'

'A variety of reasons,' said Ban-ath. 'As you have no doubt noticed the states of energy are much higher in our realm, the so-called first realm, which by the way is considered the first circle of Hell by those who live in the realm above us.'

Pug laughed. 'It's a matter of perspective, I guess.'

'Very much so.' Ban-ath's tone turned sombre. 'You have been cursed as much as blessed, Pug of Crydee. More than any mortal since Macros.'

'I'm beginning to understand that.'

'Macros was an imperfect vessel, our first attempt, and in many ways he was a poor choice.'

'Why?

'The things that made him so easy to manipulate: vanity, arrogance, and a fundamental distrust of others. You on the other hand were a new soul,

525

untroubled by so many of the things which marked Macros in previous lives. You are the result of a conspiracy of gods, for we had need of you.'

'Why?'

'Because you are a weapon, of sorts, and a tool, and you bring the one thing to this situation that no god can: humanity. We are slaves to you as much as being your masters, Pug. The relationship between the gods and humanity is one of a fair exchange. We provide expression for your deepest beliefs and needs, and you give us form and substance.'

'Why you?' asked Pug. 'If I had been asked before which god would be responsible for restoring things to this realm as they should be, I might have suggested Ishap, for balance is crucial. Or among the lesser gods, perhaps Astalon, for his justice, or Killian for her nurturing of nature. But you?'

'Who else?' said Ban-ath, giving a deep rumble of a laugh. 'Macros thought he was somehow working for the lost God of Magic, Sarig, and Nakor thought he was the instrument of Wodan-Hospur, the lost God of Knowledge.' He paused. 'You've seen only a tiny aspect of the gods, Pug, but you've seen more than most. And you've heard more, from people like Nakor and Jimmy.

'You know that even the memory of a god, or a god's dream, or a god's echo can take on form and substance, and can act as if the god were still present.

'I am here presenting to you an aspect of myself, providing an illusion to instruct you, but I am also at the same time listening to a thief in Roldem who is about to be found out by the City Watch, begging me to intervene. I am watching a man lie to his wife as he leaves to meet his mistress, who lies to him about loving him while taking his gold to give to her lover, a thug who doesn't quite believe in me, but who grudgingly leaves a copper once a month in the votive box in my shrine in LaMut, just in case. I am also listening to the pleas of a gambler about to lose his last coin and who will be beaten and killed later tonight when he can not pay back the gold he borrowed from an agent of the Mockers in Krondor when the Upright Man makes an example of him. I am sitting with a merchant who has placed gold in the hands of one of my priests to beg me to keep my worshippers away as he ships valuable spices from Muboya to the City of the Serpent River. I hear every prayer and answer them all, though most of the time my answer is "no". I also see every act done in my name, and an endless series of possibilities for every choice made. Humanity speaks to me constantly, Pug.

'All know me by a different name, or guise, or aspect. I am the god of thieves, and liars, and gamblers. But I am also the god of those who undertake impossible quests, and hopeless causes. And that is why it is I who acts on behalf of the gods of Midkemia, for if there was ever a hopeless cause it is stemming the advance of the Dread into our world, Pug.

'There are rules and they bind the gods as much as they bind mortals, and Astalon and Killian, Guis-wa, and Lims-Kragma – for all their powers – cannot ignore those rules. The laws of the universe say that we are confined to this realm, that no matter how important and puissant we may be in this, our realm, in other realms we are trespassers and hold no sway. So then, who better to enter the other realm and effect change than me?'

'The god who ignores the law, and breaks the rules,' said Pug.

'Yes,' chuckled Ban-ath. 'The Trickster. The Cheater. Only I can do what needs to be done, for it is as much my nature as it is the scorpion's nature to sting that stupid frog to death!'

Suddenly they were standing on a hill, on the edge of a bucolic valley through which ran a stream where fish could be seen jumping.

'Where are we?' Pug asked.

'It's somewhere you've been before, once.'

'When?'

'Remember,' said Ban-ath, and Pug did.

'Macros, Tomas, and I stopped here on our way back through the Hall of Worlds, after leaving the City Forever, before the Battle of Sethanon.' Pug looked around. Deer-like herbivores grazed in the meadows and birds sang in the trees. In so many ways this world resembled Midkemia. 'Why did you bring me here?'

'So that you would remember this place,' said Ban-ath, and then he vanished. From the empty air came a disembodied voice. 'Consider this a small gift for services given. I have no concern for the Tsurani, for they are not my people, but you do, as I know well. No trick this, but a heartfelt expression of gratitude. I may be a natural force without compassion, but occasionally nature is clement.'

Pug said, 'What do I do now?'

Suddenly they were back in his room, and he was in bed. His meal was finished, so he assumed while he was on this mystical journey he had actually been eating.

'You save this world,' came Ban-ath's voice from the air around him.

Pug hesitated for only a moment, then he climbed out of bed and donned a fresh robe. 'Caleb!' he shouted, and waited for his son to appear.

People ran screaming from a thundering horde of Dasati Deathknights mounted on varnin. Whatever had prohibited the Dasati from protecting the war-steeds during the early onset of this war had obviously been overcome, for now cadres of Dasati riders erupted from the constantly expanding Black Mount. Any Tsurani resistance was futile, for at best it merely stemmed the Dasati advance, while costing the lives of the defenders. At worst they were overcome and the Dasati reached their objective, which now seemed to be to capture as many Tsurani as possible and drag them back into the Black Mount.

Miranda stood next to Alenburga and surveyed the sphere, now miles across, dominating the horizon. 'In the last hour,' she said, 'I reckon it's expanded by about another mile.'

Alenburga sighed. 'I can't keep throwing soldiers' lives away. There must be another way.'

'I've tried every magic at my disposal, as has each member of the Assembly. We've lost more than two hundred magicians in the fight, and those who remain are fast losing hope.'

'Unless you have a miracle in reserve,' said the old general from Novindus, 'I think it's time to tell the Emperor he needs to evacuate.'

'I think you need to tell him yourself,' said Miranda.

Alenburga looked at Kaspar who nodded his agreement. Then he looked towards Erik, who said, 'Go on. We'll keep an eye on things.'

Alenburga turned to Miranda. 'Take me there.'

Miranda put her hand on the General's shoulder and suddenly they were standing in a garden miles away, in the middle of the old Acoma estates. White-and-gold clad Imperial Guards drew their weapons before they realized the intruders were the woman magician and the outland general; then they moved to escort the visitors.

Inside the great house, Chomata, First Advisor to the Emperor waited. 'General,' he said, bowing his head in greeting. Next he acknowledged Miranda, 'Great One.' A thin, ascetic-looking old man with a balding pate, he looked as if he hadn't slept in a week. 'What news?'

'For the Emperor,' said the General, 'and I fear it is not good.'

'He'll want to see you at once,' said Chomata.

In his private chambers, the Emperor dined alone. Alenburga bowed as did Miranda, then the General said, 'Majesty, I bring grave news.' He quickly recounted the situation and their best estimate of how long it would be before the Dasati dome menaced this very estate.

'I will not leave my people,' the Emperor said calmly. 'How many have you evacuated through the rifts?'

Miranda felt her heart sink. 'Only twenty thousand or so, Majesty.'

'There are millions in the Empire, and what of those without . . . and have you considered the Cho-ja?'

Miranda realized she hadn't. Kelewan had several intelligent races besides humans, just as Midkemia did, but here the relationships were different. The Thūn raiders from the north were a constant plague on the northernmost garrisons and occasionally made it through the passes of the High Wall, to pillage estates there. The Cho-ja were an insect-like hive culture, each hive ruled by a queen, but as Miranda understood it, somehow they were all linked in communication. Of the other races she knew little – a race of savage dwarves across the Sea of Blood in the Lost Lands, an alien race of lizard-like creatures that lived on islands across the great sea to the west . . . Feeling defeated, she said, 'Majesty, I will plead to being mortal and having limits to my abilities. No, I have not thought of these things. My first thought was to defeat these monsters who menace both your world and mine. Now I seek to save the Tsurani people. As for those others, what would you have me do?'

From behind her a voice said, 'I can help.'

Miranda turned with tears welling up in her eyes. In two strides she was across the floor and then she had her arms tightly around her husband's neck. 'I was so afraid,' she whispered, words that Pug knew no other mortal would ever hear his wife utter. Then she said, 'Magnus?'

'Yes,' he whispered back. 'He's on our island, safe.'

She sobbed once. 'Thank the gods.' Then she asked, 'Nakor?'

'No,' he said softly, and he felt her body go rigid. She was still for a moment, then took a deep breath.

She turned to the Emperor and said, 'Despite this interruption, I must continue to urge you to make ready to seek refuge on Midkemia, Majesty.'

Pug said, 'That won't be necessary.'

All eyes turned to him. 'What are you saying, Milamber?' asked the Emperor. 'Can you defeat the Dasati?'

'No,' said Pug, acknowledging his Tsurani name. 'But I have found you a haven.'

'A haven?'

'It's a fair world.' He smiled. 'I'd say it's even a little more hospitable than Kelewan. There are forests and valleys, great seas with beautiful beaches, mountains and deserts. There's game in abundance and many places for farms and orchards, to run herds and build cities. And no one else lives there.'

'Milamber, is there no other way?' asked Sezu, and for the first time since meeting the Emperor, Pug saw the mask of imperial confidence break, and behind it he spied the uncertain young man.

'I wish there was, Majesty. I wish I could say the horror I've seen can be defeated, but it cannot. It can only be frustrated, and to save other worlds in this universe from it, Kelewan . . .' He hesitated to say what he knew to be true, that this world must be destroyed to prevent the Dark One from establishing any sort of foothold in this realm. Finally he said, 'Kelewan must be abandoned. It is the only hope for your people.'

Softly, the Emperor said, 'What shall I do?' He first looked at his elderly First Advisor, then at Pug and Miranda.

Finally Pug said, 'When I trained for the Black Robe, Majesty, I stood upon the Tower of Testing, and part of that ritual showed me what is known of the history of the Tsurani people.

'It all began with the Golden Bridge, when the

people of Kelewan first came here, fleeing from some nameless terror through a vast portal, to this world.'

'This is our legend,' said Chomata.

'The Tsurani people did not originate on Kelewan,' Miranda added.

'The Tsurani people can survive on another world,' said Pug. 'Tsuranuanni is not your cities and temples, the villages and towns, for you can build again, nor is it titles and honours for those can be restored. Tsuranuanni is your people. If they endure, a new Tsuranuanni can be forged.'

The Emperor was silent for a very long time, then he nodded. 'It shall be done.'

Pug said to Miranda, 'We have much to do. I will speak to the Thūn and you must speak with the Cho-ja. I will first go to the Assembly and see if any of those remaining have knowledge of the dwarves across the sea or other intelligent races.

'Then I must go to the Hall, and find that world I visited so long ago. Once there, I will open as large a rift as I can between that world and the original rift site, near the City of the Plain.

'Have the Great Ones of the Empire begin building rifts from every major city and from any safe place away from the Dasati and tell the people to gather what they may, for the Empire must be ready, the nations must be ready, the people must be ready! We have little time left.'

'How much time do we have?' asked the Emperor.

'Less than a week, Majesty. If we linger, we die, and with us die other worlds, eventually. I have seen it. It is the truth.'

'Go,' said Sezu, who now truly looked like a crestfallen young man, a young man wearing the mantle of leadership that had been thrust on him by an accident of birth. It was clear to everyone in the room that he would rather that burden be on other shoulders at this time, but he had made his decision and he was ready to act. 'Make it so,' he said.

CHAPTER 22

WARNINGS

The chill wind blew.

Pug repeated an approach he had used many years before, of transporting himself via magic to a place on the vast tundra of the Thūn. He hiked to the north for the better part of an hour, his black robe a stark contrast to the bare grey-and-white soil beneath his feet. He was in one of the few places on this world which knew cold and ice, and it felt strange.

A band of Thūn males appeared an hour before sunset, riding towards him. They were centaur-like creatures, but rather than a marriage of man and horse, they looked more like Saaur warriors grafted to the torsos of warhorses. Each carried a round shield and a sword and they hooted odd battle chants.

Pug was ready to attempt the same tactic he had used the only previous time he had come this far north: erecting a passive barrier so that they could not harm him, or force him to defend himself with violence.

But this time they came close enough to see his black robe and veered off, speeding back the way they had come. Having no time to wait for them to send out an expendable emissary, Pug followed in a series of magic jumps, staying just far enough behind them not to provoke an attack.

In less than an hour a village came into view and Pug could see more than a score of massive sod huts with ramps leading down towards doors, so he deduced that the houses must be half underground. Smoke rose through vent holes, and Thūn children and females moved among the buildings.

An alarm was sounded and instantly the young scurried for the safety of the huts. The females took up positions in the doorways, obviously ready to defend their young if the males were defeated. Pug realized that all the Thūn's encounters with humans in black robes had been punitive, save one, the last time he had spoken to them. As part of their nature, the Thūn attempted to range south of the mountains in winter, and for a thousand years they had been repulsed by the Tsurani.

Pug was about to seek to convince them to leave lands that had been their home since the dawn of time.

He erected a shield around himself, and approached slowly. A few used slings to hurl rocks at him and one shot at him with a bow, but when the missiles bounced harmlessly off the shield, they stopped. A few feigned charges and drew up short of slamming into him, but they all hooted and challenged him.

Pug stopped just outside the village boundary

and said in a loud, calm voice, 'I seek a parlay with the Lasura.' He used their own word for themselves, like so many others meaning 'the people'. *Thūn* was a Tsurani word.

For almost ten minutes nothing happened while Pug stood motionless and the Thūn warriors shouted what he took to be insults and challenges to single combat. He knew it was ritualized and expected of braves, but he and the Thūn also knew that the average Tsurani Great One could rain fire down on this village and Pug was far from average.

Finally an older male approached and in heavily-accented Tsurani said, 'Speak, Black One, if you must.'

'I speak of a great danger, not only to the Lasura, or Tsurani, or the Cho-ja, but to this whole world. Listen and heed me, for I come to you as a friend, and offer you escape.'

Pug spoke as well as he could, for nearly an hour, and tried to keep the concepts focused and plausible, for he knew there would be serious doubt that this was anything but some Tsurani ploy to lure the Thūn south to destruction. At the end he said, 'I must leave, and I have only this to say. Send fast runners to your other villages and tell them of what I have spoken.

'If you stay here you will perish in less than eight sunrises. But if you wish to live, go to the place on the plains where the seven fingers of rock rise up from the mountains to the south. There I will leave a magic doorway. Step through it and you

538

will find yourself on a grassy plain, with lush trees and warm breezes.'

'Why would a Tsurani for the Lasura do this?' asked the old male. 'Enemies are we, and always have been.'

Pug avoided explaining he was not Tsurani born – it was a needless complication – but said, 'This land was your land before the Tsurani came, and I would make this much right: come to where the Tsurani flee, to the new world, and I will make a home for you. You will have the oath of the Emperor of the Tsurani, and this entire land I speak of will be yours alone. No Tsurani will trouble you, for it is across a vast sea and you will share it with no others. This is my bond as a Great One of the Empire, and so is the bond of the Tsurani Light of Heaven.

'Heed my words, for I must leave now,' he said, and then he willed himself back to the Assembly.

Alone in the room set aside for Miranda and himself when they resided with the Tsurani, Pug closed his eyes for a moment, hoping that the Thūn would listen. But he was almost certain they would not.

Miranda approached the hive entrance with an escort of Imperial Guards. Cho-ja hive workers scurried about the Acoma estates as they had for centuries. Miranda knew that there had been some kind of special relationship between the Emperor's great-grandmother, Mara of the Acoma, and the hive queen and later the Cho-ja magicians in far-off Chakaha, the crystal-spired Cho-ja city far beyond the eastern border of the Empire. She did not know exactly what that relationship had been, but she understood that since then the Cho-ja had enjoyed the status of an autonomous people within the borders of the Empire.

At the entrance Miranda realized she had never been this close to a Cho-ja before. They were insects, as far as she was concerned, giant ants from her point of view, yet their upper torso rose like that of a human's, with similar musculature in the chest, shoulders and arms. Their faces were like those of a mantis, with eyes that looked like faceted metal spheres, but in the place of mandibles, the Cho-ja had mouths that were very human-like. Their colour in the sun was an iridescent blue-green. 'May we address your queen?' asked Miranda.

The guard stood motionless for a long moment, then asked in the Tsurani tongue, 'Who is it who seeks audience with our queen?'

'I am Miranda, wife of Milamber of the Assembly of Magicians. I seek an audience with your queen to bring word of grave peril to all Cho-ja.'

The guard twittered in a clicking language, then said, 'Word will be sent.' He turned and clicked loudly down the hall, and several passing Cho-ja workers turned to look at Miranda. After a few minutes, another Cho-ja, wearing some sort of mantle around his shoulders, appeared at the entrance. He made a fair imitation of a human bow, and said, 'I am one who advises, and have been sent to guide you. Please follow me and be cautious, the footing here is not easy for your feet.'

Miranda was too concerned by her mission to be amused by the odd syntax and the kindness of the warning. She followed the Cho-ja advisor into the tunnels. Her first impression was of a moist odour: a hint of a spice and a nutty tang. She realized this was the scent of the Cho-ja, and that it was not an unpleasant scent.

The tunnels were lit by some sort of fluorescence emanating from a bulbous growth that hung from odd supports that appeared to be of neither wood nor stone. As she moved down a long tunnel, she saw Cho-ja diggers excavating a side tunnel and saw a small Cho-ja extruding something from his jaws, his cheeks blown out to impossible proportions as he spat a compound onto the wall, then patted it into form and realized that these tunnel supports must be made of some body secretion.

In a deeper chamber she saw strange little Cho-ja hanging from the ceiling. They had long translucent wings which they beat furiously for a while, then rested, staggering the beating of their wings so that at least one of them in a group was always moving. Miranda realized that with miles of tunnels this deep and with thousands of Cho-ja living in these vast hives, they had to keep the air moving or suffocation in the lower tunnels would be a risk.

It took a good hike downward, but at last Miranda came to the royal chamber. This was a vast excavation, easily five storeys high with a score of tunnels leading away on all sides. In the midst of this huge chamber lay the Cho-ja queen, resting upon a raised mound of earth

She was immense, her segmented body at least thirty feet long from her head to the end of her second thorax. Her chitin looked like cured hide armour, polished black, and from the withered appearance of her legs Miranda realized she never moved from this location. Her body was draped with a beautifully woven tapestry of ancient Tsurani origin. On all sides workers cared for her enormous body, polishing her chitin, fanning her with their wings, carrying food and water to her. Above and behind her, and mounted back upon her thorax, a stocky male perched, rocking back and forth as he mated with her. Small workers surrounded him, tending him, while other males waited patiently to one side to play their role in the constant, endless Cho-ja breeding.

A dozen Cho-ja males were arrayed before the queen, some wearing crested helms and others without visible ornament; all greeted Miranda with polite, silent bows. On either side of chamber, smaller versions of the queen lay upon their stomach and attendants bustled about each of them. Miranda knew these were egg-bearing lesser queens, whose non-fertile eggs were passed to the queen, who swallowed them whole, fertilizing them inside her body and then laying them again.

Miranda bowed low before the assembled Cho-ja. 'Honours to your hive, my queen.'

'Honours to your house, Miranda of Midkemia.'

'I bear a most dire warning, Majesty,' she began. Calmly Miranda related all that Pug had told her of the coming of the Dreadlord and the plans to relocate the Tsurani to their new world. At the end, she said, 'This world is lush and abundant, and there is ample room for the Cho-ja. I understand that what one queen hears, all queens hear, and that my words are even now being heard by your kin in distant Chakaha. Your magicians are legendary and we would welcome their aid in preparing the rifts to this new world for time is short and there are so many to evacuate.'

The queen continued her normal duties, then finally she said, 'We, the Cho-ja, thank Miranda of Midkemia for her warning, and we thank all who are concerned for the well-being of the Cho-ja.' She fell quiet for a long moment, and Miranda wondered if there was some sort of silent communication underway between this queen and the others. Then the queen said, 'But we must decline your kindness.'

Miranda could scarcely credit what she had heard. 'What?' she blurted.

'We will stay and we will die.'

There was a total lack of emotion in that statement, making it all the more alien for its starkness.

'But why, Majesty? Of all those on Kelewan, you are the ones who are most able to facilitate your own evacuation. You have powerful users of magic and can fashion your own rifts through which to escape.'

'Mara of the Acoma came to fetch me when I was a hatchling,' began the old queen. 'She said I was pretty and that is why I came here. Since then she visited me many times, as did her son, and his son, and his son. I enjoy those visits, as do all the queens who share the experience with me, Miranda.

'But no human has ever truly understood our nature. We are of this world. We can not abide any-where else. We were of this world when humans first came here, in the time before history, and we will die with this world. It is what must be. Would you uproot trees and move them? Would you fish the seas and put creatures of the deep in alien waters to save them? Would you move the very rocks of Kelewan to save them? You humans are visitors here, and have always been such, and it is right you should move on, but we are of this world.' She paused for a moment, then repeated, 'We are of *this* world.'

Miranda was speechless. There was such a profound finality in the queen's words, that she knew debate was pointless. Feeling defeated she said weakly, 'If you have a change of heart, we will do what we can.'

'Again, we thank you for your concerns.'

'I will be away, for I have much to see to.'

'Honours to your house, Miranda of Midkemia.'

'Honours to your hive, Queen of the Cho-ja.'

Miranda felt something very beautiful and important was about to be lost, but there were still so many things to do that she pushed aside the ache in her chest and started the return to the surface where the Imperial Guards waited to escort her back to the Emperor.

Pug felt a chill that had nothing to do with the unusually cool highland wind. Kelewan was a hot world compared to Midkemia, but these highlands were home to bitter winters and cold nights. He stood motionless and waited as a group of five Thuril approached him on foot. He waited at the edge of the town called Turandaren, which over the years had become a major trading centre between the Thuril Confederation and the Empire. Once a village on the frontier, it had evolved over the years until it was the closest thing to a Tsurani settlement in the highlands.

Over a century of peace between the two people had not lessened their distrust of each other, for that peace had been preceded by centuries of war and attempted conquest by the Tsurani. The old walls might have crumbled but they were still defensible, and the Thuril were adept mountain fighters who had never been conquered by the Tsurani.

The leader of the five men was an old warrior

by the look of him. His long grey hair was plaited and he wore a small wool cap with a long feather hanging down behind his left ear. His upper body bore clan markings and old wounds, showing that while peace with the Empire might be the norm, that didn't preclude Thuril blood feuds and border raids. Banditry was commonplace along the trade routes, as well. He wore a deep blue tartan and carried a shield and longsword, both strapped to his back. The other four men looked more like merchants than warriors. The leader halted directly in front of Pug and said, 'You're standing as if you're waiting for an invitation to enter the town, Black Robe.'

Pug smiled. 'I thought if I waited here conspicuously I'd get faster results than if I wandered around town asking questions.'

The leader laughed. 'Not a bad guess.' He rubbed his chin. 'Now, I'm Jakam, hetman of Turandaren, and these worthies are men of note.' Pug noticed that he didn't bother to introduce them. 'What can we do for you, Tsurani?'

Pug said, 'I need to find the Confederation Council and, most importantly, I need to speak with the Kaliane.'

At the mention of the Kaliane, Jakam nodded his head, as if showing respect. 'The Council meets at the Warm Springs of Shatanda, near the town of Tasdano Abear. Do you know it?'

'I can find it, if you point me in the right direction.'

'Take the road east, up into the mountains, and at the notch in the ridge, you'll find two trails down. Take the northernmost, and follow it for a week if you walk, less if you have a horse or magic. That'll put you in the Valley of Sandram and at the northern end you'll find Tasdano Abear and the Warm Springs of Shatanda. The Council should be easy enough to find, it'll be in all those tents and huts thrown up around the springs. But you'd better hurry. Council ends in six days and the leaders of the clans will return to their homes.'

'I'll be there by nightfall,' said Pug.

'Black Robes,' said Jakam, as if it were a curse. 'Anything else?'

'My thanks, and a warning.'

The four merchants stepped back and Jakam's hand moved across his chest, one motion away from drawing the sword over his shoulder. 'Warning?'

'Yes. Prepare your people for travel, for word should come from the Council soon that the Thuril people must leave these lands.'

'What? Are you bereft of reason? Are you Tsurani claiming these lands again?'

'No,' said Pug, his voice echoing with sorrow. 'They are leaving, too. Something terrible is coming into this world and all must flee. Just know that the more your people prepare, the more they will be able to take with them.'

Jakam was about to ask another question, but Pug knew that further talk would be pointless.

He spied a distant rise where the trail could clearly be seen, and transported himself there. It was an old mode of travel he had employed before, jumping from place to place along his line of sight. It was fatiguing, but effective, for like all magicians save Miranda and Magnus, he could not jump to a place he had never seen before.

He reached his goal at nightfall, as he had anticipated. He could see the many fires up on the hillside around the springs, and made his way into town. Unlike Turandaren, Tasdano Abear was a classic Thuril town comprising wattle-and-daub buildings, only the inn making concessions to more modern requirements. On the top of the hill above the town was the fortress, the Thuril log emplacement surrounded by a ditch full of bramble and thorn bush. The Thuril had been impossible to conquer because they simply refused to die defending a particular piece of land. The fortress was designed more to maul an invader before being quickly evacuated than it was to withstand any long siege. These highlanders regarded all of the highland plateaus, valleys, meadows and mountains as their home, and didn't particularly care from season to season where they resided. A town like Tasdano Abear would flourish for a decade, then vanish when people got tired of trading there. Still, over the last century, reports from the highlands indicated peace was having the long term effect of turning a semi-nomadic people into permanent residents of specific areas.

Clans traditionally had claimed ranges and meadows, but who within that clan got rights to what was often a matter of very difficult, convoluted clan politics. As most families had several blood ties to every other family in the clan, bloodshed between families in clans was rare, but brawls were a staple of the hot blooded highlanders.

Pug entered the tavern and looked around. As he expected it was crowded with many young warriors here in support of clan leaders at the Confederation Council. And while the mood was mostly festive, with this many young men from this many different families, they were always one moment away from a brawl.

The Thuril were an odd race in contrast to the Tsurani, for while the Tsurani were reticent to the point of near-silence, the Thuril were a ferociously outspoken people. Insult was an art form, and the art was to be as loud, boastful, and obnoxious as one could be, without starting a fight.

By the time Pug sat down at a long table in the corner, in the one unoccupied seat, the room had fallen silent. Never in the memory of the oldest living Thuril warrior had a Tsurani Great One walked into an inn during a Confederation Council and sat down.

Finally one of the older warriors, obviously drunk, said, 'Are you lost?' He was a red-headed, brawny fellow, with ruddy cheeks and a long drooping moustache. He wore a beaten copper necklace that sparkled in the torchlight. It was a very valuable piece of jewellery on this metal-poor world.

Pug shook his head. 'I think not.'

'So, you know where you are then?'

'This is the Sandram Valley, right?'

'It is.'

'And this is the town of Tasdano Abear, right?'

'Yes, it is.'

'And that's the Confederation Council up on the hillside at the Shatanda Warm Springs isn't it?'

'Yes, that it is.'

'Then I'm not lost.'

'Well, then, Tsurani, if you don't mind me asking, what brings you to this place?'

'I need to speak to the Council and especially the Kaliane.'

'Ah, the Kaliane, is it?'

'Yes,' said Pug.

'And supposing she doesn't wish to see you?'

'I think she will.'

'And why would that be?'

'Because I have something to say to her that she will certainly wish to hear.'

'Then why are you sitting here, you ill-gotten offspring of a musonga,' —invoking the name of a particularly stupid burrowing pest that was the bane of all farmers on Kelewan— 'and not toddling up there to tell her what you've got to say?'

'Because, you rock-headed son of a flatulent needra and a mud wallowing baloo,' —Pug rejoined with a pair of domestic animals, the stupid beast of burden and filthy, and stupid, but edible meat animal— 'it would be bad manners for me to "toddle" without an invitation to an audience, which you would know if your mother had birthed any children who could tell it was daylight while standing outside staring into the sun, and had you half the wits the gods gave to a bag of rocks. It's called "good manners".'

The warriors nearby erupted into laughter: this Tsurani not only spoke passable Thuril, he could insult with style.

The red-headed warrior didn't know whether to laugh or take umbrage, but before he could make up his mind, Pug said, 'Be a welcoming host and ask the Kaliane if she will listen to the words of Milamber of the Assembly, once husband to a Thuril woman, Katala.'

The room fell silent. An old man sitting in the corner stood up and walked over to Pug. 'How can that be? You are a young man, and Katala was a kinswoman of mine, dead before I was born. The story is told of her having wed a Black Robe.'

'I am that man,' said Pug. 'I am long lived, I remain as you see me, and was then as I am now when I was wed to her. She was my wife, and mother of my first born son, and I still grieve for her.'

The old man turned to one of the younger warriors and said, 'Go to the Kaliane, and tell her a man of importance has come from the Tsurani lands, to speak to her and the Council. He has a claim of kinship. I will vouch it is true.'

The young warrior nodded in deference to the old man, who sat down beside Pug. 'Milamber of the Assembly, I would hear the tale of you and my kinswoman.'

Pug sighed, for these were memories he rarely visited. 'When I was little more than a boy the Tsurani invaded my homeland and I was taken as slave, for the great house of the Shinzawai. It was there I met Katala of the Thuril, sold into slavery by border raiders. We met one day . . .' He told the story slowly and plainly, and soon it was clear that the memories were as vivid to him now as they had been years before, and the images of his first wife were undimmed by the passage of time.

When he had finished, warriors wept at the tale of their parting, for the proud warriors of the Thuril felt no shame in showing strong emotions. The room fell silent as the messenger returned and said, 'The Kaliane bids you come and makes you welcome to the Council, Milamber of the Assembly.'

Pug rose and walked out of the inn. He followed his guide to the top of the trail, which opened into a large meadow, dotted with hide tents, erected for the meeting of the Council. The meadow was home to natural warm springs, which in the night sent up plumes of steam and gave off a faintly metallic odour.

Night birds sang and Pug was reminded that as alien as Kelewan had been to him when he had first come here as a Tsurani captive, he had come to think of it as home for the better part of eight years. He had met his wife here and fathered his first-born, and this is where she had returned to die of an illness no priest or chirurgeon could cure.

As he was led through the sprawling community of huts, he finally found himself before an ancient longhouse. He knew enough of Thuril tradition to realize that this longhouse had been here for decades, perhaps a century, as a place where elders might come to council and seek the calming influence of the warm springs.

Once inside the long hall, Pug saw over forty Thuril leaders waiting for him, and in the centre an imposing woman of advancing years with long iron-grey hair tied in two braids. She wore a simple dress of dark red cloth, but over that a torc of beaten copper, set with precious gems. The others, both men and women, wore traditional headgear of feathers and quills, and shirts, trousers, kilts, and dresses of wool and homespun. The air in the room was thick with smoke from the large fire in a stone-lined pit in the centre of the room, and from torches on the walls.

'Welcome, Milamber of the Assembly,' said an old chieftain sitting to the right of the Kaliane. 'I am Wahopa, chieftain of the Flint Ridge people. It is my honour to host this year's Council. I bid you welcome.'

The woman to his left said, 'I am the Kaliane. You wished to speak to us?'

Pug said, 'Yes. I bring words of warning, and hope.' He began slowly. These were not a stupid people, but he was explaining concepts difficult for a magician to grasp, let alone a warrior of the highlands. But they listened without interruption, and when he finished he added, 'Safe passage will be provided to as many of your nation as can be made to muster here within the week. Bring your livestock and chattels, weapons and tools, for it is a new world opening, one that will demand much, but will give much in return.'

'Tell us of this new world, Milamber,' said the Kaliane.

'It is a fair place, with vast plains of grass, deep lakes and rolling oceans. There are mountains that touch the sky and great highland valleys where herds can run free. It is a land abundant in game and fish, and more, and there is no one living there.'

'But you are Tsurani, and your people go there. Why would you offer to share it with your enemies?' asked a chief from the second row. His tone was suspicious.

'I am not Tsurani. I am the outland magician, Pug of Crydee, taken captive during the war on the world of Midkemia. It was I who freed the Thuril warriors at the Great Games and destroyed the great arena. It was I who was wed to Katala of the Thuril, whose kinsman I met down in the town just hours ago.

'We will take anyone to this new world who

554

wishes to live,' Pug said calmly. 'I have spoken to the Thūn.' This brought an angry response, for the Thūn were a bigger plague on the Thuril than they were on the Tsurani. 'Even now others are making the same offer to the Cho-ja, the dwarves across the Sea of Blood, and any other race who wishes to escape the devastation.' Passion rose in his voice as he said, 'It was Mara of the Acoma who came to you seeking a way to meet with the great magicians at Chakaha, and she was mother to this line of emperors.

'You have had a century of truce with the Tsurani, despite occasional conflicts, but these have been no more than your own clan struggles. This world I speak of is vast, and the highlands are a great distance from where the Tsurani will reside, and if you wish, you can ignore them for another century.'

Several of the chieftains nodded, as if this were a good thing.

'Or you can reach an accord and forge a treaty that will last for generations. But none of this can come to pass if you do not leave these highlands, for death approaches rapidly and will be upon you suddenly.'

The Kaliane stood. 'I would speak with this Great One alone,' she said and her tone indicated that she was not asking for permission. 'Walk with me outside, Milamber.'

She took the lead and Pug followed. Once outside, she headed slowly down a trail leading to the larger of the many springs in the area. 'You speak fairly, Milamber, but many will not believe you,' she began. 'They will think this a Tsurani ploy to remove us from our lands, or a trap to lure us to our deaths.'

Pug was tired. He had been through ordeals no man had ever known, and despite the reinvigorating magic Ban-ath had employed, he felt exhausted in his heart and soul. He took a deep breath and said, 'I know. I can only do so much. I cannot save everyone. I make a simple offer, Kaliane. Within two days I shall open a rift,' —he looked around and then pointed to a clearing a short distance away— 'there. It will lead to a highland meadow on the world of which I spoke.' He took a deep breath. 'The Thūn will be put on a continent a vast sea away from all humans. It will be years, decades, perhaps even centuries before human refugees and the Thūn meet again. Perhaps by then you'll have made peace with the Tsurani. I do not know what the Cho-ja say, for another has sought them out. The highlands where I will open the rift is at a great distance from where the Tsurani will arrive – you can avoid them or seek them out as is your pleasure, and either make war or peace, or you can remain here and perish.' Fatigue crept into his voice. 'It is all your choice. I can only do so much.'

'I believe you,' she said. 'I will urge the chieftains to send runners and gather the clans.' She crossed her arms on her chest and looked out over the hills below. 'These have been our homes since the time of the Golden Bridge, Great One. It will be hard for some to leave.'

'Some will die,' Pug said. 'Some will not get word in time to reach here, and others will be too ill to travel. Some will refuse to leave. All of those will die. It is up to you to save the rest.'

'You do this thing, why, magician? Why do you struggle to save so many?'

Pug laughed, more out of frustration than humour. 'Who else would do it? It is my lot. And I do it because it is right that I do so.'

She nodded. 'You are a good man, Great One. Now, go, and I will do what I can. Will I see you again?'

'Only the gods know,' said Pug. 'If I can visit the highlands where you are to live, I will, but if I don't, you'll know that it is for a good reason.'

'Go with the gods,' she said, turning to walk back to the long hall and begin what would most certainly be a long and heated debate.

Taking an orb from his robe, Pug triggered it to return to the Assembly, and was gone.

CHAPTER 23

ONSLAUGHT

Jim threw a dagger.

He ducked away behind a rock as the blade struck a Dasati Deathknight in the face, taking him out of the saddle of his varnin. He was immediately trampled by other riders who ignored their fallen comrade as they rode through the canyon.

Reaching a promontory where his companions waited, he said, 'Time to be going!'

Jommy, Tad, Zane and Servan didn't need to be told twice. What had less than half an hour before been a rear echelon area, a staging point for troops heading into battle and a resting place for troops pulled out of the line, was now suddenly the front. An hour ago, all five young men had been nursing aching bodies, eating decent meals for the first time in two days, and anticipating some well-earned rest. After eating, they had found a shady spot under a wagon on which to sleep. They had become accustomed to the needra, the six-legged Tsurani beast of burden, its restless snorting and its alien odours. They were so tired it had only taken minutes for them to fall asleep.

Jim had been the first to be roused by the

shouting. They had barely avoided being trampled by Dasati Deathknights, and had escaped their nets only by scurrying up the rocky hillside which led to a ridge that had served as a natural defensive barrier on Alenburga's left flank. The only problem was that everyone else in the headquarters had gone in the other direction.

For the last two days they had been making a steady retreat. The Black Mount would expand on a fairly regular basis and the Tsurani magicians were attempting to gauge its rate so that they could predict a safe distance for each withdrawal.

The defenders' tactics had changed. They were no longer attempting to repulse a Dasati invasion, but rather were attempting to fight a screening rearguard withdrawal to give refugees time to reach the safety of the nearest rifts. Pug had established a rift that morning between Kelewan and another world, and the Emperor's edict had gone out. Magicians had carried the order to every part of the Empire and the population was mobilizing. It would be impossible to get everyone through the rifts in time, but they were going to save as many as possible.

Once the first major rift had been established, Pug had created a second one to a distant continent, then created a gateway for the Thūn. A third had been created in the Thuril highlands, and after that, other magicians were creating secondary gateways to those locations. Still other Great Ones were busy creating lesser rifts around the Empire, which terminated near the first major Tsurani rift, on the City of the Plains. That location had been selected because the area around the rift was vast and a few dozen lesser rifts could open there giving enough room for the massive influx of refugees to wait without trampling one another.

The problem seemed to be creating enough rifts to reach the new world. Pug was one of the few magicians capable of creating such a rift without help. Once he had established a rift, other rifts at nearby locations would naturally follow it to the new world, and that was beneficial, but it still took two or three magicians four or five times as long to do the work. At the last report there were seven effective rifts to the new world. But Kaspar had remarked within earshot of the young captains that seventy wouldn't be enough.

So, there was a need to slow down the Dasati, who seemed intent on capturing as many prisoners as possible to be dragged back to the Black Mount and thrown into the pit to feed the monstrosity on their home world. No one wanted to consider how horrific the situation had become. The Tsurani were warriors by tradition and temperament, and always focused on what was ahead, not behind them, but estimations ran as high as twenty to thirty thousand Tsurani having gone into the pit in the last two days. From what they had seen, the young captains thought that number low. The Dasati were anything but stupid: they were rapidly adapting their strategy and tactics to fit the situation and now their raids were massive and unexpected.

It was probably just bad luck that this newest one had brought them almost on top of the Tsurani headquarters.

Jommy looked around as they could hear the rumbling of the Dasati riders on the other side of the ridge. 'Where are we?'

Zane said, 'Tad was the last to see the map.' He looked at his foster brother and asked, 'Where are we?'

The slender blond youth held out his hand, palm outward and fingers down. 'This,' he said pointing to his middle finger, 'is the ridge behind us. Over here,' he said, pointing at the ring finger, 'is where everyone else went. We need to get from there to there.'

'With a couple of thousand Dasati Deathknights between us,' said Servan.

Jim Dasher said, 'Wait, I have an idea.'

'What?' asked Jommy. Since arriving with messages for Lord Erik, Dasher had been seconded to General Alenburga's staff, joining Jommy, Tad, Zane, and Servan as a captain.

He pointed south-west. 'The Dasati are going that way.'

'Yes,' said Tad.

'So, let's go that way,' he said, pointing north-east. 'We cut across the valley floor, and we're on the other side where we can catch up with the General and the others.'

'Brilliant idea,' said Jommy, 'but you're over-looking one thing.'

'What?'

'Everyone else at headquarters is mounted. They have horses. We don't. We'll never catch up with them.'

'Well,' said Zane, 'we certainly won't if we stand here arguing about it. I say we do as Jim says. Eventually the General will throw up another headquarters and if we just keep following the line of retreat, we'll find it sooner or later.'

With no better course of action, they boys agreed and they started back up the ridge they had just fled down. Reaching the top, they paused, crouching just below the ridgeline. They could hear no sounds of mounted Dasati, but experience had taught them that Dasati often had secondary patrols following after the raids to catch anyone who had been in hiding.

Jim was about to stick his head over the rise when he heard something. He held up his hand in a sign of caution and listened. Then he recognized the sound. Someone was humming!

He peered over and saw a lone figure moving up the trail, wearing the black robe of a Tsurani magician, and he was humming a tune. 'What is this?' Jim asked.

The others peered over and saw the figure vanishing up the trail and Jommy said, 'Was he singing?'

'Humming,' corrected Jim Dasher. 'Loudly.'

'Should we go after him?' asked Zane.

'No,' said Tad. 'If he's a magician he can take care of himself, and look where he is!'

Where he happened to be was approaching the outer limits of the 'safe' area around the Black Mount. Anywhere closer was likely to result in suddenly finding yourself inside the dome the next time it expanded. They watched the robed man vanish along the trail, then they moved over the ridge and down to the floor of the valley.

'Last time I looked, the generals were heading that way,' Jommy said, pointing to the south-east.

'Then that's the way we go,' said Dasher. 'You know, I think I've had enough of this.'

'What?' asked Servan.

'The war?' Tad suggested.

'That, certainly,' said Dasher. 'No, I mean the whole service to the Crown business.'

'Well, no one made you do it,' suggested Zane.

'Actually, someone did,' said Jim.

'Who?' Jommy asked.

Dasher shrugged. 'You lads must have figured out by now that I'm not just a thief from Krondor.'

Jommy laughed as they trudged along, keeping alert for any marauding Dasati. 'We sort of got the notion when you showed up carrying royal dispatches for Lord Erik. They don't usually hand those over to random pickpockets and bashers and tell them to scoot along through the nearest rift to a war on another world.'

'Well, it was my grandfather, really, who got

me into "the family business", I guess you could say.'

Servan said, 'Don't keep us guessing.' His tone was dry and he seemed unconvinced. He had known Jim Dasher long enough to judge him an accomplished liar.

'My grandfather is James, Lord Jamison, Duke of Rillanon.'

Jommy laughed. 'That's a wonderful tale.'

'No, I'm serious,' said Dasher. He picked up a rock and threw it, hitting a larger rock some distance away. 'I'm tired of risking my life, thugs, gamblers, whores, and all the rest of it, and I'm ready to settle down and start a family.'

'You?' said Jommy, laughing. 'A family?'

'Yes,' said Jim, beginning to become nettled. 'I even have a girl in mind.'

'This I must hear,' said Servan. 'Who, among the Kingdom aristocracy, has the Duke's grandson in mind?'

The others began to laugh.

'If you must know,' said Jim, 'she's Lady Michele de Frachette, daughter of the Earl of Montagren.'

The laughter stopped.

'You're serious? Michele?' asked Servan.

'Yes, why?'

The four former university students looked at one another, and Jommy said to Tad, 'You tell him.'

Zane said, 'You should tell him, Jommy.'

'No,' said Jommy. 'I really think it should be you, Tad. You're the first one she . . .' He looked at Jim Dasher, then said, '. . . danced with at the King's reception.'

'Yes,' said Tad, looking askance, 'but you . . . danced with her the most.'

Jommy sighed and stopped walking. 'Ah, Jim, we have all had the pleasure of her . . . ah . . . acquaintance. She attended a reception at the Royal Court in Roldem, when Tad, Zane and myself were made Knights of the King's Court.' With a grin, he also said, 'Which is where I met Servan's lovely sister, too.'

Servan's expression darkened. And it was Tad who said, 'She's, ah . . .'

'A lovely girl,' supplied Zane. 'Really.'

'Are you talking about Michele or my sister?' Servan's expression was not happy.

Tad jumped in. 'Both, about the lovely girl part, but ignore him,' he said, pointing to Jommy. 'He just likes your sister to annoy you.'

'That's not true!' protested Jommy. 'She really *is* a wonderful girl.' He mock-scowled at Servan. 'How the two of you came from the same parents is a mystery to me.'

'Enough,' said Dasher. 'Michele?'

'Ah, yes, Michele. Lovely, but . . . ambitious,' said Jommy. 'She's looking for a well-positioned husband, you could say.'

'That's what I'd say,' agreed Servan.

'And no one would be as well positioned as the grandson of the Duke of Rillanon, would he?' offered Zane.

'But before that she was . . . more open to other suitors,' supplied Zane.

'So, let's say we've all had the pleasure of . . . her company,' said Tad.

Jim's expression turned dangerous and his colour began to rise, his cheeks turning red. 'When?'

Jommy said, 'Second Day. The reception was the previous Fifth Day.'

Tad said, 'First.'

'Really?' asked Jommy. 'I thought I had supper with her first.'

'No, I did,' said Tad.

'And you?' Jommy asked of Zane.

'Fourth.'

Jim looked ready to lose his temper completely, 'So, you're telling me that the three of you—'

Servan said, 'Ah, four.' They looked at him and he added, 'Third Day.'

Jommy put his hand on Jim's shoulder and gave it a firm squeeze, as friendly a gesture as he could manage. 'Look at it this way, old son. We've saved you from a world of embarrassment, haven't we? Whoever does wed her is going to be the butt of a lot of jokes in court. Can't have that for the Duke's grandson, can we?'

Jim looked from face to face, and the colour in his cheeks began to fade. He was not by nature an idealistic sort, but he had built up a very lovely ideal of Michele. Better to find out now, he acknowledged. Finally he shook his head and said, 'Women.'

They resumed walking and Jommy said, 'Yes.'

Tad said, 'You know what the monks of La-Timsa at the university say about women don't you?'

Jommy, Servan, and Zane had heard the old joke a dozen times and in unison answered, 'Women! You can't live with them and you can't live with them.'

Jim groaned, realizing that La-Timsites were a celibate order. 'I think I'll stick to whores.'

Servan said, 'Knowing the young women of the Royal Court in Roldem, I'd say it's probably less expensive.'

'And you'll be lied to less often,' said Zane.

'Well, this is all good and all,' said Jommy, 'but have you seen any sight of a retreating army?'

'That way,' said Jim, pointing at a litter of dropped items. 'We follow what they threw away.'

'Let's hope the Dasati didn't. I'm not anxious to walk into their rearguard,' Tad said.

Conversation fell off as they trudged up a hillside and over another ridge. Then Jim said, 'You know the tune that magician was humming?'

'What about it?' asked Servan.

'I just realized I recognize it! It's a tune common in the ale houses in Land's End and Port Vykor.'

'So?' asked Tad.

'So where's a Tsurani magician learn a tune sung by drunken sailors down in Land's End?'

No one had an answer.

★   ★   ★

Leso Varen felt positively buoyant, though he was at a loss to explain why. So much of his life was made up of odd impulses that he could not explain, so he had long ago given up any seeking reasonable explanations. He knew it all began with the amulet he had found so many years ago, and the dreams that had come afterward. He had thrown it away, twice, then spent years recovering it, and once he destroyed it, he thought, only to find the shards and restore it, killing a half-dozen jewellers in the process. Something about that amulet . . .

That damned pirate Bear, the murderous monster, had it on when he died, and it was lost somewhere in the Bitter Sea. He had really desired that amulet. Wearing it had given him the first glimpse of what was possible, how death and life were so closely linked, and there was no more powerful source of power than a life slipping into death.

He never found the amulet, though he had searched in the sea for it years ago . . . There, his mind was wandering again.

He was certain there was some higher agency at work here, for he could not rest once he got an idea until he took it to fruition. Several times he had been frustrated by others, but somehow he had always endured.

As he climbed the road, Varen saw dead bodies littering the landscape. Perhaps that was why he felt so good. There was so much death every-where that he had been able to leech away fleeing life here and there. These Dasati were like children when it came to death-magic; very powerful children, granted, but their ability to find the subtle side of magic was non-existent, and they operated in a very wasteful fashion. But at least their waste had left enough ambient life-force lingering that he was physically rejuvenated to the point of no longer needing a walking stick – though Wyntakata really wasn't much of a specimen, to be truthful. Once Varen found a good lair, he'd start building up the things he needed to seize another body. He idly wondered what he could accomplish with the level of slaughter these aliens achieved.

He wondered why he was feeling the need to go back and visit the Dasati again. His initial contact with them had seemed a wonderful opportunity, but once they had established their first little dome on this world, and after he had delivered Miranda to them for study, they were downright inhospitable. He had exited without a farewell, fairly certain they were getting ready to study *him*. And he was certain they thought less well of him after he had killed two of their Deathpriests on his way out of the door.

Still, his time with them had not been a complete waste, for he knew he could work necrotic magic they could only dream of. And now appeared as good a time as any to do so, since a Dasati patrol was thundering down the road towards him.

He drew on a spark of the rage he harboured

within, called up a large supply of the life-force he had recently acquired and waited. There were twelve Deathknights riding at him, and as they approached they slowed, perhaps wondering why a lone human would stand waiting for them.

'Hello,' he said in passable Dasati, learned from the Deathpriests he had negotiated with after he had discovered their little probe-creature.

The leader pointed his sword at him. 'You speak our language?'

Sighing theatrically, Leso Varen said, 'By the gods you are a master of the obvious.' His hand shot out and a dozen tendrils of green energy sprang forth, each cocooning a Deathknight's head. Instantly swords were dropped as they reached up, clawing at the suffocating head-covers.

Within moments, they were falling from their saddles, writhing on the ground in agony as their lungs burned. Varen could feel their lives pulsing up the tendrils and his own vitality increasing. Just to be thorough, Varen did the same with the milling varnin, killing them all by draining their lives. When the last of them was dead, he smiled. 'Well, that was refreshing.'

He started humming the song again as he resumed his trek to the Black Mount.

Pug was nearly exhausted. Even after the return trip from the second plane he had not felt this depleted. The creation of rifts was a difficult enough task when carried out under normal conditions; but conditions as they stood were hardly normal.

He took a deep breath and nodded to Magnus. His son still showed the price paid by the foray into the second realm, but he had insisted on accompanying his parents to give whatever help he could.

Magnus lifted his father up, raising him so that he could see the thousands flooding across the plains. In the distance, to the north, loomed the Black Mount. It had grown again twice in the last day, its most recent increase bringing it miles closer. Pug calculated that it now covered two major cities and a score of towns along the river, as well as overlapping a huge portion of the northern plain. It rose up so high that its top vanished into the clouds: to Pug it looked like nothing so much as a giant black wall advancing down on them.

He motioned to Magnus, who lowered him.

'Can we do more?' Miranda asked.

'No,' said Pug. 'We might open another rift or two from the far west, but there are not that many people there.' He sighed. 'I fear all we can do now is wait and see how many we can get through the rift and how long it is before we must close it.'

Magnus looked into the distance. 'That thing will be down on us in two or three days.'

Pug looked at the first and largest of the rifts to the new world, and saw that people were streaming through it, but there were so many frightened, tired, hungry people waiting that the line was miles long.

He had made it clear to everyone that as soon as people were through the rift they had to move off, for the valley on the other side of the rift did not have sufficient capacity to hold all these people. He also knew that soon the people going through would be too exhausted once they were on the other side to move very far off. He turned to Magnus and said, 'Hold them up for a few minutes.'

Magnus passed orders to the Imperial Guards, who ordered the halt to people passing through. This brought instant grumbling and complaint from the otherwise dutiful and obedient Tsurani.

Miranda said, 'The next time you do that, we're going to have a riot.'

Pug nodded.

'How many have gone through already?' she asked.

He shook his head. 'I don't know, really. Two hundred thousand today, maybe. Half that many yesterday when we started.'

'Not even the population of one good-sized city.'

'Enough to start a new civilization,' said Magnus.

Miranda looked at her son and realized he was trying to make them feel that something had been accomplished. 'Only if they don't mind spending the next two or three generations in mud huts.' She looked across the plain and saw that fires were being lit as evening approached. 'Maybe some cooking and a short rest will help some of them.'

As fires appeared across the horizon to the east at first and then to the west, she said, 'There are so many.'

'Millions yet to come,' said Pug. 'We're going to lose most of them.'

'We don't know that, Father.' Magnus pointed. 'I'll go and help to open another rift to the new world. I'll go through this portal and fly myself miles away, and open another—'

'We have six spread out all over that region. It's going to take them weeks to find each other and establish some sort of communication.' He looked around. 'We can't wait too much longer to send the Light of Heaven through.'

'Will he go?' asked Miranda. 'He seemed determined to be the last through when I talked to him.'

Magnus smiled. 'I think he's going to have to fight General Alenburga for the honour.'

'It doesn't matter,' Pug said quietly. 'The last to go through . . .' He looked at the campfires now springing up in all quarters. 'Anyone who waits to be last through will die here, Magnus.'

His son said nothing.

Varen trudged along the road, watching the Black Mount rise up, getting larger by the hour yet somehow seemingly never closer. 'That is really big,' he said to himself.

At least four times in the last hour he had destroyed small bands of Deathknights, but he sensed he was overmatched as he crested a rise and saw a full hundred of them riding out of a dell. Wishing he had some of his toys from his old study in Kaspar's citadel in Olasko, he conjured up an illusion he hadn't tried in years. It was an old stand-by and easy enough to deploy. Any Tsurani would have stopped to examine the massive old dead oak that was suddenly sitting by the side of the road, but the Dasati had no idea the tree was as alien to this world as they were. They rode past and when they were safely down the road, Varen reappeared as the tree illusion vanished.

Continuing along he wondered how long it would take him to reach the edge of the sphere. Perspective was difficult, for the featureless sides gave him nothing by which to judge scale. It might be a mile on the other side of the next ridge, or it could be five miles.

Then suddenly it was dark and his lungs started to strain as his ears rang and his eyes burned. It also felt as if the grandfather of all thunderclaps had exploded right above his head.

And then hands gripped him.

Varen saw a pair of Deathknights had an iron hold on each of his arms and were propelling him forwards, expecting him to be incapacitated. But he had been inside a Dasati dome before and knew what to do, and suddenly he could breathe easily. He let the Deathknights pull him along what had up to minutes ago been a countryside road out in the bright sun. Now it was a pathway shrouded in darkness and even as he watched the leaves on the trees on either side of the road begin to blacken and shrivel.

'Oh, this is so clever!' he shouted.

The two Deathknights tightened their grips and one looked at him. He was the first to die.

Varen simply reached inside the man with his mind and stopped his heart. 'Oh, I love this place!' he said to the still-upright Deathknight. The warrior let go of Varen and drew his sword, and Leso realized he had been speaking Tsurani. He spoke in Dasati: 'I said, "Oh, I love this place!"' The Deathknight raised his sword to strike and Varen held out his hand and another encompassing cocoon of green, life-devouring energy engulfed the Deathknight.

Varen was motionless as the Deathknight died. Others nearby saw the single human standing with two dead Deathknights at his feet and ran to attack him. Varen easily snatched life from each of them until there was not a living Deathknight in sight.

'I never used to be able to do that!' he exclaimed, delighted at his new-found power. 'It must be this place!'

He looked around and adjusted his perception, and everywhere he looked he could see life energy rushing in towards the centre of the great sphere. 'That's where I need to be,' he said.

He never once for a moment considered where these impulses that had ruled his life came from.

He accepted them, and knew that when he gave into his most outrageous and destructive impulses, the more pain he caused, the more chaos he created, the happier he was. At times in the past he had found himself working very much alone, in mouldy old caves or damp huts in noxious swamps. At other times he had finessed his way into comfort, living in luxury, hosted by dupes like the Baron of Land's End or the Duke of Olasko. He had endured his share of pain along the way; and discovered that dying was no fun at all, even if he woke up in a healthy new body moments later. He had also discovered that being run through with a sword from behind was his least favourite way to die. He took a deep breath. If he had only had access to the incredible energy of life he was finding here, or rather, that incredible moment of astonishing power when life turns to death . . . if only he had possessed that knowledge and power years ago, he would now be ruling Midkemia.

'I must find out what this is!' he said aloud. He moved towards the nexus of all this strange and wonderful death-magic.

Nakor stirred. He had been unconscious, lying behind the throne upon which the TeKarana would observe the slaughter of thousands. He had no idea how long it had been since he had said goodbye to Pug and Magnus. As dry as his mouth felt, it was at least a full day, if not several. He forced himself upright and reached inside his bag. It was empty. Sighing, he took it off and pushed it away. He hadn't really been hungry, and was reaching for an orange out of habit. He sloshed a little water around in the water skin at his belt and thought it odd that he wasn't thirsty either, despite his dry mouth. Then he realized what was happening. 'Ah. That's . . . brilliant!'

He turned his head to see what was occurring in the pit. The sight made him sad. Hundreds of bodies were falling each minute, and more and more of the essence of the Dreadlord was turning to vaporous smoke and spinning upward in a mad cyclone of wind that rushed up from the bottom of the pit.

He pulled himself around the throne. He could barely see the Dreadlord any more, so much of his being was being sacrificed into the maelstrom to reach out and bind this world to Kelewan.

A sudden giddiness struck Nakor and he knew. 'It's almost time!' he whispered. He moved around, and finding it amusing, sat down in the TeKarana's throne. He didn't think Valko would mind.

He waited.

'Why don't they come?' Martuch asked.

For two days the warriors of the White and the Talnoy guards had waited for an attack from the temple Deathknights loyal to the Dark One. But no attack had materialized.

Those few Lessers left alive in the TeKarana's private apartments had been given the chore of preparing food for those hunkered down, waiting.

Bek had stood motionless in the same position, waiting for the assault. He had not eaten, drunk water, or relieved himself for two days. It was beginning to unnerve even the most battle-hardened Deathknight.

Suddenly, Bek said, 'They are not coming.'

'How do you know?' asked Valko.

The massive warrior turned and with a grin that was nearly demonic said, 'I know. You are safe. The Dark One is busy and will not return. He is leaving this world very soon. I can go now.' Suddenly a crimson light shone around the large warrior and he fell over.

A disembodied voice said, 'I am Kantas-Barat! I have returned.'

The Deathknights looked from one to another, and Father Juwon said, 'The old gods are returning!'

Hirea hurried over to Bek and examined him. Looking up, he said, 'He's dead!'

Martuch shook his head. 'That one has been dead a long time, I think. Whatever was inside him has no more use for him. I hope for a good cause.' To those assembled, he raised his voice. 'Come, it's time to end this insanity and begin rebuilding our nation.'

Most cheered, including Valko, but he looked out of the window at the city in turmoil, with fires and smoke everywhere, and he knew that despite this feigned optimism, the conflict was not yet over.

Pug dozed. He came awake with a start and looked around. 'What?'

'Father,' said Magnus. 'What is it?'

'Something . . .' He stood up and looked off into the night. 'Something's changing.'

He had been lying inside a tent hastily erected near the command pavilion occupied by the Emperor and his generals. He looked around and saw the massive rift a short distance away, torchlight casting the entire tableau into an eerie chiaroscuro, punctuated by flickering amber and red glows.

The stream of refugees was now a river, and as he silently watched, hundreds walked through the rift and into another world.

'How many?' he asked Magnus.

'No one knows, Father. Maybe a million by now, through all the gates. Maybe more.'

'Maybe less.'

Magnus shook his head in resignation. 'We're doing all we can.'

'Where's the sphere?'

'It's about fifty miles north of the City of the Plains.'

Pug almost wept. When he had last asked, it had been over a hundred miles away. He let out a long breath. 'Unless something miraculous happens, we will lose the rifts by late afternoon tomorrow.'

Magnus knew what his father was saying. All rifts off this world had to be closed before the Dark One reached them. If he was to take Kelewan, so be it. They could regroup on Midkemia and decide how best to confine him to this world, if that was possible.

But if he managed to gain access to the new Tsurani world or to Midkemia, the horror they had been watching here for days would repeat itself eventually.

Suddenly a gust of wind blew everything back as a huge thunder peal sounded around them. Lightning danced across the surface of the Black Mount and Pug shouted, 'Now! Get the Emperor through that gate!'

Imperial Guards raced to the command tent.

'What happened?' asked Magnus.

'I don't know, but we don't have until late afternoon tomorrow.'

The Black Mount was not fifty miles north of the city any more. It was now less than a mile north of the rifts, which meant that at least a million people had been swallowed up by it.

Pug felt tears come unbidden.

CHAPTER 24

OBLIVION

The Dasati attacked.

The screaming alerted Pug and the other magicians who had congregated around the Emperor's pavilion. The argument had been underway for the better part of an hour, all decorum and rank put aside.

The young ruler was being intransigent about staying to the very last, and finally Pug said, 'Majesty, no one here doubts your heart or your bravery. We know that you die each time one of your subjects is taken, but your people, more than ever, need your guidance.'

He indicated the sea of faces crowded around the large tent, looking in through the large opening, waiting to hear the Light of Heaven's order. Pug saw priests and high priests of every order, remaining close in case the Emperor ordered them to fight to the death. Pug's hand inscribed an arc in the air, encompassing everyone outside. 'Your brave Tsurani nobles are for the most part dead, and each of them gave their lives dearly. That leaves you with only children to claim the titles of Ruling Lords, and a frightened populace. Your people are good people, honest and hard-working, but they will need guidance. Order your magicians and priests, and whoever is left of the nobility, through the rift now.'

He could hear the fighting approaching, no more than a few hundred yards away. 'Soon panic will set in and no one will be able to get through the rift . . . before I must close it!'

The Emperor looked determined. 'No, Great One. I will fight.'

Pug felt exasperated. This was not the time for youthful defiance. But he realized he was talking to a young man whose every whim had been obeyed for most of his life. 'Sire, have you heard the tale of Emperor Ichindar, the ninety-first emperor, at the first peace talks between the Empire and the Kingdom of the Isles?'

'No,' said the young ruler, suddenly uncertain as to where this conversation was going.

'Good,' said Pug, and he put out his hand. The young Emperor's eyes rolled up into his head and he collapsed. Half a dozen Imperial Guards drew their swords and Pug shouted, 'Hold! The Light of Heaven merely sleeps.'

The Emperor's First Adviser Chomata chuckled. 'I know that story, Great One. It was Kasumi of the Shinzawai who knocked Emperor Ichindar unconscious so that he could be taken back through the rift to safety.'

'Good,' said Pug. 'You can explain it to him

when he revives.' To two guards he said, 'Pick up the Emperor and bear him through the rift. '

General Alenburga looked at Pug and then turned to face the throng outside the door. With the tent flaps pulled back, he had an almost panoramic view of the distant battle. He looked down at the faces of those waiting to be told what to do next. 'You, the priests and magicians and remaining ruling lords, if you love your nation, it is time. Go through the rift and care for your people. Build a new Tsuranuanni. Go!'

Many hesitated, but many moved the moment the order was given towards a smaller rift Pug had prepared to get the command staff away to safety. Magnus said, 'Father, what about you?'

'I'm staying a little longer,' Pug said. 'It's all but over here, but there are things I alone can do, and they must be done.'

'What shall I tell Mother?'

'Tell her under no circumstances is she to return here.' He looked out at the distant fighting. 'Tell her I love her and I will be home soon.'

Magnus shook his head. 'You know if I tell her not to come she will.'

'Convince her. Tell her I will be going through the rift gate in a few minutes.'

'You know I could never lie to her.'

'It's not a lie. I am going through the gate, but not this one.' He pointed over into the darkness. 'I'm going to go through the first gate, to the

Academy.' He dropped his voice. 'Tell her there won't be a "here" soon.'

'Very well,' said Magnus, embracing Pug. 'Do not get yourself killed, Father.'

Magnus departed and Pug turned to what remained of the general staff. Alenburga, Kaspar, Erik and the young officers waited, as Pug said, 'It's over, gentlemen.'

Erik von Darkmoor looked out at the distant battle. 'Yes, finally.'

Alenburga turned to the younger officers and to the Tsurani soldiers he said, 'Go through the rift to the new world. That is an order.'

As one they saluted and departed. Then to Jommy, Servan, Jim, Dash, Tad and Zane he said, 'Young sirs, your duty here is over. I thank you for your bravery.' Then, looking at Jim Dasher, he added, 'And an occasional bit of foolhardiness. Now, go. Get home.'

Pug pointed to the rift to the Academy. 'I'll need you there. Use that rift gate.'

Jommy glanced at his companions, who nodded. 'We'll stay, if you're staying.'

Kaspar said, 'Jommy, you're a likeable enough lad, but you are a terrible officer. Go!'

Jommy hesitated for a moment, then turned and moved out, the others following.

At the entrance, Erik put out a restraining hand and held up Jim Dasher. 'Tell your grandfather he has my best wishes, Jim. And tell him he has reason to be proud of you.'

Jim looked the old soldier in the eye. 'Thank you, sir.'

Kaspar and Alenburga regarded Erik. Alenburga said, 'Coming?'

Erik shook his head. 'No. I think I'll stay. If I can slow down one Deathknight for a minute or so, another dozen or two might get through the rift. I've been on borrowed time for a few years now, and I should return what I borrowed.' He glanced at Pug and said, 'If you see that annoying little gambler, tell him "thank you".'

Pug could only nod, for he had not told anyone yet of Nakor's decision to stay on Omadrabar. Only Magnus knew. He could barely speak as he said, 'I will, Erik.'

The old Knight-Marshall of Krondor drew his sword from its scabbard and moved purposefully towards the sound of battle. When he had vanished into the crowd, Kaspar said, 'There goes a great man.'

Pug could only nod, unable to find words. Finally he forced himself to speak. 'What of you two?'

Alenburga had his hand on the pommel of his sword and looked ready to follow Erik's example. 'It's difficult to imagine going back,' he said quietly, his voice still carrying despite the din outside. Panic was rising as those trying to reach the nearby rift gate could hear the sounds of battle coming from the rear. 'Leaving all these people behind . . .'

Kaspar put his hand on the General's shoulder. 'It does them no good for you to die with them, Prakesh. You have a home.'

'It's going to be too quiet, Kaspar.' He looked at his companion of this last few weeks. 'After what we've done here, trying to conquer Okanala with a band of street urchins wouldn't seem much of a challenge.'

It was Pug who answered. 'Then go through that rift to the new world, General.'

'What?'

'The Tsurani are a people in shambles. They will need strong leadership.'

'I don't think they're going to need a general any time soon,' he responded, but already Pug could see the spark in his eyes.

'Then you haven't really come to know the Tsurani, General,' said Pug. 'Before dawn on the first day, there will be plots and intrigue enough to keep you jumping for the next century. War is nothing compared to the intrigue in the Game of the Council. Have the Emperor's First Advisor tell you the story of the Riftwar from the Tsurani perspective: it was a ploy in the game, nothing more.'

Kaspar said, 'Go, and lead. They will need you.'

Alenburga hesitated, then turned and put his arms around Kaspar, grasping him in a bear hug. 'I will miss you, Kaspar of Olasko.'

'I will miss you too, General.'

The General moved purposefully through the tent, and Pug said, 'Kaspar?'

'I have no desire to be anyone's martyred hero, Pug. I will go with you.'

Pug motioned for Kaspar to follow and led him out the back of the tent towards the ancient rift gate. A trickle of people were still attempting to get through, but were being turned away by Tsurani guards who redirected them towards the larger gate to the new world. Seeing a Black Robe, the guards moved aside, and before he stepped through, Pug said, 'Go, now. Your duty here is done.'

Both soldiers, wearing the armour of the House of Acoma, saluted and moved away, both drawing their swords and running towards the sound of fighting. 'Damn, but they are an amazing bunch,' said Kaspar admiringly.

'Yes, they are,' Pug agreed.

They entered the rift.

Varen looked over the edge of the pit and found himself both repelled and attracted by it. Part of him said that he should turn and run away, as fast as possible, yet another part felt the urge to jump in. He took a deep breath and looked around.

There used to be a city here, he thought. And around it were farms and valleys and hills and villages. Now there was just this pit. Hole. Tunnel. Whatever it was, it was massive, so big that the curve of it seemed to be almost a straight line when you stood on the rim.

The power! he thought. He was intoxicated

with it. It represented a mastery of death so far beyond his dreams, and he had had some pretty incredible dreams over the ages. It was staggering. If he could somehow bring these Dasati to heel, have them serve him, he could conquer worlds.

The urge to jump became almost unbearable. If only I had a reason, he thought. Then he just jumped.

Pug appeared outside the cave, Kaspar at his side.

'Where are the guards?' Kaspar asked.

'I ordered the two young magicians back to the island when I called for as much help as possible. By then I knew we didn't need to guard these things any more.'

Kaspar shrugged. 'If you say so.'

They entered the first tunnel and moved down to a gallery. Below, ten thousand armour-clad figures waited patiently. 'What are they, Pug, really?' asked Kaspar. He had been the one who had first found the Talnoy here in Novindus, and had lugged it back with him to the Conclave.

'They are sleeping gods, Kaspar. They are the lost Dasati gods.'

'How did they come here?'

'That is a part of the story we may never know, but I believe some higher agency here conspired with them.' Pug thought it best not to mention the role played by Ban-ath. 'This was a refuge.' He looked down at a box left near the door. 'For a long time I thought the Dark One had somehow trapped these beings, but now I'm not so sure. I believe perhaps the gods of three worlds conspired to save this universe from the thing that is destroying Kelewan as we speak.'

Kaspar could only stand in mute appreciation. Pug picked up the box and opened it. Inside were a ring and a crystal. 'Nakor fashioned this crystal as a means to control these . . . beings.' He took out the ring.

Kaspar said, 'Don't! If you wear it too long, it makes you mad!'

Pug slipped the ring on. 'Don't worry. I won't wear it long.' Smiling, he added, 'You might want to cover your ears for a moment, and perhaps close your eyes against the dust.'

'What dust?'

Pug raised his hands above his head and a twisting spiral of light, white with brilliant hints of silver, shot to the ceiling of the cavern. It twisted and began to bore upward. Soon a hole appeared and from above came light. Pug increased the gap between his hands and the light began to spin faster until Kaspar saw that it was boring away the top of the mound under which the Talnoy had rested for centuries.

Dust flew and Kaspar squinted, but he couldn't take his eyes from the sight. For nearly five minutes Pug used his magic thus and when he had finished, a hole broad enough for dozens of the creatures to exit hung over their heads.

'What now?' asked Kaspar, coughing from the dust.

'Come outside a moment,' Pug said.

Kaspar followed Pug out of the mouth of the cave and a short distance up a hillside until they could look down on the hole. In the sunlight from above the Talnoy armour glinted as if newly polished.

'That's a sight,' said Kaspar of Olasko.

'It is, indeed.'

Pug extended his hand and closed his eyes. For nearly five minutes nothing happened, but Kaspar had learned long before to be patient when it came to matters of magic. Suddenly a shining oval sparkling with silver sprang into existence in the air.

Pug pointed at the Talnoy, and said, 'Go home.'

As one, the Talnoy turned towards the magician, and the first one lifted off its feet, floating upwards. As it came even with the lip of the cavern, it picked up speed and flew into the oval that was the newly-formed rift. Then came another, and the next, and as each one rose up it rose faster until the Talnoy were flying out of the cavern so fast they became a blur to the human eye.

'Even that fast it'll take a while for ten thousand of them to get through,' said Pug.

'Where are they going?'

'To Kelewan, and into the Black Mount, then down to the second realm. The ancient gods of the Dasati are returning to claim their home.'

'Amazing.'

Pug said, 'What will you do now, Kaspar? You've

590

earned your choice. Whatever crimes you were accused of, you have more than redeemed yourself in the eyes of the Conclave. If you'd stay, we would welcome you. You are a resourceful man of many talents.'

Kaspar shrugged. 'I don't think so, Pug, but thank you for the offer. I think I'll follow Tal Hawkins' example. Like Tal, if you have any need of me, I'll try to help, but for the time being, I think I need to find a new life for myself.'

Pug smiled. 'There's a young king down in Muboya who needs a new general.'

Kaspar grinned. 'You know, I had the same thought myself. Alenburga told me enough about the boy over chess for me to have a fair idea what needs to be done there.'

'Conquest and war?'

'No, that phase is over, at least until one of Muboya's neighbours gets stupid. What they need now is peace and competent administration.'

'Well, whatever they need, they'll be lucky to take you into their service.'

'Thank you, Pug.'

'For what?'

Kaspar's eyes were shining with emotion. 'For letting me take my soul back. In your stead, I would have had me hanged the moment I'd taken the citadel in Olasko. Your son and Tal Hawkins were better men than I ever hope to be, but I will try to live up to your generosity.'

'You already have, Kaspar.' Pug watched the

Talnoy still flying through the rift, and added, 'Would you like me to get you down to Muboya?'

Kaspar shook his head. 'The day is still long here, and there's a village not too far away where I can buy a horse. After what we've been through, I could use a few hours of quiet. The walk will do me good.'

'I understand,' said Pug, extending his hand. They shook. 'Fare you well, Kaspar of Olasko.'

'Fare you well, magician.' Kaspar turned and walked down the trail. By the time he reached the bottom of the hill, the last of the Talnoy was gone, and so was Pug. As he looked upward, the rift in the air vanished.

Thanking the gods for being alive, Kaspar of Olasko walked purposefully down the trail, beginning the next journey of his life.

Pug appeared in his study, where Miranda, Magnus and Caleb waited. Miranda threw her arms around her husband and held him close. 'Is it over?' she asked.

'Not quite.'

She stepped back, examining his expression. 'You're going back!' It was more of an accusation than a question. Before he could answer, she declared, 'I'm going with you.'

'No!' This came out harsher than he meant it to: an exhausted and drained woman was about to get into a serious argument with her husband. 'No,' he said again, more softly. 'I need you here. Without you, I can't get back.'

Slowly, her mood changed. 'Why?'

'Because I'm going to do something I've only done once before.'

'What?'

'Close down a rift while I'm inside it.'

Miranda stared at him. 'There has to be another way.'

'I wish there were, but we are hours, perhaps only minutes, from whatever is coming up that tunnel from the Dasati realm to this one from gaining control of the rifts. I must go back and shut them down, but the last one can not be closed from this side. You know that. It can be closed only from the Kelewan side.'

'Or from inside,' said Magnus. He was nowhere near the master of rift-magic that his father was, but he had studied it far more rigorously than his mother had. 'Father, what do you need us to do?'

'There is a pair of staves in my quarters. Please bring them to me.'

Magnus hurried out and Pug turned to his wife, 'I will be fine if you just remain here and do your part.'

Tears welled up in Miranda's eyes and she found she couldn't speak. She just held tightly to her husband's robe with both hands, as if afraid to let him go. At last, she just nodded.

Caleb came over to them. 'Can I trust you to get back here safely?' he asked.

Pug laughed. He put his arm around his younger son's neck and squeezed him tight. 'You were always the sweetest child, Caleb, and despite being a strong man any father would take pride in, it's good to see that little boy is still in there somewhere.'

Softly Caleb whispered, 'You're my father. I love you.'

'And I you.'

Magnus returned and Pug said, 'We do not have much time. Outside, please.'

They exited the building and stopped a short distance down the path in a small garden at the side of the house. Pug took one of the staves and handed it to his wife. 'I had these fashioned from an old lightning-struck oak on the other side of this island. They are twins and I need one here, in the soil of this place, as an anchor.'

Miranda planted the butt of the staff into the soil. Pug looked to where Magnus stood with his brother and said, 'Can you please help your mother, boys?'

Magnus and Caleb gripped the staff, and nodded.

'No matter what happens, for the next hour do not let go of that staff. Keep it anchored to the ground. It is my only way back.'

'Where did you learn this?' Miranda asked.

'From your father.'

She rolled her eyes, but said nothing.

'I will come back,' he promised. Then he vanished.

Mother and sons stood motionless, with

Miranda, Caleb, and Magnus holding tightly to the staff.

Pug appeared at the rift site at the Academy to find half a dozen magicians anxiously watching the flood of refugees streaming through. One of them, a tall magician named Malcolm of Tyr-Sog shouted, 'Pug! We can't keep this up! We can't get them off the island fast enough, and there are food riots beginning over in Shamata!'

'Then take the rest of them up to Landreth!' Pug pointed to the twin outward-bound rift and said, 'Once I'm through that, shut it down. Is that understood?'

'Yes, but what about this one?'

Those coming through were close to panic, pushing and shouting and almost tumbling over one another. 'I'll close it down from the other side.' Pug took a deep breath. 'I'm closing down all the rifts!'

He hurried past a situation that was almost out of control and, shouldering his staff, stepped through the rift gate into Kelewan.

He walked into a scene of insanity and chaos.

The fighting was less than a hundred yards away from the rift gate to the new world. So many people were trying to force their way through that the weak were being trampled underfoot by the strong. Pug willed himself up into the air for a better view.

The Dasati were everywhere. The Black Mount had not expanded since he had left, but he knew it was merely a matter of time. He used magical sight to see which of the rift gates were in the most peril, and saw that the one nearest to where he stood was the one most likely to be captured first.

Pug hesitated. Every moment he waited a few more Tsurani would make it through the rift into the new world. It would be a difficult life for these refugees, but it would be life. The moment he closed down this rift, he consigned everyone trying to reach it to death, most of them to the horrible fate he had witnessed down in the pit in the heart of Omadrabar. He saw a Dasati Deathknight reach the bottom of the long ramp leading up to the rift and sent out a bolt of searing white energy which caused the armoured figure to burst into flames.

That proved to be an error, for two nearby Deathpriests sent their death-magic towards him. He barely got his defensive barrier up in time, but now he could not attack the Dasati without making himself vulnerable. He considered for a moment making himself invisible again, but he knew that the work ahead of him was likely to use up all his strength, and he would have none to spare.

He closed his eyes, as much to spare himself the vision of those below once they realized all hope was gone as to focus his will, and reached out to the rift. No one on either Midkemia or Kelewan understood rifts as Pug did. This rift was one he had created and he had enabled it to be easily closed down by anyone who knew how. He willed it out of existence.

One second there was a grey void with silver light shimmering on the surface, a beacon of hope and a doorway into safety, and the next it was gone. The wail of despair that rose up tore at Pug's heart and he fought back the urge to lash out at the Dasati. They were being as evilly used by the Dark One as anyone else, and he knew that any Deathknight or Deathpriest on Kelewan was doomed to die along with the remaining Tsurani. But even so, it didn't lessen his outrage.

He went to the next rift at risk and shut it down.

Seeing the rifts begin to blink out of existence one at a time, the crowd erupted into hysteria and panic. Mothers tightly gripped their children, as if they could somehow hide from the monsters who now approached them with deadly purpose. Husbands ran, leaving wives behind, or threw themselves at the Deathknights, striking them with their bare fists, or attacking them with household implements. The old, the weak and the very young died quickly.

Pug swallowed hard and shut down another rift. He moved on to the next one. He had much to do and time was running out.

Nakor stirred. He had finally become used to how his body felt. It was a very interesting situation, and he wished he could appreciate it more, but he knew that he had something important to do very soon.

He stood up and walked to the edge of the pit. The Dreadlord was now rising up in the sea of orange and green flame, roaring defiantly, as if issuing a challenge. Nakor wondered if the gods in Kelewan could hear it. Not that it mattered, for those gods were old and tired, and unable to protect their realm. He wondered if they would go with the Tsurani people to their new world, or whether new gods would arise. He wondered if there was really any difference. It was a pity he wouldn't find out.

He studied the changing form down in the pit, for two things were happening simultaneously: the Dreadlord was releasing much of the energy harboured against this day, letting it fly up to do his bidding, creating a powerful conduit between the worlds, and as it did so, the amorphous shape was resolving itself into a more human-like aspect, albeit one of heroic stature. A vast head rose out of the blob of a body, followed by a powerful neck and then gigantic shoulders. The body that was rising mocked human form, yet paid homage to that form, for it was a thing sculpted by a master. Arms of perfect proportion followed and a fist was raised high, shaking in defiance as the Dreadlord readied himself to rise to the next plane of existence. Nakor found this entertaining in a detached way, and wondered if that detachment was a function of his no longer being alive.

Nakor wondered if he might have felt resentment, had he still been alive, but he speculated he would not. This was a unique experience. The God of Liars had left him with just enough of his own magic energy to be animated, cognitive, and logical. Nakor suspected whatever felt like emotions were most likely echoes of his own life, not genuine and heartfelt, but something his animated mind felt was needed as part of the current experience. Yet those feelings were very distant, muted to the point of detachment. But the entire experience did pique his curiosity, and he was glad he still retained the ability to be curious.

Something was coming, fast, amid the falling bodies. The Dreadlord was no longer indulging his baser appetites, but was now using the newly-dead energies as a source of power for building his passage, rather than merely feeding his gluttony. Nakor found it interesting that as the Dreadlord rose up, as his body became leaner and more hungry, the smarter he seemed to become. That would be another interesting thing to explore, had he the time.

The thing that was approaching fell from the roof, but before the Dreadlord took any notice of it, Nakor reached out with one of his few remaining tricks and pulled it towards him. It was a man in a black robe, and even though he had never seen this face before, Nakor knew exactly who it was.

★ ★ ★

Leso Varen looked at Nakor the Isalani with open-eyed astonishment. The little man had simply reached out with his mind and dragged him down to this silly throne and nothing he had tried could prevent it.

Varen was rarely rational under the best of conditions, and at the moment the conditions were hardly the best. In fact, they were about as bad as he had ever experienced. Moreover, he was very angry, though as yet he wasn't entirely sure why. 'I don't know who you are, little man, but you should not have done that!'

Varen lashed out with his most punishing death-magic, but the little man stood there grinning at him. 'Hard to kill someone already dead, isn't it?'

Varen's mind raced. Already dead? He was the master of necromancy, but he had never encountered anything like this in his life. He had animated several dozen bodies over the years, and had encountered a lich or two, but even the smartest among the undead were not usually very bright, and were always insane. He tried to seize control of Nakor, as he would with any undead being, but the little man just kept grinning at him.

'This is amusing, but your time is over. I need something you have,' Nakor said.

Leso Varen stared at him. 'What—? he began, but Nakor reached out and his hand seemed to pass into Varen's chest. Varen's eyes widened as if he were experiencing stunning pain, and he looked down as Nakor pulled his hand out.

Nakor opened his fingers and there, resting on the palm of his hand, was a tiny crystal, black and pointed at each end, looking like a multi faceted gem. Deep within the crystal a dim light burned, pulsing with a purple glow. 'We are but vessels, you and I,' said Nakor. 'The only reason we are here is to carry with us something that otherwise couldn't exist in this place. Within me I carry the tiniest spark of Ban-ath. And this,' —he held up the tiny crystal so that Varen could see it— 'is a tiny spark of the Nameless. Your master sent you here to destroy the Dark One. He may be imprisoned, insane, and countless miles from his home world, but he's still angry enough that someone else wants to take his world from him that he fashioned you. You are his weapon, Leso.'

Varen's eyes lost focus and Nakor pushed him away. 'We do not need you any longer, for now I hold the Godkiller!'

The one-time master of necromancy fell into a heap, dead at last. For a long moment Nakor regarded what he held in his hand, then he looked at the Dreadlord. 'Just a few minutes more,' Nakor promised. 'Then we will be done.'

Pug rose high into the sky. He pushed aside an almost overwhelming feeling of sorrow: thousands below him were dying by the moment. He looked at that thing that was the Black Mount and his heart sank further. It now covered hundreds of miles of the Empire. He suspected that at the current rate the entire world would be overrun within another month, perhaps less.

Ignoring the sounds of horror beneath him, he kept rising until he felt the air turn cold and thin. He created a pocket of air around him, knowing that it would not last long, and kept rising until he could see the curve of the world below.

He grieved, for while it remained alien to him in so many ways, Kelewan had been his home for years. The Tsurani were a unique and proud people, embodying the best and worst of humanity. They could be cruel, murderous, and hateful, but they also could be generous and honourable, and would give their lives for what they believed. And they had a great capacity for love.

He was musing on this when something shifted within the Black Mount. Pug used his magical vision, honed by his time on the Dasati world, to peer deep into the heart of the dome. He saw there a scene of horror so profound he could scarcely contain his outrage.

Hundreds of Deathknights rode their huge varnin through the enclosed countryside, dragging nets filled with dead and dying Tsurani behind them. The vast pit that formed the tunnel to the second realm and the Dasati world of Omadrabar stayed a fixed distance from the edge of the sphere, so the Deathknights had only the same distance to cover as before it expanded. The pit was now vast, hundreds of miles across. And Pug sensed more than saw that something was moving inside.

Nakor watched, curiously detached. It occurred to him that being dead he had little interest in anything other than the matters at hand. He wondered if he should feel regret, because he remembered being very curious when he was alive, and then he realized he had no time for thought.

The Dreadlord was using his power to drain every living thing in the vicinity. Loyal Deathpriests and temple Deathknights above all fell lifeless, their bodies descending the tunnel from Kelewan dead long before they reached him. The Dreadlord stood motionless, his figure fluid and vague, then suddenly he resolved himself into a thing of nightmare.

He was majestic, and now he looked as Nakor imagined a Dreadlord would. His body was massive, easily thirty feet tall, and shaped like a man's, though the legs had a decidedly animal shape, like a goat's or horse's, with a stifle and hock, rather than with hip and knee. The head was featureless, save for a suggestion of ears when he moved in certain directions. Around his head hovered a tiny circlet of silver light punctuated with golden flames, forming a demonic crown. His eyes were two flaming coals.

Then from his back wings of shadow sprouted, and Nakor realized these mystical pinions were designed to carry him up through the tunnel to Kelewan. As the Dreadlord prepared to launch himself upwards, Nakor stepped out from his concealed position behind the throne, stepping over the dead form of Leso Varen.

The Dreadlord launched himself up the tunnel, leaving the pit suddenly silent and empty. Then came a loud concussion, as if two massive things were colliding with each other through the tunnel. Nakor understood and made ready.

From above ten thousand black-armoured figures descended, touching down on the cold stone floor where only moments before there had been a roiling sea of Dasati life energy. Ten thousand Dasati gods had returned home, and as each touched down, their armour erupted in a glow of light – silver, green, gold, every colour imaginable – as the power of the trapped gods were released. At one time Nakor would have felt awed by such a sight, but now he just watched, sensing that his role was at an end.

Knowing it was likely to be the last act of his existence, Nakor held the black jewel on the flat palm of his left hand, and with his right, flicked it, as a child might flick a pebble off his palm. It flew straight and followed the Dreadlord's flight up the tunnel. As it rose up the tunnel, the Godkiller seemed to draw the tunnel's energy into it, effectively sealing it off behind the Dreadlord. He could never return to Omadrabar that way. The Dreadlord was finally gone from the second plane of existence. To all intents and purposes, for the Dasati the Dark One was as good as dead.

Nakor sat down and felt his mind begin to drain away. His last thought was that it had been a very interesting life.

★　★　★

Something was coming!

Pug stared down into the Black Mount, focusing hard. Then he realized it was the Dreadlord. He was using this passage between the planes of existence to leave Omadrabar and come to Kelewan! Whatever time-scale Pug might have thought he faced was completely wrong. He didn't have months or weeks, or even days, to prepare for this. The monster would arrive in moments . . .

Pug probed with every sense he possessed, looking for a weakness in the Black Mount. He could find none. Had he days or weeks to study it, with Miranda's help using what she had learned from her escape from the first sphere, then perhaps he might have found a means to shut down this monstrous thing. But he knew in his heart he might study it for years and never find what he sought. He had only one choice, a choice he had denied since this situation had presented itself. He steeled himself and began to manipulate the energies around him.

Pug let his mind reach out, and in the vast distance of space he found what he sought. He conjured the single most powerful spell he had ever fashioned, one he had imagined, but never thought he would ever use. Circling Kelewan was a single moon, locked in a perfect orbit by the balance of forces exerted by both the sun and the planet. Pug tipped that balance.

Millions of miles away in space a massive rift appeared before the moon, and just inside the top of the dome of the Black Mount its twin manifested. Pug lowered himself down to a position by the rift that led back home, and knew he had to be quick.

He could not leave this last rift open, for to do so would doom Midkemia to the same fate about to befall Kelewan.

Millions of miles away, the moon struck the rift gate. Only part of it was forced through, but its velocity was enough to drive an impossible amount of stone, equal to the tallest mountain on Kelewan, through it in scant seconds. Pug stepped inside the rift just as the moon's vast shard appeared inside the Black Mount and slammed down at incalculable speed into the pit. The Dreadlord had only an instant to sense that something was terribly wrong. A massive increase in air pressure around the Dark One gripped the gigantic being as if an enormous hand squeezed him. Then for the briefest instant a wall of light fell upon him.

The moon shard and the black gem shard Nakor had released struck in the same instant. The Dreadlord was no mortal being; but in that instant he was crushed.

The universe began to tear.

No one on the planet's surface felt pain. For one moment the world had been a landscape of terror, struggle and death, and in the next moment, everything was gone. A cloud of hot gas travelled a path around a distant yellow-green sun where minutes before a world and its moon had existed.

★　　★　　★

Pug found himself in a grey nothingness, devoid of any sensation, light, dark, cold or heat. He had experienced this once before, and then he had reached out with his mind to find his old teacher, Kulgan.

This time he had a more compelling target for his mind: his wife and sons. He gripped tightly the staff that was twin to the one at home. He let his magic senses run through the ancient wood and could feel Miranda, Caleb and Magnus out there, the three people he loved more than anyone else in that world. He sensed them . . . somewhere . . . there! He could feel the echo of the staff in his hand and the touch of his loved ones on it, and reached for them. Then with a tearing pain, he was standing by them, shivering as if he had been exposed to the most profound cold possible.

He said, 'It is done,' then collapsed into his son's arms.

EPILOGUE

It was a quiet afternoon lunch. Pug had slept the entire night and next day through, and deep into the morning before arising. He felt numb, and knew that the full weight of what had happened would not fall upon him for a few more days, or even weeks. He was old enough to understand that the mind and heart healed in their own good time and that when they were ready to deal with what he had done, they would.

Caleb, his wife Marie, and the boys, Jommy, Tad, and Zane, along with Magnus and Miranda, were quiet, lost in the gentle conversation of a family just pleased to be with one another. It was an overcast day outside, but sombre weather seemed appropriate to Pug.

At last, he asked Miranda, 'How many Great Ones got through in the end?'

Miranda stopped chewing for a moment, then swallowed. 'I believe forty-one got through the rift to the Academy, and perhaps another hundred or so through the rift to the new world.'

Jommy said, 'They're going to have to come up

with a name for the place. They can't just keep calling it the "new world", now, can they?'

Pug smiled. He was very pleased that his three foster grandsons had survived.

'How about others?' he asked.

Miranda said, 'We've no official tally. Maybe ten thousand Tsurani got through the rifts to here and that other one up in LaMut. Most of them want to go to the new world, to the King's relief, I'm sure, though a few want to stay in LaMut. A lot of those who were with Kaspar are staying with him down in Novindus. He's going to have quite an army when he arrives to take service with the Maharaja of Muboya.'

Magnus said, 'Will we ever know, Father, how many . . . ?'

Pug just shook his head briefly. 'Died? No, we never will.'

The best estimate was that just over two million Tsurani had made it through to the new world, but that meant for each one who was saved, five had died at the hands of the Dasati or when the planet was vaporized. He looked at Miranda. 'And the Thuril?'

Miranda forced a smile. 'Apparently they're a little more practical about things than we gave them credit for. Seems the majority of them got through in time. Given their culture, they'll probably adapt to their new highlands faster than the Tsurani will to the rest of their continent.'

'What about the Thūn?'

'No one knows. We'll have to send someone down there to see.'

Pug didn't ask about the Cho-ja, for he already knew the answer. It saddened him greatly that such a majestic alien race had chosen to die with their world. He stared off through a rain-spattered window for a long time, then took a slow drink of wine and said, 'I'm going to miss that little cheat.'

Caleb laughed. 'Not when we're playing cards, you're not.'

'Or throwing dice,' said Jommy.

Pug sighed. 'I know I lived almost fifty years before meeting him,' said Pug, 'but it feels like he has always been around.'

Miranda reached out and squeezed her husband's hand. 'He still is, in a way.'

Pug lifted his mug. 'To Nakor.'

'Nakor!' they all toasted.

Jommy said, 'We lost two good friends that day.'

Pug said, 'Nakor was Erik's oldest surviving friend, did you know that?'

'No,' said Jommy. 'I bet there were some stories about those two.'

'One or two,' said Pug, rising. 'I have a couple of things I would like to take care of in my study, and then I think I'll rest.' As others started to stand up, he motioned for them to stay where they were. 'I'm tired, not injured. Finish your meal.'

He went up to his study and opened the door. Behind the desk, in his chair, sat a brown haired man.

'Ban-ath!'

'Yes,' said the God of Thieves. 'I felt you deserved to know one thing. The Dark One is destroyed, or at least as destroyed as a Dreadlord can be. He's been cast back into the void, so for all intent and purposes, he is gone.'

'How? Certainly not—'

'Your little trick with the flaming planet? Very unexpected, and I will confess I was impressed. I thought you'd try to open a fissure in the earth, having the Holy City fall into the molten core of the planet and take the Dreadlord with it, or drown it at the bottom of the sea, but turning the entire world into dust, that was . . . remarkable.'

'So we are at last safe?' asked Pug.

Ban-ath laughed. 'Never,' he said, then vanished.

Pug stood there wishing he had the means to understand if what the God of Liars had said was true or not. Then he saw the box. He crossed to it, hesitated for a moment, then opened it. Inside was a scroll. Feeling a sinking sensation in his stomach, he took it out and unrolled it.

In his familiar handwriting was a message.

'So maybe you deserve to know two things,' it read. 'You didn't write these notes and send them back through time. I did.'

It was signed, 'Kalkin.'

Pug sat down and tried not to laugh.

Wrath of a Mad God

ALSO BY RAYMOND E. FEIST
FROM CLIPPER LARGE PRINT

Exile's Return
Flight of the Nighthawks
Into a Dark Realm